In Some Other Life

In Some Other Life

Jessica Brody

FARRAR STRAUS GIROUX
NEW YORK

Farrar Straus Giroux Books for Young Readers
An imprint of Macmillan Publishing Group, LLC
175 Fifth Avenue, New York, NY 10010

Printed in the United States of America by LSC Communications,
Harrisonburg, Virginia
Designed by Elizabeth H. Clark
First edition, 2017
1 3 5 7 9 10 8 6 4 2

fiercereads.com

Cataloging-in-Publication Data is on file at the Library of Congress

ISBN: 978-0-374-38076-2

To Morgan Matson,
for your boundless plotting wisdom . . . and friendship

Two roads diverged in a yellow wood,
And sorry I could not travel both . . .

—ROBERT FROST

CONTENTS

If...

Then . . .

Date: November 14
From: My Friend the Printer
To: Kennedy Rhodes
Subject: RE: Fourth Follow-Up

Dear Ms. Rhodes,

Thank you for your fourth follow-up email today. As I mentioned in my response to your previous three follow-ups, we are ready and eager to receive the files for your next issue of the *Southwest Star* school newspaper and we foresee no problems in the printing process.

I can guarantee you that our printers are routinely checked, serviced, and repaired, and are all currently functioning properly. We speak to our ink supplier daily and he has given us no indication of a sudden worldwide ink shortage, as you suggested. Nor has there been any sign from our paper supplier of a paper mill strike.

May I suggest that you refrain from Googling "possible catastrophes at print shops" from now on and rest assured that our shop is safe from burglary, power outages, hackers, bug infestations, hurricanes, volcanic eruptions, geomagnetic reversal, and asteroid impacts.

I'm sure your dreams *have* been known to be "prophetic" as you alleged, but we run a tight ship here and I am positive that we will not be attacked by paper pirates anytime soon (if that's even a thing, which I doubt).

I understand how important this issue is and I can certainly appreciate the fact that your life, career, and future happiness rest on it being "kick-ass," as you put it.

We thank you again for your continued patronage. It is an honor to be the official printer of the award-winning *Southwest Star.*

Best of luck with your big upcoming issue. We look forward to reading it.

Regards,

Eric Nettles
General Manager
My Friend the Printer

If...

If I Fail

Relax. Deep breaths. In. Out. In. Out.

It's only the most important week of your life. No big deal. If you fail epically, it's not the end of the world. You'll just wind up miserable, poor, alone, unhappy, and probably diseased.

What's so horrible about that?

Oh God, this meditation thing *isn't* working.

I open my eyes and stare at the ceiling. How do those Tibetan monks do this all day long? How do they not drive themselves crazy with what-if questions?

What if the issue isn't good enough?

What if we don't win the award for the record-breaking fourth year in a row?

What if I totally bomb my admissions interview?

What if I don't get into *any* college and I have to spend my life scrubbing chewed gum off the underside of desks?

What if . . .

"Oh, what a beautiful morning!" My dad opens my bedroom door and glides in, spreading his arms wide and singing totally off-key at the top of his lungs. "Oh, what a beautiful day!"

He's been waking me up the same way since kindergarten. Thankfully it's not always the *same* song. He has a whole repertoire of morning hymns, most of them originating from musicals that had their heyday decades before I was born.

"I can't do it," I say with a groan. "I can't handle the pressure. Just sign me up for janitor school now and get it over with."

My dad laughs and opens the vertical blinds. I pull the pillow over my head to block the light. "Did anyone ever tell you that you worry too much?"

"Yeah, you. Daily."

He removes the pillow from my face. "Well, you should listen to me. I'm a very wise man." He pulls the covers off me and yanks on my dead arm. "C'mon. Let's go. Up and at 'em, soldier. If I can face today, then *you* can face today."

The realization hits me like a punch in the gut.

Oh God. That's right. It's my dad's big night. I totally forgot.

I suddenly feel guilty for lying here lamenting about my own stress when my dad is dealing with a major career turning point of his own. Tonight is his first big gallery show. He's been trying to make it as a photographer since pretty much before I was born and this show could change everything. It doesn't really help that the subject matter of his photos is a little on the unusual side. I mean, we all think he's talented, but it's taken a while for the rest of the world to catch up.

"Crap," I swear, jumping out of bed. "Dad, I'm so sorry. I forgot. I'm a terrible daughter. Are you ready? Are you excited? Are you nervous?"

He shrugs and shakes his head. "Nope. Not nervous at all."

Always the cool cucumber, my dad.

That must be a recessive gene because I certainly didn't get it. Frankie, my little brother, on the other hand, he's pretty much my dad's mini-me. Well, if you replace a photography obsession with a theoretical physics obsession.

"How do you do it?" I ask. "How do you stay so calm?"

He shrugs again. "I don't know. I guess I have faith that whatever happens was meant to happen. Oh, and of course I have faith in Magnum."

Magnum is the name of Dad's favorite camera. He named it after Thomas Sullivan Magnum IV, the main character of the eighties TV show *Magnum, P.I.*, about a private investigator played by Tom Selleck. He chose the name because Magnum always sees the truth. Just like his camera.

Magnum is one of those fancy models with a bunch of letters and numbers in the name. I can never remember *which* numbers or letters, though, which is why I'm grateful he calls it Magnum. Dad has loads of cameras, but Magnum is like his best friend. He never leaves the house without it. It's basically an extra appendage.

I sigh. Okay, I can totally do this. I can be chill and relaxed and have faith. I can trust that . . .

Dang it! I forgot to tell the printer that we're testing out a brand-new layout in this month's issue. They'll need to double-check all the new margins. I have to email Eric again.

I grab for my phone and open my inbox.

Dad laughs and walks out of the room, kissing me on the top of my head as he passes. "Breakfast in ten." Then he closes the door.

I tap out the email in a flurry and hastily press Send just as I realize I misspelled my own name at the bottom. The email zoomed off so fast I couldn't really see, but I'm pretty sure I signed it from Jennefry. Instead of Kennedy.

I sigh and compose a new email. Eric is going to hate me. If he doesn't already.

Hi Eric. That last email was from Kennedy. Not Jennefry. Just in case you got confused and thought some evil nemesis named Jennefry staged a coup and took over as editor in chief of the paper. Nope. It's still me. Thanks.

I press Send and take a deep breath, glancing up at the wall above my desk, at the three framed issues of the *Southwest Star* that I hung there. Like every morning, the sight of them instantly gives me strength and calms my nerves.

I exhale and return my attention to my phone, opening my SnipPic app and scrolling through my notifications. I got seven likes on my latest picture. One from Laney, my best friend since freshman year. One from Austin, my boyfriend. And a few from members of the newspaper staff, including Mia Graham, my features editor, who is in line to take over as editor in chief of the paper when I graduate in May.

The picture is one Laney took of me in the newspaper office last night. We had to stay until eleven o'clock and the issue is *still* not finished.

I scroll through my feed, skimming past the various photos of people I follow, mostly fellow newspaper staffers, until I find the one I'm looking for. It's the latest selfie from CoyCoy55. She's standing in front of the amazing grand brick staircase of the Windsor Academy Prep School, dressed in her pristine blue Windsor Academy blazer with a pressed white-collared shirt underneath. Her gorgeous auburn hair is blowing in the early November breeze and she's smiling that perfect, pink-lipped, white-toothed smile. She already has fifty-two likes and her caption reads:

> Another beautiful day at W.A.! Can't wait to hear our guest lecturer this morning! He's a state senator! #LoveMyLife #WindsorAcademy

A state senator!? Seriously? Who's next? The president?

The other week, they had an astronaut as a guest lecturer, and last year Daphne Wu, my all-time favorite author, came to speak. I came this close to sneaking into their famous amphitheater-style "Lauditorium" just to catch a few words. We *never* get guest lecturers at Southwest High. Besides, where would they even speak? In our crummy cafeteria where all the tables and chairs squeak? In our pathetic excuse for a theater that smells like dirty socks because it's right next door to the boys' locker room?

With a sigh, I close the SnipPic app and toss my phone on the bed. I bet CoyCoy55 doesn't have to worry about newspaper issues and print shops and impressing alumni interviewers. I bet she doesn't have to worry about anything! Everyone knows that when you go to the Windsor Academy, colleges simply roll out the red carpet for you. You probably don't even have to fill out an application. Every top college in the country probably just hand delivers you an acceptance letter via some white-gloved messenger service.

Meanwhile, across town at Southwest High, we're all grappling for the measly handful of spots the Ivy League colleges reserve for public school kids.

I close my eyes. *Relax. Deep breaths. In. Out. In. Out.*

You can do this. You've got this. Everything is going to be . . .

Crap.

I forgot to tell the printer we need a hundred extra copies for the award committee members. They're going to have to order more paper.

My eyes flash open. I grab for my phone again and start tapping out another email, praying this won't be the excuse Eric uses to finally add my address to his spam filter.

If the Universe Smelled

Sometimes I wish I went to the Windsor Academy just for the uniforms. I mean, I practically wear the same thing to school every day anyway—jeans, T-shirt, boots, and an old leather jacket that used to belong to my dad back when he was in his "edgy phase," as he likes to call it—but it would be nice to have an *excuse* to wear the same thing every day and not feel like you're doing it out of basic laziness and a severe allergic reaction to shopping.

My hair goes straight into a side braid, and my books go into my camo-green messenger bag. I grab my interview study guide from my nightstand, where I tossed it last night after I'd stared at the pages for so long the words started to look like they were growing arms and legs.

I check my phone to see if Horace, our design editor at the newspaper, has written me back about the fifteen graphics he still hasn't gotten around to designing for this month's issue, but there's nothing. Typical Horace.

Looks like I'm going to have to spend my entire free period

making graphics. Just what I need today: to go to battle with Adobe Illustrator.

There's also been no word from the school's IT guy about the error I was getting last night when I tried to upload our files to the school server.

I groan, slip my phone into my bag, and head downstairs where I'm greeted by the delicious smell of chocolate chip waffles. Dad always puts chocolate chips in the waffles on a big day. He thinks it brings good luck. "Nothing bad ever happens when chocolate is in the equation" is his entire theory about life.

I pull out the stool next to Frankie and sit down at the kitchen counter in front of my pile of newspapers. I subscribe to five national papers that I usually skim each morning over breakfast. As editor in chief of the *Southwest Star*, I think it's important to keep up to date on what the big-name presses are doing. But today I have to study for my alumni interview, so I push the stack aside as I ask, "Where's Mom?"

Dad pulls a perfectly formed work of art out of the waffle iron and plops it onto a plate. "She had to go into work early so she could be home in time for the show tonight."

It's not unusual for Mom to be gone by the time I get downstairs. She's a partner at a top law firm, which basically means she works crazy hours making sure large corporations pay for their screwups. Dad has always been the stay-at-home parent for Frankie and me. He built his photography studio right in the basement so he could work from home. He likes to joke that his commute is only thirty seconds and there's hardly any traffic.

Dad tops the waffle with maple syrup and whipped cream sculpted into some ambiguous shape and sets the plate down in front of me.

I scrutinize the whipped cream. "Hmm," I say, rotating the plate in a circle. "A giraffe?"

"I was going for 'Darkened Nature of Sorrow.'"

I snap my fingers. "So close."

The truth is, I'm way too anxious to eat, but I don't want to hurt his feelings so I cut a small bite.

Frankie has noise-canceling headphones on over his wild, uncombed hair that's sticking up in a million directions. He's hunched over his board game while he shovels forkfuls of syrupy waffles into his mouth.

My dad reaches over the counter and pulls Frankie's headphones off his ears long enough to remind him to "Chew!"

I peer over to study Frankie's latest creation. It looks like he's redrawing the Forest of Relativity again. He's been working on his theoretical physics board game for almost six months now. It's called What's the Matter? and he must have tried to explain the rules to me countless times but I still have no idea how to play. The best I can tell, it's like Chutes and Ladders except with wormholes and hadron colliders.

Frankie is not a normal eleven-year-old child.

He catches me watching him and yanks his headphones off, turning the board around so I can see his latest work. He's an incredible artist. He gets that from my dad. "What do you think?" he asks eagerly.

I give him a thumbs-up and pop the minuscule bite of waffle into my mouth.

"Now when you land on a proton space, you don't have to get a Nucleus card to bypass the Bridge of Dark Matter. You can just cut through the Forest!"

"Oh, thank God," I tell him while chewing. "I always get stuck on the Bridge of Dark Matter."

He rolls his eyes. "That's because you never remember to use your Gravity Eraser card."

"I've had that card?"

"Duh. Everyone starts the game with one."

I slap my forehead. "Now you tell me."

Frankie will probably never have to worry about getting into a good college. I'm sure MIT will recruit him by the time he's fourteen.

I, on the other hand, have to work doubly hard for everything.

"Dad," I say, sliding my interview crib sheet across the counter. "Quiz me."

Dad is eating his waffles standing up, like always. He sets his plate down and picks up the page. He clears his throat and pulls his face into a serious expression, putting on the pretense of a snooty professor. "Ms. Rhodes," he begins in an obnoxiously stuffy accent. "Thank you for your interest in Columbia University's Undergraduate Journalism Program."

I stifle a giggle. Frankie looks up from the Forest of Relativity, obviously not wanting to miss this farce.

"My first question for you today is," Dad goes on, "what is your biggest regret in life?"

I take a breath. I know this one. I've studied this particular question the most. You see, I did a bunch of research online and gathered all of the popular questions asked in college admission interviews. This one appeared the most.

"My biggest regret," I begin my scripted answer, "is probably working too hard and not taking enough time for myself. You see, I'm the editor in chief of my high school newspaper, the *Southwest Star*, and ever since I took over in my freshman year, we've managed to win the National Spartan Press Award three years in a row. And although I'm very proud of this accomplishment, success comes at a price and I'm afraid I don't have a lot of free time to do fun things. But I hear they have this great new invention called television now."

I let out my rehearsed chuckle at that last part and then exhale in relief. That might have been my best delivery yet. Let's hope I can do it exactly the same way tomorrow afternoon at the alum's house.

Dad nods his head approvingly. Even Frankie looks impressed.

"Not bad," Dad praises, and then remembers his stuffy-professor persona and clears his throat again. "I mean, Well said, Ms. Rhodes. Well said, indeed."

I beam. "I read that you should always take a question that

is meant to focus on a negative and spin it so it focuses on a positive. And you should always put a little humor into each answer."

Dad slides the paper back to me and transforms into himself again. "You're going to blow this up. There's no way you won't get in."

"You know," Frankie begins knowledgeably, "in some other parallel universe, you *already* got in."

"How is that possible?" I ask. "If I haven't even had the interview yet."

Frankie sets his fork down with a clank and I'm immediately sorry I asked. I can tell by the look on his face, he's about to get all timey-wimey technical with us. I guess with our family's DNA, it was too much to ask for a *normal* little brother who watches cartoons and puts posters of famous jocks on his wall. No, Frankie's walls are covered with pictures of Stephen Hawking and Michio Kaku.

I worry about the kid. I do. How is he *ever* going to survive middle school next year in one piece?

"You see," he begins, with the same flair my father had when pretending to be a snooty professor. The only difference is, Frankie's isn't an act. "The multiverse theory states that *all* possible outcomes—infinite potentials—already exist in other dimensions. So when you scheduled the interview for tomorrow, you unknowingly created a parallel universe. Which means that another you could have—and *did*—schedule the interview for last week. So *that* version of you has already had your interview and has already been accepted into Columbia."

I stare at him in bewilderment. "That doesn't make any sense. Early decision letters for Columbia don't arrive until December 15. So even if my interview was last week, I still wouldn't know if I got in for another month."

Frankie's face falls. "Oh." He bites his lip in deep concentration as he thinks this over. Dad and I share a smile as I take a sip of orange juice.

"What else do you need to do before tonight?" I ask Dad.

He unplugs the waffle iron and starts wiping it down. "Not much. Just some last-minute framing. Oh, and if you have time, there's one more photo downstairs that needs a caption. Mind taking a stab at it?"

"Not at all," I say, licking my fork. "I'll take a look before I go."

Dad got the visual photography skills of the family but he's terrible with the written word. Thankfully, that's my forte, so we make a good team. I've been writing photo captions for him since I was in elementary school. I think I've captioned every single piece that's going to be in tonight's exhibit.

I stand up and carry my plate to the sink, trying to hide the barely touched waffle from my dad. But his keen photographer eye notices everything.

"You're not hungry?" he asks.

I shake my head. "Too much on my mind, I think. It was delicious though!" I pull out the trash compactor drawer, dump in the waffle, and put the plate in the dishwasher. Dad hates dishes left in the sink.

He gives me a disapproving look. "Promise me you'll eat lunch."

I draw an imaginary X across my chest. "Promise. What time is the show?"

"It starts at eight."

I wince. It's Drop Dead night at the paper, which means it's the last night before the files are due to the printer, so we work and work and work until we basically drop dead. But I can't miss Dad's show. I refuse to. So we'll just have to work extra hard and extra *fast* so I can get out on time.

"I might be a few minutes late, but I'll be there."

Dad pulls me into a hug and kisses the top of my head. "You do what you have to do."

"I've got it!" Frankie says suddenly, startling both of us.

"You've got what?" I ask.

"In a parallel universe, you were born a year *earlier*, which means you got accepted to Columbia *last* year and are already there right now!" He grins, looking extremely proud of himself.

"But Mom and Dad weren't married a year earlier," I point out.

Frankie slumps back on his stool with a frown. "Huh." Then a moment later, he says, "I know! In a parallel universe—"

"In a parallel universe," Dad interrupts, "you've already finished your breakfast *and* brushed your teeth, *and* done something about that hair."

Frankie self-consciously pats at his head, pushing down the crazy strands that are sticking up, but they just boing right back.

"I think you're going to have to take a shower," Dad tells him.

Frankie groans and stuffs the last bite of waffle into his mouth before pushing off the stool. "In a parallel universe, no one has to take a shower," he gripes as he trudges up the stairs. "Showers were never even invented!"

"That would be a pretty smelly universe," I call after him.

"You're a pretty smelly universe!" he calls back.

I close the dishwasher and am about to kick the trash compactor shut when something under my half-eaten waffle catches my eye. An envelope. It's covered in sticky syrup and melted whipped cream, but I can still make out the familiar logo in the top left corner.

"*Another* offer?" I ask Dad, nodding toward the letter. "What'd they promise this time? A fully paid time-share on the moon?"

"A company car of my choice."

Jeffrey and Associates is an advertising firm that's been trying to recruit my dad for years. Every few months they send another job offer with even *more* zeros at the end. But Dad always turns them down.

"I would never work for those corporate, soul-sucking buffoons," he likes to say with pride. "Your old man is not a sellout. I refuse to let Magnum be used to hawk laundry detergent and cat food. No way. Nohow."

I snort and close the trash drawer. "Which photo needs the caption?"

Dad sprays the counter with all-purpose cleaner and wipes it down. "It's the one that looks eerily like varicose veins."

"Well, there's your caption right there. 'Eerily Like Varicose Veins.'"

He stops cleaning and fakes a stroke of inspiration. "Oh yeah! What on earth do I need you for?"

If My Locker Door Actually Opened

Dad's studio is immaculate. Just like the rest of the house. Everything on his desk is aligned in perfect symmetry, his shelves have labels on them, and you could basically eat off the spotless red rug on the floor. He says he thrives on hyper-organization. I don't have to be a geneticist to know how I turned out the way I did.

Most of the photos for the show tonight are already at the gallery, but there are a few still here. I immediately locate the piece that needs the caption and chuckle when I look at it. He's right. It does look a lot like varicose veins. It also looks a lot like . . .

I tilt my head, getting a sudden idea.

I find a pad of sticky notes on his desk and write down my caption, smiling to myself. He's going to love it.

I stick the paper to the framed photograph, wipe my hands, and hit the last switch on the multi-light panel as I leave.

My work here is done.

*   *   *

When Mom got promoted to partner at her law firm last year, she bought a brand-new Lexus SUV and gave me her old Honda Accord, which I promptly named Woody, after Bob Woodward, the famous journalist.

I love my car. Not because it has any fancy car-things like souped-up wheels or upgraded cup holders or whatever, but because I've made it my own. I found a really cool steering wheel wrap online that looks like newsprint and matches my phone case. I also got a custom license plate frame that says "Keep Calm and Carry a Notebook and Pen." And my sparkly pink car charger was a gift from Laney. It was kind of a private joke between us, a combination of the facts that I hate anything pink and sparkly and that I'm always draining my battery checking emails.

I normally pick Laney up on the way to school since she doesn't have a car, but last night she texted me to tell me she was catching a ride early with her dad so she could work on her final story for the issue. It made me smile. Laney is probably the only other person on staff as dedicated to this newspaper as I am. We should have been co–editors in chief, but she insisted I take the job and she'd be my news editor, which is just so Laney. She's the kind of girl who'd much rather man the spotlight than have it pointed at her.

I don't know what's going to happen next year if I get into Columbia and she gets into UCLA. We'll be light-years apart.

But I can't think about that now. I have too many other things on my mind.

My usual route to school takes me right past the entrance

to the Windsor Academy and, as I approach, I keep my gaze trained on the stoplight in front of me, biting my lip in anticipation.

I preemptively ease my foot off the gas pedal, hovering over the brake.

C'mon. C'mon. Turn red. Turn red.

The light flickers to yellow and I eagerly slam on the brakes, causing someone to honk behind me. They clearly thought I was going to run the yellow. But I wouldn't do that. Because I'm a responsible, law-abiding driver.

As soon as I come to a stop, I glance out the window and take in the famous brick-and-stone sign that reads "Windsor Preparatory Academy: Grades 7–12." My gaze wanders through the black iron gates and up the beautifully landscaped driveway, until I can just barely make out the parking lot and a hint of Royce Hall, the campus's iconic main building, with its impressive curving brick staircase and white columns. I don't really need to see it, though. I know what it looks like because I've pretty much memorized their website. And I follow the school on SnipPic, where the administration is always posting fabulous pictures of students eating lunch in the state-of-the-art student union, or peering into microscopes in one of their high-tech science labs, or swimming laps in their Olympic-size indoor swimming pool.

Southwest High doesn't even have a SnipPic account. Because honestly, what would they post? A close-up of the stuff they try to pass off as "beef Bolognese" in the cafeteria? A snapshot of that one desk in the AP chemistry classroom that's *always* broken but that I *always* end up getting stuck sitting in and *always* forget that it tips over when you lean too far to the left?

The Windsor Academy has been ranked one of the best schools in the country. The acceptance rate is in the low single digits. Sure, I applied. Of *course*, I applied. I've wanted to go to Windsor since kindergarten. I filled out an application the second I entered the sixth grade. I checked the mail every day for months, waiting for the letter. And then . . .

Well, it's complicated. And I don't like to dwell on it.

The light turns green and I take one last look at the greener-than-green grass and step on the accelerator.

By the time I get to Southwest High a few minutes later, Austin, my boyfriend, is already parked and waiting for me in front of the school.

"Hey, gorgeous," he says, giving me a peck on the lips. I try to hide my wince at the scent of coffee on his breath—I loathe the taste, smell, and even sight of coffee—but he notices. "Sorry," he says, blowing into his hands and smelling them. "I stopped at Peabody's on the way to school."

"That's okay," I say brightly, trying not to make a big deal of it. "Maybe just keep some breath mints in your car, you know?"

He makes that *tsk*ing sound with his teeth that drives me bonkers and shoots me with gun fingers. "Good idea."

I let out a sigh and check the inbox on my phone. There are two new emails from Eric at My Friend the Printer, letting me know that he received *my* two new emails, but still nothing from Horace about the graphics or the IT guy about the server issue. I feel my grip tighten around the phone.

I hate thinking about all those files just sitting there on the hard drives. Anything could happen to them. An electromagnetic pulse could wipe out every computer in a five-mile radius. Hard-drive pirates could break in and pillage the school. A freak flash flood could . . .

"Rough morning?" Austin asks, interrupting my paranoia spiral.

I pocket my phone and take a deep breath. "Yes."

"What parallel universe was Frankie in today?" he asks as we walk through the front doors.

I laugh. "One where there are no showers."

He chuckles. "Classic."

I can't help but smile. Austin knows me so well. That's why we've been together for the past three and a half years. Because we're totally, absolutely, one-hundred-percent in tune with each other.

"So are you coming over tonight?" he asks.

Huh?

I stop midstep in the hallway. Tonight? Did we make plans? I don't remember making plans. I quickly pull my phone back out and click the calendar app. The only thing on my schedule for today is Drop Dead night at the newspaper and then Dad's exhibit at the gallery. "What's tonight?" I ask.

He looks a little hurt. "They're releasing the new season of *How Is This My Life?* on Netflix, remember? Eight new episodes are releasing at seven!"

I sag in relief. Thank God. It's only that stupid comedy special he loves so much. To be honest, I really don't know why. It's not even that funny. The comedian, Tom Something-or-other, just makes really lame fart jokes the whole time. I mean, c'mon, fart jokes? For a whole hour? Isn't that a tad bit lazy?

Anyone can write fart jokes.

Frankie can write fart jokes.

Okay, maybe not. Frankie would probably just go off on some tangent about nitrogen and cows raised for beef and global warming.

"Here comes the big one," Austin is saying in his best impression of the comedian. "Here comes the whaaaaammmy!" Then he busts up laughing, even releasing a tiny snort. "God, that guy is good."

"I'm so sorry," I tell him, trying to sound torn up about it. "I can't come."

His face falls in disappointment. "But it's my favorite show. And stand-up comedy is more fun when you watch it with other people!"

"I know," I say, instantly feeling guilty. "But it's Drop Dead and then I have my dad's gallery show tonight."

Okay, so I know this sounds bad, but I'm secretly relieved that I have these big important plans and can't sit around all night watching Tom What's-his-face anthropomorphize bodily functions. It's not that I don't like hanging out with my boyfriend. Obviously I do. It's just that he insists on binge-watching the entire eight-episode season the second it releases. And when you don't find it funny to begin with, eight hours of the same stupid jokes can pretty much make you want to guzzle a bottle of toxic newspaper ink.

When you've been together for as long as we have, it's natural for you to find differing interests. I mean, it's not like we have to agree on *everything*.

"I'm sorry," I tell Austin again, noticing he still looks disappointed. "I would be there if I could!"

This makes him smile. "I know. It's all good."

We arrive at my locker and I dial in the combination and pull on the handle. It doesn't open. It doesn't even budge. Not that this is anything new. It never opens. The lockers at Southwest High are about a million years old and I don't think they've ever been cleaned or repaired. They were probably once a lovely shade of turquoise, but now they're all this ugly sludge/rust color.

I sigh and try the combo again, yanking hard on the lever. Still nothing. I let out a groan. "I hate this stupid thing!"

"You gotta push in, *then* pull up," Austin says, scooting me aside. He dials my combination and tries his technique, to no avail. He sets his backpack on the ground, rolls up his sleeves, and makes another attempt. This time he shakes the lever so hard, the entire row of lockers bangs around. Finally, after he pounds his fist against the metal three times and kicks it twice, the door pops open.

Do I seriously have to do that every time I want to open my locker? I should just risk scoliosis and carry all of my books around in my bag.

The Windsor Academy doesn't even have lockers. They removed them two years ago when they initiated their new high-tech education system called the Windsor Achiever. Everything is completely digital and synced across all devices. I read about it on their website.

I empty my bag of everything except my notebook for the newspaper and the book I need to return to the library.

"Gotta run," Austin says, leaning in to kiss me, but then he remembers his coffee breath. "Right," he says, pulling away. "Breath mints. I'm on it."

I slam my locker door shut. It bounces against the latch and then breaks off entirely, clattering to the floor near my feet. I sigh dramatically and just walk away.

At least it'll be easier to get my stuff this way.

If I Didn't Have Laney

Laney and I both have first period free. We usually spend it in the newspaper office, which is located on the second floor of the school, next to the display case that features our three Spartan Press Awards. I stop in the library on the way to return the copy of *Moby-Dick* that I checked out three weeks ago. After this I only have one book left on the "25 Books to Read Before College" list. It was published by the *San Francisco Chronicle* ten years ago. I found it online when I was twelve and Googling "How to Get Accepted to the College of Your Dreams." The only title I have left to read is *Robinson Crusoe* by Daniel Defoe, but I haven't been able to find it in our school library. The computer says there are three copies on the shelf, but they all seem to have magically disappeared and the librarian insists she doesn't have enough money in the budget to replace them.

I check the shelf once again before leaving, even wandering from the Ds into the Es and Cs, but there's still no sign of those alleged three copies.

I guess I'll have to get it from the public library.

Laney is working hard at her computer station when I bust

through the door of the newspaper office. "I only have two hundred more words to write," she says without looking up from the screen. "Then I can put this section to bed."

"Excellent," I say, taking a deep breath. I love coming into this office. It feels like my second home. The sound of computer keys clacking, the smell of the ink from the small printer we use for our proof pages, our past issues decorating the walls. But I also always feel ten pounds heavier the moment I walk through the door. The stress cloaks me like a wet blanket.

"Did you come up with an idea for your last piece?" Laney asks.

"How about locker doors that fall off when you close them?"

"That's not news."

I slide into the computer station next to her, mumbling, "I know. Did Horace create the graphics yet?"

She shakes her head and goes back to typing. "Does Horace ever do anything around here?"

I let out a groan, grab the keyboard, and bring it up to my forehead, banging twice. "Ugh."

Laney expertly pats me on the back with one hand while the other keeps typing. "It'll be okay. We're going to finish this and then, after it's sent to the printer, we're going to strap Horace upside down to the flagpole . . . by the balls."

Despite myself, I let out a laugh.

I don't know what I'd do without Delaney Patel. She's my rock. She always knows exactly what to say to make me feel better.

And she loves saying balls.

I log in and take a deep breath as I wait for the machine to boot up. That meditation book my dad gave me said something about oxygen being Mother Nature's remedy to everything. But I honestly don't think Mother Nature ever had to put out an award-winning school newspaper every month.

I suck in another deep inhale and scowl. I can still taste Austin's coffee on my lips.

No, wait a minute. That's not coming from me.

I sniff at the air. "Do you smell . . . coffee?"

Laney immediately covers her mouth. "Oh, sorry. I went to Peabody's this morning. It must be me."

I look over at her, tapping furiously to finish her story. "That's weird," I say. "Austin went to Peabody's this morning, too."

She stops typing as an unreadable expression blankets her face. "That is weird," she says flatly.

"Did you see him there?"

It takes her a moment to respond, like she's trying to remember. She must be more stressed than I am if she's having trouble remembering the face of a guy she's known for three years. "No," she finally says. "I must have just missed him."

The computer finishes booting up and I click on the file for this month's issue. Thankfully, it opens and all the work we did yesterday on the new layout is still there. I let out the breath I've been holding since last night and stare at the front page. Last night I was happy with it. Now everything looks wrong. What is the story about the new science teacher doing on the front page? That's not front-page news.

I start shuffling things around, but stop when I get the strange sensation that someone is watching me. I look up to see Laney staring at me from the next terminal. "What?" I ask, smoothing down my hair.

She blinks a few times and shakes her head. "Nothing. Do you want me to email Horace and ask him to come down here after first period?"

I grunt. "No. I'll make the graphics myself. Like always."

Laney nods for what feels like a lifetime and then goes back to typing.

"Lanes," I say, studying her curiously. "Is everything all right?"

"Yeah," she says, but her voice is unusually high. "Everything's great. I'm just stressed about the issue."

I sigh. "I know, me too."

She rubs my back again. "Don't worry. It's going to be good."

I shake my head. "It can't be good. It has to be *great*."

"It's going to be amazing! First class! Genius! And the balls of every member on the SPA committee are going to fall right off when they read it."

I smile. "Thanks."

Laney grins and goes back to working on her story.

Seriously. Thank *God* for Laney. She's the only person in my life who can keep me sane.

If We Don't Win

Not to brag or anything, but the Southwest Star was kind of on its last legs when I took over. I turned this whole paper around. With the help of Laney, obviously.

The truth is, Laney and I weren't even planning to *be* on the newspaper. The whole thing was kind of an accident. We were both looking for the debate club but we ended up walking into the newspaper office instead. It's actually how we met.

The creative writing teacher, Ms. Testerman, had been trying to keep the newspaper afloat for months. They had this sad little online site with the totally uninspired name of "The Southwest News," and no print edition. The school board was about to shut down the club because no one was actually *reading* the paper.

When Laney and I walked into room 212 after school on the first day of freshman year, thinking it was the debate club meeting, Ms. Testerman was trying to rally the five completely lethargic students who called themselves the newspaper staff by asking for story ideas.

I happened to have *just* been complaining to Austin earlier that day about the disproportionate funds that went to the football program as opposed to the library, so I raised my hand and pitched the story.

Ms. Testerman was positively thrilled and told me to look into it, which I did.

That story ended up winning us our very first Spartan Press Award. It turned out the head football coach was illegally siphoning off funds from other programs in the school. So while the tennis team and the cheerleading squad had to sell lollipops or frozen cheesecakes to be able to go to *their* state finals, the football team always seemed to have plenty of money to do whatever it wanted.

After the story ran, the head coach was fired and the money was returned to the rightful departments. Now I always snicker quietly to myself when a football player comes up to me in the hallway and asks if I want to buy a lollipop.

By my second month as a freshman, I was unanimously voted in as editor in chief. Now, more than three years later, with three award-winning front pages framed and mounted on my bedroom wall, I have the enormous burden of releasing a kick-ass issue every month.

But this issue is more stressful than most. Because this issue is the one we send to the Spartan Press Award for consideration. And once you've won it three years in a row, people kind of *expect* you to win it again.

The issue is due to the committee in two weeks and the winners are notified by email on December 15, which just *happens* to also be the day Columbia early decision letters arrive.

Let's see those Tibetan monks deal with *that* kind of pressure.

After school, once the entire newspaper staff has assembled in the office, I call for everyone's attention. "Okay. I know everyone wants to get out of here at a reasonable hour, so I'll try to make this short. First, I want to thank you all for being here on Drop Dead and giving up whatever you had to give up today. Second, the new layout has been causing some formatting issues with the sections, so please quadruple-check *everything* before saving. I know it's kind of a hassle, but I really think the new layout will impress the judges at the SPA. The old layout was getting stale, and if you want to keep winning you have to keep evolving, right?"

There are a few apathetic echoes of "Right" on top of Laney's overly enthusiastic one. I flash her a grateful smile and she nods back at me.

"I have an idea," Horace interjects, without even looking up from his monitor. I know he's playing his stupid computer game instead of actually working on a story. I can see it reflected in his glasses. "Why don't we write a story about how no one reads newspapers anymore because everything's online?"

I can feel my temperature rising. Laney gives me a look that says, "Just let it go. It's not worth the fight."

Horace is technically our design editor. But all he really does around here is annoy people with his bonehead comments while he plays Excavation Empire.

I've tried to play. Just to see what the fuss is about. And I don't get it. You build things. With bricks. And then you wait for people to tear them down. It's like a digital version of the sandbox when we were four.

I would have fired Horace ages ago if I was actually allowed to fire people. But it's school rules. Since newspaper isn't a sport it's considered a "club," and the rules clearly state that anyone who wants to be in a club is allowed to be.

Trust me, I've read the rules over and over again. Extensively. I even asked my mom, the lawyer, to help me find a loophole, but she claims the document is ironclad and even looked a little impressed when she read it.

So bottom line, Horace is on the newspaper staff whether I like it or not.

"Thank you, Horace," I say tersely. "That was very helpful."

"No problem, chief," he says, before pounding angrily on the keyboard and shouting at his screen, "I hope your city gets bulldozed by the Inferno Dragon!"

"Okay," I say brightly. "Remember to save your files every three minutes so you don't lose any work. As soon as your section is done, message me so I can add it to the final file. Let's try to get out of here before dark."

"I don't know what we'd do without you," Laney says, coming up to me after the staff has dispersed. "You save this paper's balls like every single week."

"We work as a team," I remind her. "But, thanks."

She touches my arm. "I better go proof this article so I can get home in time for *How Is This My Life?*"

I let out a groan. "Oh God. I forgot you watch that thing, too."

Laney looks practically offended. "Of course I watch it. It's only the best show on Netflix." She lowers her voice an octave. "Here comes the big one! Here comes the whaaaaammmy!" Then she laughs so hard, she snorts.

"That show is so stupid! I can't believe both you and Aus—" I break off, my mind suddenly putting pieces together. I can't believe I didn't think of it before.

"Laney!" I say urgently, grabbing her arm.

I can feel her stiffen. "What?"

"You *have* to go over to Austin's and watch it with him!"

She's silent for a full five seconds before stammering, "W-w-why would I do that?"

God, based on her reaction, you would think she's secretly hated my boyfriend's guts for the past three years and was too afraid to tell me.

"Because," I say, as though it's obvious. And it *is*. At least to me. "You both *love* that show. And I feel bad because I have my dad's gallery thing tonight so I can't watch it with him. But if *you* go over there, then you can watch it *together*!"

It really is one of my finer ideas, if I don't say so myself.

"No," Laney says brusquely, picking up a stack of papers off a nearby desk and straightening them like it's the most important job in the world. "I don't think that's a good idea."

"Yes it is!" I insist. "You guys even quote the same stupid line from his bit. You're clearly *meant* to watch this together."

Laney lets out a weird chipmunk laugh. "Yeah, right. Me and

Austin? We're not meant to do anything together. We have like *nothing* in common."

Why is she acting so strange? The three of us hang out all the time and she's never acted like this. What's the big deal?

"Um, you have *me* in common. And apparently also this lame comedy show." I grab her hand and tug on it. "Please do it. It would mean so much to me. You're just going to be watching the show tonight anyway, right? Why not watch it with Austin? You know stand-up comedy is more fun to watch with someone else. Please, please, please!"

Laney stares down at my hand. Is it just me or does her breathing look a little erratic?

I tilt my head. "Laney? What's going on?"

She lets out that weird rodent laugh again. "Nothing. Nothing's going on. I'm fine. I'm totally, one-hundred-percent finesies."

Finesies?

"So you'll go?" I confirm.

She gnaws on her bottom lip. "Yeah. Why not? I mean, if it'll make you happy."

I let out a sigh. "Yes. It will make me very happy."

"Great," Laney says, but I hear a hint of uneasiness in her voice. Maybe she really *does* hate Austin. Maybe she's just been too polite to tell me this whole time. Sure, he can be a little weird sometimes and he has a knack for saying and doing the most embarrassing things in the middle of the hallway. And he to- tally overuses the phrase "for all intents and purposes," except he says, "for all intensive purposes," which is actually *not* the phrase. And he . . .

Well, anyway, the point is, he's my boyfriend and I love him and if Laney has a problem with him, then a few hours of hanging out with him might do some good.

Laney scurries back to her computer and slides into her seat. I stand in the front of the room, watching my team at work.

Relax. Deep breaths. In. Out. In. Out.

The issue is on track. Austin has someone to watch his comedy show with. It looks like I might get out of here in time to make it to Dad's show.

Everything is working out great. All it needed was a little delegation.

If They Knew the Truth

Miraculously we get the issue done by seven thirty-two and I race out of the school with the flash drive in hand and zoom over to the printer on the other side of town. I always hand deliver the final files to Eric for every issue. Too much can happen when you email or upload to the cloud.

A virus could corrupt the formatting. The email could end up sitting unseen in someone's spam folder. Aliens could decide today is the day they finally hack Earth's cyberspace.

All very likely possibilities.

Thankfully the gallery is only a mile away from the printer, so after dropping off the drive, I make it there slightly before eight o'clock. I park on the street a few buildings away and sit in my car for a moment to decompress. It's been a long day and I need to get my head back on straight before I go in there.

I turn up the music on Woody's stereo and close my eyes, trying to collect my thoughts and transform myself from the title of "Editor in Chief" to "Supportive Daughter."

I flip the visor down and check my reflection in the mirror. I didn't have time to change so I'm still wearing my jeans and brown leather jacket. Not that I'd have much to change *into*. My closet basically consists of what I'm wearing right now.

I do take the time to rebraid my hair, though, just so I feel like I've done something.

As I walk toward the gallery, I swipe on my phone to see that CoyCoy55 has posted a new picture. This one is of her and her best friend, Luce_the_Goose.

I don't know either of their real names, just their profile names. Luce_the_Goose is obviously something like Lucy but I have no idea what CoyCoy's real name could be. I'm convinced, however, it's something really cool and unique like Cleo or Lark, or maybe something über literary like Ophelia or Brontë.

In this picture, they're doing one of their hilarious Caption Challenges. That's when one of them suggests a silly caption and they have to act it out for the picture. This one is called "Meteor! Heading right toward us!" They're both pointing at the sky and screaming. I chuckle when I see it. The Caption Challenge pics are always my favorite. It shows how much fun they have together.

With a sigh, I shut off my phone and toss it into my bag.

You made your choice, Kennedy, I remind myself for the billionth time. *This is your life.*

I've tried unfollowing CoyCoy55. I have. Several times. But it's like an addiction I can't kick. One time, a few months ago, Laney caught me looking at CoyCoy55's feed. We were sitting on the grass in the soccer field eating our lunch and I was complaining that the grass at our school was too coarse and itchy and was giving me a rash. I took out my phone to look at one of

CoyCoy55's many photos of her and Luce_the_Goose lounging on the perfectly green, *soft* grass at the Windsor Academy and Laney glanced over at my screen and laughed at me. "Do you ever think that maybe people at Windsor are stalking *our* Snip-Pic feeds, wishing they had *our* life?"

I snorted at this. It was almost too ridiculous to respond to, but I did anyway. "No," I said confidently. "They're too busy living their amazing lives to worry about what *we're* doing."

Laney is really the only person who knows about my obsession with the Windsor Academy. But even she doesn't know the full extent of it. For instance, she doesn't know that I purposefully drive a specific route to school every day in hopes that the light will turn red in front of the gates so I can steal a peek inside. She doesn't know that I practically have CoyCoy55's entire school schedule memorized. She also doesn't know that I fall asleep almost every night wondering what my life would be like if I went there. If I was one of them. If I wore that uniform and sat on that lawn and ate in that gorgeous student union.

I would never tell Laney any of these things. I would never tell *anyone* any of these things. They'd surely have me locked away. Or at the very least send me to some kind of stalkers anonymous group.

But that's only because they don't know the full story. No one does. Not even Laney. I never told a soul what really happened.

Laney, like everyone in my life, still thinks I never got in.

If Eyes Could Talk

Dad's show opens to the public at eight p.m. I walk through the back doors of the gallery with two minutes to spare. It's a spectacular space. The walls are white, the floors are wood, and the ceilings are unfinished, making it look like we're inside a chic factory.

I walk through the large, open room in amazement as Dad's artwork stares at me from all sides. Literally.

The series is called "Portals."

Dad takes these mind-blowing photographs of people's eyes. Although you would never really know it when you first look at them. The pictures are so zoomed in and enlarged, they no longer look like eyes. They turn into completely other things. Forests. Rivers. Blades of grass. Sunrises. Solar systems.

Different people see different things. That's the beauty of what Dad does.

It's like a really psychedelic Rorschach test.

I stop when I see the photograph that I captioned this morning, giggling slightly when I remember that Dad thought it looked like varicose veins. Instead, I chose to caption it "Purple Rain," because it resembles violet-colored lightning streaking across the sky, and also because my dad loves that song by Prince. Apparently it was playing when my parents first met in a bar during Dad's "edgy phase." It's kind of ironic that this particular eye belongs to our garbageman—the epitome of suburban living and the polar opposite of an "edgy phase."

I continue down the wall, smiling at the photographs, remembering the subject behind each one. I pass my mom's eye, which looks like a sunflower; Dad's eye, which looks like planet Earth from space; Frankie's eye, which looks like a galaxy—no surprise there—until I finally get to my own eye. It's a bright, almost electric blue, with spindly white threads dancing across it, like a spiderweb strung across a cloudless blue sky.

I beam proudly when I read the small white placard underneath.

Make a wish.

I wrote that caption as a little inside joke between Dad and me. He always thought spiderwebs were lucky, and when I was a kid I used to make wishes on them. He took the photograph a few months ago, and the next day he found out he was getting this show. "See?" he said to me that day. "I always knew you were lucky. There's the proof. Right there."

"So?" Dad says, coming up behind me. "What do you think?"

I turn and smile at him. "It's amazing, Dad. It's . . ." But I can't even finish the thought because my voice cracks and I feel tears welling up. I'm just so proud of him. He's been waiting so long for this moment.

Dad seems to get the point anyway and pulls me into a hug. "Thanks, kiddo."

The doors to the gallery open, and from that moment on there's a constant stream of people coming and going, chattering excitedly about my dad's art. I stand in the corner and just watch the whole thing. Everyone is agog at the photos. They tilt their heads and move back and forth from the walls, trying to see the various pictures hidden within each piece. Dad spends the evening bustling about, explaining his intention with each one and changing people's perspective.

By the time the clock hits eleven, every single piece in this gallery has been sold. The art dealer said she's never seen anything like it from a new artist. I want to tell her that my dad *isn't* a new artist. He's been doing this for years. *This is just the first time you dumbos have taken notice.*

I watch as my dad delivers the news to my mom, who's dressed in her typical black work suit, sipping champagne as she makes polite small talk with some snobby art critic. As soon as he tells her, all of her professionalism and lawyerly composure goes right out the window and she turns into a teenage girl at a rock concert. She squeals and leaps into his arms. Dad twirls her around and then she kisses him hard on the lips.

"Yuck," Frankie says next to me, averting his eyes, and I laugh. I know you're supposed to be grossed out seeing your parents display affection for each other, and normally I am. But not now. Now, I'm just fascinated by it. And so inspired.

My dad hasn't earned a dime since my mother met him. Sure, he takes care of everything at home. He makes us breakfast and dinner and does the laundry and helps us with our homework—well, he helps *me*. Frankie stopped needing help when he was in second grade. But he's turned down every single job offer those stupid Jeffrey and Associates people have sent him. He's refused to sell out and become a corporate photographer in exchange for a steady paycheck. Because he believed in his art. And so did my mom. She supported him—and *us*—completely on her own, without ever complaining about it.

And now it's finally paid off.

Frankie buries his face in my jacket and I ruffle his hair. "Is it over?" he asks.

I watch Mom jump back down, keeping her arms tightly around my dad. "Yeah," I tell him. "It's over."

He lifts his head and gags. "In a parallel universe that *never* happened."

"I think it's nice," I tell him, "that Mom is so supportive. It's important to him and she gets that . . ."

My voice trails off as I remember my conversation with Austin in the hallway today. How quickly I dismissed his comedy show for being lame and juvenile. He loves that show. He's been looking forward to the new season for eight months. Sure, it may not be a photography exhibit at an art gallery, but it's important to *him*. And I haven't been supportive at all.

While my parents are talking to the art dealer, I slip out the back door and get into my car. I check the clock on the dash. It's a little after eleven thirty. There are eight episodes in the season and they're each an hour long. Austin said the episodes were being released at seven. That means, if I hurry, I can still watch the last few with him and Laney.

I speed the entire way there, feeling a small prick of excitement as I park the car in Austin's driveway and tiptoe toward the basement door. I know he'll be in there. That's where he always watches TV. The idea of surprising him is making my heart start to hammer.

It's kind of romantic. Me showing up for him at the last minute. Zooming across town to be a loving, supportive girlfriend and show him that I really do care about his interests. Even the ones that don't interest me.

As I ease open the door into the main area of the basement, I can hear Tom What's-his-butt cracking one of his signature fart jokes from the TV room next door. "The key to farting in public," he says, "is making sure you have a fart scapegoat nearby." The audience roars with laughter. I wait to hear Austin's loud booming laugh and Laney's signature chipmunk giggle-snort. They'll definitely find that stupid joke funny. But there's absolute silence in the next room. That's weird. Maybe they went upstairs to get a snack. But then, why wouldn't they pause the show?

I creep through the basement toward the TV room, listening intently. I can definitely hear *something*. But it's not laughter.

It almost sounds like—

OH. MY. GOD.

I screech to a halt in the doorway as I take in the heart-ripping, gut-wrenching, life-changing sight that lies in front of me.

The TV is on. Tom Who-the-heck-cares is still cracking one lewd joke after another, but Laney and Austin aren't catching a single word he says.

Because they're too busy kissing.

If I Had Chosen Right

The very first thought that enters my mind as I watch my boyfriend kissing my best friend is:

You chose wrong.

Not the wrong boyfriend. And not even the wrong best friend.

But the wrong life.

I must make some kind of noise and it probably sounds something like a mouse being electrocuted because suddenly they're not kissing anymore. They're looking at me. And I'm looking at them and the TV is still going and an announcer kicks off the beginning of a new episode by yodeling, "How Is This My Life?"

And I think, *Yes, exactly.*

How is this my life?

This wasn't supposed to be my life. I wasn't supposed to be here. I'm supposed to be at the Windsor Academy. I'm supposed to be with CoyCoy55 and Luce_the_Goose. We're all supposed to be studying together in the student union or touring art museums or something.

Instead, I'm standing here like an idiot and they're sitting there like idiots and no one is sure which idiot should talk first. It's like one of those lame standoffs in an action flick when the cop and the bad guy are both pointing guns at each other and they're saying things like "I know what you did" and "I'm going to blow your brains out" and "You'll never get away with this" and "Just watch me."

I never understood those scenes. I always thought, *Why doesn't someone freaking shoot already and put an end to this?*

But now, I'm suddenly gaining a new appreciation for that particular type of stalemate. If I shoot first—if I speak or cry or yell—there's a chance they'll immediately shoot back. And then it'll hurt more. And we'll all be dead.

So I do what no cop has ever done in the history of action movies. I drop my weapon and just start running.

I can hear a single pair of footsteps following after me. I can't tell whom they belong to. Who was sent as the envoy? Who cares enough to follow me? My stupid makes-obnoxious-sounds-with-his-teeth, likes-cheap-fart-jokes boyfriend? Or my stupid laughs-like-a-chipmunk, coffee-breath best friend?

The coffee breath.

Holy crap, it was right in front of me and I didn't even see it.

That's why Laney was acting so strange today in the newspaper office.

They didn't just both go to Peabody's this morning. They went *together*.

Which means, this kiss might not be the first.

Looks like *I'm* the bigger idiot, after all. Although I guess I already knew that. I made the decision that got me here, didn't I? I'm the one who chose this life.

"Kennedy! Wait!" the footsteps speak. And the voice belongs to Laney. I should have known she'd be the one to come after me.

Somewhere deep inside, I find the strength to stop. To turn around and face her. To ask the one question I know will haunt me forever if I don't ask.

"How long?" I demand.

She stops, too, keeping a safe distance. "We never wanted to hurt you," she whimpers. It's a foreign sound coming from her. Like she's on the verge of tears. But Laney never cries. She's too strong. She's the rock in the friendship and rocks don't cry. "*I* never wanted to hurt you," she amends.

"How long?" I repeat through clenched teeth.

Laney stares into my eyes for a long moment. She bravely holds my gaze even though her face is tormented. Then, when she can't hold on any longer, she drops her head and whispers, "Three months."

And then I'm running again. And Laney is calling after me again. But I don't stop this time. I don't want to hear her pitiful explanations and empty apologies.

I get in my car, start the engine, and throw the gearshift into Drive. As I peel away from the curb, my headlights just barely catch Laney's silhouette on the sidewalk. Her body is slumped in surrender. Her hands are covering her eyes. Like she's actually crying.

Like she has any right to cry.

A moment later, my phone starts exploding with texts. I pull it out of my bag and shut off the ringer. I won't read them. Because I don't care what they say. I don't care about anything Laney has to say ever again. Or Austin for that matter.

Although strangely enough, it's not the Austin part that hurts the most. It's the Laney part. Austin's betrayal just feels like a sunburn on top of a massive gouge in my arm. It stings, it's uncomfortable, but it's overshadowed by this bleeding, oozing, festering wound underneath.

She's my *best* friend. My partner in crime. My news editor.

Why would she do this?

As I turn into my subdivision, a beam from one of the streetlamps bounces off something sparkling inside my car. I look down to see the glittery pink phone charger that's plugged into the center console.

The gag gift from Laney.

Because she knows how much I hate pink things that sparkle. I hate that marketers just expect girls to buy stuff because they make it in a glittery color. Like we're nothing more than moths attracted to shiny things. I even wrote a piece about it in the *Southwest Star*.

I slam on the brakes and the car lurches to a halt. With my heart still pounding and my inhales and exhales sounding like I'm breathing through a scuba mask, I yank out the charger, roll down the window, and chuck it as far as I can. Which admittedly isn't very far because I'm not that good at throwing stuff and the wind catches the cord and nearly blows it back in my face.

Now it's lying on the ground in the middle of the street. The pink glitter flashing in the streetlights.

No, I think. *Not good enough.*

I throw the car in Reverse and back up. Then I floor the gas pedal and race forward until I hear the satisfying crunch under my tires.

Then I back up and do it again. And again. And again. Back and forth. Back and forth. Until the crunching sound subsides and there's nothing but dust left and the stupid thing finally stops sparkling.

If I Had Said No

The house is quiet when I get home. There's an empty champagne bottle on the kitchen counter. For a brief moment, I forget everything that happened in the last thirty minutes. I forget about Laney's betrayal and Austin's lies and three and a half years of friendship down the drain.

My dad had an amazing night tonight. He reached a career milestone. Everything's going to change for him now. Some people thought he was crazy. Turning down job offers all of those years. Rejecting the opportunity for a steady paycheck and a steady job just so he could take pictures of eyeballs. But in the end, everything worked out. He believed in something with all his heart and it paid off.

He made the *right* choice.

I run upstairs to my room and collapse on my bed. I pull my phone out of my bag and immediately click on CoyCoy55's Snip-Pic feed. I scroll through the photos, finding one of my favorites from a week ago. It was another Caption Challenge with her and Luce_the_Goose. They were studying in the Windsor Academy's stunning high-ceilinged student union. Their signature school-issued navy blue laptops are open on the table. In the picture, they're both swooning theatrically—CoyCoy55 collapsed in her chair with her hand to her forehead like she fainted in a Jane Austen novel and Luce_the_Goose sprawled across the table, fanning herself.

The caption reads: "My Book Boyfriend Just Proposed!"

I should be in that photo. I should be fake swooning right alongside them.

Seething, I toss the phone aside, stand up, and head straight for the bottom drawer of my desk. That's where I keep the letter.

I gently run my fingertip back and forth over the blue and silver Windsor Academy logo embossed right onto the paper as my eyes skim the words on the page that I still have memorized all of these years later.

Congratulations . . .
A place has opened up . . .
You have shown tremendous potential . . .
We are thrilled to offer you admission . . .
Please respond by . . .

The truth is, I *didn't* get into the Windsor Academy. At least not at first. I got wait-listed at the end of the sixth grade. I was beyond devastated because I knew there was no chance I'd ever get in.

No one *ever* gets off the wait list. Because no one ever leaves. The Windsor Academy is the kind of school that unlocks doors that don't even have handles. If you're lucky enough to get accepted right out of elementary school then you stay put. All the way until high school graduation.

But then, two years later, right before the end of eighth grade, the impossible happened. This letter arrived informing me that a space was available. And, if I so chose, I could start freshman year of high school with the young elite.

It was a miracle.

But as my fickle luck would have it, it wasn't the first miracle that had happened to me that week.

The first miracle had arrived five days earlier, also in the form of a letter. I opened my locker to find the note carefully folded up inside. My name was written on the outside, surrounded by a lopsided heart.

I tore it open and my heart hammered in my chest as I read the words I'd been waiting to hear for nearly two years.

Wanna go to the movies with me tonight?

It was from *him*. Austin McKinley. If there was ever anything I wanted more than the Windsor Academy, it was Austin McKinley. I had loved him from afar since the first day of seventh grade. I had fallen asleep to fantasies of kissing him every night. I had scribbled our names in thousands of hearts on thousands of notebook pages and Photoshopped our faces together more times than I'd ever admit.

And now, he wanted to go out. With *me*.

Of course I said yes. I agonized over the date for hours. What would I wear? What would I say? Where would I put my hands? When my mom dropped me off at the theater later that night, I saw him waiting for me in the lobby, standing next to the refreshment stand looking jaw-dropping in jeans and still-wet hair.

After the movie, he told me what a good time he'd had and asked if we could hang out again. Then he leaned forward and pecked me on the lips, lighting a hundred fires all over my body. When he pulled back and I looked into his clear-as-crystal blue eyes, that was it. It was all over.

When the Windsor Academy letter came, I immediately knew.

I could never say yes to both of them. I would have to choose.

Turning down the Windsor Academy was the hardest thing I've ever done. Although truthfully, I never actually turned them down. The letter had an expiration date. Respond by this day or your spot will be given away. I simply didn't respond.

I hid the letter in my bottom drawer and never told a soul.

Maybe because somewhere deep inside, I always knew it was the wrong choice. Maybe because I assumed if anyone knew, they would try to talk me out of it. And I didn't want to be talked out of it.

I wanted Austin.

I knew our budding relationship would never survive if I went to Windsor at the end of the summer. Even though it was only a few miles away from Southwest High, I was smart enough to understand how these things worked. Long-distance relationships in high school—even three-mile-radius ones—were doomed to fail.

Of course I had doubts at first. Of course I still wondered if

I'd made the right choice every time I passed by Windsor on the way to school. But I dealt with it.

As my relationship with Austin blossomed and evolved and we eventually became one of the longest-standing couples at Southwest High, my self-doubt slowly faded until it was background noise. Until I could barely hear it.

I fold up the letter and place it back in my desk drawer. I don't even realize I've been crying until I turn around and the room is blurry. I sniffle and wipe at my eyes. And that's when I see the framed photograph sitting on the floor near my closet. It wasn't there this morning, but it's there now, leaning against the wall. I recognize it immediately.

It's my eye.

My extreme close-up blue spiderweb of an eye. The one that was on display at the sold-out gallery show tonight.

Curiously, I step closer to it until I see the small Post-it note with Dad's neat handwriting attached to the top left corner of the frame.

Couldn't bear to sell this one. —Dad

Then my gaze falls to the little white placard at the bottom of the frame. The caption I wrote for him:

Make a wish.

I feel tears well up all over again as I collapse in front of the photograph and stare into my own eye. Into my own past. Into my own messed-up choices. Dad always thought spiderwebs were lucky. That I was his lucky charm. And while that might be true, when it comes to *me*, it turns out I'm my own curse.

I brought this on myself.

I chose wrong.

If I Don't Care

By noon the next day, I'm a whole new woman. I've showered. I've dressed. I've done my hair (and *not* in a braid). I've even moisturized my face. Something I've never done in my life but, as it turns out, is pretty dang refreshing.

I don't have time to be angry or bitter or forlorn. I don't have time to play the victim and lament over my crappy choice in friends and boyfriends. My Columbia interview is in an hour and I am *not* going to blow this. I may not have gone to the Windsor Academy, I may have screwed that one up, but I'm not going to make the same mistake twice. I'm not going to let a stupid guy— or girl—mess up any more of my life.

I am going to Columbia University. I am going to be a journalist. I don't need Austin. I don't even need Laney. I just need these well-thought-out, relentlessly rehearsed, foolproof interview answers and I'm good to go.

I sit at the kitchen counter, spooning soup into my mouth while I quiz myself on my crib sheet. Dad signed me out of school today. We both knew I wouldn't be able to concentrate on AP calculus or AP history while this interview loomed over my head.

So I've spent the morning psyching myself up. And *not* thinking about Austin and Laney.

Okay, I thought about them a little bit. Namely, as I was destroying every shred of evidence that Austin was ever my boyfriend and Laney was ever my best friend . . . which was basically half of the things in my bedroom. But now that *that's* done, I can get on with my life. I can move forward.

I haven't even read a single text message from either of them. I deleted them all *and* blocked their numbers. That's how over it I am. That's how little I care.

"Kennedy?"

"Gah!" I jump at the sound of Dad's voice, spilling soup on my interview questions. "Dad," I say scornfully, "you scared me. Don't sneak up on a girl like that when she's prepping for the biggest interview of her life."

Dad flashes me a weird look. "I came into the kitchen singing and tap dancing. I wasn't exactly stealth."

In addition to singing completely off-key, Dad also tap dances. Poorly.

"Oh," I say, wiping down the page with my napkin.

"You were kind of in a trance there," Dad points out. "You must really be laser focused on this thing."

"Yes. Laser focused." I sit up straighter and add, "On the interview."

"Right," Dad agrees, sounding confused. "On the interview. What else would you be focused on?"

"Nothing," I reply breezily. "Nothing at all. I have absolutely *nothing* else to focus on except this interview."

Okay, so I haven't told my parents about what happened last night. I will. Eventually. I'll call them sometime next year from my dorm room at Columbia.

I finish wiping the soup from my paper and stare at the questions again as Dad starts assembling his usual sandwich. He's been eating the exact same lunch every day for the past three years. Wheat bread, turkey, pickles, *then* cheese, lettuce, tomato, mayonnaise, and a dash of Worcestershire sauce. He calls it "the Duke."

"The gallery owner called today," Dad tells me as he tops his sandwich with the second piece of bread. "She's had nonstop orders since last night."

"That's terrific!"

Dad beams. "It is. But it means I'll be working a lot in the next few days to try to keep up."

I finish my soup and carry the bowl to the dishwasher. "Have I told you how proud I am of you?" I say, giving my dad a kiss on the cheek just as he takes his first bite of the Duke.

"Wait," Dad garbles with his mouth full. "That's supposed to be my line."

I shrug. "Sorry. Beat you to the punch."

I carefully place my interview crib sheet in my messenger bag and toss the strap over my shoulder. "Okay, I'm off to get into Columbia!"

Dad grins widely with a piece of Worcestershire-soaked lettuce hanging out the side of his mouth. "Break a leg!"

"I think you only say that to actors."

Dad nods pensively. "Okay then, break a pen! Bust a laptop! Burn a book!"

I shake my head. "Stick to the photography, Dad."

"Flip a table!" Dad calls after me as I head for the front door. "Destroy a chair! Crash a car! No, wait, don't do that!"

"Bye, Dad!" I say with a laugh. "See you in a few hours."

If I Spoke German

The Columbia alum lives in one of those grand mansions on the west side of town. She's a tall, willowy, dark-haired woman dressed in an African print kaftan with black leggings underneath. She greets me with a kind smile and a handshake.

"Welcome, Kennedy!" she says. "I'm Geraldine Watkins, but you can call me Watts. All my friends do."

"Thank you . . . Watts," I reply as she leads me into the house.

The first thing I see when I step into the living room is her wall of diplomas. And I literally mean an entire wall. She must have every degree there is to get. The spaces that aren't occupied by PhDs or master's degrees are filled with framed photographs of Watts in all sorts of exotic-looking places. Rain forests and mountains and deserts.

I suddenly become ten times more intimidated than I was when I pulled up to the curb a few minutes ago.

"Wow!" I say, stopping to look at a picture of her posing next to a cactus, surrounded by sand dunes. "Is this New Mexico?"

She stops in her tracks, her body visibly stiffening. "That's the

Kalahari Desert." Then, as if she's afraid I might be *extra* clueless, adds, "In *Africa*."

I immediately feel my face flood with shame. "Oh," I fumble. "Right. Well, it's a beautiful photograph. That must have been a wonderful trip."

Her face pales. "We went on an anti-poaching mission and stumbled upon over twenty slaughtered elephant carcasses."

"Oh," I say again, berating myself. But honestly, how was I supposed to know that from a stupid picture? It's not like she's standing *next* to one of the elephant carcasses. "That's very . . . sad."

Sad?

I'm a writer and I couldn't come up with a more creative adjective than *sad*?

"Hmm," Watts says ambiguously as she takes a seat on a large red armchair in the center of the room and gestures for me to take the couch across from her, next to a droopy potted plant.

"I think your ficus needs some water," I say with a chuckle, trying for a joke.

But Watts clearly doesn't find it amusing. I can actually see her jaw clench. "That's *not* a ficus. It's a *Ceropegia woodii*. It's a South African flowering plant. I brought it back from Swaziland. It's supposed to look like that."

The terseness of her tone makes my stomach seize. Apparently instead of studying interview questions I should have been studying exotic plants and anti-poaching expeditions. I wonder if I should just throw in the towel and leave now.

But then, a moment later, the most adorable fluffy white

dog comes galloping into the room, and my spirits lift. I love dogs! And dogs always love me.

I smile and bend down. "Hello, there! Aren't you the cutest thing I've ever seen?"

The dog makes a vicious snarling face and snaps at me. I let out a yelp and jump back onto the couch.

Great. Now I've pissed off the dog, too.

"Sorry about that," Watts says, scooping the little white fluff ball into her lap and scratching his head. "This is Klaus. He doesn't like to be approached by strangers. Unless you have organic duck treats. And he only speaks German."

I clear my throat awkwardly. "German?" I confirm.

"Ja. Ich habe ein Jahr in Heidelberg studiert und spreche jetzt mit Klaus Deutsch, um die Sprache nicht zu vergessen."

Oh God. I have no idea what she just said. Did the interview already start? Was that the first question? Was I supposed to learn German? None of the websites said *anything* about an interviewer asking questions in a foreign language!

Watts laughs. "How rude of me. I'm sure you don't speak German."

I sag in relief. "No. I'm sorry. I don't."

"I was saying I studied abroad in Heidelberg for a year and I practice the language with Klaus. So I don't lose it." She turns her face back to the dog who gives her a wet kiss on the lips. *"Nicht wahr, Klaus? Nicht wahr? Runter!"*

The dog dutifully jumps down from her lap.

"Sitz!" Watts says. The dog sits.

"Braver Hund!" Watts praises as she takes a piece of mystery

meat from the pocket of her kaftan and gives it to the dog. I've never seen anything devour something so passionately as Klaus devours that treat.

Watts laughs again. "He simply loves those organic duck treats. I buy them at the farmers' market. They cost a pretty penny but he won't do tricks for anything less."

I nod as though I understand. As though I, too, have a small yappy dog with expensive taste who only speaks German.

"Hol dein Spielzeug!" she says to Klaus, and the dog scuttles out of the room, returns a second later with a stuffed pineapple, and begins gnawing on it.

Watts turns her attention to me with a smile. "That'll keep him busy for a while." She grabs a manila folder from the nearby coffee table and flips it open, glancing briefly at my application inside. "So tell me, Kennedy. Why do you want to go to Columbia?"

I take a deep breath and sit up straighter. This is one of the questions I anticipated. And I am *ready.* "Well, I want to be a journalist and Columbia has one of the best journalism programs in the country. Plus, I'm a huge fan of the East Coast and the significance that the city of New York has played in our nation's history."

I release the breath. Excellent start. Just as I rehearsed. Watts nods and jots down a few notes on my application.

"And have you always wanted to be a journalist?"

I'm prepared for this question, too. "Actually, no. I've always loved to write, but I stumbled upon journalism by accident. You see, on the first day of freshman year, my best friend Laney and I were looking for the debate team meeting . . ."

My voice trails off.

My best friend Laney.

More like my traitorous, backstabbing former *best friend Laney.*

"Go on," Watts prompts me.

I blink, feeling the moisture begin to pool in my eyes.

Get it together, Kennedy! Do NOT cry in this interview.

"Sorry, where was I?"

"You were saying you were looking for the debate team meeting," Watts prompts with a friendly smile.

I clear my throat. "Right. Sorry! We were looking for the debate team meeting and instead we wandered into the newspaper office and . . ."

And then she stole my boyfriend and lied to my face for three months, all the while pretending to be my friend.

No! Stop it! Stop it! Stop it! Do not let Laney ruin this for you.

"And the rest was history!" I finish quickly, adding a grin so big and fake that it feels like my cheeks are going to break.

Watts smiles and writes something down. "So, I've been reviewing your application and I have to say, I'm impressed by all that you've accomplished."

I beam. "Thank you."

"I mean, editor in chief of the *Southwest Star*? It's an excellent paper."

"You've read it?" I blurt out, feeling my muscles uncoil. Maybe this isn't going as horribly as I thought.

She laughs. "Yes, and it's extremely well done. Especially that story in the last issue about the feral cats living in the park."

My face falls. That was Laney's story. And apparently she was already hooking up with Austin when she wrote it. Was she lying in his bed with her laptop while she typed it? Was he kissing her shoulder while she emailed it to me with her signature smiley-face-with-glasses sign-off?

"So tell me," Watts goes on, setting the folder down on her lap. "You've accomplished so much in such a short time. You must have made some sacrifices in order to do all of that. What would you say is your biggest regret thus far?"

I knew she'd ask this. I just knew it. I puff up my chest and refresh my smile. "I would have to say my biggest regret is . . ."

Not going to the Windsor Academy and choosing a stupid boy who turned out to be a two-timing scumbag.

I clear my throat and start again. "My biggest regret would have to be . . ."

Trusting my best friend and believing her when she told me she didn't even want *to go to Austin's stupid house to watch the stupid comedy special.*

Watts smiles and nods for me to continue.

"My biggest regret," I try for the third time, "is probably working too hard and not taking enough time for myself . . ." I trail off again, my vision clouding over.

"What do you mean by that?" Watts prompts. She probably thinks I'm a total moron by now. I can't even finish a freaking sentence!

I look down and realize my hands are shaking. I tuck them between my legs. "I mean, my biggest regret is not *thinking* of myself. Or of my future."

Wait, no. That's not in the script.

"Go on," Watts encourages.

"I've made some pretty crappy choices," I say before realizing I just said *crappy* to my alumni interviewer.

Watts looks startled but composes herself quickly. "What kind of choices?"

"All the wrong ones!" I blurt out, throwing my hands in the air. *Oh God. Stop talking. Stop talking NOW.*

But I can't. I can't stop now. It's all tumbling out of my mouth faster than I can even comprehend what I'm saying.

"My entire high school experience was a mistake. One giant, freaking mistake. I didn't do what I was supposed to do. I didn't choose the right path. I chose the wrong one. And now I'm at a crappy public school where the locker doors don't even stay on and the grass is itchy and the desks are broken and you never remember *which* desk is broken, so you sit in it again and again, and it tips over every time and everyone laughs at you while you think about how you could have been somewhere else. You could have been at the best school in the state. But you aren't. You chose the boy. The stupid, stupid boy who misuses simple phrases and laughs at fart jokes. Because you were *fourteen*! These kinds of life-altering decisions shouldn't rest in the hands of people who have barely finished puberty. They can't handle it. They choose wrong. And now I'm stuck in this life that I wasn't supposed to be in to begin with, and you'll probably reject me because that's what my life has become. So I might as well get used to it, right?"

When I finish ranting Watts is staring at me. Even Klaus has stopped chewing on his stuffed pineapple and is gaping at me with his head tilted.

Apparently, he *does* understand English.

"I should probably go." I stand and grab my bag. Watts doesn't even make a move to stop me or walk me to the door. She just sits there with her mouth open, gawking at me like I'm some poached animal carcass left to rot in the desert.

Which, believe me, is *exactly* how I feel right now.

If Zombies Were Real

It isn't until I reach my car that everything hits me at once. That's when I fully realize what just happened. That's when my own voice echoes back in my ears.

Oh God. Oh. God.

OH. MY. GOD!

What was I thinking? What was I *doing?* It was like I was having an out-of-body experience. I wasn't in control of any of my arms or legs or stupid flapping lips. It just poured out of me.

I sit in my car and stare out the windshield at the street. I feel numb. I feel pointless. I feel *sick.*

I open the car door and retch all over Watts's curb.

Well, if I didn't totally turn her off already, then that should do the trick.

I close the car door and press my head back hard against the seat. Why didn't I reschedule the interview? Why didn't I just call her up and say, *You know what? I'm not feeling my best today, how about we postpone until next week?* What was I thinking going to the most important interview of my life the day after I found out that my boyfriend has been cheating on me with my *best* friend? Who does that?

Stupid people, that's who.

Stubborn people.

People who make horrible, life-changing decisions they can't take back.

People like me.

There's no chance I'll get into Columbia now. Why would they let in someone like me? A crazy, babbling, bitter fool who pisses off the dog and mistakes the Kalahari Desert for New Mexico.

I hastily wipe at the tears that are streaming down my face and turn the key in the ignition. I don't even know where I'm going to go. I'm certainly not going to go home, where my dad can grill me about how the interview went. And there's no way I'm going to school and facing Laney and Austin. I just want to drive and drive until I've lost the way back.

I shift into gear, yank on the steering wheel, and slam my foot on the gas.

Twenty minutes later, I find myself parked in front of the Windsor Academy. I don't know how I got here. I don't remember making any of the turns or changing any of the lanes. It's like my body steered here on its own.

I stare up at the black iron security gate and the impressively large sign with the school's initials—WA—positioned in the center.

I could drive up, push the call button, and ask the receptionist to open the gate, but I have no idea what I'd say. "Hi, will you let me in so I can cry on your beautiful lawn?" So I just continue to stare at the sign, wondering what things would be like if I were on the inside, instead of the outside. If I *weren't* a massive screwup.

Right then, an SUV pulls up to the call box, and a moment later the gate swings open. I make a hasty decision and plunge down on the accelerator, just managing to squeeze through before the gate starts to close again.

The exhilaration of being inside these walls hits me immediately. Of course, I've been inside before. Once. In sixth grade when we got to tour the campus before I submitted my application. It hasn't changed much. The grass is still the most vibrant shade of green. The flower beds are still blooming with color. There are no students milling around in their gray and blue uniforms right now. They must be in class. I check the clock on my dash. It's two forty p.m. They probably have at least another period before the end of the day.

I park and wander up the paved walkway to the main entrance. The Windsor Academy has seven total buildings on campus. Royce Hall—the iconic one that's on the home page of their website—is the colonial-style building that was clearly modeled after the famous Ivy League colleges in New England. I slowly make my way up the grand curving brick staircase to the front entrance.

It's immaculately clean and white inside. And it smells so good. Like fresh paint and new carpet. I bet they change the carpets here once a week!

The receptionist is not at her desk—she's probably grabbing

a fancy coffee drink from that gorgeous student union that looks like a train station—but I remember where the dean's office is. I remember where *everything* is. It's like my visit here in the sixth grade was the one time in my life when I had a photographic memory. My brain just right-clicked and saved forever.

When I reach the dean's office, I find the door closed. I reach out to knock but a voice stops me. "I wouldn't do that if I were you."

I turn around to see a tall, lanky guy in a Windsor uniform sitting in the small two-chair waiting area.

"She's on the phone. Dean Lewis doesn't like to be disturbed when she's on the phone." The way he says this last part, I get the feeling that he's mocking her.

"Oh," I say. "Right. Thanks."

I take a seat in the chair next to him and place my backpack on the floor. I can feel the boy's eyes on me from the moment I sit down. Like he's sizing me up. He's probably thinking the same thing I'm thinking.

What is she doing here? She doesn't belong here.

"So, what's your story?" he asks.

I turn and look at him closely for the first time, noticing that *he* doesn't look like he really belongs here either. I mean, he's wearing the traditional boy uniform—gray slacks, a white button-down shirt, a silver and blue striped tie, and a navy blazer with the official Windsor Academy crest sewn over the left breast pocket—but there's something about the way it fits him, or the way he's choosing to wear it, that just doesn't work. His blazer is too big on his lanky body, his shirt is wrinkled and untucked and the buttons are misaligned. His tie is hanging loose around his neck, and his pants are covered in what looks like pizza grease stains. Plus, his hair is kind of a mess. It's dark and longish, curling over the collar of his blazer.

All of the boys I've seen in CoyCoy55's SnipPic feed look so sharp and put together. Their hair is cut short and always gelled into place. The knots in their ties are always tight and precise. They look like catalog models. This guy looks like he just rolled out of bed after sleeping in yesterday's uniform.

He's staring intently at me and I soon realize that I haven't answered his question. "Um, I'm here to talk to the dean," I say vaguely, trying to keep my voice light and conversational.

He snorts and gestures to the waiting area. "Well, *that's* obvious. But *why*? Normally anyone waiting around here who's not in uniform is a sixth grader applying for admission." He leans back in his chair with a dark chuckle. "All of those young innocent hopefuls, so eager to have their hearts blackened by this soul-crushing institution of higher learning."

I gape in surprise. Was that supposed to be a joke?

"I'm not a sixth grader," I tell him. "I'm a senior."

He gives me a once-over. "But you clearly don't go here."

Ouch.

Okay, that stings.

I cross my arms over my chest and direct my attention forward, determined to just ignore him. "No, I don't."

"Well, you're lucky."

I turn back to him with a scandalized look. "Are you serious?"

He doesn't even blink. "Dead serious. Trust me, you do *not* want to go here."

This guy is starting to grate on my nerves. "And why not?"

"Because this place sucks out your soul and turns you into a zombie. A very intelligent zombie with excellent future prospects. But still a zombie."

I let out a sharp gasp. "It does not."

I think back to all those photos on CoyCoy55's SnipPic feed. She definitely didn't look like a zombie. She looked amazing. Like she was having the time of her life every single day.

What is this guy's problem? Does he not realize how fortunate he is to go here? Does he not understand what a gift he has? I take in his slothful, slacker appearance once again and feel a trace of resentment rise up in my throat. If he hates it here so much, why doesn't he just drop out? I would gladly take his spot.

"It certainly does," he counters. "I've been here since the seventh grade. I've seen it happen. The spirit-crushing. The mind control. The destruction of dreams. It's pretty gross."

"But," I argue, flustered, "this is one of the top ten private schools in the country."

He drops his head back and lets out a mocking laugh that sends prickles of agitation down my arms. "So you read that list too, huh?" Then he leans forward and stares at me with his dark, intense eyes. "Did you ever stop to wonder who's actually creating those lists? Maybe they're zombies, too."

I shake my head and angle my body away from him. I'm not listening to this nonsense anymore. He's clearly deranged. He's probably on drugs. I mean, look at him. He looks like he walked through a car wash with his clothes on.

"So, what's your name?" he asks in a totally normal voice, as if he wasn't just likening this school to a bad horror movie.

I blow out a huff. "Like I'd tell you."

He seems to find this amusing. I can hear the smile in his voice. "Ah, I get it."

Against my better judgment, I face him again. "You get what?"

"You're a zombie *wannabe*." He tilts his head to the side, thinking. "Hey, that's actually a really great band name."

I feel my face getting hot. "I'm not a zombie wannabe," I snap. "Just because I want to better myself and go to a great school doesn't mean—"

"So you *do* want to go here?" he says, like he's just solved the cold case of the century. "That's why you're here, isn't it? You're hoping there's an open spot. Well, I'll tell you right now. There's not. Zombies rarely ever leave. That would require independent thought and that's not a zombie's strong suit."

I press my lips together hard. I want to scream at this guy. But I know that won't do any good. So I go back to ignoring him.

He's quiet for a moment. I hope that means he's decided to ignore me, too. But then he says, "So where do you go to school now?"

I don't respond. I can feel him watching me again.

"Let me guess. Southwest High."

I grit my teeth. I will not give him the satisfaction of engaging. I will not.

My silence causes him to laugh again, and out of the corner of my eye I see him swivel and face forward, leaning back in his chair and kicking his feet out in front of him. I steal a peek at his shoes. They're caked in dirt.

"Trust me," he says quietly. "You're better off."

Right then, the office door swings open and we're greeted by Dean Lewis. I recognize her from her picture on the school website. She's a pleasant-looking woman with shoulder-length blond hair, a slender face, and reading glasses hanging around her neck by a bejeweled cord.

She looks like everything else in this place: lovely and wonderful and perfect.

Dean Lewis glances between me and the obnoxious guy. "Who was first?" she asks kindly.

"She was," the guy says, and I brave another look at him. This time in surprise. "You're in much more of a hurry to get in there than I am," he explains.

Well, I'm certainly not going to argue with that.

Despite how agitated this boy has made me, I force a breezy smile onto my face, grab my backpack, stand up, and follow Dean Lewis back into her bright and spacious office, which, I immediately remark, smells like daisies.

If I Don't Fit In

I take a seat at the large mahogany desk in the center of the office as Dean Lewis sits across from me. She closes her navy blue laptop and gives me her undivided attention.

"So," she says warmly. "What can I do for you, Ms. . . ."

"Rhodes," I say, trying to infuse my voice with a confidence that doesn't exist. "And I would very much like my space."

She tilts her head. "I'm sorry?"

"I was admitted here. I have an acceptance letter. And I want to go. I can start tomorrow. I just need a uniform."

Dean Lewis squints at me from across her desk, obviously trying to make sense of me. "What's your first name?" she finally asks.

"Kennedy, like the president."

She reopens her laptop and begins typing. After a second, she frowns at the screen. "Yes. My records show that you *were* accepted three years ago but you never responded to the letter."

"I know. I'm sorry about that. I, um . . ." I search for a good excuse. "I did actually respond, but my letter got lost in the mail."

She doesn't believe me for a second.

"The point is," I go on, "I made a mistake. A huge one. Probably the biggest mistake of my life."

Dean Lewis opens her mouth to speak but I don't let her get a word out. "You don't understand. I'm supposed to go here. I know it. I chose the wrong life. And now I need to fix it. I *have* to fix it. That's why I'm here. If I can just enroll, if I can just be a Windsor Academy student, I know everything will be better."

Dean Lewis clasps her hands together on her desk and gives me a pitying look. I know what she's about to say before she even says it.

"I'm sorry"—she glances at her screen—"Ms. Rhodes. But we filled that slot three years ago."

"Please," I try again, my voice breaking. "There has to be another spot. You have to make room. I'll do anything. I'll sit on the floor of the classrooms. I won't cause any trouble. Please."

She grimaces. "I'm afraid we can't just *make room*. The Windsor Academy class size is one hundred students. And we have one hundred students enrolled in each grade."

My shoulders slouch in defeat and I feel the tears well up in my eyes again. I blink furiously, trying to shoo them away, but they're relentless, and soon everything in this office—Dean Lewis included—is under water.

She makes a sympathetic clucking sound. "Oh. Sweetie. I really am sorry. I wish—"

"You wish there was something you could do," I interrupt. "I know." With a shudder and a sniffle, I stand up, turn around, and walk out the door. But not before adding, "Me too."

When I leave the office, the boy with the dirty uniform

gives me a salute. I keep walking. I shuffle down the hallway, past the receptionist—who has returned from her coffee break—and out the front doors. I stand atop the grand brick staircase and look out over the grounds of the school.

This beautiful, magnificent school. From my vantage point, I can see the ultramodern Bellum Hall where the science classes are taught and the Sanderson-Ruiz Library, built in the regal Georgian architecture style. The Fineman Arts Center where all studio art and dance classes are held, and the student union where everyone studies and eats lunch. I can even see all the way to Waldorf Pond, with its glittering geyser fountain in the center.

I can't believe I gave this up.

And for what? I have absolutely nothing to show for it now. I've lost everything I care about in the past twenty-four hours.

My boyfriend.

My best friend.

My shot at Columbia.

My future.

I take one last look at the campus and start down the stairs. Back to my crummy life in my crummy school. But before I reach the bottom, I hear a soothing melodic chime that pulls me to a stop.

Is that the bell?

The doors behind me burst open and a horde of uniformed students come flooding out of Royce Hall and down the steps. They're all talking and laughing and making jokes.

See, I think with a flash of annoyance. *They're not zombies.*

They look so happy.

And for just a flicker of a moment, I feel happy, too. I can almost imagine myself as one of them. Rushing to my next class, prattling eagerly about something inspiring a teacher said today. I feel like I'm part of something. A community of people who care about their education and their future.

Then I glance down at my outfit and remember who I really am.

I'm an outsider. I don't belong here. I'm not part of this club.

I let out a defeated sigh and continue down the stairs. But a second later, something catches my eye. A girl with pale skin and bright auburn hair coming up the steps. She adjusts her schoolbag as she chats animatedly with another student.

My whole body freezes.

I can't believe it. It's really her.

CoyCoy55 in the flesh!

And she's coming right toward me!

I hold my breath, feeling a wave of dizziness pass through me as she gets closer. As she passes *right* by me. As her navy blue blazer brushes against my arm.

In fact, I'm so distracted watching her disappear into the building that I don't even notice the guy barreling toward me from the top of the stairs. He shoves up against me, trying to get past and my foot slips. I grasp the handrail to keep from toppling over, but it only seems to throw me further off balance. My left foot skids against the edge of the step and then my entire leg shoots out from under me. I lose my grip on the handrail and feel myself falling backward. I grapple for something to hold on to, but my hands only paddle the air. I hear a gasp from someone nearby as I bump down multiple brick steps, my butt bouncing painfully against each one. Humiliation trickles over me. I can't believe I'm falling down the grand staircase of the Windsor Academy! In front of *everyone*!

This is exactly the kind of thing that gets turned into an animated GIF and ends up on a Buzzfeed list.

Just when I think my impromptu butt slide is finally coming to an end, the last step hits me hard, flinging my upper body back. I feel something in that exact moment. Like a gust of air. A comforting warm breeze. Except it's not blowing over me. It feels like it's blowing *through* me. Then I hear a loud *thump* as my head smacks into brick, and everything around me fades to black.

If I'm Not Fine

God, my head hurts. It feels like someone put my brain in a juicer. And my legs are cold. Why are my legs so cold?

I try to open my eyes, but it's as though my lids are weighed down with boulders. I'm only able to open them a sliver before a beam of light sends a thunderbolt of pain through me.

Ugh.

I'm so not doing that again.

"Look, she's opening her eyes!" says a girl's voice I don't recognize. She sounds impatient. "I told you she was fine. Just give her an aspirin and let her go."

"For the last time, Sequoia," says another female voice. It sounds much older than the first. "She's not going to class."

"You don't understand," the girl argues. "Our PEs are due by the end of *today*. Mr. Fitz doesn't accept late work."

Mr. Fitz?

PEs?

What's a PE?

I try to open my eyes again, but all I can manage is an eyelash flutter.

"I'm sure Mr. Fitz will make an exception this time," the older woman says.

The girl huffs. "You clearly don't know Mr. Fitz."

What is going on? Where am I? Who are these people?

"Miss Farris," the woman says in a take-charge kind of tone. "Go to class."

"But—" the girl protests.

"Nuh-uh. I'm keeping Ms. Rhodes under observation for at least another hour."

Ms. Rhodes?

This woman knows me. How does she know me?

I hear loud footsteps, then the sound of a door opening and closing. I rack my throbbing brain, trying to remember where I am and how I got here, but I come up with nothing. I try once again to open my eyes, this time making significantly more progress, but the light is still blinding.

Is that sunlight? Am I outside? Am I lying on the ground?

That can't be right. The surface beneath me feels soft and squishy. Like a bed.

Why are my legs so cold?

I blink a few times, waiting for my eyes to adjust to the light. It's not the sun. It's coming from a fluorescent panel in the ceiling. My head is still hammering but my surroundings finally come into focus. I'm inside a white room with various medical instruments hanging on the wall. A hospital room?

No.

A nurse's office?

Suddenly a face comes into view. A woman hovering above me. She has kind eyes and wrinkles around her red-painted lips.

"Hello there. How do you feel?" She smiles wide.

I try to sit up. Not a good idea. The room wobbles and I quickly lie back down.

"Oh no," the woman says, "don't try to get up. Just lie there. You took quite a tumble down those stairs. You kids are always in such a hurry around here."

Stairs!

Yes, of course. I remember now. Brick stairs. *Hard* stairs. I saw CoyCoy55 and I got distracted. Then someone pushed past me and I fell.

I hit my head.

On the grand staircase of the Windsor Academy!

In front of *everyone*!

The humiliation plows into me and shame prickles my cheeks. How many people saw? How many people took a video? Will this be my claim to fame? Kennedy Rhodes. She didn't get into Columbia but she sure falls down stairs like a boss.

My head starts to throb again. I really need to get out of here. I can't stay a minute longer and risk even further embarrassment.

I try to sit up again. The room swims but I do my best to ignore it.

"Sweetie." The woman—obviously the school nurse—gently pushes on my shoulders. "I really think you need to rest. Thankfully there was no bleeding but you could still have a concussion.

I spoke to the school doctor and she said you need to be kept under strict observation."

I touch the back of my head and feel a giant bump forming.

The nurse makes a clucking sound with her tongue. "I swear they put way too much pressure on you kids," she murmurs, almost to herself. "It's that darn Ivy League quota they're always pushing on you. I don't agree with it. Not one bit. It's no wonder that poor girl did what she did. I blame the administration. I really do. But does Dean Lewis ever listen to anything *I* have to say? No. I'm just the school nurse. What do I know about running an elite institution of higher learning?"

She's rambling now and I have no idea what she's talking about.

"I really should go," I say, trying to be as polite as possible.

She sighs. "If this is about your PE, then I'm sure—"

"Look, I don't even know what that is," I snap. "I just need to go."

The nurse cocks her head to the side and gives me a very worried look. "Oh dear. Perhaps you *do* have a concussion."

"I don't think so." I push myself off what I now see is a leather cot. "I'm sure I'm fine."

I mean, I feel fine. Apart from the massive headache, obviously.

"What day is it?" the nurse challenges.

I sigh. This is pointless. "November 15."

The date has been seared into my memory. The day of my Columbia interview. The day I watched my future get flushed down the proverbial toilet.

"And where are you?"

"The Windsor Academy."

She purses her lips. I've clearly debunked her theory. "What is your name?"

"Kennedy Rhodes!" I say, growing impatient. "I told you. I'm *fine*."

"What class are you supposed to be in right now?"

Class? Why would she care what class I'm supposed to be in? I don't even go here. Is this a trick question? Is she trying to trip me up so I'll be forced to stay?

I opt not to answer. Instead I look around for my camo messenger bag. I'm fairly certain I had it when I went to the dean's office, but I can't seem to find it. All I see is a gray laptop bag in the corner that is most definitely not mine.

"See," the nurse says indignantly. "You're clearly *not* fine. You don't even remember that you're supposed to be in Mr. Fitz's AP language arts right now."

What on earth is this lady talking about?

I shake my head. "I think you have me confused with someone else."

She tilts her head again, this time with more sympathy than concern. "No. I think *you're* the one who's confused. Do you remember what happened?"

"Of course I remember," I say instantly, but inside my mind, there's a small flicker of doubt.

Do I remember?

The nurse crosses her arms over her chest. "Tell me then."

"I came here to talk to the dean. I wanted to see if the school had any spaces open. Then on the way out, I tripped and fell down the stairs. End of story."

She squints at me. "Spaces open? Do you have a friend who wants to attend Windsor?"

"No," I say, irritated. "*I* want to attend Windsor."

The nurse covers her mouth with her hand and sucks in a sharp breath. I fight the urge to roll my eyes. I know it's hard to get in here, but she doesn't have to react like *that*. Do I really not look like someone who could get into the Windsor Academy? I'm about to tell her, quite indignantly, that I *did* in fact get accepted here, thank you very much, but just as I open my mouth to speak, she says, "Oh, sweetie. I really think you should lie down."

There's something about her words this time that strikes a nerve. She sounds genuinely concerned about my well-being, and maybe even a little bit spooked.

"What's going on?" I demand, but I can hear the uneasiness in my voice as anxiety starts to bloom in my chest.

"Lie down and get some rest. I'm going to call the doctor again."

My stomach flips but I stay standing. "No. I won't lie down until you tell me what's going on. Why are you looking at me like that? Why do you need to call the doctor?"

She doesn't answer. She turns to a phone in the corner and dials a number, keeping her vigilant gaze pointed at me the whole time, as though she's afraid I might spontaneously combust.

"Yes, hello. This is Nurse Wilson again. One of our students . . . yes, the one who hit her head. I'm afraid she might be suffering some memory loss."

One of our students?

Memory loss?

My chest starts to constrict. My eyes dart around the room in a panic. What happened?

One of our students.

But I'm not a student here. She's definitely confusing me with someone else. She has to be. Can't she tell I don't go here? If I did I'd be wearing—

I glance down at my clothes and let out a gasp.

Where are my pants?

Why are my legs completely bare?

My gaze travels up until I see a swatch of gray fabric. It's a skirt. I'm wearing a skirt. I *never* wear skirts.

It takes a few seconds but I soon realize that this isn't just any skirt. This is *the* skirt. The Windsor Academy gray wool skirt. And tucked into it is a white button-up shirt, covered by a . . .

No! It's not possible.

I pat my arms and shoulders, feeling the thick fabric under my shaking fingers.

I'd recognize that navy blue blazer anywhere.

I touch the familiar emblem sewn onto the pocket and feel a chill run through my body. I know what it says. I don't need to look. But I do anyway. I rip off the blazer and hold the emblem up to my face, reading every word five times.

THE WINDSOR ACADEMY
EST. 1972

What is happening?

Did I steal this? Is there some poor kid lying unconscious in a closet somewhere wearing *my* clothes?

The jacket slips from my grasp and falls to the floor. I start backing up until my cold, bare legs hit the edge of the leather cot and I collapse onto my butt. The room is spinning again. Out of control. I can't make sense of simple objects in the room. Everything is one giant blur.

I think maybe this woman is right. I think maybe I should lie down.

Because I am most definitely *not* fine.

If I Escape

Relax. Deep breaths. In. Out. In. Out.

Let's think about this rationally. I fell down the stairs. I bumped my head. I'm clearly confused. Maybe even still unconscious. Maybe I'm lying in a heap at the bottom of the grand staircase, making all of this up in my head.

So it's some kind of psychedelic, whack-to-the-head dream.

But if this *is* a dream, why does my head hurt so much?

And why are my legs so cold?

Why does everything about this room—this whole place—feel so *real?*

The nurse hangs up the phone and approaches me, taking my hand and giving it a pat. "You're going to be fine. The doctor is on her way."

Doctor?

Oh no. That's not good. I've already been humiliated enough. All I need right now is to be carried out of the Windsor Academy on a stretcher.

I sit up again and hop off the cot. "That's okay. I'm totally better now. See, good as new." I knock against my head with my fist, immediately regretting it because my skull knocks back with a painful thump.

The nurse looks unconvinced. "What about your memory loss?"

"Memory loss?" I force out an overeager laugh. "You believed that? I was totally faking it! Ha ha! Pretty good, huh?"

I need to get out of here. I need to figure out what is happening and I can't do it with Nurse Nosy-Pants over there staring at me like I'm in a science experiment.

"But," she argues, "just a second ago, you didn't remember you were even a student here."

I wave this away like it's the silliest thing I've ever heard. "Of *course* I remember I'm a student here. I'm wearing the uniform, aren't I?" My voice cracks at the end. I clear my throat as I scoop up the navy blazer that I dropped and take a step toward the door, hoping she doesn't try to tackle me to the ground. "Well, I better go. Gotta get to Mr. Futz's AP language arts."

"You mean Mr. Fitz?"

I laugh again. It sounds incredibly strained. "Yes. Him. And *you* better call back that doctor so she doesn't come all the way over here for nothing."

I bolt out of the nurse's office and glance down the empty hallway. I have no idea where I am. Yes, I've studied the online campus maps extensively, but the nurse's office is not one of the things they advertise.

I take a left and start jogging down the corridor, slowly recognizing the interior as Royce Hall, the campus's main building, which means I haven't gone far.

I just need to find my way to the parking lot. Then I can get in my car, drive home, take a long hot bath, and try to figure out what in the world is happening to me.

I spot an exit at the end of another long hall and veer right. I walk briskly, trying to ignore the incessant pounding in my head. But right before I reach the door, I hear the chimes again—that beautiful melodic song—and a second later the hallway is flooded with students.

Did another period just end? How long was I unconscious?

I keep moving toward my escape, but I have to swim through the masses of uniformed bodies rushing to go the opposite way. I've almost made it to the exit when a voice calls out behind me. "Crusher!"

I keep pushing on, wiggling through the narrow gaps in the bodies.

"Crusher!" the voice comes again, sounding closer this time.

I'm just reaching for the door handle when the same voice screams, "KENNEDY!" and I feel a tug on my shirtsleeve.

I turn around and nearly pass out all over again.

Because standing there before me, looking right at me as though she knows me, as though she expects me to know *her*, is none other than CoyCoy55.

"Thank God, you're okay. I told that stupid Nurse Wilson you were fine. I mean, you hit your head but it's not like it was *that* hard. But she wouldn't let me take you to class. How did you finally escape? Did you drug her? Did you knock her unconscious with the fire extinguisher? You know what? I don't need to know the details. The point is now you can turn in your PE, but you don't have much time."

CoyCoy55 has been talking a mile a minute and I've been struggling to keep up. Either because of the whack I took to the head or because I'm still in shock over the fact that she knows my name when we've never even met before. Sure, I semi-stalk her on SnipPic, but she doesn't know that.

Does she?

CoyCoy55 tugs on my sleeve again. "Come on! You have less than"—she checks her phone and lets out a squeak—"three minutes! We need to hurry!"

In addition to my tongue not being able to form words, my legs don't seem to want to move either. It's like my feet have fused to this shiny tile floor.

"Crusher," she urges impatiently. "You know Mr. Fitz. He won't accept your PE if it's even a minute late."

I know Mr. Fitz?

I don't know any Mr. Fitzes. Also, why does she keep calling me Crusher? And what is this PE everyone keeps talking about? What does PE even stand for?

Physical education?

Psychology exam?

Pork enchilada?

I hold my head in my hands, trying to squeeze some sense into it. "Hold on a second," I'm finally able to say. "How do you know me?"

CoyCoy55 stares at me for a long time, her mouth pulling into a pout. Then after a moment, she breaks into nervous laughter.

"Oh, I get it. You're messing with me. Pretending you really *do* have brain damage or something. Har-dee-har-har-har. Very funny. But it won't work. I know you better than anyone, Crusher, and it would take more than a tumble down the stairs to mess with that big brain of yours."

I blink rapidly, trying to follow even a smidgen of what she's saying, but I come up decidedly short. There were just too many things coming out of her mouth that I want to pick apart and analyze.

She gives me another tug on the arm. "Let's. *Go!*"

But I'm still in too much shock to move.

"Fine," she resigns. "Maybe you do have brain damage or whatever, but it's going to have to wait until after you turn in the first draft of your PE. It's 20 percent of our grade, remember?"

No! I want to scream. *I don't remember! I don't understand a single thing that's happening right now.*

"I . . ." I stammer, trying to figure out which part of this messed-up situation I should address first. "I don't have my PE."

CoyCoy55 waves this away like it's an annoying fly. "Of course you have your PE. You showed it to me this morning on the way to school."

On the way to school?

"I . . ." I falter. "I didn't come to school today. I went to my Columbia interview."

Didn't I?

CoyCoy55 gives me a pitying look. "No, sweetie. That was another dream. You've been having nightmares about that interview for months."

I stifle a gasp. How does *she* know that?

"Your interview isn't for another two days. Relax."

"What?" I ask, my mouth falling open.

I haven't even had *the interview yet?*

"Oh God." She puts her hand to her mouth. "Maybe you bonked your head harder than I thought." She leans forward and speaks to me slowly in short, simple sentences. "This morning you were with me. We came to school. I drove. You read me the first page of your PE in the car. It's very good." She twists her mouth thoughtfully. "Maybe even better than mine, but I don't want to talk about that."

I'm trying to focus on her. I really am. But my eyes keep glazing over and my head seems to throb in pain with every word that she says.

I drove to school with her? Why don't I remember that?

Maybe I really do have a concussion.

But what about all the stuff I *do* remember? Bombing my interview? Driving here and sneaking through the gate? Talking to Dean Lewis?

CoyCoy55 is still staring expectantly at me, waiting for me to produce this mysterious PE thing out of thin air.

PE.

Physics experiment?

Parabolic equation?

Pulmonary embolism?

"I . . ." I begin again, glancing around for help. "I don't know where I put it."

She rolls her big green eyes. "It's in your bag, silly." Then she looks me up and down and her eyes widen. "Wait, where *is* your bag?"

I shake my head. "I don't know."

CoyCoy55 looks at her phone again and presses her lips tightly together like she's trying to hold back a scream. "Okay, last I saw, it was in the nurse's office. I carried it in after you fell. Did you leave it there?"

"You were there when I fell?" I search my muddled thoughts for the memory of my spill down the stairs. I remember seeing CoyCoy55 on the stairs. I remember her brushing past me and continuing into the building. Did she run back out when she heard all the commotion?

"Of course I was there!" she practically yells, throwing her hands in the air. "You were walking right next to me. We were on our way to English. Then that idiot knocked into you and you slipped. I tried to catch you, but you fell so fast."

I close my eyes and squeeze my head again. What is she talking about? That's not how it happened at *all*. Is she lying?

CoyCoy55 glances at her phone again. "Okay, we'll rehash the details of your untimely almost-demise later. Right now, we need to get your PE and get it to Fitz's room." She taps her large white teeth thoughtfully with her fingernail. "You probably shouldn't go back into the nurse's office. Nurse Wilson might inject you with a sedative to try to detain you."

"Really?" I blurt out.

CoyCoy55 shoots me a look out of the corner of her eye. "No, not really. But she definitely will try to keep you there. So I'll go get your bag and you wait here."

Without another word, she spins on her heels and takes off down the hall.

I stand there for a few seconds, my thoughts chaotically banging around my head like rocks in a blender. I stare down the hallway at CoyCoy55's vanishing form. Then I turn and stare at the door to the outside.

I could do it. I could run away right now. I could bust through that door, find my car, drive straight home, and stick my head under a cold faucet until the world starts making sense again. Or I wake up.

Whichever comes first.

I take a tentative step toward the exit but I don't get very far, because a split second later, CoyCoy55's breathless voice comes echoing down the empty hallway. "Crusher! I've got your bag. Let's go!"

I glance back at the door, trying to figure out which of my current conflicting desires is stronger—the desperate urge to get out of here or the burning curiosity to learn more about this strange planet I've seemed to crash-land on.

"CRUSHER!" CoyCoy55 shouts from the end of the hallway. "I'm trying to save your brain-damaged butt right now and you're *not* helping."

The curiosity wins.

The Choices That Define Us—First Draft

Kennedy Rhodes

AP Language Arts, Period 7

Mr. Fitz

Page 1

It's my belief that everyone gets at least one big fate-altering decision in their life. A defining choice. A major crossroads that will determine the course of their future. Or maybe even the future of the whole world. Like what if Bill Gates had never dropped out of Harvard to start Microsoft? What if Christopher Columbus had sailed east instead of west? What if Abraham Lincoln had decided he didn't really feel like seeing a play that night?

History would have been changed. Worlds would have spun off-course. Life, as we know it, would be different.

As it turns out, my big life-defining choice came three and a half years ago. Yes, I realize that's a lot of pressure to put on the scrawny shoulders of a fourteen-year-old, but we have no control over *when* our big life-defining moments come, all we can control is what we do with them. *How* we choose.

Fortunately, I chose right. I chose to attend the Windsor Academy. And my life was forever altered for the better.

Sometimes it feels like my life didn't really begin until I came here. Until this remarkable, prestigious school opened its doors to me and welcomed me in. That's when I met my two amazing best friends and discovered my passion for robotics, the stock market, entrepreneurship, the economy, and, of course, school fund-raising. But more important, that's when I truly began to discover *myself*.

If I'm Someone Else

My eyes devour the words on the paper clutched in my hand as my brain reels like a slot machine, trying to find the right combination, trying to make everything line up.

But it doesn't line up.

I keep losing.

Are these really my words? Did I really write this?

But that's impossible. This paper isn't even about me. This is about someone else. It's about another life.

A *better* life.

So it's fiction, right? A short story.

I eagerly flip to the second page, but before I can read a sentence the paper is snatched out of my hand. "Relax," CoyCoy55 tells me. "It's only a first draft. If there are any typos left, you know Fitz will find them. Not that there *would* be any. Your first drafts always read like final drafts."

"I wrote that?" I ask, leaning over to try to get another glimpse of the paper.

She rolls her eyes and replies in a sarcastic tone. "Yes. You wrote it. You're a genius. Okay? Enough ego-stroking. We both know you're a better writer than me, you don't have to rub it in."

"But I wasn't—" I start to argue.

CoyCoy55 lifts a hand to silence me. "Let's just turn it in, okay?"

She hands me the gray laptop bag that she retrieved from the nurse's office. It's the same one I remember seeing on the floor in the corner after I woke up.

"That's not mine," I say.

"Of course it's yours," she says. "See." She points to the flap and I nearly choke when I read the words stitched right into the fabric.

KENNEDY "CRUSHER" RHODES

"Oh," I reply lamely, taking the bag.

"And you better put your blazer back on before you go into Fitz's room."

I slip my arms through the sleeves and slide the unfamiliar jacket back on. It feels so strange. And yet so *right*. Like I was born to wear it.

"C'mon," CoyCoy55 says, and leads me up to the second floor of Royce Hall and through the door of room 211.

The classroom is unbelievable. I mean, I've seen Windsor Academy classrooms in pictures before and a few on my tour in the sixth grade, but nothing compares to this. It doesn't even look like a classroom—apart from the whiteboard and the posters of quotes from famous authors on the wall. But other than that, it looks like someone's fancy, formal dining room. There are no desks, just a huge oval-shaped wooden table in the center with thirteen chairs around it.

This is where they teach English?

Where do they teach astronomy? At NASA?

The room is so stunning, I lose my footing as soon as I step inside and nearly bite the dust all over again. Fortunately this time, CoyCoy55 reaches out to catch me. "Whoa there, Crusher. Maybe we should start calling you Stumbler."

"Hello, ladies." I hear the deep, silky voice come from the corner of the room and I turn to see a young male teacher sitting behind a large mahogany desk. He has dark blond hair and hazel eyes framed by wire-rimmed glasses that he pushes up the bridge of his nose as we approach. "What can I do for you?"

"Kennedy is here to turn in her Personal Essay."

Personal Essay! PE!

Duh!

The man turns his gaze on me. "Sequoia said you had a little accident on the grand staircase. I'm sorry to hear it. Are you okay?"

Sequoia.

Se-*quoi*-a.

I let out a gasp and whip my gaze toward the girl who dragged me in here. "CoyCoy55! I get it now!"

*I've been trying to figure that out for *years*!*

CoyCoy—*Sequoia*—gives me a panicked look, then turns to Mr. Fitz. "You'll have to excuse Kennedy's behavior. She hasn't really been herself since the fall."

Mr. Fitz narrows his eyes at me in concern. "Have you seen the nurse?"

"Yes!" Sequoia answers. "And she's totally fine. She just needs to sleep it off." She shoves the paper back into my hand and nudges her chin toward the teacher.

"Uh," I stammer, and take a giant step forward to hand the essay to Mr. Fitz. I really don't want to give it up. I want to keep reading. But I have a feeling if I don't turn it in, Sequoia might actually have a pulmonary embolism.

"Here you go." I force a smile, proffering the paper. "One *Personal Essay*. Written by me."

He glances down at it and then at the clock on the wall. It's two minutes past three o'clock. I can see his tongue jab against the inside of his cheek.

"Well, it *is* two minutes late."

Sequoia opens her mouth to protest but he continues before she can speak. "But I'm willing to make an exception just this once. Given the circumstances."

Sequoia breathes out a heavy sigh next to me. "Thank you, Mr. Fitz."

"Thank you," I echo.

Mr. Fitz tilts his head and studies my face with a mix of curiosity and something else I can't quite identify. "Are you sure you're all right?" he asks.

"She's fine!" Sequoia insists, pulling on the sleeve of my blazer.

"I understand it must be hard for both of you," Mr. Fitz goes on. "After what happened to Ms. Wallace—"

"Thank you, Mr. Fitz," Sequoia interrupts, sounding flustered and desperate to end this conversation. She gives my blazer another tug and drags me out of the room. "See you tomorrow!" she calls out, closing the door behind us.

What was that about?

Who's Ms. Wallace?

I'm about to ask Sequoia this very question when she collapses against the wall and sighs like she's just prevented a nuclear weapons crisis. "Phew. That was close. Good thing you're Mr. Fitz's favorite student. I don't think he would have accepted that paper late from anyone else."

"I'm his favorite student?" I ask in disbelief.

She snorts. "Obviously. You're only the best writer in the class. He *adores* you. I could have come in with a bleeding gash on my forehead and he'd be like, 'Oh, sorry about your damaged brain, Sequoia, but your paper is still late.'"

"Well," I say, feeling awkward. "Thanks for helping me get it to him."

She grins. "What are best friends for?"

"Best friends?" I blurt out. "We're best friends?"

Sequoia breaks into a totally charming, infectious laugh. "You really crack me up, Crusher." Then she loops her arm through mine and guides me back to the stairwell. "Come on. I'll take you home. You could really use a nap."

If the House Is a Disaster

I'm grateful that Sequoia offered to drive me home. I'm definitely in no condition to drive my own car right now. In fact, I can't even seem to find it. I must have forgotten where I parked. Among so many other things that seem to have slipped my mind today.

I recognize Sequoia's car from her SnipPic posts. It's the white BMW parked in the back of the lot. She opens the passenger door for me and I drop the bag I'm holding on the floor and collapse inside, resting my head against the cool surface of the window.

Sequoia drives in silence. I half expect her to ask me for directions, because how does she know where I live? But no, she makes all the right turns like she's navigated them a thousand times, until she pulls up in front of my house.

"I'm worried about you, Crusher," she says, shifting the car into Park.

But I don't answer, because I'm too busy gaping at the car parked in the driveway. *My* car. Woody, the Honda.

How did it get back here?

I parked it in the Windsor Academy parking lot. I remember doing it. It's how I *got* to Windsor in the first place. Did Dad come and pick it up for some reason? Did the school call him to tell him about my fall?

"Kennedy," Sequoia says, reaching over from the passenger seat to pass a hand in front of my face.

I blink and look at her. "Huh?"

"You're not yourself."

"You can say that again," I mumble.

She bites her lip, clearly struggling with something. "Is it just the fall or is there something else bothering you?"

I stare blankly back at her.

She huffs. "Look, I know it's weird. It's weird for me, too. She should be here. She should be bouncing around in the backseat, making us listen to that horrible punk music she likes, or coming up with those ridiculous caption challenges. But she's not. And it's not our fault. We have to remember that. She made her choices. And they were *her* choices."

I blink rapidly, trying to keep up. But it's a lost cause.

"Promise me you'll *try* to get some sleep," Sequoia goes on. "Take a Dormidrome."

I let out a resigned sigh. "I don't even know what that is."

Then, before she can respond, I grab my bag and drag myself out of the car. When I close the front door behind me, I rest my head against it, waiting for the pounding to subside. It doesn't. I need to find some aspirin.

I wander into the kitchen and screech to a halt when I see my mom sitting at the table, working on her laptop. I glance at the clock on the microwave. It's a little after four. What is she doing home?

When she sees me, she jumps up and throws her arms around me. "Kennedy! Are you okay? Your school called."

I step out of her embrace and point in the general direction of the driveway. "Is that why the Honda is outside?"

She tilts her head, like she doesn't understand what I'm asking.

"Did you go pick it up?" I rephrase.

Mom studies me, pursing her lips. "Nurse Wilson said you hit your head. How do you feel?"

"You know who Nurse Wilson is?"

Mom's eyebrows knit together in concern. "Of course I know who Nurse Wilson is. She's worked at Windsor since before you started."

I have to lie down. Like now.

Without a word, I shuffle toward the stairs, but pause when I notice the state of the living room. It's a complete disaster. There are dirty dishes on the coffee table and law books spread out all over the floor. Half of the throw pillows from the couch have been tossed haphazardly around the room.

"What happened in here?" I ask. "Were we robbed or something?"

My mom, who has been watching me vigilantly, walks over and peers at the living room. She doesn't seem fazed in the slightest. "What do you mean?"

"What do I mean?" I repeat, my voice rising. "It's a mess!"

She rakes her teeth over her bottom lip. "I can clean it if it bothers you."

"Of course it bothers me!" I shriek. "Doesn't it bother *you?*"

Mom closes her eyes for a long drawn-out moment. "I think maybe you should rest. You're getting awfully worked up."

Worked up?

Well, that's the understatement of the century. My entire life has been pulled out from under me and I have no idea why or how! Obviously I'm getting worked up!

I turn around and stare into the kitchen, hoping something will make sense, but it's just as uncharacteristically chaotic as the living room. Dishes stacked up in the sink, pans left on the burners, piles of unopened mail on the counter. Dad is going to *freak* when he sees this.

I'm about to ask where he is when I catch sight of the closed basement door, and then suddenly everything clicks into place.

Dad always shuts the basement door when he's working really hard and doesn't want to be disturbed. He told me this morning that the art dealer asked for more pieces and he'd be busy for a while. He's probably been locked in his studio all day trying to pump out more photos. That's why the place is such a mess.

Mom takes me by the arm. "Come on. I'm sure everything will look better after a few hours of sleep." She coaxes me up the steps and down the hall, past Frankie's closed door with the familiar poster that says "Never Trust an Atom. They Make Up Everything," and to my room where I proceed to collapse onto my mattress—uniform, shoes, and all.

I close my eyes, trying to ignore the panic that's coating my throat like tar.

Relax. Deep breaths. In. Out. In. Out.

Maybe she's right. Maybe everything will look better after a few hours of sleep.

If I Freak Out

Except I can't sleep. Because something is seriously wrong with my bedroom. It feels like one of those games with two pictures that *look* identical but have several subtle differences. Like my desk is in the same place but my laptop is gone. My bookshelf is in the same place but there are different books on it. Instead of white vertical blinds, there are thick black curtains pulled over my windows, blocking out any hope of sunlight.

Uneasily, I stand up and walk over to my closet door. I don't know why I feel the need to hold my breath when I open it, but I do. I take a deep inhale and slowly ease the door open, like I'm a cheerleader in a horror movie who's about to get hacked into pieces.

A tiny gasp escapes my lips when I peer inside.

There's no chain-saw-wielding serial killer, but what I find might be even scarier.

My clothes are gone. My T-shirts, my jeans, even my dad's old leather jacket. They've all been replaced by stuff I've never seen before. Dresses, skirts, sparkly tops, and . . .

I stifle another gasp.

Windsor Academy uniforms!

Just like the one I'm currently wearing.

I slam the closet door and lean against it, like I'm trying to stop the monsters from escaping.

Deep breaths. Deep breaths. Deep breaths.

In. Out. In. Out. IN. OUT!

I hear something in the hallway and jump, letting out a yelp.

I run to my bedroom door and yank it open to find Frankie padding to his bathroom in the hall. At least *he* looks the same. He's barefoot and wearing his galaxy pajamas. He always changes right into pajamas the second he gets home from school. He's done it since kindergarten.

"Frankie!" I cry, and grab his arm. "You have to see this."

I pull him into my room and watch his reaction carefully, fully expecting his eyes to open wide and for him to say something appropriate, like "Whoa! What happened in here?"

But he doesn't. He simply stares at me.

"Well?" I prompt, gesturing frantically to . . . *everything*.

Frankie lets out a whine and does a little bounce. "Kennedy. I have to *pee*."

"There's no time for peeing," I scold. "I'm totally freaking out here."

Frankie rolls his eyes, giving me the impression that he's heard these very words from me before. "Just apologize and get it over with," he says.

I give him a funny look before glancing back around my room. "Huh?"

He sighs impatiently. "To Sequoia."

"How do you know Sequoia?" I ask accusingly.

"I don't have time for this." He moves toward the hallway. "I have to pee."

I step in front of him. "Stop. Answer me. How do you know Sequoia?"

He tilts his head and looks at me like I might actually be crazy. "She's one of your *best friends*," he says, putting extra emphasis on the words as though I might have never heard them before.

"What about Laney?" I ask, the name immediately bringing a bitter taste to my mouth. Laney isn't my best friend anymore. She's not *anything* to me anymore.

"Who?" Frankie asks.

"Laney!" I repeat, losing my patience. "You know, my best friend." I scowl, and quietly add, "Until she hooked up with Austin."

But Frankie hears it. He hears everything.

"Who's Austin?" he asks, exasperated, like he thinks this is all a stupid game.

But it's not a game. It's my life! And it's seriously messed up right now.

"Don't be ridiculous. You know Austin. You *love* Austin. He's only been coming over here for the past *three* years. You play nerdy science games together. And you have long philosophical debates about whether time travel is possible."

"Hold up." Frankie's voice turns serious. "Time travel is

completely possible. In fact, right now, one hundred years in the future, the time travel gene is being developed by an evil corporation called Dio—"

"Frankie! Focus!" I yell, holding his head firmly between my hands. "Austin. Tell me you know Austin."

He rubs at his eyebrow. "Nope. Doesn't ring a bell."

My hands fall from his face. "You're joking, right? This is a joke. You're playing some kind of prank on me."

But I can tell from his bewildered expression that he's just as lost as I am.

How does he not know Austin? What happened when I bumped my head? Did I make up an entire life that doesn't even exist? Austin and Laney and the comedy show and walking in on them kissing? Did none of that actually happen?

I take a deep breath.

Okay, think. I'm a journalist. I investigate stuff all the time. It's my job to get to the truth. This is just another story to crack. All I have to do is look at the facts and . . .

My train of thought is suddenly derailed when my gaze lands on the wall above my desk and my eyes nearly pop out of my head.

I'm not sure why I didn't notice it before. Too many other strange distractions, I guess. But now I see it. Now I can't see anything *but* it.

My *Southwest Star* issues have been taken down. I framed the three issues that won the Spartan Press Award and hung them above my desk. Now they're gone.

There's only one single frame in their place. It's much smaller than my other frames and there's some kind of cream-colored paper behind the glass. I can't quite read it from this distance so I take a step closer. Then another. Then another. Until my eyes can make out the familiar words that I committed to memory years ago.

Dear Ms. Rhodes,
Congratulations! It is on this date, May 12, that we are
pleased to inform you a place has opened up in our
freshman class next semester. Because you have shown
tremendous potential, we are thrilled to offer you
admission . . .

I run toward it, pressing my fingertips against the glass. It can't be the same letter. I never framed that letter. I always kept it in the bottom drawer of my desk. Because no one even knew it existed. Because I never told anyone that I got in.

I drop to my knees and dive for the bottom drawer. The one that's always hidden my deepest, darkest secret. My choice.

I yank it open and rummage around, finding nothing but a few flash drives, a lockbox that I've never seen before, and some spare pens. I pull everything out and reach my hand way back into the drawer. Until my fingertips touch wood.

It's not here.

I glance up at the frame on my wall again. It's not here because it's *there*. The same letter. In a new place. With a new purpose.

"It's like . . ." I begin aloud. But I can't say it. Because it's crazy. It's ludicrous. It's not possible. It doesn't fit within the safe confines of my logical, rational world.

So instead, I close my eyes and whisper it to myself. Quietly, in the far back corners of my mind where no one else can hear.

It's like my choice has been reversed.

If Frankie Is Right

When I open my eyes the room is empty. Frankie is gone.

Whoa. I grab on to my bedpost for support. First my blinds, then my clothes, now my brother has vanished, too!

I think I'm trapped inside some kind of government experiment.

Then, a few seconds later, I hear the toilet flush and I exhale in relief and stumble back into the hallway just as Frankie plods out of the bathroom. I grab his arm again and pull him back to my room.

"Frankie," I say, my voice rattling. "I'm like *really* freaking out here."

Frankie sighs. "I told you. Apologize to Sequoia for whatever you're fighting about and she'll stop crying."

Sequoia and I are fighting?

Okay, slow down. One mystery at a time.

"It's not that. I think . . ." I let out a breath. "I think I'm losing my mind."

Frankie does not look in the least bit fazed by my admission.

"This morning," I go on, "everything was different. This

room was different. This bookshelf was different. My closet had different clothes in it."

Frankie squints at me, like he's not following.

I huff impatiently and try a different tactic. "Where do I go to school?"

He gives me a dubious look. "Is this that game you play where you make us remind you of how smart you are and how lucky you are to go to the Windsor Acad—"

"Aha!" I shout, making him flinch. "You see! *This morning*, I didn't go to the Windsor Academy. This morning, I went to Southwest High. And I was best friends with Laney who cheated on me with Austin who you don't even seem to know exists!" I flail my arms wildly. "And now everyone is acting like I go to the Windsor Academy except no one is even supposed to know that I got *into* the Windsor Academy because I hid the acceptance letter so people wouldn't think I was crazy for choosing to go to Southwest High for a boy! Except now the acceptance letter is hanging on my freaking wall like . . . like . . ." I pause, trying to make sense of my own chaotic thoughts. "Like my whole life is on a different track or something."

Frankie stares at me, his face all scrunched up the way it is whenever he's working on the Sea of Quantum Entanglement section of his board game. "What did you just say?" he asks, an eerie twinge to his voice.

"Nothing," I mumble. "Never mind. I'm not making any sense."

"No," he insists. "Say it again."

I collapse onto my bed, breathless and fatigued. "I said it feels like my life is on a different track or something."

Frankie's eyes grow wide and then he starts mumbling, like he's having an argument with himself. "Could it be? No, it can't be. But what if it is? It's not. I mean, it's only a theory, right? It's not like it's been proven. She could just be having a delusional breakdown. I mean, I wouldn't be surprised—"

"Frankie," I interrupt. He blinks and focuses on me, like he forgot I was even there. "What are you talking about?"

"I . . ." he begins hesitantly, raking his teeth over his bottom lip. "I think I might know what's happening here."

"You do?" I ask.

He exhales loudly. "Yes. I mean, I have a *theory*, and you know theories are only speculative. I'll have to gather more data, do some more research before I can make any conclusive . . ."

"Frankie," I urge him.

But he's already off again. Lost in his own thoughts. It happens a lot. "But if I'm right, this could be huge. I mean, *supernova* huge. If we could somehow prove this and submit it to a scientific journal, this could change everything. Everyone would read it." He sucks in a sharp breath. "Stephen Hawking would read it! Maybe he'd even come to visit!"

"Frankie!" I yell in an attempt to bring him back.

"Oh, right. Sorry." He grabs me by the shoulders, his fingers digging into my skin, as his eyes light up. "Kennedy, I don't think you realize what you've done."

I scoff. "We've established that part already."

"It's quite possible you've altered the fabric of space and time."

"English, Frankie."

"Fine. To put it simply"—he flashes me a mocking smile—"*very* simply." He spreads his arms wide like a televangelist welcoming new followers. "I'm pretty sure you've traveled to a parallel universe!"

I think my brother anticipated some kind of fanfare after that because he's staring at me with this expectant look on his face. But I just stare back at him, my expression completely blank. Then I let out a sigh and stand up from the bed.

"Frankie," I warn. "Enough with the parallel universe crap! I need real explanations."

"This is a *real* explanation," he maintains. "And it's not *crap*. It's a scientific breakthrough!" He runs over to my desk and grabs a notebook and pen from the top drawer and starts writing furiously. I peer over his shoulder to see a mess of incomprehensible scribbles, diagrams, and equations.

I snort and go back to pacing. "There's another explanation. There has to be. It must have something to do with hitting my head on the stairs today. I mean, Dorothy hit her head and woke up in Oz, so I could feasibly hit my head and wake up in"—I glance around my vaguely familiar bedroom—"well, whatever this place is."

"Parallel universe," Frankie supplies with his head still bent over the notebook.

I ignore him and keep pacing. "*Maybe* I hit my head so hard I'm lying in a coma in the hospital right now. Maybe this is all some really messed-up coma delusion. Maybe—"

My rant is suddenly cut off by a strange chirping noise. I freeze and spin around, searching for the source. "What was that?" I ask, panicked.

Frankie rolls his eyes, sets down the notebook, and walks over to the schoolbag on the floor. "Don't be so dramatic!" he admonishes, flipping it open. "It's just your SnipPic alert. Somebody probably commented on one of your photos."

He pulls out a hideous pink sparkly contraption and proffers it to me.

I shake my head. "That's *not* my phone."

"Yes, it is."

"It's pink."

Frankie nudges the device toward me. "And sparkly. Now take it."

I hesitantly take the princess-colored monstrosity, turning it around in my hands. It's definitely the same model as my phone, but this cover is vomit-inducing.

"Who picked out this case?" I ask.

"You did," Frankie says, sitting on my bed and resuming his scribbles.

"As a joke?" I confirm.

He purses his lips. "I don't think so."

The phone lets out another startling chirp and I nearly drop it. I fumble to swipe it on and navigate to the SnipPic app where I have—

Holy crap. Seventy-five notifications???

From who? I don't even know half that many people!

I click on the app and scroll through my feed. I don't recognize a single picture in here. This is definitely not my profile. This phone has to belong to someone else. That's all there is to it.

But I stop when something oddly familiar catches my eye. I scroll back three photos and stare in astonishment at the screen.

I remember this photo. I first saw it on CoyCoy55's feed a week ago. She was in the student union with Luce_the_Goose, posing for one of those Caption Challenges they always do.

As I study the picture, a shiver runs through me, chilling me to the bone.

It's the same photo. The same table. Even the same caption. With one major difference.

I'm in it.

If I Start to Believe

The phone slips from my hand and bounces on the carpet. I lunge for it and stare at the picture again. I can't believe it. It's really me. Posing right alongside CoyCoy55 and Luce_the_Goose for one of those Caption Challenge games.

This is the one where the caption reads: "My Book Boyfriend Just Proposed!"

Exactly as I remembered it, CoyCoy55 is tipped back in her chair, pretending to have fainted, while Luce_the_Goose is lying on the table fanning herself. And then there's me. I'm standing behind CoyCoy55's chair, swooning dramatically.

It's like I've just been Photoshopped into the picture. Cut and pasted right into their lives.

Frankie glances over my shoulder to see what I've been so speechlessly staring at for the last few minutes.

"Uh-*huh*," he says knowingly, clucking his tongue. "Now you believe me?"

"B-b-but," I stammer. "I don't understand."

"It's quite simple really," Frankie begins. "The multiverse

theory states that every decision we make creates a brand-new alternate reality where—"

"Never mind," I interrupt. "Don't try to explain it. It'll only confuse me."

Frankie shrugs and goes back to his work. "Suit yourself."

I scroll through the rest of the photos in the feed, my eyes growing wider with every swipe of my finger. There are so many pictures in here that I've never seen before. All of me. Or, at least, someone who looks just like me.

It's as though she's me but, at the same time, *not* me.

She's some *other* me.

Sitting on the greener-than-green lawn of the Windsor Academy, eating lunch in the student union, studying in the gorgeous Sanderson-Ruiz Library, getting ready to listen to a guest speaker in the Lauditorium.

I look up and glance around my new room. Frankie may need to run through equations and complicated theorems for the rest of the night, but all the proof I need is right here. In these photos. In my closet. On my wall.

I go to the Windsor Academy.

I am a Windsor Academy student.

I walk through those doors every morning and sit in those classrooms and wear those uniforms and live that life.

I *chose* wisely.

I never gave up on my dreams to be with Austin. He never cheated on me with my best friend. I never bombed that alumni interview.

That happened to a different Kennedy. In a different life.

Even if this *is* all just a drug-induced coma dream, I don't care. This is the life I always knew I was meant to lead. The life I always wanted for myself. And now I finally have it.

It's finally *mine*.

If My Reflection Changes

Barruuugah!

Barruuugah!

What is that noise? It sounds like a herd of trumpeting elephants stomping through my bedroom. I tear my eyes open. It's pitch-dark. And my head is pounding like the elephants are stomping directly on my skull.

I try to go back to sleep, but a moment later I hear it again and bolt upright.

Those are definitely elephants. A whole parade of them. And they're definitely trumpeting. Why are elephants trumpeting in my room? What time is it? It's too early for trumpeting elephants.

I reach for my phone on my nightstand, grappling in the darkness until I find it. I swipe on the screen and blink against the bright light. When my eyes finally adjust, I can see the time.

Five thirty a.m.

Then the elephants come a third time.

What. The. Heck?

That's when I notice my screen is flashing. The alarm is going off. Who set the alarm for five thirty a.m.? My fingers fumble around until the screen goes dark and the noise blissfully stops. I roll over and immediately fall back asleep. But after what feels like mere seconds, I'm awoken by another intrusive sound.

This time, it's a dog barking.

No, not just one dog. *Ten* dogs. All trying to one-up each other for the noisiest, most obnoxious bark.

For crying out loud!

I reach for my phone. It's five forty a.m. and the alarm is going off *again*.

I bat at it until the dogs shut up. I've just drifted back into a peaceful sleep when Frankie bursts through my bedroom door, breathless and looking like he hasn't slept a wink. "Kennedy! Oh, good! You're up."

I groan and roll back over. "I'm not up. I'm going back to sleep."

That's when the rooster starts crowing. I glare at my phone. How many animals are in this thing?

I silence the sound of the crowing as Frankie sits on my bed, clutching the same notebook he stole from my desk last night. I can see through my bleary vision that he's filled almost *half* of it with more incomprehensible scribbles and formulas. "I've been at it all night," he explains, quickly transitioning into his professor voice. "Now, I did some research. There's a very small *fringe* theory out there about something called overlaps—"

I grab the pillow and pull it over my face. "Frankie. It's too early. Go away."

"But your alarm went off."

"Why is it even going off this early?"

"Because that's when you wake up," he says, like this is a well-known fact.

"At five thirty in the morning? Why would I wake up so early?"

"Because the Windsor Academy starts at eight and Sequoia always picks you up at six thirty so you can have breakfast and study in the student union before first period." He taps the notebook in his lap. "So, an overlap is when the exact same thing happens at the *exact* same moment in two different universes, creating a sort of intersection in the—"

"The Windsor Academy?" I interrupt, bolting upright. I turn on my bedside lamp and blink into the light.

Is it real? Am I still here? Did I wake up from the weird coma dream?

I bound out of bed and open my closet door with a grand flourish, an enormous grin spreading across my face when I see the rows of clean, pressed uniforms hanging up where my boring drab jeans and T-shirts used to be.

I let out a whoop. "I'm going to the Windsor Academy!" I start jumping up and down. "Oh my God. This is so exciting! What do I do? Where do I go? What do I wear?" I peer back into my closet and slap my forehead. "Duh. The uniforms."

"Kennedy!" Frankie snaps.

I'd almost forgotten he was here. I turn around to find him still sitting on my bed with his notebook. "What?"

"I think I figured out how you got here."

I grab a skirt, blouse, and blazer from the closet and lay them out on my bed. Then I prance into my bathroom and run the shower. Frankie follows after me.

"It was the stairs," he goes on, his eyes glazed over from the lack of sleep. "You hit your head at the exact same time in the exact same place in both lives, allowing you, in that one brief instant, to travel from one universe to another!"

"You're adorable," I say, kissing his wild, untamed hair.

He backs away, looking grossed out. "Kennedy. This is serious."

"Very serious," I agree wholeheartedly, spinning him around by the shoulders and scooting him out of the bathroom.

"I need more information, though. More data points. If you could give me some details about your other life then I could quantify them, insert them into a spreadsheet and—"

"I have to get ready for school," I say brightly, cutting him off again. "Correction, I have to get ready for the *Windsor Academy*. Good luck with all that." Then I close the bathroom door.

I take a quick shower and dry myself off with a towel. After the steam clears, I look in the mirror, ready to give myself a triumphant smile, but I literally startle at my own reflection.

Whoa.

I look horrible.

That spill down the stairs really took its toll on me. I have dark purple shadows under my eyes, my skin is ghastly pale, and my eyes are all bloodshot.

I pull open the top drawer where I usually keep my eye drops and leap back when I see what's inside. The drawer is practically overflowing with makeup. I've never worn makeup in my life. I've always thought it was so fake and misleading.

I rifle through the contents, picking up a few bottles and reading the labels. "Full cover concealer, gel serum concealer, eye brightener, undereye protector."

Jeez. Other Me is kind of obsessed with concealer.

I swipe on my phone and scan through my new SnipPic feed, studying my face in the photographs more closely. I'm definitely wearing eyeliner and eye shadow and blush and lip gloss and . . .

I gasp when a sudden realization comes to me. The pink phone case. The drawer full of makeup. Dresses in my closet.

"Am I a"—my gag reflexes kick in—*"girly girl?"*

Okay, calm down.

So what if I wear a little makeup? It's not the end of the world. If that's the price I have to pay to go to the Windsor Academy, I'll take it.

I peer at my frightening reflection again and shudder.

Maybe a little makeup isn't such a bad idea.

I sigh and start dabbing some of the skin-perfecting hydrating cover-up on my face, concentrating on the dark shadows. Then I add some mascara, a little eyeliner (nearly poking my eyeball in the process), and some lip gloss.

When I brave another glance in the mirror, there's been some improvement, but the sight of my pale face still kind of terrifies me. I locate some kind of brownish powder and sprinkle it on with a brush. It brings a little color back to my skin.

Much better.

After I get dressed, I blow-dry my hair and grab my school-bag, noticing again the name stitched right into the fabric.

KENNEDY "CRUSHER" RHODES

As I head down the hall, I stop at Frankie's room. He's at his desk, hunched over his notebook, his tongue hanging out the side of his mouth as he scribbles.

"Frankie?"

He doesn't look up. "Yeah?"

"Why does Sequoia call me Crusher?"

"Everyone at Windsor calls you Crusher," he replies absently.

"Why?"

"Because you crush everything you do. You're kind of a super-star over there."

I feel a giddy jolt of electricity run through me.

A superstar? At the Windsor Academy? Me?

I bite my lip to stifle the goofy grin that threatens to take over my entire face. This just keeps getting better and better!

"Why?" Frankie asks, his head suddenly popping up. "Do people not call you Crusher in your old life? What do they call you? What do they call me? Is my name even still Frankie? Am I still a physicist?" He gasps. "What if I'm something else? Something boring like a geologist!"

"Have a great day!" I say, as I continue down the hallway.

"Wait!" Frankie calls after me, appearing in the doorway.

I grudgingly turn around. "What?"

"What *is* different about me?"

I squint at him. "What do you mean?"

"I mean, the multiverse is a complicated place. Everything is interconnected. Even things you may not realize are connected. You pull one string and suddenly half of your life has changed. So what's different about me?"

I give him a quick once-over, taking in the galaxy pajamas he put on the moment he got home from school yesterday, his hair that always seems to look like he's been electrocuted no matter how many times he brushes it, and the tiny bits of toothpaste crusted to the corner of his mouth. Then I shrug. "Nothing. Nothing is different about you."

He sighs impatiently. "Look closer, Kennedy. There's got to be something."

I shake my head. "There isn't. You look exactly the same."

"Fine," he says, gesturing behind him. "Look at my room."

I groan. "Frankie. I don't have time for this. I have to—"

"Just look!" he commands.

I follow him into his bedroom and glance around at the same Stephen Hawking and Michio Kaku posters on the wall, the same deep space wall decals and comforter, his telescope near the window pointed toward Saturn (his favorite planet), even the same balled-up papers littered around the trash can from when he got frustrated with whatever he was drawing and missed the bin.

"The same," I pronounce.

"Look carefully."

"Frankie," I reply, irritated, "I'm telling you, there's nothing different about you or your room."

"Everything is a variable!" he practically shouts. "What about my bookshelf?"

I turn and scan the shelves filled with titles written by both famous and unknown physicists and his collection of *Scientific American* magazines. "Same."

"What about the calendar on my wall?"

I glance at it, recognizing it immediately. "Each month features a moon from another planet? Yeah, that's the same, too."

Frankie looks stumped. He spins in a circle, examining his room with the scrutiny of a forensic investigator. Then, as his gaze lands on his desk, his face lights up. "My board game! I bet I wasn't making my own board game in your other life."

"What's the Matter?" I ask indignantly.

He slumps. "Oh." He grabs the notebook from his desk and scowls at it. Then he sits down and resumes his mad scribbling.

"Good luck, buddy," I say with a chuckle, ruffling his hair.

As soon as I get downstairs, I cringe when I notice again how unusually messy the house is. I peer over at the basement door. It's still closed, which is weird because it was closed when I went to bed last night. I came downstairs to say good night to my parents and Dad was still in there.

Did he work all night?

I take out my phone and send him a quick text message.

Me: Everything going okay?

Surprisingly he writes back right away.

Dad: Yup. Working hard as always!

Wow. That must have been some order from the gallery owner.

He's not going to be happy when he finally emerges to find the house in shambles. I make a mental note to straighten up when I get home from school today so he doesn't have to deal with it.

My phone dings again and I glance at the screen.

Dad: Sorry I won't be able to make it tonight. Have a great time!

I stare vacantly at the phone.

What's tonight?

I'm just about to check my calendar app when I hear a horn honk outside. I glance out the window to see Sequoia's white BMW idling in the drive. With a giddy yip, I check my full-length reflection in the hall mirror, sucking in a sharp breath.

The uniform and the hair and the makeup and the bag with my name stitched onto the side. It's all just too good to be true!

If I am trapped in a strange coma dream, I apologize to everyone gathered around my bedside, praying for me to wake up. Because I really hope I never do.

I give the sleeves of my blazer a firm tug and head out the front door, ready and eager to start my new (and improved) life.

If I Take Twenty-Two Selfies

Driving through the gates of the Windsor Academy in Sequoia's car is like driving into a fairy tale in a horse-drawn carriage. I swear I hear music playing and angels singing, and when I look up at the sky the clouds appear to part.

The whole way here Sequoia has been chatting about arrangements for some party. I have no idea what she's talking about, and to be honest, I haven't really been listening. I've been far too focused on the absolutely outrageous notion that I'm actually going to the Windsor Academy! I'm going to sit in those amazing classrooms and study in that gorgeous student union and listen to some of the most prestigious teachers in the country speak.

Sequoia parks the car and checks her reflection in the visor mirror. Meanwhile, I can't stop staring at this incredible tree that we've just parked under. I crane my neck to see it in all its glory through the front windshield. It must be the most beautiful Spanish oak tree I've ever seen! It's so massive and majestic and the leaves are the most vibrant shade of autumn yellow. Even the *trees* on this campus are superior.

"Crusher," Sequoia says with a tinge of annoyance, and I realize she must have been talking but I have absolutely no idea what she said.

"Huh?"

She peers out the windshield. "What are you looking at?"

"This tree," I say wistfully. "It's . . ."

But before I can even find a word worthy of its magnificence, Sequoia lets out a weird squeaking noise and quickly slams the gearshift into Reverse. "Ugh, you're right! It's going to shed all over the hood of my car."

She backs out of her spot and pulls into another one three spaces down.

"Much better," she says, putting the car back into Park.

I open the door and step onto the asphalt, feeling like I'm stepping onto white fluffy clouds. I glance around the parking lot, taking in the trees, the buildings, the sprawling green lawns. I couldn't see any of it yesterday because I was in too much shock. But now I see all of it. Every brick in every building. Every lamppost lining every walkway. Every spectacular blade of grass.

I let out a deep sigh. Is this what it feels like to die and go to heaven?

"Are you okay?" Sequoia says, approaching me cautiously like she's afraid I might explode. "You're acting really weird."

I glance at my best friend, giving her a once-over. From the top of her shiny auburn hair to the bottom of her standard black Windsor Academy loafers.

She subconsciously touches her face. "What? Do I have toothpaste on my cheek or something?"

I've dreamed of this moment for so long. I've pictured my-self in this very spot, standing next to CoyCoy55, ready to walk those pathways and strut through the halls of those buildings, and now the moment is finally here.

"Crusher, you're scaring me," Sequoia says. "What's going on?"

I should tell her the truth. After all, she's my best friend. I have the SnipPic feed to prove it. She would understand, wouldn't she?

"Sequoia," I begin pensively, shifting my schoolbag up my shoulder. "Have you ever made a choice that you've regretted?"

She looks at me like I'm deranged. "Um, only every single day, why?"

"No, I mean like a really big decision. Something that changed the course of your whole life."

She nods once, her face turning ashen. "Yes."

"What if you could go back and do that decision over again? Would you do it?"

Sequoia stares at me for a long moment. Her bottom lip starts to tremble, and then, out of nowhere, she bursts into tears.

I stand in stunned silence for a moment before rushing to put my arm around her shaking shoulders. "Hey, hey. It's okay. Don't cry."

"I already told you I regretted going to my sister's piano re-cital instead of studying for that French midterm. I don't need you to rub it in more!" She's crying so hard, I'm barely able to comprehend the words coming out of her mouth. "You said you thought it would be okay. Even though I dropped four spots! Four whole spots! Because of that stupid Steven Lamar!"

"Whoa, whoa," I say, panicking. I have no idea what she's talking about. "Slow down. It's going to be fine."

"Do you think Harvard will notice? Do you think it will cost me my admission?"

"No!" I rush to say. "No. I'm sure it'll be fine. I'm sorry I brought it up."

She sniffles and wipes her eyes, taking a huge shuddering breath.

Okay, so maybe trying to tell Sequoia the truth was *not* the right move. I think I should probably keep this whole universe-hopping thing—or whatever it is—to myself.

Sequoia pulls a compact out of her bag and wipes the smudges of eye makeup from her face. When she clicks the compact shut, it's like a switch has been flipped. The transformation is startling. One second she was a blubbering sack of tears and now it's like it never even happened.

She refreshes her smile. "Let's take a selfie."

I gape at her, unsure of how to respond. I don't want to say anything that might set her off again. "Are you sure? We don't have to."

She rolls her eyes at me. "I know we don't *have* to. I want to."

"Okay," I say hesitantly.

I follow Sequoia to the front of Royce Hall and we pose with the grand staircase in the background.

"What's the caption?" I ask.

"What do you mean?"

"The challenge. The Caption Challenge. Don't we always do a funny . . ." But my voice trails off when I see the look on

Sequoia's face. Her skin has turned a ghostly white color and she looks like she's about to start crying again.

"Let's just take the picture," she snaps, startling me.

Um. What was that about?

I smile when Sequoia extends her phone out and takes the photo. She shows it to me for approval.

"Cute!" I say, trying to keep my voice light and airy so she doesn't spontaneously combust into tears again.

But when she looks at it, she scowls. "The angle isn't right. Let's do it again."

"Okay," I agree, and get back into position. We stand shoulder to shoulder, smiling into the camera as Sequoia positions the phone high above our heads, tilting it this way and that to frame Royce Hall perfectly behind us. She clicks and rotates it around to check the results.

"Even better!" I rave.

She jabs the inside of her cheek with her tongue. "There's a weird shadow on our faces." She turns the camera back around and I resume my stance next to her.

"Turn your face to the left," she instructs me, and I do. "No, too much to the left. And don't do that weird thing with your face. It's making the wrinkle between your eyes more pronounced."

I have a wrinkle between my eyes?

"What am I doing with my face?" I ask, trying to relax my forehead.

"You're smiling too hard. Make it look more natural."

"But this is my natural smile."

"No. Do your Crusher smile."

What does my Crusher smile look like?

I try to relax my face a bit as Sequoia aims the camera. "Yeah," she encourages, "like that. Now raise your chin up. And tilt your shoulders toward me."

My mouth is starting to hurt from all the smiling, but I do what she asks. She angles the phone a few more times before finally snapping the picture. I feel my body collapse afterward, like I just ran a marathon.

"Good?" I ask as she examines the photo.

She bites her lip and I cringe. Is she really going to make us take that again? Does she do this with *every* selfie?

"I think we need wind," Sequoia says. "The whole thing will come together if wind is blowing through our hair."

"Wind," I repeat dubiously. "So we're just supposed to wait around until—"

Right then, on cue, a light breeze blows through the campus and Sequoia squeals, "Quick! Get into place."

I resume my position and try to duplicate the last smile. She clicks the photo just as the breeze brushes past us, blowing our hair back from our faces.

I hold my breath as she studies the latest attempt.

"I guess it'll do." She subsides, and begins tapping at the screen. "Tagged."

I hear my phone chirp and I pull it out of my bag to look at the final result. I admit, I still look pretty tired, even with the pounds of concealer. Sequoia, on the other hand, looks flawless. Not a smear of makeup, not a single tearstain. No one would ever be able to tell that a few minutes ago she was bawling her eyes out.

But as my gaze drifts down to the caption, I'm instantly able to forget about Sequoia's mini-meltdown as my excitement level rises again.

Game faces on. Getting ready to tackle another day
at the W.A.!
#LoveMyLife

That hashtag has never felt more appropriate.

If My Laptop Attacks Me

The minute Sequoia and I walk into the student union, I have to choke back the sob that rises in my throat and the tears of joy that well up in my eyes. It's just like I always imagined. No, *better* than I imagined. The floor-to-ceiling windows, the massive round pendant lights hanging from the rafters, the chic blue and silver decor (to match the school colors). There's even a rec room with a Ping-Pong table, *and* a store selling Windsor Academy–monogrammed everything!

Sequoia heads straight for the café along the back wall. It's cafeteria style and she grabs a tray and slides it along the metal poles. I watch her closely, figuring my best bet is to follow her every move so I don't mess anything up.

"Egg white and spinach frittata," she tells the woman behind the counter.

"The same," I say quickly, while inside my head, I'm screaming, *They serve egg-white frittatas here?!*

The Southwest High cafeteria only sells prepackaged muffins and stale bagels for breakfast. This is too cool.

As the woman prepares our meal, I glance around the rest of

the café. They have a hot and cold cereal station with every oatmeal topping you could imagine, a toast station with like a hundred different kinds of bread and jam, a waffle station with real maple syrup and fresh berries, and even a juice station with a push-button juicing machine.

This is like eating breakfast in a five-star hotel!

The woman hands us our plates of food and Sequoia pushes her tray down to the beverage station and orders us two double cappuccinos with extra foam.

"Actually," I tell the barista behind the counter, "I'll have a chai tea."

For a moment, I think Sequoia's eyes might bug right out of her head. "You're having *tea*?"

I can tell instantly that I said the wrong thing. "Uh, yeah."

"But you *always* have a double cappuccino in the morning."

I try to control my gag reflexes. Coffee? Gross! There's no way I'm drinking that. I'll throw up all over my beautiful uniform.

"I thought I'd try something new today," I say, attempting to sound nonchalant.

Sequoia continues to gape at me like I've suddenly grown a third arm. "B-b-but," she stammers, "how will you make it through AP chem without a cappuccino?"

Jeez, by the sound of her voice, you would think I told her I was skipping oxygen.

"I think I'll manage," I say confidently.

The barista delivers our drinks and I scan the café for a place to pay, but Sequoia prances off with her tray, heading into the main seating area of the student union.

Is this included with our tuition?

I follow Sequoia and watch her plop down at a table and pull her laptop out of her bag. She turns it on and begins typing furiously, taking short breaks only to shovel forkfuls of frittata into her mouth and guzzle sips of her cappuccino.

She really wastes no time getting started with the studying, does she?

"What are you doing?" Sequoia asks, glancing up at me. It's only now I realize I'm just standing here staring at her, with my tray still in my hands.

I quickly take a seat. I guess I should get started on the studying, too. I kind of hoped I could explore the student union a little more but that would probably be weird, given that I'm supposed to have been coming here for more than three years.

With eagerness bubbling inside me, I open my bag. It's honestly the first time I've even looked in here. I guess I shouldn't be surprised when my eyes land on my very own navy blue Windsor Academy laptop, but I am.

I gasp as I pull it out and run my fingertips across the smooth surface. The school logo is stamped right into the top left corner and my name is engraved in the center. This is the coolest thing ever! I can't stop touching it.

But I freeze when I realize Sequoia is gaping at me again. I flash a hurried smile and pretend to be wiping off a smudge. "Got it," I say brightly.

I open the laptop and power it on, feeling my heart race faster with each passing second that it takes to boot up. I drum my fingers anxiously on the table until the desktop finally appears.

Then, before I can even get a good look at the screen, I'm suddenly bombarded by a stream of notifications.

Ding!

Ding!

Ding!

Ding! Ding! Ding! Ding! Ding!

The sound is so loud, students from neighboring tables turn to stare at me. I search frantically for a mute button, but the pop-ups are coming so fast and furious, I can't seem to do anything but sit paralyzed and watch them fill up my screen.

Read chapters 4–6 for AP history

Write paper on technology in the Civil War (20+pages . . .
   single spaced!)

Read 50 pages of *Treasure Island*

Study for AP chem quiz

Are these homework assignments?

Sequoia glances at my screen and her eyes widen in panic. Her reaction instantly makes me feel better. At least I'm not the only person alarmed by this attack. It's probably some kind of computer glitch.

But then she says, "Jeez, Crusher. What did you do last night? Watch TV?"

"Uh," I stammer, trying my best to close the pop-up windows. But it's like trying to play a game of Whack-a-Mole. For every notification that I close, another three pop up in its place.

"Did you not study at *all*?" Sequoia asks.

"Uh," I repeat, trying to come up with a believable excuse. "I wasn't feeling well. You know, after the whole stair-falling thing."

Actually, now that I mention it, my head *is* starting to hurt again. I rub the back of my scalp. The bump is still there, although thankfully it's getting smaller.

Ding! Ding! Ding! Ding! Ding!

Sequoia, finally losing her patience, reaches over and presses a combination of keys, silencing the beeping machine.

But the notifications keep coming. It takes me a while, but I finally manage to track them all to a program called the Windsor Achiever.

That's right! I think with sudden realization. That's the app I read about on the school's website. It's supposed to store everything I need for school.

I open the program and click through the various tabs, marveling at how impressive it is. It's like the most robust organizational app ever.

There's a Task tab with all of my homework assignments (twenty-two are currently marked in red as "overdue"), a Textbook tab with access to my digital textbooks, a Schedule tab that lists my classes, times, and room numbers (that will come in handy today), and even a Clubs & Activities tab that lists every extracurricular I'm currently enrolled in. And there's a *lot*. Investment Club, French Club, Young Entrepreneurs Club, Model U.N., National Honor Society, National Economics Challenge (what on earth is *that?*), Astronomy Club, and Robotics Club?

As in like *robots?*

Seriously?

Other Me has been *quite* a busy bee.

And finally, there's a tab at the end labeled Rankings. I curiously click on it and have to cover my mouth to block another involuntary gasp. It's our class ranking! The entire senior class arranged in order of highest to lowest GPA.

And at the very top, with a significant lead, is *my* name.

A huge grin spreads across my face.

It's almost too good to be true! Other Me did all the work and now I'm going to reap the rewards. No wonder they call her Crusher. With all of those clubs and *that* GPA, there's really no other way to describe it.

I'm *crushing* it in this life.

"What?" Sequoia asks, obviously having noticed my ridiculous grin. She leans over to get a glimpse at my screen and lets out a harrumph. "*Please* don't remind me. Stupid French midterm. Stupid Steven Lamar."

I see her lip start to quiver again and I quickly angle the screen away.

"Don't ask me how he pulled that 98 percent out of nowhere," Sequoia goes on, seemingly holding herself together. "I have theories but I won't sink that low."

I skim the list, seeing Sequoia Farris ranked at number 6. I scroll to the bottom but stop when I notice that there are only ninety-nine names listed.

I could have sworn each class at Windsor had one hundred students. Didn't Dean Lewis tell me just yesterday that there are one hundred spots in the senior class and they were all taken? That's why I couldn't enroll. Because no one ever drops out. There's rarely *ever* an open spot at Windsor.

So why are there only ninety-nine names here?

I'm about to ask Sequoia this very question when she leans over again and points to the little red 22 hovering over my Task tab. "You better get cracking on that if you want to *keep* that number-one spot."

I blink out of what feels like a trance. She's right. I really should stop futzing around with this awesome app and get to work. I click on the Task view and scroll through the long list of overdue assignments. It seems to go on forever.

There's no way I can do all of these things before first period starts in—I click the Schedule tab—an hour! It's virtually impossible. Hermione Granger with her Time Turner couldn't even finish this in time.

Relax. Deep breaths. In. Out. In. Out.

I just have to take it one thing at a time. I quickly scan the list of tasks. A few reading assignments, a few papers to write, a calculus problem set to finish, a chemistry quiz to study for. And what are *these* weird tasks?

EN-1118-DQ
CH-1121-MD
FR-1122-AK

What do they even mean? They're obviously written in some kind of shorthand that Other Me uses to save time, but to me, it's like an alien language. How can I do the assignment if I don't know what the assignment is? And it's not like I can ask Sequoia. She already thinks I left my mind on the steps of Royce Hall.

Well, I'm sure I'll figure it out as soon as I get to one of my classes and the teacher is like, "Okay, everyone turn in your EN-1118-DQs!" For now, I'm going to have to skip it.

I continue scanning the list, looking for something to tackle that seems relatively simple, but I'm interrupted by a shrill voice coming from behind me. "Oh my gosh! Crusher! Are you okay? I heard what happened yesterday. I was so worried!"

I turn around to see a short girl with a cute blond bob and a headband. She's holding a paper coffee cup and staring at me wide-eyed like I'm a newly unveiled exhibit at the museum.

"She's fine," Sequoia answers for me, sounding a little protective. "Just a small bump to the head. Nothing to concern yourself with."

The girl exhales dramatically. I don't even know her but I can tell it's fake. "Thank goodness. I thought maybe you had brain damage or something."

Is it just my imagination or did she sound a bit hopeful when she said that?

I glance out of the corner of my eye just in time to see Sequoia roll her eyes. "Her brain is fine. And she's still number one in the class so . . ."

She lets this hang in the air, along with a thick awkwardness that makes me squirm.

"Okay, good," the girl says with another overly theatrical sigh.

"After what happened to Lucinda, I couldn't bear to think . . ." But then she looks at Sequoia and her voice trails off.

I follow her gaze, noticing the tears brimming in Sequoia's eyes. And her lips are pressed so tightly together they seem to disappear completely.

"Well," the girl chirps, sounding anxious. "I gotta go. See you in chem!"

She scurries away and I glance back at Sequoia, wondering if I should scoot my chair over and comfort her. But then, a moment later, she sniffles and goes back to work, that switch flicking just as suddenly as it did in the parking lot.

"God," she says, typing into her laptop. "She is such a vulture. One mention of you falling down the stairs and she's already planning her valedictorian speech."

I stutter out a laugh. But that's not the part of the conversation that's bothering me. There's something else going on around here. Something people aren't talking about. And it's not my bump to the head.

"After what happened to Lucinda, I couldn't bear to think . . ."
Lucinda . . .

Who is Lucinda?

Making sure Sequoia is fully engaged in her work, I pull my phone out of my bag and click on the SnipPic app. I scroll back to the picture I saw last night—the one where we're doing those over-the-top swooning poses, pretending our book boyfriends had just proposed. It was taken at this very table. Except it had *three* people in it. Sequoia, me, and Luce_the_Goose.

Luce_the_Goose.

Luce . . .

Lucinda . . .

A chill runs up my spine. What happened to this person? Why isn't she here? And why does Sequoia react so strangely every time someone mentions her?

I check the time stamp of the picture of the three of us. It was taken on November 9. Exactly one week ago. I scroll down, scrutinizing the photos that were posted before that. The smiling, short-haired Lucinda is in almost all of them. I scroll back up, studying the photos taken *after* November 9.

Lucinda is not in any of them.

It's like she simply disappeared.

If I Master Being a Student

After that explosion on my laptop, I know I should be focusing on making a dent in this epic task list, but I'm too distracted by this Lucinda girl and trying to figure out why she stopped appearing in my SnipPic photos. It's the same with Sequoia's feed. No trace of Lucinda in the past week. I click on Luce_the_ Goose's profile to try to get some clues, but her photos just stop completely after November 9. She hasn't posted anything in over a week, which feels odd since before that date she seemed to have posted at least five times a day.

I'm tempted to ask Sequoia about it, but I don't want to risk setting her off again or looking completely insane. If Lucinda is in all of these pictures on my feed then she's clearly my friend, which means I should probably know where she is. If I start asking questions, I might find myself right back in Nurse Wilson's office. Or worse, the hospital.

Needless to say, by the time the chime rings for first period, I've made very little progress on my work. The only tasks I've managed to tick off the list are "Turn in PE" because I did that yesterday and "Read 50 pages of *Treasure Island*" because I read that book last year. It was number 17 on the "25 Books to Read Before College" list that I found in seventh grade.

I started studying for my chemistry quiz, which is first period, but I didn't get very far. Fortunately, I found a study guide that Other Me had stored on her laptop and I was able to review some of the questions and answers before Sequoia and I set off for class. Thank God Other Me is as organized and meticulous as I am.

Other than that, though, I'm pretty much screwed today. I'm hoping if I just explain to the teachers what happened yesterday—the head-bumping part obviously, *not* the traveling-between-universes part—they'll take pity on me and give me some extensions.

According to the schedule in my Windsor Achiever app, which I've discovered is also on my phone, I have AP chemistry, followed by a study period (which the school calls Student Mastery Hour), then AP American history, lunch, AP French, then another Student Mastery Hour, then AP calculus and AP English.

When I see it all written out like that, it's incredibly daunting, but also incredibly exciting. And I definitely appreciate those built-in study periods. I'm going to need them. Other Me is clearly even more ambitious than I am. She's like me with better opportunities. And if she can do this, so can I.

AP chemistry is in Bellum Hall, the math and science building. It's hands down the coolest building I've ever walked into. It looks more like a space museum than a school building. And don't get me started on the AP chemistry classroom itself. I feel like I'm walking onto the set of a forensic crime show! Every lab station has its own iPad! Not to mention the teacher, Mr. Hartland, who used to teach chemistry at Cambridge University. You know, where Stephen Hawking studied. No big deal.

We do have a quiz, so I'm grateful that I crammed in those few minutes of studying before the chime rang. Also Other Me is amazing at taking notes. Everything that was covered in the quiz was in her study guide, so I'm feeling pretty confident about the results.

For the first Student Mastery Hour, I'm dying to check out the Sanderson-Ruiz Library, but Sequoia insists we study in this little alcove on the second floor of Royce Hall so we can be closer to our AP history classroom. There are tons of these little alcoves throughout the school. Windsor calls them study bays. They each have a small couch, two armchairs, a coffee table, and a single-serve coffee machine with an impressive selection of coffee pods.

Sequoia brews herself an Italian dark roast (hasn't she had *enough* caffeine today?) and I opt for a green tea, which makes Sequoia's eyes bug out of her head all over again. We make ourselves comfortable on the couch and I try to focus on my AP history reading, but this headache that started before first period has only gotten worse and now it feels like someone is slowly drilling a hole through my skull. By the time the chime rings again, I've barely managed to finish half a chapter.

History is in another amazing classroom. This one is made to look like someone's living room. Instead of desks, a bunch of sofas and armchairs are set up in a circle. We spend the entire class period debating the Civil War. Yes, *debating*. Not being quizzed or lectured. The students here actually have opinions about the Civil War. *Differing* opinions. And they're very vocal about them.

The teacher, Ms. Clemenson, just sits on the arm of one of the couches, looking amused and mediating when the discussion gets a little *too* passionate.

By the end of the period, I decide that Walt Disney World has nothing on the Windsor Academy. *This* is the happiest place on earth.

These are my people.

When lunch rolls around, Sequoia rushes off to an appointment with her college counselor and I check my app to see I'm scheduled to be in Fineman Arts Center, room 117, for an Investment Club meeting. I have no idea what one does in an Investment Club but I'm about to find out.

I make a sandwich from the epic sandwich bar in the Windsor Café, then dash out of the student union to find the Fineman Arts Center. According to all the online campus maps that I've memorized, it's supposed to be right next door, but those maps must not be proportionate because I feel like I'm running forever.

By the time I get to room 117, I'm completely breathless.

"Sorry! Sorry!" I say as I burst through the door. "I know I'm late—" But the words are snatched from my lips when I see that the room is completely empty. Well, *almost* empty.

There's one guy. He's sitting at a large round table, typing at a laptop.

I recognize him immediately and a wave of revulsion passes through me. He's that guy I met yesterday when I was sitting outside the dean's office. He looks exactly the same, like he hasn't showered in weeks and slept in his uniform last night. He peers at me from over the top of his computer and I swear I see a flicker of annoyance flash in his eyes before he goes back to work.

"Where is everyone?" I ask.

He doesn't answer, keeping his head bent toward his screen.

I glance around at the empty room. "Is this the Investment Club?" If it is, it must not be very popular.

He finally stops typing. "No. This is *Writer's Block*."

"*Writer's Block?*" I repeat.

He scoffs and rolls his eyes. "The *literary* magazine," he clarifies, and I don't miss the condescending way he says *literary* like I've never heard the word before.

I feel a small jolt of excitement. A literary magazine! My app must have had the wrong club listed. But it makes perfect sense that I'd be part of a literary magazine. I am, after all, a writer. "Oh! Right. Sorry. My mistake." I slide into a chair on the other side of the table and pull out my laptop. "Am I early?"

But the boy watches me with a confused expression that quickly morphs into irritation. "What are you doing?" he asks.

"Uh . . ." I'm starting to feel uneasy. "I think this is where I'm supposed to be."

He barks out a laugh. "I highly doubt that."

His reaction takes me by surprise. "Aren't I a member of the literary magazine?"

"Is this a joke?"

My stomach swoops. "I don't think so."

The boy gawks at me, his eyebrows knitting together like he's trying to decipher the foreign Martian language coming out of my mouth. "Why would *you* be on a literary magazine? You have absolutely *zero* writing experience."

"That's not true!" I begin to argue. "I'm the editor in chief of . . ."

But my voice trails off as the realization punches me right in the gut.

The *Southwest Star*.

It's not mine anymore.

That's why the framed issues had disappeared from above my desk, replaced by the framed acceptance letter from Windsor. I guess since I go to school here, I don't run the newspaper at Southwest High anymore.

I know that makes sense, I just . . .

Well, I hadn't really thought about it until now.

I wonder who's running the *Southwest Star* now. Probably Mia Graham, my features editor, or maybe even Laney. As much as the very thought of her sends a quiver of anger through me, I know she would do a good job.

"The editor in chief of what?" the boy prompts, looking amused. "The *Zombie Press*?"

My temper flares. "No," I say indignantly. "I'll have you know I have *plenty* of writing experience."

He goes back to typing. "Writing papers on the Civil War doesn't count."

My headache throbs inside my skull. Why is he implying that I'm not a member of the literary magazine? Is he playing some kind of prank on me? Well, whatever. If I'm not a member yet, that doesn't mean I can't sign up now. Investment Club can wait.

I plaster on a bright smile. "Fine. If I'm not a member, then I'd like to join."

He lets out a snort that grates on my nerves and continues typing. When I make no move to leave, he glances up. "Wait, are you serious?"

Now I'm just kind of offended. "Yes. Dead serious."

He studies me. Like *really* studies me. His eyes are narrowed, his lips are pressed in a hard line. I start to feel self-conscious and surreptitiously check my teeth with my tongue for pieces of food.

"No," he says after a long moment, and then goes back to work.

"No?" I spit back, astonished. "What do you mean no?"

"I mean, you can't join. I'm saying no."

I gape at him. "Can you do that?"

"I'm the editor in chief. I can do whatever I want."

"B-b-but," I stammer, "why?"

He sighs and shoots me a look that says, *I really don't have time to deal with this.* "Because I just don't think you'd be the right fit for this particular publication." I can hear the hostility in his voice. If he's been trying to hide it, it's out of the bag now.

I cross my arms over my chest. "You don't even know me!"

He laughs at this. A dark, vicious, villain-in-a-lair-stroking-a-cat kind of laugh. "Oh, trust me. I know you."

"How could you possibly know anything about me," I argue. "We just met—" But the words halt on my lips. I was going to say we just met yesterday, because that's when *I* remember meeting him, but then I remind myself that *this* me has been a student at Windsor for more than three years. That's plenty of time to make friends with everyone . . . or, as it would seem in this boy's case, enemies.

He gives me a strange look.

"Never mind," I mutter. "Why don't you think I would be a good fit? I'm a good writer."

"Fine," he says, leaning back in his chair. "I'll let you join the magazine—"

I break into a grin. "Great!"

"*If,*" he goes on, holding up a finger, "you can tell me what my last name is."

My jaw drops open. He can't do that! That's not fair. I don't know anyone's last name. I barely know anyone's first name. I just started here!

He stares me down like a challenger in a duel, tilting his head with an amused smirk. "Well?"

I swallow. Okay, I'm not sure how to get around this one. But the bigger question is, why does he just *assume* that I wouldn't know his last name? I mean obviously I *don't*, but he doesn't know what I've been through. He doesn't know I'm a foreigner from another universe. As far as he's concerned, I'm Kennedy Rhodes, the girl he's gone to school with since the ninth grade. *She* should definitely know his last name. And his first name, for that matter.

"You can't do it, can you?" He laughs again. This one is even darker. And I swear I hear the faintest trace of sadness underneath. "Un-freaking-believable."

I open my mouth to protest but nothing comes out.

"That's *amazing*," he says bitterly. "You've gone here how many years? We've been in how many of the same classes—not to mention the *other* things we've done together—and you can never be bothered to remember my last name?"

What?

That can't be true. He's lying. He's tricking me somehow. And what *other* things is he talking about?

"I-I . . ." I stammer. "I do remember. I just temporarily forgot. I hit my head yesterday and—"

He doesn't look convinced. "Oh, that's a good one."

"I did! I swear. It was right after I saw you outside of the dean's office."

The shift in his body is *almost* imperceptible. I *almost* don't notice the way his jaw tightens and his fingertips dig into his palms.

"I mean," I correct myself, "it was right after Student Mastery Hour."

But he doesn't seem interested in my correction. He doesn't seem interested in my head injury at all anymore. "How did you know I was in the dean's office?" he snaps, and I sense the panic in his voice.

"I don't," I try to cover for myself.

According to Sequoia I was with *her* yesterday when I fell.

"You just said . . ."

"I was mistaken," I say, rubbing at my temples to fake confusion. Although to be honest, they're *really* pounding now. "I was confusing you for someone else. Like I said, I bumped my head. Details are getting mixed up in my brain."

I watch his lips twist in contemplation, noticing for the first time the dark stubble on his cheeks. Looks like someone forgot to shave this morning.

I think he's about to say something else but he never gets the chance, because right then the classroom door opens and a group of students—the rest of the literary magazine, I presume—bustles in, talking animatedly about something. They all screech to a halt when they see me.

"Well," the boy says, rising from his seat. I notice his demeanor instantly shifts at the appearance of the other students. Like he's an actor preparing to take the stage. "It was nice chatting with you. But I have a meeting to lead."

"So," I say, confused, "can I join the magazine?"

He walks to the whiteboard, turning back to me long enough to say "No," before uncapping a dry-erase marker and scribbling something on the board.

I can feel everyone's eyes on me as I close my laptop and slide it back into my bag. Trying to blink away the tears of humiliation that are welling up in my eyes, I keep my head down and start for the door as the rest of the students take their seats.

"And for the millionth time," the boy calls out just before I leave, "it's Dylan *Parker*. Let's see if your zombie brain can remember that tomorrow."

If I Boycott Boys

What on earth is that guy's problem? Why does he hate me so
much? Why did he have to embarrass me in front of the whole
literary magazine? He called me a zombie! I'm not a zombie! He's
just mad that I don't remember his last name. But I'm sure there's
a logical explanation for that. I'm sure Other Me had good reason not to remember him. Maybe she's been so busy cramming
all sorts of useful knowledge and information into her brain, she
doesn't have any room for names. Maybe she was mad at him
and only *pretended* to forget his name. Maybe he did something
horrible to Sequoia and they got in a huge fight and now Other
Me is siding with her best friend. As best friends *should* do.

"So what's with that Dylan Parker guy?" I ask Sequoia casually as we walk through the parking lot toward her car at the
end of the day. Despite being what feels like *decades* behind in
my homework, I somehow managed to survive six class periods
and two more club meetings relatively intact, thanks to my excellent improvising skills and a few extensions from teachers.

As it turned out, I *was* supposed to be in the Investment Club
during Activity Hour today. *And* I'm the president. Apparently,

in my haste to get there, I barged into the wrong room. A mistake I certainly won't make again.

Sequoia is barely listening to me. She's scrolling through her SnipPic app, reading the countless comments she received on our selfie this morning. "Good call on that tree." She looks up long enough to point to a black sedan parked in our original space that's now covered in leaves and dirt.

I flash a perfunctory smile and return to the matter at hand. "So what's his deal anyway?"

"Whose deal?" she asks, as though she didn't even hear my first question.

"Dylan Parker," I repeat. I looked him up on the Windsor Achiever app during my second Student Mastery Hour. I was surprised, actually, to see that he's ranked in the top twenty of the class. I assumed, judging by the way he dresses and his general opinion of the school, that he'd be at the bottom.

Sequoia unlocks the car. "I don't know anyone named Dylan Parker. Is he a freshman?"

I open the passenger-side door. "No, he's a senior."

Sequoia drops into the driver's seat. "Doesn't sound familiar."

So Sequoia doesn't know him either? Well, now I don't feel as bad. But seriously, what is with this guy? Is he a ghost?

"He runs the literary magazine." I make one last effort to prompt her as I buckle my seat belt.

"We have a literary magazine?"

I laugh. "Yes. It's called *Writer's Block.*"

She pushes the start engine button. "Oh, right. The weird-looking guy?"

"Is he weird-looking?" I ask. "I don't think he's that bad."

She shrugs. "I guess he'd be all right, you know, if he actually gave a crap about his appearance or his education."

"He's ranked number 19," I put in, even though I have no idea why I'm defending him. He was horrible to me.

"I don't know how," Sequoia says. "He never participates in class."

I suddenly remember what he said to me outside the dean's office yesterday. About how he thought this school sucked out your soul and turned you into a lifeless zombie. I instantly feel myself getting flustered again. He's probably some spoiled rich kid who's been given everything he's ever wanted in life and has never had to work for anything. He probably doesn't even have to try. He probably already has acceptance letters to every single Ivy League college in the country.

He has no idea how lucky he is to go here. There are so many people who would *kill* to be here. If he hates it so much, why doesn't he just leave?

"Wasn't that the guy you went on a date with?" Sequoia asks suddenly, like the memory just popped into her head.

"A date?" I screech.

With that *guy?*

"Yeah." She backs out of the parking spot and maneuvers through the lot. "In ninth grade. It was right before we became friends. Remember?"

My mind is spinning. Other Me went out with him in the ninth grade? Is that why he was so nasty to me? Did Other Me break his heart or something?

And isn't it kind of weird—and a little insensitive—that she wouldn't remember his last name after they went on a *date*?

It must not have been that memorable an experience.

"Uh," I falter. "Vaguely. Remind me?"

Sequoia pulls up to the Windsor Academy gates and waits for them to open. She scrunches up her face like the effort of trying to heave this memory out of her brain is almost painful. "I remember you going on one date with someone—I think it was that Dylan guy—then you met me and I showed you the error of your ways." She turns and flashes me a beaming smile.

I force a laugh. "The error of my ways. Right. You mean, because he's so . . ." I search for the right word.

Reprehensible?

Obnoxious?

Rude?

"Undatable?" I finish.

She flips on her signal and turns left onto the main road. "No," she says, flashing me a strange look. "Because dating is a huge waste of time."

"Oh," I say lamely. "Right."

"That's why we made the Boycott Pact. No boys until college."

My mouth falls open. Is she being serious? Has Other Me really never dated anyone since ninth grade? No wonder she has so much time for all of those clubs.

"You know, you owe that first place ranking to me," Sequoia brags. "Imagine if you'd continued dating that loser. You'd never have been able to accomplish everything that you have. You'd be too busy worrying about your stupid relationship."

"Yeah," I agree. Even though, in reality, I don't have to imagine it. I already know what that choice looks like. I've *lived* it.

Although, for some reason, I find myself wondering what that one date with Dylan Parker was like. Did we have fun? Was he sweet and romantic? Did we *kiss*?

The thought sends a tremor of disgust through me.

Eew. I can't imagine kissing that guy. His lips are probably all chapped and gross and he probably smells from his obvious aversion to bathing.

Well, whatever happened on that *one* date, Other Me was smart to listen to Sequoia and steer clear of boy-related drama. I made that mistake when I chose Austin and look how well that turned out. She's right. Boys are a *huge* waste of time.

"How crazy was that Civil War debate in history today?" Sequoia asks, changing subjects and lanes at the same time. It's like she's already forgotten about our previous conversation. As though she's barely given Dylan Parker a second thought.

And that's exactly what I intend to do.

Not give him a second thought.

If I Feed My Addiction

My phone rings as soon as Sequoia turns onto the highway. The call is from the home line, which means it's my brother. Both my parents always call from their cells.

"Hi, Frankie," I say into the phone.

"I eat oatmeal for breakfast every morning!" he announces like he's kicking off a newscast.

I scrunch up my face. "Huh?"

"That's got to be different, right? In this universe?"

I rub my forehead. My headache is the size of Texas now. "No, Frankie. That's the same, too."

"Hmm," he says, sounding discouraged. Then, a second later, he blurts out, "I refuse to use hand dryers in public bathrooms!"

"Because two years ago you read an article that they suck dirt up from the floor and then blow it on your hands."

"I don't have a cell phone!" he practically shouts, his voice cracking.

I chuckle. "How do you think I knew it was you when you called just now? You're the only one in the house who uses the landline."

Silence.

Then he mumbles, "I'll get back to you," and hangs up.

"What was that about?" Sequoia asks as I lock my phone.

"Nothing," I mumble.

"Frankie being Frankie?" she asks with a playful smile.

I laugh, grateful for *one* thing I don't have to explain today. "Exactly."

I glance out the window and it's only now I notice that Sequoia has completely missed the turnoff for my street.

"Where are we going?" I ask.

"To my house," she says as though it's obvious. "So we can get ready together."

Get ready? For what?

Sequoia darts a suspicious glance at me, as if she can read my bewildered thoughts. "The school fund-raiser," she prompts, sounding a little perturbed.

I sit up straighter in my seat. A what?

"You can't possibly have forgotten. You practically organized the whole thing."

I organized a school fund-raiser? On top of everything else?

Next I'm going to find out I'm swimming in the summer Olympics!

"Uh," I say lamely, "of course I didn't forget." I grapple to unlock my phone and click the calendar app. Lo and behold, there it is. Right in my schedule.

7:00 p.m.—Windsor Academy Fund-Raising Gala

"What is with you today?" Sequoia asks. She's exited the highway and is stopped at a red light, staring at me like I'm an alien invader disguised in a Kennedy Rhodes bodysuit, which coincidentally is kind of how I feel.

"Sorry," I say, massaging my temples. "I've had this massive headache all day and it won't go away."

Sequoia studies me for a long moment, evidently trying to decide whether or not this is a good enough explanation.

"I think it's from the fall yesterday," I add, hoping this will persuade her.

She squints at me. "How much coffee have you had today?"

Coffee? What does that have to do with anything?

"None," I say.

"NONE?!" she screeches. "Well, no wonder! It's nearly five o'clock! It probably feels like a herd of rhinoceroses have been playing rugby inside your brain!"

Actually, that's exactly how it feels.

The light turns green. "Crusher," Sequoia admonishes, stepping on the gas. "Today is *not* the day to go cold turkey. This event is *way* too important."

Then I'm suddenly slammed into the door as Sequoia makes a split decision and yanks hard on the steering wheel, maneuvering her BMW across three lanes of traffic and into a parking lot.

"Well, that certainly didn't help my headache," I say, rubbing the spot where the window crashed into my skull.

"What do you want?" she asks, and I glance up to see that

we're in line at a Starbucks drive-through. "And *no* tea this time. That's how you got into this mess."

Is she right? Am I simply having caffeine withdrawals? How much coffee do I normally drink every day?

I lean over her to study the menu, searching for the least coffee-sounding coffee drink. "A Pumpkin Spice Latte, I guess."

Sequoia conveys my order to the little speaker and I have to work extra hard to conceal the shock when she tacks on a triple espresso shot for herself.

Triple espresso? I can't even begin to count how many milligrams of caffeine this girl has consumed today. And she's not that big a person. I'm surprised she hasn't rocketed into orbit by now.

Sequoia pays the cashier and hands me my drink before shooting hers straight up and tossing the empty cup into the backseat. I take a tentative sip, fully expecting to hate it, but it's actually not half bad. I mean, I can still taste the coffee, but with all that milk, syrup, and whipped cream it's pretty buried.

"Better?" Sequoia asks, navigating through the parking lot.

"Actually, yeah," I say, surprised. It's not like my headache is instantly gone, but there's something far less urgent about it. As if this was what my body was craving all along.

I stare down at the paper cup in my hand, reading the initials PSL scribbled onto the side. Laney once wrote a story for the paper about the nationwide pumpkin craze. She was convinced the whole thing could be traced back to this little drink. I wonder if that story still exists, even though I'm no longer editor in chief.

"Sequoia?" I say, glancing up from my cup. "Does the Windsor Academy have a school newspaper?"

She turns onto the main road, flashing me a strange look. "No. Why?"

I shake my head and take another sip from my drink. "No reason."

If Sequoia Played Piano

Sequoia lives in one of those really nice gated communities with a country club and a golf course. I try to hide my reaction as she pulls into the driveway of her house because I'm supposed to have been coming here for more than three years, but it's difficult. The house is spectacular. It's three stories, with dramatically steep angles on the roof and a white stone façade.

When we walk through the front door, I feel like I'm walking into a museum. The interior is all rich creams and dark woods and red accents. And the most beautiful piece of classical music is playing from a speaker in the next room.

"Sorry about that," Sequoia says, sounding slightly annoyed. "My sister is home from school for Thanksgiving break. She's been at it nonstop."

I follow her through the spacious living room into the kitchen, passing a round, turret-shaped nook where a girl is seated at a magnificent white grand piano.

Someone is playing *that song?*

I could have sworn it was a recording.

"Your sister," I repeat curiously, taking a step toward the piano room. I can't see the girl's face because her back is to us, but from behind, they could practically be the same person. She has the same willowy frame as Sequoia and the same reddish-brown hair.

I watch, mesmerized, as the girl's fingers move over the keys in graceful strokes, and I can't help but be completely swept away by the sound.

"Kamilah," Sequoia whines. "Can you give it a break for three seconds?" Then Sequoia leans in to whisper to me, "We haven't had peace and quiet around here since she got back from Chestnut Ridge."

Chestnut Ridge?

The fancy boarding school? Wow. No wonder she plays so well. That's one of the hardest high school music programs to get into.

"You know," Kamilah huffs, shutting the cover with a hard *clack*, "I don't come up to your room and tell you to stop studying, do I?"

"My studying is *quiet*," Sequoia retorted.

Kamilah turns around and I stifle a gasp when I see her eerily familiar face.

"You're twins!" I say, before I can stop myself.

Whatever argument Kamilah was going to make next is completely ripped from her mouth. She gapes at me. "What's with her?" she asks Sequoia.

Sequoia is looking at me with a matching expression. Glancing between them is kind of freaky. It's like standing between two mirrors. "She's . . ." Sequoia says haltingly. "She . . . didn't have her caffeine this morning."

She grabs me by the arm and drags me up the stairs until we're safely behind the door of her room. "What was that?" she asks accusingly.

"Sorry," I mumble, looking at the floor.

"You've only known Kamilah for three years."

"I know. It's just, sometimes I forget how much you look alike."

Sequoia is quiet for a long moment. When I brave a glance up at her, she's staring at me with an unnerving expression. "Okay, I'm going to chalk up your weird behavior lately to head trauma and stress. But I swear, if you crack on me, too, I will never forgive you."

Crack on her, too?

What does that mean?

But before I can pry further, the soft melodic sound of another classical piece floats up the stairs. Sequoia lets out a groan and opens her bedroom door long enough to yell, "Why don't you try getting a life and leaving the house for once?"

The piano gets louder in response. Sequoia slams the door again and gives me an apologetic look. "We're just going to have to blast some music to mask the sound."

"I think it's kind of nice," I say wistfully. "She's obviously very talented."

Sequoia shoots me a look of disgust. "Ugh. You're beginning to sound like my crazy parents. God, it's so much better when she's locked away in that boarding school with all the other smug musical geniuses. Then I don't have to listen to them fawn over her like she's God's gift to the world."

I'm getting the feeling that this is not your average sibling rivalry. "They fawn over you, too," I say.

I know I can't be sure that's true, but I can't imagine how it wouldn't be. I've been watching CoyCoy55 for the past three years. She's smart. And beautiful. And inspiring. How could parents not be proud of a child like that?

She snorts. "Hardly." She opens her closet door but just stares inside, like she forgot why she went in there to begin with.

"Sometimes I wonder how they chose, you know?" She says it so quietly, I'm not sure she even meant for me to hear. "We were infants. How did they pick her to be the musical one and me to be the academic one?" She turns and lets out a sad laugh. "I've seen the home videos, we were both banging around on pots and pans with a vengeance. Was her banging that much more melodic than mine?"

From the way she's talking, I'm pretty sure this is a conversation we've had before. Probably even numerous times, so I know better than to ask her for an explanation. Instead, I try to offer comfort.

"Being academic is just as impressive," I tell her.

She removes two plastic garment bags from the closet and lays them down on her bed. "Yeah, maybe if I was at the top of the class like you. But trust me, number six is nothing to brag about in this house. Not when you've been told your whole life that you're being pitted against your twin sister."

"Your parents never said that," I argue, feeling confident in my statement. Because honestly, what kind of parent would say that?

"Maybe not in those exact terms, but the message has been pretty clear." Sequoia lets out a deep, burdened sigh. "If I can just get into Harvard, everything will be fine. I'll finally prove them wrong."

I walk over and put my arm around her. "Of course you'll get into Harvard."

"You don't know that," she accuses, tears welling up. "A million things could go wrong. My SAT scores might not be high enough. I could flunk a test next week. I could bomb my admissions interview."

I cringe at the reminder of being in Watts's living room, variations of the word *crap* spewing out of my mouth like a broken fountain.

"Yeah, but you're forgetting the most important thing," I tell her.

She wipes the moisture from the corners of her eyes. "What?"

I squeeze her shoulder. "You go to the Windsor Academy! Do you know how good that looks on a college application? Do you know how many Windsor students get into Ivy League colleges every year?"

"Eighty-nine percent," she replies automatically, like she's a robot giving a preprogrammed response.

"Wow! Really?"

She shoots me a strange look and I conceal my surprise. "That's right, 89 percent! See! That's a *huge* percentage! Because the Windsor Academy is an amazing school."

She sniffles. "Not as good as Chestnut Ridge."

"*Better* than Chestnut Ridge," I assure her.

She seems to contemplate that for a moment, a far-off look in her eyes. Then she asks, "Do you ever feel like a racehorse?"

I'm not following. "A racehorse?"

"Yeah. Like someone has invested all this money in you, everyone is watching, but no one really cares what you do or how you do it, just as long as you cross the finish line first?"

There's something very sad about her question. It strikes a chord in me. I rack my brain for an appropriate response, but before I can get anything out, Sequoia unzips the first garment bag and says, "C'mon. We should start getting ready or we'll be late."

If I Turn Into a Princess

I realize I'm not exactly an expert when it comes to dresses but these two are absolutely *amazing*. Sequoia has dressed me in a sleek, strapless navy gown with a gathered waist while she's wearing a stunning layered coral dress with a sequined hem.

Are we going to a school fund-raiser or the Academy Awards?

She also offered to do my hair and makeup, for which I'm grateful, because she did a much better job than I could ever do. My hair is pinned up in a side chignon with loose strands framing my face and my eye makeup is dark and sultry. Looking in the mirror, I can't believe what I see. I can't believe I'm wearing a dress like this. In my other life, I considered changing out of my jeans and Dad's ratty old leather jacket the height of refinement. Now, I look like a celebrity!

I never thought I'd feel this way, but it's kind of fun getting all dressed up. I guess it makes a big difference when you actually have somewhere to go.

The fund-raiser is being held at the country club in Sequoia's community. Evidently, that's why we decided to get ready here. It's only a short drive from her house. The entire way there, I'm panicked that I won't know what to do or what to say, but it becomes obvious the moment I walk through the door of the ballroom that Other Me, being the rock star that she is, already took care of everything.

I stand in the doorway in absolute awe. At Southwest High we sold candy and cheesecakes to raise money. This is like a society ball.

The giant room is decorated in Windsor Academy navy and silver. The tables are covered with glittery fabric and crystal glasses, and the waiters, dressed in white tuxedos with navy blue bow ties, are bustling around, putting final touches on the table settings.

The guests start arriving a few minutes later, and by eight o'clock the room is packed with beautiful people swathed in beautiful clothes. Everybody here is either a Windsor student, teacher, parent, or alum.

I make small talk with faculty. I eat delicious passed hors d'oeuvres. I steal away for the occasional dance floor romp with Sequoia. And I post so many SnipPics, my feed is overflowing. I just want to document everything. I want to freeze this moment and capture it in a frame.

This is, by far, the most glamorous thing I've ever done.

It's truly something else.

Normal high-school seniors don't attend events like this.

That's because you're not normal anymore, a voice in the back of my head reminds me.

I don't think it's fully hit me until right now.

My life at the Windsor Academy isn't just about digital

textbooks and award-winning teachers. It's about so much more than that. Robotics Club, and Investment Club, and fancy fund-raising galas.

With the dress and the fancy party and the pumpkin in my latte, I'm beginning to fully understand how Cinderella felt when she was poofed right out of her sad failure of a life and into a brand-new exciting one.

So what if I don't run a newspaper or write for a literary magazine? I'm living a true fairy tale!

After dinner is served, I wander through the aisles of the silent auction, clutching my expensive crystal glassware and marveling at all the amazing items that companies have donated. We're not talking about a little teeth-cleaning at the local dentist or a gift basket from the grocery store. These donations are legit. Ski trips to Steamboat Springs, spa packages for two, even shopping sprees with a personal stylist! And some of the silent auction bids are over ten thousand dollars!

When I ran the *Southwest Star*, I was over the moon when we raised a tenth of that in a month! I remember how touch and go it was for the first few issues after I became editor in chief. We were living month to month, never knowing if we would be able to raise enough money to put out another issue. Printing physical copies cost money. Money the school wouldn't give us. We sold ads to local businesses to keep ourselves afloat: ortho-dontists and nail salons and restaurants. I had to bang on doors and convince business owners why advertising in a "washed-up" medium was a good idea. The staff called me the Closer because I refused to leave until I got a check. For the most part, I simply pestered those poor people to death. But it worked. Because when you believe in something as much as I believed in that paper, you do what it takes.

And clearly, Other Me believes in this.

She believes in the Windsor Academy. Otherwise, why would she put so much effort into organizing a fund-raising event for it?

I stop and study the bid sheet for a bottle of red wine. It must be a pretty good wine because the highest bid is currently twenty-five hundred dollars from someone named—I bend down and squint at the messy handwriting—*Dylan Parker?*

That can't be right. Why would *he* be bidding on a bottle of wine that he can't even drink in support of a school that he doesn't even like?

"It's my dad," says a voice, startling me. I jump back and accidentally land on the hem of my strapless dress, nearly pulling it right off my body.

A hand reaches out to steady me. When I finally catch my balance I see that it belongs to Dylan. He's dressed in a black tux that, like his Windsor uniform, looks wrinkled and thrown on. His bow tie isn't even tied.

"Whoa there," he says. "We wouldn't want you to fall twice in one week." There's no sympathy in his tone, only smugness.

"Thanks," I mutter, and turn back toward the auction table. But I can still feel him there behind me. For some reason I get the impression that he's watching me. Waiting for a reaction.

"It's pretty incredible, isn't it?" he asks after a moment. "That my dad will spend twenty-five hundred dollars on a bottle of wine that he'll never drink?"

"It's for a good cause," I retort tightly, without looking at him. He scoffs. "Sure. Yeah. A good cause. There are children starving all over the world. The wild elephant population is dwindling because of poachers. The oceans are full of oil and trash, and half the fish species on the menu tonight are being over-fished, but hey, let's give our money to rich kids because God forbid they have to use year-old iPads in their science classrooms."

"If you're so against this fund-raiser, why are you even here?" I fire back.

"Trust me, there are plenty of places I'd rather be. But I wasn't really given a choice. My dad is a very *proud* Windsor alum. As was my grandfather."

"So you're a legacy?"

He groans. "God, I hate that word."

I sigh and keep walking, hoping to get away from buzz-kill Dylan. I can't believe I ever went on a date with this guy!

I bend over to read the description on the next item and nearly drop my crystal glass. "Holy crap! Someone got Daphne Wu to donate autographed copies of *all* of her books?"

She's hands down my favorite author. I remember when Coy-Coy55 posted a picture of her in the Windsor Lauditorium when she came to speak last year.

Dylan steps up next to me and flashes me a strange look. "Seriously?"

"What? Not a fan?" I roll my eyes. "What a surprise."

"Actually, I'm a huge fan. I was commenting on your reaction."

I do my best to ignore him. Chances are he's going to make some obnoxious comment about how I'm a zombie and zombies shouldn't have favorite authors or some nonsense like that. I take a sip of my drink and move on to the next item up for bids—a set of designer luggage.

He follows, keeping his gaze trained on me. "I mean, didn't *you* get Daphne Wu to donate the books?"

I spit out my drink. *"What?"*

He gives me another confused look. "I thought you got *all* the donations."

"I did?!" I clear my throat when I see his reaction. "I mean, that's right. I did. Yay for me."

Meanwhile, inside, I'm screaming.

How on earth did Other Me manage to convince someone to donate a ski vacation worth over ten thousand dollars?

I'm beginning to think she really might be superwoman.

Dylan is still staring at me with that inquisitive expression, like he's not quite sure what to make of me. I avoid his probing gaze by looking at the highest bid on the designer luggage set, blinking in surprise again when I see Dylan Parker's name.

"So your dad is Dylan Parker, too?" I ask, peering up at him.

"Yup." He makes a *popping* sound at the end of the word. "Dylan Parker III."

"Doesn't that make you a fourth?"

"The zombie can count!" he says, like he's just discovered life on Neptune.

I scoff and turn to confront him. "I am *not* a zombie."

He laughs. "Are you kidding? You're like the *queen* of the zombies. Just look at all this!" He spreads his arms wide, gesturing to the entire room.

"What's wrong with it?"

"What's wrong with it?" he spits back. "You don't see the irony in raising money for a school that costs fifty thousand dollars a year to attend?"

Fifty thousand dollars?

I don't remember the tuition being that high. Although to be honest, I never spent a ton of time on that section of the website.

"Well . . ." I struggle to find a defense, but I just don't have one.

"Well, exactly," Dylan says. "It's ridiculous. This shindig alone probably costs over a hundred thousand dollars. And you'll probably raise, what? A hundred and twenty-five? That's some zombie math for you."

I cross my arms, feeling my breathing grow shallow. Why do I always get so flustered around this guy? Why can't I just ignore him and be done with it?

"Look," I say, losing my cool. "I happen to really like it here. I'm *grateful* to be attending the Windsor Academy. And I'm not going to let *you* or anyone else spoil that for me. This school is amazing. It provides opportunities that most people would kill for. And if it takes a little extra money to make that happen, then I'm *honored* to donate my time and energy to help."

I turn on my heels and stalk off, feeling proud of myself. Feeling in control and powerful and on top of the world again.

"Why don't you ask Lucinda Wallace what she thinks?"

I freeze on the spot, my breath suddenly trapped in my lungs.

"Why don't you ask her how *amazing* this school is?" Dylan lets out a dark laugh. "Oh, that's right. I forgot. You and your BFF Sequoia would rather pretend she never existed."

I spin around and open my mouth to respond—not sure if anything will come out besides hot air—but I'm never given the opportunity. Because right then a loud voice echoes through the entire ballroom. "Good evening, Windsor Family!"

I turn toward the stage to see Dean Lewis standing in front of the microphone, looking radiant in a long, shimmery gown.

"Thank you so much for coming," she goes on. She's so poised and calm. Like she was born to be up on that stage. "On behalf of the entire Windsor faculty, we are delighted that you could join us tonight for this very special occasion."

There's a smattering of polite clapping throughout the room, and I glance around me to find that Dylan has disappeared into the crowd.

"Although to be honest," Dean Lewis says, "this whole night wouldn't have been possible without one very special person."

Sequoia pushes through a group of people to come stand next to me. She flashes me a giddy smile and nudges me with her elbow. "She's talking about you!"

I feel my legs go numb.

What?

No. She can't be.

"Her friends call her Crusher," Dean Lewis goes on with a twinkle in her eye. "Because, let's face it, she *crushes* everything she does. Including this beautiful, brilliant gala. There's no doubt she represents everything the Windsor Academy stands for and we will miss her terribly when she graduates in May. Please give it up for the fabulously accomplished and ridiculously talented student fund-raising captain, Miss Kennedy Rhodes!"

The room bursts into raucous applause. Somewhere near me, I'm pretty sure Sequoia is telling me to do something, but I can barely even hear it over the sound of rushing water in my ears.

I feel a nudge at my back. "Go," Sequoia urges. "Get your butt up there."

What? No way!

It's one thing to stand up in front of a room full of student newspaper reporters, it's quite another to stand up in a room full of tuxedo-and-ball-gown-clad people who bid twenty-five hundred dollars on a bottle of what is basically just fermented grape juice.

Panicked, I look to the stage, where Dean Lewis is shielding her eyes from the spotlight and scanning the crowd. "Where is she?" She gives a hearty laugh. "Probably off convincing someone to donate to next year's gala. Kennedy?"

I instinctively start to back away but Sequoia gives me another nudge in the back. "Go on! You deserve it!"

I stumble toward the stage, my legs feeling like solid blocks of ice beneath me. As I climb the steps, I seriously think that I might faint. Is this what an out-of-body experience feels like? Because I am nowhere *near* my body right now.

Dean Lewis claps as I make my way toward her. "This girl," she announces to the room, "not only organized this entire event, but she also secured every single donated item on that auction table."

More applause. "There are still a few auction items open, but we've already raised one hundred and twenty-five thousand dollars for the Windsor Academy tonight!"

The room goes crazy. Meanwhile, my head is spinning.

One hundred and twenty-five thousand dollars.

I don't want to do it. I hate myself for doing it, but I can't help it. It's like my eyes move all on their own, without my permission. I scan the crowd for Dylan. And when my gaze finally lands on his, he gives me the subtlest of smirks. It's got "I told you so" written all over it.

I shake my head and force myself to look at anyone but him. Every other single person in this room is applauding and cheering and singing my praises.

So what if he accurately guessed how much we would raise? That doesn't mean anything. He doesn't know for sure how much this event cost to put together. Maybe it was organized with donations. Maybe it didn't cost us a penny.

One hundred and twenty-five thousand dollars is an incredible amount of money.

And I'm responsible for that.

That's definitely something to be proud of.

"Please join me in raising a toast to Kennedy Rhodes!" Dean Lewis sings and hands me a glass of soda water. Hundreds of hands launch into the air and I stare into the crowd, my gaze, once again, involuntarily finding Dylan. He raises an invisible glass and gives me a wink.

I huff silently and turn away.

I don't care what Dylan Parker has to say. He's an outcast. A minority. A rebellious spoiled ingrate who doesn't appreciate what he's been given.

As I raise my glass to the Windsor Academy and clink it against Dean Lewis's, I've never felt better about my choices.

Then . . .

Then I Find Out the Truth

By the time the last guest leaves, it's already way past midnight and I'm exhausted. As beautiful as this dress is, I can't wait to get out of it and put on something more comfortable.

Even though it's completely out of her way, Sequoia insists on driving me home.

"That was amazing," she says, as she turns out of the country club parking lot. "Simply amazing."

"Yeah," I say dazedly, staring out the window at the passing streetlamps. This whole day and night has felt like a dream.

A dream I never want to wake up from.

Except I can't stop thinking about the things Dylan said to me. They're buzzing around me like an annoying fly I can't swat away.

As much as I don't want to believe anything he said, Dylan was right about one thing. Sequoia and I *do* act like Lucinda never even existed. It's strange. Sequoia has barely even mentioned her in the past two days, and every time someone brings her up she quickly shuts it down.

It's not right. If Lucinda was our best friend and something bad happened to her, we should be talking about it.

Sequoia lets out a contented sigh. "Aren't you glad that's over with? All that buildup. All that worrying. It's nice to just sit back and bask in your success, isn't it?"

"Yes," I agree absently. "It's a good feeling."

I take a deep breath and grab the edge of the seat for support. "It's a shame Lucinda had to miss it."

The energy in the car snaps like a twig. I can almost hear it breaking. I peer at Sequoia out of the corner of my eye and notice her jaw has tightened and her grip around the steering wheel has turned deadly.

"I don't want to talk about it," she murmurs.

I swallow timidly. "I think maybe we should."

"Why would you do that?!" Sequoia snarls, taking me by surprise. She's no longer quiet. No longer basking in the glow of the evening. Now she's turned into something else. Something fierce. "Why would you ruin the night like that?"

"I'm sorry," I offer. "But I just—"

"There's nothing to talk about. There's nothing more to say. Lucinda made her choice. And it was entirely *hers* to make. We had nothing to do with it. She knew what she was getting into. She knew what the Windsor Academy honor code says about cheating, she knew it meant automatic expulsion, but she bought the stolen exam anyway. There's no point in feeling sorry for her. She brought this on herself."

My brain is swimming in Sequoia's words, trying to make

sense of them and string them together with everything else I've learned over the past two days.

Lucinda got expelled for cheating?

She bought a stolen exam?

I feel my chest squeeze at the notion. I mean, I always knew Windsor was a tough school and the students were under a lot of pressure to succeed (I've only been here for a day and I can already feel it!), but I never would have imagined anyone would resort to cheating.

I try to keep my reaction inside so it doesn't show all over my face, but it's like trying to keep a tornado in a bottle. There are just so many questions I'm dying to ask her. My journalist brain is drowning in them, desperate to get to the bottom of the story.

Who sold her the exam? How did they get it? Has this happened before? Is Lucinda the first one to get expelled?

But I can tell from the look on Sequoia's face as she pulls up to the curb in front of my house that she's done talking. Even if I could find a way to phrase the question so it didn't make me sound like a lunatic, I doubt she would even answer.

Which means I'm going to have to find the answers another way.

"I'll pick you up at six thirty tomorrow," Sequoia says tersely, refusing to look at me.

"Okay." I grab my bag with my school clothes in it and reach for the door handle just as a thought comes to me. "Hey. When is it my turn to drive?" I assume we must take turns. It wouldn't be fair for her to drive every day.

But she gives me the strangest look, like she has no idea what I'm talking about, and says, "Don't be late. I need to study for the French exam in the morning."

I decide to let it go. If Sequoia wants to drive, she can drive.

"I won't," I assure her, and step out of the car.

The house is quiet when I enter. I check the clock on my phone to find it's almost one in the morning. Everyone is already asleep. I'm dying to wake up Frankie and ask him what he knows about Lucinda, or wake up my dad to tell him about my amazing night, but it's late. And I'm so tired.

I peel off Sequoia's gown and hang it neatly in my closet. Then I collapse onto my bed without even bothering to wash my face. I climb under the covers, feeling the weight of this long day settle in around me like an unwelcome bedfellow. I switch off my bedside light, fully expecting to be asleep by the time my head hits the pillow.

But sleep never comes.

Then My Dad Gets an Imaginary Assistant

When Sequoia drops me off at home after school the next day, I'm tired but raring to go. According to my calendar, my Columbia interview with the very same Geraldine Watkins starts in one hour and I am going to *rock* it.

I hardly got any sleep last night. I lay awake for hours with the events of the day on a constant, exhausting loop: all those unfinished tasks in my Windsor Achiever app, Dean Lewis's toast, Dylan's smirk from the audience, Sequoia's irrational response to my comment in the car.

But I've had four Pumpkin Spice Lattes today, I'm geared up, and I've vowed to put that all behind me. At least until after the interview.

I'm *not* going to screw it up again. This time, I am ready. This time, I know exactly what I need to do to impress the socks off the world-traveling, German-speaking, exotic-plant-collecting Geraldine Watkins. I spent both of my Student Mastery Hours today prepping. There's no doubt in my mind. This thing is in the bag.

When I walk into the kitchen, I find my mom sitting at the

table again, working on her laptop. The sight is so off-putting, I almost walk out and walk back in, convinced I've entered the wrong house.

I can tell she's in deep concentration mode, probably working on a legal brief. She always gets two matching lines between her eyebrows when she's in the middle of a brief. Like an eleven stamped into her skin. She flashes me a hurried smile when I enter but doesn't stop typing.

That's two days in a row she's been home at this hour. She normally doesn't get back until after Dad has made dinner *and* cleaned up the kitchen.

I look to the basement door. It's closed. Is he really still down there working? That seems like an awfully long time. You'd think he'd come out to at least say hello.

This has got to be the longest he's ever been in there. I mean, he's locked himself down there before to work, but never for two whole days. Is that why Mom is working from home? To pick up the slack? I guess that makes sense.

"How long is Dad going to be working?" I ask, nodding to the basement.

Mom lets out a snort, like I've made some kind of inappropriate joke, and keeps typing.

Well, that was weird.

I decide to call him. I don't want to go to my Columbia interview without talking to him first. So he can wish me luck. Or tell me to break a leg or flip a table or whatever. I smile at the memory of the last time I saw him, when I was leaving the house for the doomed version of this interview.

As I head upstairs to my room, I pull out my sparkly pink phone, click Dad's mobile number, and press the phone to my ear. It rings and rings until finally his voice mail picks up. I'm about to end the call when something strikes me as odd about his outgoing message. It's changed.

It used to be short and funny, my dad yelling in a panicked voice, "Who is this?! How did you get this number?!" and then the beep.

Now, my dad sounds so serious and official as he says, "Hi. This is Daniel Rhodes. I'm unable to answer the phone right now. Please leave your message and either I or my assistant will call you back as soon as possible. Thank you."

His assistant? Since when did he get an assistant?

Then I let out a short bark of a laugh as I drop my bag on my bed. Oh, I get it. It's a joke. Very funny, Dad. He thinks he's some big shot now that he's sold all of those photographs and he's trying to sound über important.

"Your imaginary assistant maybe," I mutter, as I end the call without leaving a message.

I strip out of my uniform and find a smart-looking black suit in my closet. I have to hand it to Other Me. She certainly knows how to dress herself better than I ever did. I should have worn a suit to the first interview. Instead I wore my *nice* jeans and a *less* ratty T-shirt. That was my first mistake right there.

I apply another layer of concealer under my eyes—those pesky purple shadows only seem to be getting worse—and grab my new and *improved* crib sheet from my schoolbag, giving it another once-over.

This is it. Time to put my future back on track!

When I get back downstairs, Mom has moved from the kitchen to the dining room. I can hear her yelling at someone on the phone. She's probably chewing out some poor paralegal for filing the wrong motion or something. I know better than to bother her when she's on a work call, particularly one that sounds like that, so I tiptoe into the kitchen, grab Woody's keys from the counter, and head for the garage.

I glance again at the closed basement door, really wanting to see my dad for just a minute before I go, but I'm running behind schedule. I still have one critical stop to make before I go to the interview.

I'll just have to tell him about it when I get home. Hopefully I can convince him to come out for dinner. I mean, he has to eat, doesn't he?

I continue into the garage, unlock Woody, and drop into the driver's seat. But the moment I close the door behind me, I notice that something is off. The car looks . . . *different*. And all my stuff is gone.

My newspaper-print steering wheel cover. My Columbia-logo key chain on the keys. My supply of Big Red chewing gum in the center console.

Curious, I get out of the car and walk around the hood to examine the license plate frame. It used to say "Keep Calm and Carry a Notebook and Pen," but now it just says "I bought mine at AutoWorld Honda!"

That's right, I think with a sudden influx of sadness. I don't run the newspaper anymore. So why would I buy a license plate frame that says "Keep Calm and Carry a Notebook and Pen"?

No, I tell myself, before I travel too far down that melancholy road. *Enough moping. You were given a second chance to guarantee your place at Columbia. Don't screw it up!*

Right.

I get back behind the wheel, start the engine, and back out of the garage.

I don't have time to worry about key chains or missing license plate frames. I have an alumni interview to rock.

Then I Get a Do-Over

"Welcome, Kennedy!" Watts says, opening the door wide. "As I mentioned on the phone, I'm Geraldine Watkins, but you can call me Watts. All my friends do."

I shake her outstretched hand with fervor. "So nice to meet you, Watts. What a lovely home you have."

She beams. "Why, thank you."

I step inside and stare at the wall of framed photographs and diplomas. "Wow!" I exclaim. "You've been everywhere!" I point to the picture of Watts in the desert surrounded by cacti and sand dunes. "Oh my gosh! Is that the Kalahari?"

She looks impressed.

I give myself an invisible point in the invisible tally.

Current Kennedy: 1. Former Kennedy: 0.

"Yes, it is! Have you been?"

"Not yet," I say, with a desolate sigh. "But I've always wanted to go. It's so horrible what's happening out there with the poaching. All those poor elephants being slaughtered for their tusks."

I did a little research on the topic so I could be well versed on the issue. It really is *horrific.*

She nods solemnly. "Yes, it is. Terribly sad."

"Did you know that over twenty thousand elephants are poached every year? Just so people can have a useless ivory trinket?"

She puts a hand to her heart. "It's awful, isn't it?"

"Atrocious," I agree.

She lets out a sigh. "It's so nice to see someone your age show an interest in such an important issue. Can I get you anything to drink?"

"I'm fine. Thank you."

Almost immediately after we take our same seats in the living room, the little white dog—Klaus, if I remember correctly—comes scampering into the room. He stops short when he sees me, giving me an evil glare and growling under his breath.

"Klaus!" Watts says, patting her lap. "Leave the nice girl alone. I'm sorry. He's not very good with strangers. He only speaks German so—"

"*Was für ein süsser Hund!*" I exclaim, trying desperately to remember the handful of useful German phrases I Googled today. I pat my shins to call the dog to me. "*Komm her, Klaus!*"

The dog tilts his head curiously, like he's trying to figure out if I'm for real or not. For a second I panic, thinking he's not going to come. Thinking I misremembered the phrase and actually told him he was a disgusting dog who licks himself too much. But then I remember the treats I hid in my bag. Watts said she got them at the farmers' market, so I made a special trip on the way over here. I had to zigzag frantically through all the stalls, asking each vendor if they sold organic duck treats for dogs, but eventually I found them.

I reach into my bag and pull out a long strip of dried meat. Klaus's ears immediately perk up when he smells it.

"Willst du ein Leckerli?" I ask the dog if he wants a treat.

Klaus lets out a small whimper of excitement and darts toward me, leaping onto my lap and devouring the treat. I hesitantly reach out and pat his head. He seems to be okay with this. Actually, he leans into my hand and starts rubbing his head against it like a cat.

Meanwhile, Watts is sitting in the chair across from me, looking stunned.

"My best friend has a dog," I lie. "She loves these organic duck treats so I always have a few on hand."

"I . . . I," Watts stutters. "I've never seen him do that with *anyone*. He's normally so averse to new people."

I smile and try to act like this kind of thing happens all the time. Like I'm just a natural German-speaking dog whisperer. "Well, what can you do? I'm a dog person!" I turn to Klaus. *"Sitz!"*

He sits. I give him another treat and he lies down next to me and goes to work on it.

Watts continues to stare. "And you speak German? I didn't see that on your application."

I tilt my head, scratching the dog behind the ears. "Oh? I must have forgotten to include it. It feels like such second nature to me sometimes, I almost forget that not everyone speaks it."

Okay, scale it back a notch, Kennedy.

That might be taking things a bit far. The last thing I need is for her to want to conduct the entire interview in . . .

"Wo haben Sie Deutsch gelernt?" Watts asks.

Crap.

Time to change the subject. Fast. I glance around the living room, looking for something else to talk about. Something to get her mind off the German thing. My eyes light up when they fall upon the potted plant next to me.

"Wow!" I exclaim, pointing to it. "Is that a *Ceropegia woodii?*"

Watts's mouth falls open and a strangled, shocked gasp gurgles out. "It is," she finally manages to utter. "I can't believe you knew that. Hardly anyone outside of South Africa knows what that is."

I wave my hand at this, as if to say, *Well, everyone is stupid. Except for us.* "I'm just fascinated by Swaziland horticulture."

She balks at this. "You are?"

"Oh, sure. All horticulture, actually. But especially the Swaziland kind."

"Have you ever been?"

I sigh. "Unfortunately, no. Not yet anyway. But you know, journalists get to travel all over the world, so maybe one day I'll get to cover a story in South Africa."

She gives me a strange look, like now *I'm* the one speaking a foreign language. After a long, uncomfortable silence, she grabs the folder from the coffee table and flips it open. I watch anxiously as her eyes graze over my application.

"Journalist? But I thought you were applying to be an economics major."

Economics major?

That can't be right. She must have the wrong application. It must be someone else's. Without thinking, I reach out and grab the folder from her, turning it around so I can read the name on top.

My entire body goes numb and the folder nearly slips from my grasp.

There it is. My name.

"B-b-but . . ." I stammer, my eyes whizzing over the rest of the page. Everything else is correct. My birthday. My address. My phone number. But on the line that reads "Intended Major," someone has typed . . .

"Economics," I read aloud, the word feeling fat and awkward on my lips.

Why would I write that? I hate economics. I had to take Intro to Micro-Economics last year and I almost failed. Okay, I almost got a B, but still. I despised every second of that class.

I'm applying to Columbia for *journalism*. That's what I've been working so hard for. Ever since . . .

My thoughts trail off as the reality of the situation sinks in.

I never went to Southwest High.

I never stumbled into that newspaper office.

I never became the editor in chief of the *Southwest Star*.

I never applied to be a journalism major.

I stare vacantly at the application in my hands. At the line that says, quite clearly, "economics."

I typed that. I inserted that into the application. That was *my* choice.

It's all been *my* choice.

My gaze flickers farther down the page to the line that says "Name of High School" and the very crisp black letters that follow it.

The Windsor Academy

Also *my* choice.

It was the better choice. I'm sure of it. I'm still sure of it.

Except, suddenly, I feel a strange anxiety bloom in my stomach. That gross, sticky feeling that something isn't right. That something is off.

Doubt.

I recognize it almost immediately. It fueled me for so long. It became part of my daily existence. Part of my identity.

And now it's back.

"Excuse me," Watts says, looking slightly confused as she reaches out and removes the folder from my death grip. "I'm just gonna take that back now."

I blink and focus on her. On the room. On the dog. On my purpose here at this very moment.

Stop, I command myself. *This is your chance to make things right. To redeem yourself. Don't blow it on a feeling that will probably go away in a few hours.*

So what if I wrote economics on my application? It's still the same school. It's still the same dream. I can just change my major after I get in.

If I get in.

I straighten up in my seat and refresh my composed smile.

"Sorry about that," I say professionally, feeding Klaus another duck treat from my bag. "Where were we?"

Watts gives me another inquisitive look but then eases back into interviewer mode. "Why don't you start by telling me why you want to go to Columbia?"

I take a deep breath, trying to ooze confidence and togetherness. I'm going to have to work extra hard to make up for that mini-cuckoo breakdown.

I clear my throat. "Well, I want to be a journalist—" I stop, quickly amending my answer. "An *economics* . . . um . . . person. And Columbia has one of the best economics programs in the country. Plus, I'm a huge fan of the East Coast and the significance that the city of New York has played in our nation's history."

I watch Watts's reaction carefully. She nods and makes a note in my file.

So far, so good.

"Well, it's obvious you're quite accomplished. I mean, top of your class at Windsor, Robotics Club, Investment Club, French Club, Young Entrepreneurs Club, student fund-raising captain." She pauses to take a dramatic breath.

I chuckle modestly. "Yes, I've been a little busy."

"You must have had to make some sacrifices in order to do all of that. What would you say is your biggest regret thus far?"

I take a deep breath. That's right. The regret question. It's what sent me off the deep end the last time around.

Well, not this time.

This is my moment. It's time to get my life back on track.

I clear my throat and infuse my voice with a cool, calm confidence, accessing the pre-scripted answer I spent so long writing and perfecting.

"My biggest regret is probably working too hard and not taking enough time for myself. You see, I'm the editor—" I stop and restart. "I mean, I'm a member of all those clubs you mentioned, plus the student fund-raising captain for the school. And although I'm very proud of these accomplishments, success comes at a price, and I'm afraid I don't have a lot of free time to do fun things. But I hear they have this great new invention called television now."

I breathe out a sigh of relief. I made it. I did it. I finished the answer without going psycho. Watts even laughs at the last part.

See? This is what happens when you don't let your cheating ex-boyfriend and backstabbing ex–best friend get in the way.

You can actually *succeed* at your college alumni interview.

Ten minutes later after I've knocked five more questions out of the park, Watts closes the folder on her lap and returns it to the coffee table. "Well, that was terrific. Just terrific. You clearly have Columbia written all over you."

Butterflies start flapping eagerly in my stomach. "Really? Thank you!"

"And Klaus certainly agrees," she adds with a laugh, nodding to the sleeping white lump of fur curled up against my leg. "With credentials like yours, you're practically a shoo-in. I can't see any reason why you wouldn't get in. I'll be submitting my passionate recommendation for acceptance to the admissions office."

Then I Open the Basement Door

By the time I burst through the garage door and into the house, the news is practically bubbling out of my mouth. I toss the car keys in the air and yell, "I'm going to Columbia!"

But then I see my mom's grim expression and I immediately lower my hands, the car keys dropping to the floor with a *clank*.

She's standing in the middle of the kitchen with her briefcase in her hand like she's ready to go somewhere and she's glaring at me. Eighteen years of living in the same house with the same parents is enough to know when you're in trouble. And I'm definitely in trouble. Although I can't, for the life of me, figure out why.

"Did you take my car?" she accuses.

"No," I reply meekly.

Her death glare doesn't let up. "Oh really? Then why wasn't it in the garage when I was called down to the office for an important meeting with a client and had no way to get there?"

"I-I-" I stammer, glancing at the keys on the floor by my feet. I suddenly understand how suspected criminals wrongfully accused of murder must feel when the judge glowers down at them. "I . . . I took *my* car."

She snorts at this, like it's the funniest thing she's ever heard. "Your car?"

"Yes," I say defensively. What part of that didn't she understand?

She throws her phone into her briefcase. "You know what? I don't have time to deal with this right now. I have a roomful of angry partners downtown wondering where I am." She stalks toward me, bends down, and scoops the keys up from the floor.

"Mom, I'm sorry," I try to say, even though I don't have the foggiest idea what I'm apologizing for. I just know that when Mom is in a mood like this, you apologize. Fast.

Although to be honest, I haven't seen her this angry in a really long time. Sure, she's the volatile parent of the two of them, but Dad always seems to know when she's reaching the end of her rope. It's his superpower. And he's always there to feed her more rope.

"We'll talk about it when I get home," she barks, stomping down the hallway toward the garage. "Make dinner for your brother!"

Then the garage door slams, making me jump.

For a long time, I stand there in stunned silence. What just happened? Did she not hear me? Did she not understand what I said? I just told her I was going to Columbia and she acted like I announced I had decided to become a heroin addict.

I'm so confused.

And why do I have to make dinner for Frankie? Is Dad still holed up in the basement? I turn toward the closed door, feeling a small shiver run up my arms.

Something feels really wrong. Like I'm missing a big piece of the picture and nothing is adding up anymore.

My dad has been down there in that basement for more than two days and I haven't heard so much as a floor squeak. Has he come out to eat? Is he still alive down there? And why do I seem to be the only one who even cares?

I drop my bag on the floor and walk toward the basement door, resting my hand tentatively on the knob. If he really is hard at work, he's not going to be thrilled about me barging in on him. When you're in the zone, the last thing you want is to be pulled out. But this is kind of important.

I mean, an alumni interviewer from Columbia University just told me that she's going to recommend me for admission. That's a pretty big deal, right?

He would want me to interrupt him for this. I know it.

I inhale a decisive breath and yank on the handle, flinching at the creaking noise the door makes. It sounds like it hasn't been opened in months.

"Dad?" I call as I start down the stairs.

But the deeper I go into the bowels of our house, the more my stomach starts to tangle in knots. It's really dark down here.

Has he set up some kind of photography darkroom?

"Dad?" I say again, but there's no response.

Did he fall asleep?

I fumble for the panel of light switches on the wall. There

are six switches, one for each of the professional photography lights and one for the overhead light.

But my hand brushes against cold concrete.

C'mon, I tell myself with a flash of annoyance. *It's around here somewhere.*

I turn on the flashlight app on my phone and swing it around the wall. Left, right, up, down, all the way to the ground. But there's nothing. The wall is bare.

With panic squeezing my chest, I wave the flashlight around the dark basement, getting brief glimpses of unidentifiable objects and grotesque shadows. I spot a string hanging from the ceiling and pull on it.

A single bulb illuminates the room and I suck in a sharp breath as my phone slips from my grasp and lands on the concrete floor.

It's not just that my dad isn't in his studio.

There *is* no studio.

Then My World Flips Upside Down

I remember the day my dad announced he was going to turn the basement into a photography studio. He was loading the dishwasher after dinner and my mom had just gotten home from a long day in court. She was gobbling up leftover chili, Frankie was sitting at the counter drawing, and I was multitasking, as usual: helping Dad with the dishes, texting with Austin about our weekend plans, *and* sending a mass email to the newspaper staff about our next issue.

It was three years ago. I was still a freshman.

There was no buildup or segue or transition. One minute there was the sound of Mom desperately trying to get food into her overworked system, and the next minute Dad was saying, "I think I'm going to remodel the basement."

"Oh?" Mom asked, looking up from her half-empty chili bowl. "For what?"

"I want to dedicate myself full time to the Portals project."

"I love that idea!" I chimed in.

"Hey," Frankie protested, dropping his pencil. "Full time? What about us?"

Dad laughed. "Okay, three-quarters time."

"Three-fifths time," Frankie countered.

"Six-eighths time," was Dad's response.

But Frankie was not fooled. He hardly ever is. He crossed his arms. "That's the same as three-quarters."

Mom and I both stifled a laugh.

Dad looked defeated. "Three-fifths it is."

Satisfied that he had won the negotiation, Frankie resumed drawing.

"Anyway," Dad went on. "I want to sell a bunch of our old stuff and consolidate all those boxes to give myself more room. I can use that entire space as a studio with lights and backdrops and a small desk to set up my laptop."

Mom nodded with a mouthful of chili. "I wuv it," she mumbled, then swallowed. "It would be good for you to have your own space."

"Exactly."

"I can help," I offered, as I scrubbed down a plate and handed it to Dad.

He beamed at me as he put it in the dishwasher. "That'd be great."

"We can build a special shelf just for Magnum," I suggested.

"Shelf?" Dad repeated with mock disgust. "There'll be no *shelf.* He needs a shrine."

I rolled my eyes and deadpanned, "Oh right. What on earth was I thinking?"

"Clearly, you weren't."

Then I flung a handful of soapy water at him.

*   *   *

I blink into the dreary, low light of the basement as a cloud of confusion settles over me. Where is everything? It's like all of our hard work three years ago has been erased. The rickety shelves full of dusty boxes are still attached to the wall where Dad's desk should be. Mom's old treadmill is still sitting untouched in the corner with a bunch of junk piled up on the runner.

We sold that treadmill. I remember!

An adorable newlywed couple from Craigslist came and picked it up. They argued over which room in their new house it should go in.

Yet, there it is. Like it never left.

And that ancient cracked leather recliner that Dad used to have in his bachelor pad before he met Mom is still here, too. Even though I distinctly remember the dump truck coming to pick it up. Mom said it was the happiest day of her life. Dad went into mourning for five hours.

Through the dust and clutter, I spot a box on one of the shelves that says "Danny's Photos" and run over to it. I pull it down, crouch on the ground, and tear open the flaps. It's filled with Dad's early photography. The pictures he took on the road when he traveled with his band during his "edgy phase," the pictures he took of Mom in the first few months of their relationship, and the pictures he took of Frankie and me as kids.

I tilt the almost-empty box to see what else is in there and freeze when I notice what's lining the bottom. My breathing grows shallow as I reach inside and pull out the first few photos of Dad's Portals project. They're yellowed and dirty and some of the paper is bent in the corners, but there's no denying it. I'd recognize my mother's eye anywhere.

It always looked like a sunflower.

Dad started out small. A few photos here and there, mostly of Mom. He didn't start getting really serious about the project until after he converted the basement into his studio. That's when he started taking pictures of anyone he could persuade to sit for him. Neighbors, friends, the gardener, and every delivery man who was unfortunate enough to have our house on his route.

I fall back onto my butt, clutching the small stack of yellowing photographs in my hand, trying to make sense of my rambling, chaotic thoughts. Trying to rein in the wild questions that are galloping through my mind.

What happened down here?

Where are the rest of Dad's photos?

Why is his studio suddenly gone?

And most important, if Dad hasn't been down here this whole time like I thought, then where is he?

Then a Baby Cries

My phone is still lying on the ground. I grab it and click on Dad's name. It rings and rings and then goes to voice mail. "Hi. This is Daniel Rhodes. I'm unable to answer the phone right now. Please leave your message and either I or my assistant will call you back as soon as possible. Thank you."

I quickly hang up. That message gives me the creeps.

It *is* a joke, isn't it?

I jump when, a second later, my phone vibrates in my hand and I see my father's name on the caller ID.

"Dad?" I ask, my voice shaky.

"I only have a few minutes between setups, but I saw you called twice. What's up?"

I pull the phone away from my ear and check the caller ID again, just to be sure it didn't display another name. Because, let's be honest, the man on the other end of the phone is *not* my dad. He sounds way too frazzled and stressed and *serious*. Like this whole talking-on-the-phone thing is just a big inconvenience.

"Everything okay?" I hear him ask through the speaker.

I quickly return the phone to my ear. "Yeah. Everything's

fine. I just haven't seen you in a while. I went down to the basement and—"

But I'm suddenly cut off by a loud wailing in the background. It sounds like a baby crying. And then Dad shouts, "No! No! We're not shooting him until eight! Right now it's only the mother! Can someone quiet that kid down? I'm on the phone!" There's a muffled noise and then my father says, "I'm sorry, honey. What were you saying about the basement?"

A chill starts at the top of my spine and travels all the way down to my toes. "Dad," I begin warily. "Where are you?"

He sighs. "Still in New York, unfortunately. The Cuddles Diaper gig is taking longer than we expected, which means we had to push back the cat food job in Boston until next week. Tell your mother I'm sorry."

New York?

Boston?

Diapers?

CAT FOOD?

"I-I," I splutter, trying to find the words to form a question I don't even understand. "I'm confused. Why are you in New York?"

He laughs. "I ask myself the same question every day. But I just go where the big bosses tell me to go."

Big bosses? What big bosses?

Dad has never had a boss. He always loves to brag about how he's his own boss. Then he makes stupid jokes like "Who's the boss?" and "Bam! I just photographed that thing like a boss!"

Is he making another one of his lame jokes?

I'm about to ask this very question but then I hear a loud crash on the other end of the phone.

"Crap," Dad swears. "Sorry, honey. I gotta go. An incompetent PA just knocked over a ten-foot wall of diapers. Give Frankie a hug for me. Bye." I hear another muffled noise, followed by my dad shouting, "What is going—"

Then the call is ended.

I sit in the dimly lit basement, staring at my darkened phone screen as I attempt to run back through that bizarre conversation in my head. But each time I replay it, it becomes more puzzling.

Why is Dad in New York with screaming babies?

Why isn't he *here* in this basement surrounded by the watchful eyes of a hundred family, friends, and strangers?

With sudden determination, I launch to my feet and bound up the two flights of stairs until I'm bursting through Frankie's bedroom door. He's seated at his desk, shuffling the deck of Cosmic cards from his What's the Matter? board game.

"Frankie!" I say breathlessly. "I need to ask you something."

When he sees me, he immediately brightens and sets the cards down on the desk. "Kennedy! Oh good, you're home! I've made a list!"

He grabs his notebook from the bedside table and flips it open.

I squint. "What kind of list?"

"All of the things I'm *positive* are different about me in this universe."

"Frankie, I—"

But he quickly shushes me. "Just listen." He glances down at his notebook. "One, my compulsive need to buy a new toothbrush every six weeks."

"That's the same. Look, I need to ask you something about Dad."

"Two, my extreme dislike for fabric softener commercials."

"The same! Now, can you focus, please? This is important."

He frowns at his notes, discouraged. "The same? How could that be the same?"

"You don't like when companies use inanimate-objects-come-to-life to sell domestic products."

"That bear is freaky!" he cries defensively.

"Frankie," I urge. "What does Dad do for a living?"

"He's a photographer," he replies dismissively, glancing back at his list. "Three, my inability to pronounce the word *wor-chest-sure*." He tilts his head. "Wor-chest-shire?"

I grab the notebook from his hand. "He's a photographer?" I confirm.

"Wor-*kest*-sure?"

"Frankie!" I shout.

He finally focuses on me. "What?"

"You said he was a photographer?"

"Yes. Dad's a photographer."

"What's the name of his camera?"

"Magnum. It's named after some lame TV show from the eighties."

"And he takes pictures of eyes, right?"

Frankie looks like I'm speaking in code. "Eyes?"

"Yeah, you know, eyeballs."

"Like an ophthalmologist?"

"No. Like close-up pictures of eyes. You know, where they no longer look like eyes. They look like . . . other things."

He still doesn't seem to follow me and I feel my heart race.

"What do they look like?" he asks, suddenly interested.

I clench my fists to keep from screaming. "What does Dad photograph?"

Frankie shrugs. "Whatever they tell him to. Diapers. Dog food. Tires. Hamburgers."

"Who?" I demand. "Whatever *who* tells him to?"

"The company he works for," Frankie replies as though it's obvious.

My breathing grows shallow. I want to curl into a ball and disappear. "What company?" I ask, barely audible, barely even a squeak.

Don't say it.

Don't say it.

Don't say it.

"Jeffrey and Associates," Frankie replies.

The walls start to close in on me. The Stephen Hawking poster glares at me with a smug expression that says, *You really didn't think this would be easy, did you?* I collapse onto Frankie's bed, feeling the weight of the universe cave in around me.

He said it.

Then I Count the Stars

No. He can't work for them. He turned them down. A hundred times. He always turns them down. He rips up their offer letters and throws them in the trash. I've seen him do it countless times!

"You're lying." I fix my gaze accusingly on Frankie. "Dad would *never* work for those soul-sucking corporate buffoons."

He chuckles. "That's exactly what Dad calls them."

I shiver. I know that's what Dad calls them. That's where *I* got it.

"If he *knows* that they're soul-sucking corporate buffoons, then why does he work for them?"

Frankie shrugs. "The art thing wasn't working out. They sent him the offer and he took it."

I hold my head in my hands like I'm trying to stop my brains from bursting out of my ears. "No, no, no. The art thing *did* work out. It did! It just took a little time. I don't understand why he wouldn't wait. Why he didn't have confidence in himself."

Frankie shrugs. "There's no telling what chain reaction causes someone to do something differently in one universe or another.

There are an infinite number of possible factors that could have contributed to Dad's decision to take a job that forces him to be on the road more than half the year."

"More than half the year?!" I cry, feeling like something heavy is sitting on my chest, pushing down. "Is that why Mom works from home?"

"Only in the afternoons when I get home from school. Why? Mom doesn't work from home in your life?"

I throw my hands up. "No! She's always at the office and ever since she made partner, we hardly see her at all."

"She made partner?"

I blink at him with sudden comprehension. "She's not a partner at the firm?"

Frankie shakes his head. "She's a senior associate."

"So she never got a promotion and bought the Lexus?"

Frankie whistles. "Whoa. Mom drives a *Lexus* in your world?"

"Yeah," I whisper, as more pieces fall into place. "She gave me the Honda and I named it Woody. That's why she was so upset. I really *did* take her car."

I fall onto my back and stare up at the constellations of little plastic stars that Frankie glued to his ceiling. Then he lies down next to me and we stargaze together.

"I don't understand," I say, tears brimming in my eyes. "Why would Dad take that job offer? He promised me he would never sell out. It doesn't make any sense."

"It makes sense in the grand cosmic scheme of things. That's where everything has meaning. We just can't always see what that meaning is."

I glance at my brother out of the corner of my eye. I don't know what I'd do without him. I'd be so lost right now. I mean, I'm lost even *with* his explanations.

"For instance," he goes on, "who knows why in this life I read all the Harry Potter books six times, while in the other life . . ." He leaves the sentence hanging, prompting me to finish it.

"That's a trick question," I say flatly. "Once you found out there were seven Horcruxes, you had to read the series seven times. You said it had universal significance."

"Dang it!" He punches the air with his fist. "There has to be *something* different about me in this universe! There has to be a variable!"

I let out an exhausted sigh. "To be honest, I'm kind of glad there isn't. I'm not sure my heart can take any more radical changes to this family."

I don't understand how my one stupid decision could change so much.

My dad sold out to a soul-sucking corporation.

My mom never made partner because she had to stay home in the afternoons to watch Frankie.

My life has gotten infinitely better while my parents' lives seem to have gotten worse. How is that possible?

We lie there in silence for a moment as I try to sort through everything that's happened since I fell on those stairs. Sequoia and Lucinda and the fund-raising gala and my Columbia application that said "economics" instead of "journalism."

"Frankie," I say after a moment.

"Mmm?" He sounds distant and pensive. He's probably still trying to figure out what his "variable" is.

"What's my thing?"

He lets his head loll toward me. "Your *thing*?"

"Yeah," I say, curling onto my side to look at him. "You know, my *thing*. My passion. The one hobby that I put all my effort into."

He shrugs and turns back to the ceiling. "You have lots of things."

I think about the Activities tab in my Windsor Achiever app and how I literally had to scroll down the page to see them all. "But there must be *one* thing that I like better than the others. One thing that gets me out of bed in the morning."

He laughs. "The menagerie of animals in your phone is what gets you out of bed in the morning."

I swat him with the back of my hand. "You know what I mean. You have your board game and in my old life I had this newspaper. A really amazing, award-winning school newspaper. What do I have in this life?"

"Hmmm." His mouth scrunches to one side. "I can't think of only *one* thing. You really do everything."

I roll onto my back again and stare up at the fake stars, tracing their patterns with my eyes, trying to identify their shapes and meanings. But somehow, they seem misaligned. Out of order. Constellations that have wandered out of their formations, until they're just chaotic clusters with no rhyme or reason.

"Do you miss Dad?" I ask Frankie after a while, and then,

with a breaking voice I add, "Do *I* miss Dad?" I clear my throat. "I mean, Other Me."

"Sure. Of course. We *all* miss him. It was bad at first. But then I guess we kind of got used to it."

My throat starts to sting. I can't imagine getting used to Dad not being here every day. Not waking me up with badly sung show tunes in the morning. Not listening to him crack lame jokes while he makes us waffles.

Not being . . . well, Dad.

That word—that title—has always been synonymous with a very clear picture in my mind. A picture of a man who loves what he does, but loves his family more. A man who takes care of us. All of us. Who calms my mother down when she's stressed about work. Who quizzes me before tests. Who helps Frankie with his eternally unfinished board game. Who cooks dinner and keeps the house clean. Who's talked me down from so many metaphorical ledges, I've lost count.

A man who makes everything seem possible and nothing seem impossible.

Who chased his dream through the darkest valleys and over the highest mountains, and through the most shadowy woods, until he finally caught it. Until he sold out his very first gallery show.

Now all of that is gone.

And somehow I'm responsible, even though I don't know why.

I sit up before any more weight can push down on my chest.

"C'mon," I say, nudging Frankie. "Mom says I have to make you dinner."

He pushes himself up and shoots me a skeptical look. "What are you making?"

"Only the greatest sandwich in the world. It's called the Duke. It's one of Dad's specialties."

Frankie still doesn't look convinced. "I don't remember Dad ever making that."

I smile. It's strained at best. "That's okay. Because I do."

Then I Find My Hidden Stash

I know I should be studying. I know I'll completely regret it in the morning when my Windsor Achiever app attacks me like a NORAD alarm during an alien invasion. But after stuffing ourselves on Duke sandwiches and toasting Dad with cups of apple juice, Frankie and I zonk out in front of the television and watch bad reality shows. It's strangely the only programming we can actually agree on.

By nine o'clock, Mom is still at the office, and I can't stop yawning.

"Time for your Dormidrome," Frankie says, grabbing the remote and flipping to the science channel.

"There's that word again. What's a Dormi—whatever?"

Frankie squints at me. "A Dormidrome."

"Yeah. Sequoia said something about that the other day when she dropped me off after school. What is that?"

"Oh," Frankie replies knowingly.

"What?"

But he doesn't respond. He turns off the TV and beckons for me to follow him.

"What are you doing?" I ask.

"Just come with me."

When we get to my bedroom, he yanks open the top drawer of my nightstand and I leap back as though a snake has slithered out.

"What is all that?"

"Your sleeping pills."

I gape in disbelief at the contents of the drawer. There's no way those are mine. There are like seven different bottles in there. "I take *all* of those?" I squeak.

"Well, not at once!" He starts pointing at the various pills. "This one is for when you can't *fall* asleep. This one is for when you wake up in the middle of the night and can't fall *back* asleep. This one is for napping. This one—"

"Okay. I get it!" I shut the drawer, narrowly missing his finger. I am *so* not taking any of those. "Does Mom know I have all those pills?"

Frankie chuckles. "Who do you think got them for you?"

An hour later, I lie in bed, thinking about everything sitting in my task list that I still haven't checked off yet. There's a little voice in the back of my head telling me that I should probably do some reading before I go to sleep. Maybe just one AP history chapter. Or a few pages of *Bel Ami* by Guy de Maupassant for AP French. But I'm too tired.

Tomorrow will be the official catch-up day. Tomorrow I'll work extra hard and plow through all of those pesky little alerts.

Now that my interview is finished and the fund-raising gala is over, I can focus one hundred percent on my schoolwork.

I curl onto my side, sighing into the pillow. It feels so good to just close my eyes and go to sleep. Just drift off into peaceful dreams.

Any minute now the sweet, sweet darkness will come and pull me under.

Any minute now.

Seriously, what's taking so long?

I groan and roll onto my back. My body is so tired. My eyeballs are so strained. Yet I can't seem to fall asleep.

You can do this, I tell myself. *Deep breaths. In. Out. In. Out.*

Just relax and allow your brain to switch off. Just think of peaceful meadows and chirping birds and . . . my unfinished AP calculus problem set and my paper on the Civil War and . . .

Gah! This isn't working.

I sit up, turn on the light, and open the top drawer of my nightstand, staring at the pharmacy of sleep aids. I've never taken anything to help me sleep before. What if they're not safe? What if they chew at my brain like mice gnawing at the wires inside the wall? You don't even realize you have a problem until the whole house goes dark.

That's ridiculous. They must be safe if my mother got them for me.

And Sequoia knows about them. In fact, she probably takes them, too. I bet everyone at Windsor takes *something* to help them sleep. It's a small price to pay to go to such a prestigious school and be handed a golden ticket to the college of your choice.

A very small price to pay.

I reach out and grab one of the bottles, twisting off the cap and pouring a small white tablet into my palm. I toss it onto my tongue and grab the nearby glass of water, positioning it against my lips.

But I can already taste the bitter, acidy flavor of the pill in my mouth. I can already feel the chemicals seeping into my bloodstream.

I spit the capsule back into my hand.

You don't need it, I tell myself. *It's all in your head.*

Maybe Other Me is used to taking these kinds of things, but I'm not. I've gone eighteen years without taking a single sleeping pill, there's no reason to start now. It's not like I have to do everything she did. I can make adjustments to this life as I go. There are no rules to this dimension-hopping thing. At least none that I know of.

I toss the pill on the nightstand and turn off the light, determined to do this the old-fashioned way.

It's just falling asleep. It's not like it's hard.

Then I Try Another Combination

Barruuugah!

Barruuugah!

Oh God, I need to set a different ring tone for that alarm. I slap the phone on my nightstand in an effort to quiet the trumpeting elephants but I only manage to knock the thing onto the ground.

Barruuugah!

Barruuugah!

"Shut up!" I shout, twisting my body off the bed so I can silence the phone.

Just five more minutes.

My eyes drift closed.

And then . . .

Woof! Woof! Woof! Woof! Woof!

The dogs start barking almost immediately. It's no use trying to sleep in this jungle. Letting out a groan, I rub my eyes and switch on the lamp, blinking against the bright light. My head is throbbing. I feel like I'm wearing a helmet made out of cement. How does Other Me do this every single day?

Oh right. She takes a massive amount of drugs.

Maybe I should have taken one of those sleeping pills, because I really feel like I barely slept at all. And now I'm expected to function? Think? Form coherent sentences that don't consist of "rawrabadablada"?

No wonder Other Me drinks so much coffee.

I jump into the shower and let the scalding hot water rain down on me until I start to feel alive again. Although it doesn't do anything to help my reflection. When the steam clears from the mirror and I can see my face, I nearly shriek at the sight. I look so haggard and old. Like I've been smoking two packs a day since I was three.

Thank God, it's Friday. I have the whole weekend to catch up on sleep.

Friday . . .

Friday . . .

Why does that day feel so important? Why is it niggling at me like an itch that's just out of reach? I grab my phone and stare at the calendar. According to the app, I have a Robotics Club meeting after school, followed by the Young Entrepreneurs Club.

But that's not it.

I stare at the date. November 18.

November 18.

November 18.

The day is howling in my mind like one of those animal alarms in my phone. But I can't put my finger on why.

I dart over to my desk and search through every drawer, looking for a clue to what could possibly be nagging at me. But I can't find anything. I do, however, stumble upon that weird lockbox again that's in the bottom drawer of my desk. I remember finding it three days ago when I was searching for the Windsor acceptance letter I used to keep in here. The one that's now framed and hanging above my desk where my issues of the *Southwest Star* used to be.

The *Southwest Star*!

Of course! Today is November 18. The day the new issue was supposed to come back from the printer.

I feel an ache of longing at the thought of missing that.

The day the new issue arrives is always one of the most rewarding moments of being on a newspaper staff.

Right now, somewhere in another universe, thousands of crisp, fresh-off-the-press copies of the *Southwest Star* are being loaded into a van to be delivered to the front office of the school.

Right now, somewhere in another universe, another me is prepping the box that will ship one hundred copies to the Spartan Press Award committee members for what could be our fourth win in a row.

I can almost smell the scent of the fresh ink. Feel the silky paper on my fingertips.

I think about the last time I was in that office. Before I walked in on Laney and Austin kissing. Before I bombed my first admissions interview. Before I hit my head on the steps of Royce Hall, sending me into this other version of my life. If I had known it would be my last few moments in that office, I would have treasured them more. I would have lingered a bit.

I would have said goodbye.

I stare into the bottom drawer of my desk, my gaze falling again on the black lockbox. I've never had a lockbox before. I wonder what Other Me is hiding in there. It must be something important if it has to be locked up.

I pull it out and examine the clasp. It's secured with a four-digit combination. I try all of my regular numeric passwords: 1010 (my birthday), 2222 (my favorite number—22—repeated), 0715 (Frankie's birthday), but none of them work.

Now I'm even more desperate to find out what's inside. But just then, my phone chirps with a text message from Sequoia and I glance at the clock.

I'm late!

I jump to my feet, shove the box back into the drawer, and close it with my foot. Why does it feel like time is my enemy in this life? There's never enough of it to sleep or finish homework or break into mysterious lockboxes.

I pray that in Robotics Club I'm working on a robot replica of myself. Because I could seriously use a clone right now.

Then I Fight a Zombie Hunter

Between our morning study session in the student union, one
Student Mastery Hour, and lunch, I've managed to cross a whop-
ping ten items off my Windsor Achiever task list by the end
of sixth period. Which would feel like tremendous progress if
twenty more tasks hadn't appeared overnight. They're like can-
cer cells. They multiply on their own.

And I still haven't figured out the meaning of the tasks written in that strange shorthand. There's about a dozen of them
still on my list and three more appeared this morning.

HI-1122-JE

SP-1123-TSL

AL-1121-GE

I don't have a clue what these assignments are. None of the
teachers have mentioned them but they keep popping up.
Clearly Other Me programmed them in at some point; I just
wish I knew what they were for.

For our final Student Mastery Hour of the day, I tell Sequoia

I need to check out a book from the library, so I'm just going to study there for the period.

"Are you still trying to finish that reading list?" she asks.

I assume she's talking about the "25 Books to Read Before College" list that I found in the seventh grade. It feels good to know that Other Me kept that up. At least *that* much hasn't changed.

"Yeah," I lie, because I don't want to have to tell Sequoia the truth. That honestly I just need some time by myself without any distractions. Plus, I'm secretly dying to see the inside of the Sanderson-Ruiz Library. It's the newest building on campus. It wasn't even built when I toured the school in sixth grade.

The library was always my favorite building to look at online. I remember staring at pictures for hours, dreaming of sitting in those high-backed leather chairs, browsing titles in the dark wood bookcases, or staring through the dramatic skylights in the high ceiling. But nothing could have prepared me for the moment when I actually step foot inside the building for the first time.

I literally freeze in the doorway, my jaw dropping open. It's the most miraculous sight, the pictures don't even begin to do it justice.

I spend about ten minutes wandering around, running my fingertips against the wood paneling and the spines of the books, watching the large, flat screens on the walls cycle through recommendations and advertisements for upcoming events. For a while, I forget why I even came in here. Then my phone vibrates and I remember the daunting task list that awaits me.

I hitch my bag farther up my shoulder and head off to seek out a quiet, secluded place to work. I find a fantastic little study bay toward the back, hidden behind the mystery section. It has a small two-seater couch, a coffee table, and two end tables with matching reading lamps.

With a quiet yip of excitement, I fall into the couch and make myself comfortable. I check the clock on my phone, calculating that I have forty-seven minutes left of Student Mastery Hour before I have to be in AP English.

I power on my laptop, take a deep breath, and pick up where I left off with my AP history reading. But before I can get through even two paragraphs I hear a gruff, irritated voice say, "Oh great. My anti-zombie device must be broken."

Annoyed by the interruption, I lift my gaze to find Dylan Parker standing there. His uniform is rumpled and untucked like always and his dark hair looks like he drove to school with his head sticking out the window. Like a dog.

I lower my laptop screen. "Excuse me?"

"This is *my* secret spot. I doused the entire place with an anti-zombie formula of my own design, but apparently it's not working."

I press my lips together and tilt my screen back up. "Maybe I'm not a zombie. Maybe *that's* the problem."

"Oh, you're definitely a zombie." He slides his bag off his shoulder and collapses down on the seat next to me. I realize this is supposed to be a couch for two, but it's definitely not big enough for both of us. He's suddenly everywhere. His elbows are bumping into me as he searches for something in his bag. And that smell. It's . . . it's . . .

Okay, actually, it's kind of nice. What is that anyway? Some kind of citrusy spring mountain soap?

So he bathes. So what?

"Um, hello!" I close my laptop and scoot over as far as I can. "I was kind of sitting here."

He looks unfazed by my complaint. "It's a two-seater couch. And like I said, this is *my* spot." He pulls a tattered, dog-eared paperback out of his bag, flips it open to a bookmarked page, and begins reading. Even though I've scooted as far away from him as possible, he still feels *way* too close.

"I don't remember seeing your name written anywhere," I point out, moving closer to the armrest. But unless I actually want to climb on *top* of it, there's not much farther I can go.

He shrugs and keeps reading. "If you don't like it here, you can always leave."

"No," I argue. "I was here first. *You* have to leave."

He turns another page. "No, I don't."

"Fine," I huff, getting comfortable and reopening my laptop.

"Fine," he echoes.

I continue reading about westward expansion after the Civil War, taking deep breaths to try to calm myself down.

Dylan sighs dramatically, leans back on the couch, and props his dirty sneakers on the coffee table, right on *top* of my schoolbag.

I cringe and reach for the bag, yanking it out from under his

243

feet. He lets out another sigh and stretches, spreading his legs wide so that one of his dirty shoes is now directly in front of me.

I press my lips together again and attempt to ignore him. He's trying to be obnoxious. He's trying to get me to leave. Well, it's not happening.

If anyone's leaving it's him.

I lean back as well, propping my feet on the coffee table next to his and reaching my elbows out as far as they will go. As I type my chapter notes, I try to bump his hand every time I hit the Enter key, but he somehow keeps managing to dodge me. Finally, after several tries, I make contact, knocking his book out of his hands and onto his lap.

I expect to hear some kind of dissatisfaction come out of him. A grunt, a groan, something. But no. He just calmly picks up his book, finds the spot where he left off, and continues reading. This time, however, he places the novel in his other hand and sprawls his left arm across the top of the couch, until it's wedged under my head.

I lean forward in disgust, feeling my hair for any residue from his hands.

"I'm sorry," he says smugly. "Does that bother you? I like to get comfortable while I read. If that bothers you, you can always—"

"It doesn't bother me," I snap. "In fact, I like to get comfortable, too." I turn my body ninety degrees and lean my back against the armrest. Then I place my laptop on my stomach, kick off my shoes, lean back, and rest my socked feet right up against his legs, so my toes are practically digging under his thighs.

"Ahhh," I say, wiggling my toes. "Much better." I pick up my head to look at him. "I'm sorry. Does that bother you? Do my feet smell? If so, you can always leave."

I can see frustration start to sour his face, but he appears to be doing his best to conceal it. He crosses his right leg over his left. "Nope. Doesn't bother me at all."

I give him a fake sugary smile. "Good." I continue typing. I have to admit it's actually really hard to type like this. I have to hoist my head up to see the screen, which is starting to give me a neck ache, but there's no way I'm backing down now.

He'll leave eventually. I just need to stick it out.

Dylan leans forward to pull a pack of gum out of his bag and removes two pieces. At first I think he's going to give me one, like some kind of peace offering, but then he stuffs both pieces in his mouth and begins to chew as loudly as the human jaw is capable of chewing.

The sound is positively infuriating. All that wet smacking and jaw flapping. *Ugh.* I can't *believe* I went on even one date with this guy! Did I spend the whole time trying not to gag?

I tell myself to take deep breaths. He's trying to get a rise out of me. Don't let him. Stay the course. Claim this space.

I reach into my bag, pull out my earbuds, and stuff them into my ears. I blast my music full volume. It's so loud, there's no *way* he won't be able to hear it.

I steal a peek at him around the corner of my laptop screen. He's calmly reading and turning pages, bopping his head to the beat of my music. *My* music. He can't *enjoy* my music. That is most definitely *not* allowed.

Annoyed, I switch to another song. A syrupy, bubble-gummy pop song that no guy on the face of the planet would ever *bop* his head to.

I turn up the volume. It's so loud in my ears I think I might actually break something important, but I stick it out. I steal another peek at him. His head has stopped moving and his expression has turned slightly, like he's just bit into an especially bitter pickle. Then, a second later, he purses his lips thoughtfully and starts teetering his head from side to side in rhythm with the beat.

God! Why is he so set on making my life difficult?

I remind myself not to get worked up. I can't hear his gum chewing anymore, so I'll just continue my work. I focus back on my digital textbook, pretending to be totally engrossed in the content.

Until I feel a damp spatter on my legs and jump.

Eew. What was that?

I peer up at the ceiling to see if the roof is leaking before I realize it's not raining today. Besides, this building is brand-new. There wouldn't be a leak in the roof. And that's when I see the giant pink bubble out of the corner of my eye, followed by another wet sprinkle on my bare skin as it pops. He's blowing bubbles and his disgusting saliva is spraying all over me!

I quickly sit up and withdraw my legs, yanking the earbuds from my ears. "That's repulsive," I say.

He looks surprised. "What?"

"You! You're repulsive!"

"I'm sorry. Is my gum chewing bothering you? If it is, you can always just—"

But I don't wait for him to finish. With a grunt, I stuff my laptop in my bag and get the heck out of there. I tell myself I'm not leaving because of him. I'm leaving because I need to study. I'm way behind and I don't have time for his childish games.

But even so, I don't look back for fear of seeing the victory plastered all over his smug face.

Then My Dream Is Excavated

When Sequoia drops me off at home later that afternoon, I don't even bother going inside. I wait for her to drive away, then I hitch my bag up my shoulder and start walking down the street.

I know I could ask my mom to borrow the car, but she's still pretty ticked off about me stealing it yesterday. Plus, she might ask where I'm going and I'm not sure I want to explain. I'm not sure I *could* explain.

As soon as I walk through the front doors of Southwest High ten minutes later, all the familiar sights and sounds and smells hit me at once. The last bell rang about five minutes ago, so the hallways are packed solid with people. I'd almost forgotten how crowded it is in this place. The Windsor Academy is so spacious. There are six grades instead of four but each class has only a hundred students in it. The entire Windsor student body is barely the size of *one* class here.

Falling into my usual routine, I bow my head and shove my way through the masses toward the stairwell. I know exactly where I'm going. I just need to see it. I need to say goodbye. I need to know my newspaper is in good hands. Then I can move on with my life.

I need closure.

The smell of these hallways always made me feel sick and the ugly tile floors always gave me a headache, but today the effect hits me harder than usual, and by the time I reach the second floor I'm breathing only through my mouth and fighting back waves of nausea.

I pass by Ms. Mann's science classroom and peer inside, remembering how only half of the microscopes even worked. I pass by my old locker, laughing to myself when I notice the door is gone in this universe, too.

Thank God, I don't go here anymore.

Thank God, I hit my head and found myself living a better life.

I turn the corner and head toward the newspaper office. I can see the display case up ahead. The one where we keep our three Spartan Press Awards. I used to pass it every day. I used to stop and stare into the glass at those gorgeous three statues standing so proud and tall. Like they were carrying the weight of the world and hardly even noticed. The sight of them was enough to cheer me up on even my lowest of days.

I can still remember how it felt to hold the first one for the very first time. To see that tiny gold plate with the words "*Southwest Star*, editor in chief Kennedy Rhodes" engraved in it.

I felt just like that golden woman on the pedestal.

I felt like I could conquer the world.

But as I approach the newspaper office, my feet start to drag and a ripple of unease passes over me. There's something very strange about the display case.

The trophies inside look . . . *different*. They're not beautiful gilded women standing atop podiums, reaching their arms to the sky. They look like weird lumps that some child crafted out of gold play dough.

I urge my feet to move again, running to the case and pressing my hands against the glass. Then I see the banner strung across the top, and my entire body goes numb.

**Congratulations to Our State Wrestling
Champions—5 Years in a Row!**

Wrestling?

Those are wrestling trophies? But this is supposed to be a newspaper display case. It belongs to the newspaper. We use it to show off our trophies and our best issues, and anything else devoted to the *Southwest Star*. Why is it suddenly filled with wrestling stuff?

Did they move our display case?

Did they move the newspaper office?

I hurry to the door marked with the number 212, my home for the past three and a half years. Or at least it *was*. In some other life. For some other me.

School is out, so the newspaper team should be assembling here any minute. With a deep breath, I pull open the door and step hesitantly inside, instantly bombarded by all the memories

I made within these walls. Thousands and thousands of them clobbering me at once. The time we misspelled a word in our front-page story about teen literacy. The time we were so desperate for an extra article to fill out the sports section, we invented a badminton team. The time Horace's game overheated one of the computers and the hard drive melted. The time we challenged the yearbook staff to an epic, cutthroat battle of Taboo and lost.

The time Laney and I accidentally walked through that door for the very first time.

Ever since then, this place has been a refuge for me in the middle of this chaotic building. A place where my voice mattered and my opinion was important and my words were read.

That one twist of fate is what set my whole other life on course.

Now, it's someone's else fate. Someone else's course.

I glance around the classroom, the unease inside me growing by the second. There's something very off about this place. It feels so . . . so . . .

Sterile is the word that pops into my head.

The computers are still lined up in the same formation, the carpet is still in desperate need of replacement, but the room? It lacks a sense of purpose. A sense of *life*.

Where are all the scribbles on the whiteboard? The hundreds of story ideas thrown out by staff members. Where are all the issues hanging on the walls? The team's proudest moments on display. Where are—

Just then, the door bursts open and a group of five or six boys tumble inside, talking animatedly while stuffing chocolate in their mouths and sipping soda from plastic cups.

They stop when they notice me and look to each other for an explanation. But none of them seem to be able to give one. Finally, one boy—clearly their leader—pushes his way to the front, and as soon as I see his face my mouth drops open.

"Horace?" I ask in disgust. "What are you doing here?"

He seems to startle at the sound of his own name and studies me for a long moment. "I'm sorry, do I know you?"

I roll my eyes. "Horace. It's me. Kennedy . . ." But I immediately catch my mistake. Of course he doesn't know me. I'm a stranger to him. He never sat in my newspaper club and made annoying jokes while he used my computers to play his stupid Excavation Empire game. Laney and I never stayed up late at night plotting his demise . . . or, at the very least, his removal from the paper.

He was never a constant nuisance to me because I never went here.

"I'm sorry," Horace says in his usual haughty tone. "I don't know any Kennedys. You know, except the president. But he's dead."

Thank you, Captain Obvious.

"Now, if you'll excuse us," he goes on. "We have a meeting in here."

I watch in shock and disbelief as the boys disperse throughout the room, taking seats at the computer stations.

Wait, what are they doing?

What meeting could they possibly have in here?

OH. MY. GOD.

Is Horace the editor in chief of the newspaper?

No. That can't be. I will *not* allow it. I'll file a complaint. I'll stage an intervention. I'll destroy this place before I let Horace take charge of *my* newspaper.

I'm about to voice my dissatisfaction right then and there, when suddenly one of the machines finishes booting up and I hear a familiar sound. That obnoxious synthesized melody that used to play over and over again in my nightmares.

I turn and stare at the monitor, a strange gurgling sound coming from the back of my throat.

"Is that . . ." I ask, struggling to get the words out. "Is that Excavation Empire?"

The boy—a short frumpy kid with glasses—glances up at me in annoyance. "Uh. Yah."

My gaze whips left and right, watching in horror as all the screens light up and that annoying seven-note song reverberates around me in surround sound.

When I speak again my voice is a shattered replica of itself. "Is this an Excavation Empire *club*?"

"Yeah," Horace mumbles from his station, taking a sip of soda. "And I don't remember your name on the invite, so . . ." He makes a clucking sound and tips his head toward the door.

"B-b-but you can't," I stammer, getting flustered. "You can't do that. This is the newspaper office."

Horace flashes me a strange look from the top of his computer. "What newspaper?"

I stomp my foot in frustration. "The *Southwest St*—" But my voice cuts off when I remember that *I* named it the *Southwest Star*. I changed the name from the *Southwest News* after I became editor in chief. After I wrote that story about the football coach siphoning the funds and won us the first Spartan Press Award and saved the paper from . . .

A bitter, cold frost settles in around me, chilling me to the bone.

From closing.

From folding.

From ending.

"The *school* newspaper," I say meekly.

Horace scoffs at this, taking another slurp of soda before saying the words that I know will haunt me forever. "This school doesn't have a newspaper."

Then I Set Myself Straight

As I stand in the middle of the classroom that used to be my second home, Horace's words echo in my mind.

"This school doesn't have a newspaper."

They hit me hard. Like a blow to the chest. The kind that knocks the wind out of you. That takes away your ability to even scream.

"Don't look so shocked," Horace says, his fingers moving rapidly across the keyboard as he launches into his game. "Newspapers are dead. No one reads them anymore. So, get lost."

I feel like I'm collapsing in on myself.

I feel like I'm falling.

I feel like I'm going to throw up.

"You're such a big fat cheater!" Horace yells at his screen. "Let's see what you think of my Storm of Prophecy!"

"More like Storm of Absurdity," another guy fires back.

I can't watch this.

In a daze, I stagger out the door, down the stairs, and back into the parking lot. I can barely put one foot in front of the other. I can barely get my lungs to move oxygen in and out.

This was a mistake. Coming here was a huge mistake. I should have left the past in the past (or in the other universe) where it belonged. I just wanted closure and all I got was my worst nightmare come true.

My newspaper is gone.

It never even *was*.

And now my computers are being used to build imaginary cities with imaginary bricks so imaginary bulldozers can tear them down.

That shouldn't be allowed to be a club. Who approved this? Who thought this was a good idea? Those are the best computers in the school! They shouldn't be used for something so pointless, not to mention . . . *violent*.

They're in there destroying cities. That club is promoting teen violence. If those boys all grow up to be criminals, it will be entirely the fault of this school. I'm tempted to write a very strongly worded op-ed piece on the whole thing, until I miserably remind myself that I don't have a newspaper to publish it in.

I plop down on the front steps of the school and try to calm myself.

Deep breaths. In. Out. In. Out.

This isn't my world anymore. I don't go to this school. I don't sit in those classrooms. I shouldn't care what the computers are being used for.

I rush to pull my phone out of my bag, open the Windsor Achiever app, and click on the Rankings tab.

1. Kennedy Rhodes.

There it is, I tell myself. *Your new life. Your new accomplishment. This is what you're proud of now.*

With a determined huff, I stand up and brush the dirt from my uniform. I don't have time to sit around here and mope. I have things to do. Tasks to complete. People to impress. I'm at the top of my class at the Windsor Academy! That's a big freaking deal. And if I want to keep it that way, I need to remember my priorities.

I march through the parking lot, ready to put this whole escapade behind me. Ready to get back to my new and *improved* life. But a moment later, I spot something that pulls me to a halt. I squint across the row of parked cars, certain that I must be imagining it. Or that I'm simply too far away to see it clearly.

I take a few more steps, trying to get a better view. But the closer I get, the more convinced I am that what I'm looking at is absolutely, one-hundred-percent real.

It's *them.*

My ex-boyfriend, Austin McKinley, and my former best friend, Laney Patel.

And they're kissing again.

Then I Become a Stalker Again

I remember when we won our first Spartan Press Award. I remember sitting there in that newspaper office, my hand clutched tightly in Laney's, waiting for the email to arrive.

When the notification finally popped up in my inbox and I opened it to see the words "The *Southwest Star* from Southwest High School," I nearly fainted. All the blood left my head. I could barely even stand up. Laney had to help me out of my chair. She kept me from falling.

She was always my rock. I leaned on her daily. For so many things. And yet, she never wanted to share in the glory. After the trophy came in the mail, I offered to let her take it home for the weekend, but she refused. I offered to have them engrave her name alongside mine, but she refused that, too.

She was always so intent on letting me shine. Like a moon circling the earth. Never feeling direct sunlight. Always basking in someone else's glow.

But not today. Not right now. She's glowing plenty on her own. In fact, I think I might need sunglasses to protect my eyes from all that glow radiating off her.

For a moment, as I stand there watching them make out in the parking lot, I'm convinced that I've fallen back into that other universe. That I've been tossed right back into that nightmare where I'm stuck at this school and Laney and Austin cheated on me and I've blown my chances at going to Columbia.

But then I glance down and see that I'm still wearing my Windsor uniform. And the questions start to bounce around my brain like pinballs in a machine.

Are they together in this life, too?

How long have they been dating?

How did it start?

Did she steal him from someone else like she stole him from me?

My whole body is numb. My breathing is ragged. My heart is pounding.

When they finally manage to break apart, I duck behind one of the cars, afraid that they might see me. Which, I quickly realize, is actually pretty stupid. Laney doesn't even know me in this life. She's not my friend. We never met. Those three and a half years of friendship, when she stood by me through everything, are gone. Vanished. Erased.

Still, I can't bring myself to come out from behind the cover of this car. Crouched down like a spy, I peer at them over the hood. I watch as Laney whispers something to Austin that I can't hear.

Then Austin grins and shouts in a booming voice, "Here comes the big one! Here comes the . . ."

Laney immediately joins in, "Whaaaaammmy!"

They practically fall on top of each other in fits of laughter. I can hear Laney's signature chipmunk giggle from here.

My stomach flips.

Apparently their taste in television shows hasn't improved much in this universe. They're still quoting that stupid *How Is This My Life?* show.

Still laughing, Laney says, "That last episode was funny as balls!" Then she buries her face in Austin's chest, and he kisses the top of her head.

I can't do this. I can't take this anymore.

I need to get out of here.

Staying in a crouch, I zigzag through the cars until I'm out of the parking lot. Then I sprint the entire way home.

When I burst through the front door a record eight minutes later, I'm breathless and dizzy. My mom is in the kitchen, yelling at someone on the phone again. I barrel past her and charge up the stairs, past Frankie's room where he's working diligently on his *What's the Matter?* board game, straight to my bedroom.

"Kennedy!" Frankie jumps up from his desk when he sees me. "I've made a new list!"

"I don't want to hear it right now!" I call back.

But like always, he ignores me, following me into my room as he reads from his notebook. "My obsession with argyle socks."

I sigh. "The same."

He frowns and crosses it off his list. "My inability to surrender in Monopoly."

I roll my eyes. "One time we had a game that lasted twenty-two days."

His body wilts as he crosses this off, too.

"Frankie," I plead. "I really can't deal with this right now." I grab his shoulders, turn him around, and march him out of my room.

"My fear of barbershops?" he asks, barely looking up.

"The same!" I close the door on him.

"My laptop decal?" he calls from the hallway.

"It's Newton's apple falling from the tree!" I yell back.

I can hear him harrumph before stomping back to his room and slamming the door.

With a groan, I toss my bag onto my bed and dig out my phone. I open SnipPic and search for Laney's profile. I click on it and scan the photos, my heart sinking with a thud when I notice her profile picture.

It's the two of them. They're dressed up and posing in front of a fake city skyline. I recognize that backdrop. I once had a very similar picture in front of that backdrop. Except it was a photo of *me* and Austin. It was taken at prom last year.

They went together, I think with a sudden wave of nausea.

I quickly start scrolling through her feed like a crazy stalker, desperate for more information, more details. It's overflowing with photographs of the two of them. Laney and Austin skiing together, Laney and Austin at the community pool in the summer, Laney and Austin at Peabody's café. I scroll back and back and back until I find the very first one of them together.

It's dated sometime during the second semester of freshman year.

Which means they've been dating for the past three years.

As I stare at the photos, I feel a hot, jealous rage rumble through me.

She didn't just steal my boyfriend. She stole my whole life.

But I can't tell if I'm jealous of her because she's with him, because she *took* him, or if I'm simply jealous of *them*. For what they have. For what they're sharing in all these pictures.

They look so dang happy.

Were Austin and I *ever* that happy? And come to think of it, have I ever seen Laney look that happy?

When I search back through my memories of my former best friend, why do they always seem to revolve around me? Her cheering *me* up. Her making *me* feel better. Her telling *me* the newspaper is going to be amazeballs.

For more than three years, Laney was my rock. My support system. The person I leaned on for everything. But as I continue to scroll through her feed, watching tender moment after tender moment pass by, I suddenly find myself wondering, Who was Laney's rock? Who did *she* lean on?

I mean, sure, we were always there for each other. I would have helped her through anything. Except I suddenly can't recall one time when our roles were reversed. When I was the strong one and she was the one falling apart, freaking out, waking up in the middle of the night with panic attacks that the front-page headline is misspelled. She was always the one who answered the phone. Who calmed me down. Who logged in to the server to assure me that the headline was fine.

She was so busy being sturdy and strong for me, who was being sturdy and strong for her?

The answer hits me like a slap in the face.

No one.

Until now, apparently.

Because now she has him. She has Austin. *My* Austin. *My* boyfriend.

But as I continue to stare at them, feeling more and more like a creepy Peeping Tom, that possessive word—*my*—starts to lose its meaning. It starts to feel like a pair of jeans that no longer fit, that you've stashed away on the top shelf of your closet, just in case. But every time you bring them down, they never quite look right. And eventually, you have to give them away.

With a lump in my throat, I toss the phone on the bed. I sit in silence for a long moment, listening to the faint sounds of the house. The whir of the heater, the footsteps of people downstairs, the thumping of my own heart banging against my rib cage. And then the sound of my mother's voice calling me down to dinner.

I push myself from the bed and start for the door. I look back once at the phone still lying on my bed. Then, before I can second-guess myself or overanalyze my actions, I run back, navigate to Laney's profile again, and click "Follow."

Then the Dean Plays Hardball

I assumed I'd be able to catch up on my sleep this weekend, but apparently that was wishful thinking, because when the elephants trample through my room at five thirty a.m. on Monday, I feel more wretched than ever. And don't get me started on my face. Let's just say the purple shadows under my eyes have been upgraded to black holes.

The good news is, I finally feel like I'm caught up on my schoolwork. I studied nearly nonstop all day Saturday and Sunday, ticking off tasks from my to-do list like no one's business. Now, I can confidently say that I'm in control of the app. Instead of it being in control of me.

After our morning study session in the student union, Sequoia and I pack up our stuff and head to Royce Hall for AP history. But just as we're ascending the grand staircase, Dean Lewis's voice comes over the speaker system.

"Attention, Windsor students and faculty. I am calling an emergency school assembly. Please head straight to the Lauditorium. Thank you."

I look to Sequoia, who's wearing an uneasy expression. "What do you think that's about?"

She appears pensive, like maybe she has a theory, but then she shakes her head and turns around on the steps. "No idea."

The Lauditorium is housed in a cylindrical structure attached to the student union. It's a beautiful round amphitheater with stadium seating laid out three hundred and sixty degrees around the stage.

I would be excited to be sitting in these plush comfy seats for the first time if the energy in the air wasn't so ominous. It's clear Dean Lewis's unexpected summoning has put everyone on edge. Even the teachers. Small hushed conversations reverberate around the room as everyone attempts to speculate what this could be about.

Dean Lewis takes the stage. She has a lapel mic fastened to her immaculate purple pants suit. I'm in awe of the students' respect for her. The din around the rotunda immediately quiets down without her even having to say anything.

Everyone is so reverent and attentive.

Well, everyone except *him.*

As I scan the crowd, my eyes immediately fall on Dylan, sitting in approximately the same row as me on the other side of the circle. He's staring at something in his lap. Probably his phone.

I can't believe the nerve of that guy. The least he could do is show some respect for Dean Lewis. I mean, the woman went to Vassar, Harvard, *and* Yale. She's basically a legend.

I shoot him a dagger look from across the Lauditorium. I don't really expect him to see it since his eyes are averted, but for some strange reason he happens to look up at that exact moment, and his gaze just happens to land right on me.

He gives me another one of his obnoxious smirks. I roll my eyes and focus back on Dean Lewis.

"Thank you all for coming," she begins in a somber tone. "I apologize for the late notice, but something has come to the administration's attention that simply cannot be delayed."

I watch her intently, trying to focus on what she's saying, but I can't help stealing another peek at Dylan. He's gone back to staring at whatever is in his lap and suddenly I'm desperate to know what it is. What is so über important to him that he can't take ten minutes out of his day to listen to the dean of the school?

I lean forward, trying to peer through the heads blocking my view, but I still can't get a good look at his lap. I sit up extra tall, craning my neck to the left and right. I can *almost* make it out. I just need a few more inches. I ease onto my feet and just catch sight of a newspaper lying open on his legs, when Sequoia yanks me back down, hissing, "What are you doing?"

"Nothing," I say casually. "I was stretching my legs."

She lets out a frustrated huff and goes back to listening to the dean.

"Unfortunately," the dean goes on, "the section of the Windsor Academy's honor code dealing with unlawful testing procedures has been breached once again."

What?

I look to Sequoia to gauge her reaction, but her face is blank.

"Cheating," the dean says forcefully, "will *not* be tolerated at this school."

My chest tightens.

"We have an 89 percent Ivy League acceptance rate here and a *zero* tolerance policy for this kind of behavior." She pulls her reading glasses off and lets them hang around her neck. "I'm disappointed to report that stolen exams have been discovered in the possession of three additional Windsor Academy students who have all been expelled."

A gasp echoes throughout the room. I admit one of them came from me.

Who would buy stolen exams? It's unethical and illegal, not to mention deceitful. Don't people want to succeed the right way? The honest way? If you cheat just to get into an Ivy League school, then you can never truly feel the satisfaction of your accomplishment.

"This cannot continue," the dean says, turning to glare at each and every one of us. "I've spoken with the administration and a decisive action plan has been made."

Good, I think, nodding along with her words. They should take action. They should do whatever they need to do to put an end to this. I'm still so horrified that this kind of thing even happens here.

"Whoever has been stealing and selling unauthorized copies of Windsor Academy exams," the dean continues, "we strongly urge you to step forward and confess to your crimes."

That's it? That's their big plan? Asking the culprit to confess? He's never going to turn himself in. Who would do that?

"So," Dean Lewis says, casting her gaze around the room, "would anyone care to step forward and take responsibility for their illegal actions?"

The Lauditorium is utterly silent. No one even dares to breathe. Everyone is glancing out of the corners of their eyes to see if someone is willing to stand up.

No one does. Dean Lewis looks extremely disappointed.

She clears her throat. "I am giving the offending student until the end of Thanksgiving break to contemplate their actions and make the right decision. Step forward and confess your crimes to a staff member by first period Monday morning."

A small titter breaks out among the students.

"Otherwise," Dean Lewis goes on, silencing everyone immediately, "starting next week, we will begin docking one percentage point a week from every student grade until the person responsible decides to make the right choice."

Another gasp permeates the silence of the Lauditorium. The students are no longer sitting politely in their seats. They're now looking at each other with accusing, openmouthed stares. Murmurs of "That's not fair" and "This is ludicrous" start to percolate through the crowd.

Dean Lewis raises a hand, bringing the complaints to a halt. "I realize this comes as a shock, but this has gone on long enough. If you have any information about who is behind this, then I beseech you to come forward and save your peers."

Sequoia turns to me with tears brimming in her eyes. She's about to lose it.

I still can't believe anyone would do this. It doesn't seem worth it. Why would a student, fortunate enough to go to this amazing school, risk their future and all of their hard work just to sell a few tests and make a quick buck?

The second the thought enters my mind, my gaze immediately swivels back to the boy sitting across the room from me. The one who couldn't be bothered to even pay attention to the dean's speech. Curiously, he's paying attention now.

He's no longer reading the newspaper in his lap. Like every other student in this room, his eyes are trained on Dean Lewis. But *unlike* the other students in this room, his expression isn't one of shock or fury or accusation.

It looks suspiciously like pride.

Then I Make a Life-Changing Decision

It was him. It has to be him. He's the only person I know with enough motive and disdain for this place to risk getting caught. It makes perfect sense. Dylan hates Windsor. He hates all the students here. So what better way to make a mockery of this zombifying institution than to steal exams and sell them to the students?

By the time the assembly lets out, I'm so mad I could punch him.

"I can't believe this is happening!" Sequoia is full-on crying now. Actually, she's pretty close to hyperventilating.

I take her by the elbow and guide her into the adjoining student center, sitting her down at a table. "Relax," I tell her. "Deep breaths. In. Out. In. Out."

She tries, but it just comes out as a shudder. "What am I going to do? I'm already dangerously close to a B in four classes. If they start docking percentage points, I'm doomed! I'll never get into Harvard. I'll never become a senator. I'll never be able to run for president!"

"Hey!" I say, grabbing her chin and forcing her to look at me.

"Stop. Of course you will. You're going to be the best president this country has ever seen."

She sniffles, trying to focus on me through her glassy, tear-filled eyes. "Have you ever heard of a president who got a B in calculus?"

"I . . ." I stammer. "I'm sure there are plenty of presidents who got worse than a B in calculus. Besides, you're not getting a B. I'm sure someone will come forward."

She shakes her head and wipes her runny nose. "No they won't."

"You don't know that," I argue.

She gives me a doubtful look. "This is the Windsor Academy."

"Exactly! This is the Windsor Academy. The students here are the most upstanding in the country. Someone has information and they'll bring it to the dean."

She drops her head into her hands and sobs.

I sit next to her and rub her back. "Maybe Dean Lewis was bluffing. Maybe they won't dock anyone's grades."

"Dean Lewis doesn't bluff," comes Sequoia's muffled response.

I bite my lip and stare into the massive student union. People are still shuffling out of the Lauditorium, looking completely distraught and hopeless. Everyone except Dylan, that is. I spot him the moment he saunters in and strolls over to an empty table. He pulls out his newspaper and spreads it on the table, looking like he couldn't care less that the vibe in this place is akin to a bomb threat.

My eyes narrow in his direction.

I know when someone is guilty. It's a journalistic talent. You have to be objective about a situation, but you also need instincts like a tiger. And right now, my instincts are roaring at full volume.

This cheating thing would make a perfect front-page story. I can already see the headline:

Slacker Boy Nabbed in Prep School
Cheating Scandal

That's the kind of headline that wins Spartan Press Awards.

I glance over at Sequoia, who's still blubbering into her hands, and I'm suddenly struck with an idea. It's so incredibly genius, I'm not sure why I didn't think of it earlier. Probably because I was so busy trying to wrangle my unruly task list and build robots in Robotics Club and make wise investments in Investment Club and launch my Internet company in the Young Entrepreneurs Club, that I completely overlooked my true passion. The one thing that has always made me happy.

"Sequoia," I say, standing up from the table, "I'll be right back."

With a swift, decisive motion, I toss my bag onto my shoulder, march out of the student union, across the lawn, and up the steps of Royce Hall.

I barge into Mr. Fitz's classroom like a girl on a mission, but it's empty. I must have beaten him here from the student union. I take a seat at the table and wait.

Mr. Fitz arrives a few minutes later. "Ms. Rhodes," he says, looking surprised to see me. He takes a seat behind his desk. "What can I do for you?"

I stand up and watch as he types in a username and an excessively long password to unlock his laptop. It momentarily distracts me from my reason for being here.

"Are all the teachers' passwords that long?" I ask.

He sighs. "Yes. They made us change our passwords *again* last week. They think whoever is stealing the tests was able to hack the server where the teachers keep their files. Now the passwords are ridiculous. It's like Fort Knox around here."

I bite my lip, trying to process what he's just said. Is that a clue somehow? Does Dylan have some kind of secret hacking skill that no one knows about?

"Anyway," he interrupts my short reverie, "did you need something?"

"Oh! Yes!" I say, suddenly remembering my brilliant idea. I puff out my chest and stand up straighter. "I'd like to start a Windsor Academy student newspaper."

Then I Get Stonewalled

I'm so excited as I stand before Mr. Fitz and declare my decision, I can hardly contain myself. This is going to be even better than the *Southwest Star*! It's going to be legendary. I even started brainstorming names on my walk over here. So far I like *The Windsor Express*, *The Windsor World*, and just *The W*.

I came to Mr. Fitz because he's the head of the English department, so I assume he'd be the one to talk to about starting a new writing-oriented club. And as soon as he signs off on it, I'm going straight to Dylan Parker to get to the bottom of this test-stealing scandal.

If I work extra hard—like *really* hustle—I might even be able to get an issue out in time for the Spartan Press Awards deadline at the end of this week!

And why wouldn't I win? I know exactly what it takes to win. I'm a winner. No, I'm a *crusher*!

And I will crush this, too.

Mr. Fitz closes his laptop and leans back in his chair, looking extremely intrigued by my idea. Even he thinks it's a winner.

In fact, he's probably sitting there right now, wondering why he didn't think of it himself.

"You want to start a student newspaper?" he confirms.

I nod. "Yes. And I already know what my first story is going to be."

His eyebrows rise inquisitively. "And what is that?"

"The test-stealing scandal."

He looks hopeful. "Do you know who's behind it?"

"Not yet," I admit. "But I want to investigate. And I want to publish my findings in a school newspaper." I hitch my bag farther up my shoulder. "So, what's the protocol? Do I need like a faculty sponsor or something?"

He reopens his laptop. "No."

I blink in confusion. "No, I don't need a faculty sponsor?"

"No, you do need one of those. You'll need a faculty member to sign an activity activation form and then you'll need to file it with the dean's office, but I'm saying no. I won't sign it."

My mouth falls open. "Why not?"

"Because I don't think it's a good idea."

I stand there speechless for a few seconds before resolving, "Fine. I'll just ask another faculty member."

"And I'll make sure they say no, too," he says evenly.

"B-b-but, you can't do that," I protest, shocked. "Doesn't every student have a right to form a club?"

"Yes," he admits. "Every student but *you.*"

So much for being Fitz's favorite. This man obviously has some kind of vendetta against me.

"Why?" I demand, tears of frustration springing to my eyes.

"That," he says, pointing at my face. "Right there. That's why."

I sniffle. "Because I'm crying? You won't let me start a newspaper because I'm a sensitive person who shows her emotions? Would you rather I be a heartless robot who never shares her feelings and walks around all day acting like a . . . like a . . . *zombie?*"

Fitz doesn't even blink. He stays perfectly calm and replies, "No. I won't let you start a newspaper because you're too hard on yourself. You're already stretched far too thin and I'm worried about you."

"Well, I'm fine!" I insist, wiping my cheeks with the backs of my hands. "And I'd be better if I could just do what makes me happy. And right now, that's starting a newspaper."

Fitz rubs his eyes with his thumb and forefinger, looking like he's trying to summon strength. "Look, I'm going to be honest with you. You're what the administration calls an 'at risk' student. Your ambition has the tendency to get the better of you. You stress easily. You let the pressures of succeeding here compromise who you are. I've seen it happen too many times. Like with Lucinda Wallace. I let her down. We all did. We didn't get involved soon enough. Maybe if we'd recognized the signs earlier, we could have saved her from self-destructing."

I squint at him, unable to believe what I'm hearing.

He's crazy. He doesn't know anything. He doesn't know me. I want to scream at him to take a look around. Everyone here is stressed out. Everyone wants to succeed. Sequoia just had a complete meltdown in the student union! Why am I being singled out? Because I'm too ambitious? Last I checked, ambition wasn't a bad thing. Ambition is what won me three Spartan Press Awards in a row. Ambition is why I'm at the top of my class in one of the most prestigious schools in the country. Ambition is the reason Geraldine Watkins is recommending me for admission to Columbia University!

Mr. Fitz sighs. "I don't want to see the pressure get to you, too. I don't want to see you crack. I worry that one more thing on your plate, one more responsibility, will be the thing that breaks you."

"Well, you don't have to worry about me," I say, as sternly and calmly as I can when all I really want to do is scream and throw something. "I'm not going to crack. I'm *not* Lucinda. I'm my own person. I'm *Kennedy*."

Mr. Fitz nods, like he wholeheartedly agrees. "Exactly. And I'm trying to save you from her."

I bristle and spin on my heels. "Don't bother!" I call back over my shoulder as I march toward the door. "I don't need saving."

Then I Question
My First Suspect

By lunch the next day, I've made a decision. I'm going it alone. I don't need a faculty sponsor. I don't need approval from the school. Some of the best articles in history were written under-cover. Corporate sponsorship just leads to censorship. If I do this on my own, the news will be that much more organic.

And who knows? If I'm able to break this cheating-scandal story, maybe Mr. Fitz will reconsider. Maybe he'll realize the error of his ways and sponsor my club. And if not, then I'll just release it on the down low. I'll start some anonymous tell-all website. I'll be the information vigilante. Let them try to un-cover my identity. Let them try to take down my site. I'll just create a new one. I'll pop up somewhere else. With a new URL. My readers will follow me. They're loyal like that.

Or at least they will be after I release my first issue.

What's most important is that I provide legitimate, trust-worthy news.

And I know exactly where to start.

When I march into room 117 of the Fineman Arts Center, Dylan is already there, typing into his laptop. Thankfully, the rest of his magazine club hasn't arrived yet, which is perfect because my business is with him. Not them.

He glances up briefly before grabbing a baby carrot from a little plastic bag on the table and popping it in his mouth. "You again?" he asks with his mouth full. "I'm still not letting you onto the magazine."

I try not to let my disgust for his loud, openmouthed chewing get the better of me. I'm here as a journalist now. And I need to act like it. Journalists don't let their sources get them all riled up. They stay calm and professional.

"For your information," I reply as politely as I can, "I've formed my own club. A school newspaper."

He lets out a bark of a laugh. I fight every impulse *not* to let this offend me.

"What?" I ask, staying calm. "What's so funny?"

He shakes his head. "Nothing."

"Anyway," I go on, clearing my throat, "I'm writing a story on the cheating scandal and I was hoping to interview you about it."

I keep my eyes fixed on his face, searching for clues. A flash of a grimace. A hint of recognition. They're called micro-expressions. Detectives rely on them to catch guilty criminals. They're brief involuntary facial movements that only occur when a person is deliberately or unconsciously trying to hide their *true* reaction.

But it takes a shrewd eye to be able to spot a micro-expression, and I obviously miss Dylan's because all I see is confusion. "Why me?"

I play innocent. I can't let on that he's my number-one suspect. Otherwise, I'll get nothing out of him. I plaster on a smile. "I'm interviewing a lot of people. Just to see where it leads. Sometimes people know things that they don't realize are important. It's my job to extract those details and piece them together."

He squints at me, like he's trying to figure out whether or not I'm being serious. Then he pops another carrot into his mouth and begins chewing languidly, like a cow with a mouthful of cud.

I try to keep my smile intact, but every chomp on that carrot is like nails on a chalkboard. What is with this guy? Does he not know how to chew like a normal person? Was he like this on our date? If so, I should be grateful Sequoia convinced me not to go out with him again.

I take his silence as an invitation and sit down next to him at the table, pulling out a brand-new Windsor-monogrammed notebook that I picked up in the student union this morning.

"So," I begin breezily, "when did you first become aware that tests were being stolen and sold to students at school?"

He's still staring at me, like he's trying to piece together his own front-page story. "You think I did it," he announces after a long, torturous moment.

"No," I splutter helplessly, laughing off his accusation.

"Yes," he maintains, pointing a carrot at me. "That's why you're here."

"I told you. I'm interviewing lots of people. Not just you."

He nods at the notebook in front of me. "Then why is that thing empty?"

I glance down at the first page and berate myself. I should have flipped to some random spot in the middle. "I . . ." I flounder. "I already filled another notebook."

"Yeah, I'm so sure. You think just because I dress like a slob and dis the school on a daily basis that *I'm* the most obvious suspect. Now, I'm not a professional journalist like *you*, but that doesn't seem like very good journalism work to me. It actually seems pretty biased. And a bit lazy."

I take deep breaths, reminding myself to stay calm. Journalists are composed. And objective. They get to the story. They don't let the story get to them.

He smirks. "Why don't you look at one of your zombie friends like Sequoia? She's got guilt written all over her."

"She does not," I reply, a bit more harshly than I would have liked. I quickly reel myself back in. "Sequoia is completely distraught over this whole thing. She has a *lot* to lose. Unlike you."

"So you *do* think it's me."

I press my lips together. Maybe I went too far with that last part. He obviously can see my distress because he starts laughing.

"I'm sorry," I say as civilly as I can, "are you *laughing* at me?"

He stops and looks me straight in the eye. "Yes."

The grip on my pen tightens. "To be honest, I don't appreciate that."

He flashes me that stupid smirk again. "Well, to be even more honest, I don't really care what you do and don't appreciate."

My temper flares. I can feel my face getting hot. Why does

he have to be so impossible? "Look," I seethe, "I know it was you. And I'm going to get to the bottom of it. With or without your help."

He sticks a baby carrot in his mouth like a cigar before chomping down. "So, then why are you sitting here? Why aren't you marching over to Dean Lewis's office yourself to turn me in? I mean, if you're so *sure* I'm the culprit."

This is pointless. I'm not getting anything from him. With a huff, I close my notebook and return it to my bag.

"Ah," he says, chewing loudly. "I get it. You don't want to implicate yourself. You're afraid if you turn me in, Dean Lewis will suspect you of *buying* the tests from me." He nods like he's solving a big murder case. "Very shrewd."

I shove my chair back and stand up. "I shouldn't *have* to turn you in. You should turn in yourself."

"And why should I do that?"

"Because you're guilty!" I say exasperatedly, throwing my hands in the air.

He sighs and looks at something on his laptop screen like he's already finished with this conversation. "If you say so."

I grunt. "I saw you."

He glances at me. "You saw me selling tests?"

"No," I amend impatiently. "I saw you smirking during Dean Lewis's speech. Like you were so proud of yourself."

"So you were watching me," he says, like this is some big breakthrough. "Do you have a crush on me? Is this something we should talk about? You know, get it out in the open. I'm flattered, truly, but you're not my type. I'm not really into the whole zombie-chic thing."

I feel my breathing growing heavy. "I do *not* have a crush on you."

He sighs. "I don't know. You were getting really cozy with me on that couch in the library the other day."

I stomp my foot. "I was there first!"

"Whoa. Easy there, *Crusher*," Dylan says, and I don't miss the condescension in his voice. "I wouldn't want you to burst a blood vessel or anything. Besides, you were wrong."

"About what?" I demand.

"That smirk you saw when you were checking me out."

"I wasn't—"

"Hey, I'm not judging. It's a free country. You can lust after whoever you want."

I close my eyes, trying to regain my composure. "You repulse me," I say through clenched teeth.

When I open my eyes, I swear I see a flash of genuine pain flicker across his face, but it's gone so fast I can't be sure. "Ouch," he says in a mocking tone. "That was harsh."

An apology bubbles to my lips, but I swallow it down. Why should I apologize to him? He started it. He called me a zombie!

"Anyway," he continues. "It wasn't pride."

I squint at him.

"The smirk," he reminds me. "It was mirth."

"Mirth," I repeat in disbelief.

"Yes. It means amusement."

"I know what it means," I snap.

"Just checking. You seemed a little confused there."

I cross my arms over my chest. "And why were you smirking mirthfully?"

He grabs another carrot and points it at me. "Good question. Allow me to elaborate." He gestures to the chair I vacated. "Care to sit back down?"

"No," I snap.

"Suit yourself. You see, the only way I've been able to survive in this zombie factory is by creating little games for myself. One of these games is to score zombies on the level of their mental breakdowns. I rate them on a scale of one to ten, one being fairly benign, ten being like full-on looney-tunes crack-up. Crying over a test grade? That's a minor offense. I give that a two. Adderall addiction?" He teeters his head from side to side. "Common but not earth-shattering. A three. Pulling a Lucinda Wallace? That gets you a solid seven. But this illegal-test thing. I mean, this has kind of blown my scale out of the water. If this person has cracked as much as I think they have, then I might have to create a brand-new scale. Hence, the reason for my mirthful smirking. I'm simply impressed by this zombie's ability to blow my mind. After everything I've seen around here, I thought my mind was explosion-proof."

I let out a sigh. This conversation is clearly going nowhere. I don't know why I even bothered. "So you're denying it," I confirm.

"The mirthless smirking? Oh, no. I fully confess to that."

"No," I growl. "Stealing the tests."

"Oh, that. Yeah, I'm afraid I just don't care enough to steal exams."

"That's exactly why you *would* do it! Because you don't care."

He doesn't seem to follow my logic. He pops the last of his carrots in his mouth and chews pensively. "But why? What would I get out of it?"

"Watching everyone around you fail, for starters."

He twists his mouth to the side. "I admit, that's a plus."

"Not to mention bragging rights."

"Bragging rights? Who would I brag to?"

I gesture to the still-empty classroom. "I don't know! Your magazine people. You must have a friend in this group. Someone as warped as you."

"Ah, see, that's where you're wrong," he says. "These people aren't my friends. They're my mask."

"Your *mask*?" I repeat dubiously.

"They help me blend in. After six years at this school, you learn to be a real expert at blending. As long as it *looks* like you fit in and have friends and are 'involved' in something, the administration pretty much leaves you alone."

"So the magazine is fake?" I ask, taking out my notebook, poised to write something down. "A cover? To distract from your *other* operations?"

He grins, like this is all a big game to him. "Touché. But no. The magazine is very real."

"I've never read it," I challenge.

"I'm not surprised."

285

I scowl. "So let me get this straight. You have no friends? You just *pretend* to have friends."

"I do what I have to do."

"You do realize that's kind of pathetic."

I notice his tongue jab against the inside of his cheek and I feel a small twinge of satisfaction. But it fades away the second he fires back with, "Not as pathetic as holding on to a crush for three and a half years. I mean, we had *one* date. And it was a *long* time ago. I think it might be time for you to move on."

With a huff, I pull my bag onto my shoulder and lean onto the back of the chair, trying to look as menacing as I can. "You can joke all you want, but I'm going to prove you're behind this. I won't let you take down this school."

"Ooh," he says, sounding extremely interested. "Does this mean I'll be seeing even *more* of you?"

"Oh, shut up!" I snap, turning on my heels to march away. But before I even get to the door, he calls out, "I'll give you a four."

"What?" I ask, spinning back around.

"Your breakdown. It's a four. But I'd be willing to reexamine in the future. If you want to try again."

Then I Make a Plan

Dylan Parker is guilty. There are no two ways about it. But he's obviously also a master manipulator and a very good liar. I just need to figure out a way to *prove* that he's lying.

The good news is tomorrow is the Wednesday before Thanksgiving, which means school is out until Monday and I have plenty of time to work on my investigation. The bad news is my Windsor Achiever app has been dinging incessantly ever since I got home from school today.

I really don't want to study, but I figure I should probably knock out some schoolwork before I get too consumed with this story. So I make a bargain with myself. I set a timer on my phone for two hours, vowing to work until it goes off, and then I'm free to do whatever I want.

I check my Achiever app. The second drafts of our personal essays are due at the end of next week. That should be easy enough. Mr. Fitz gave me an A on my first draft and his comments were light. I should be able to revise it in less than an hour.

Thinking about Mr. Fitz makes my muscles coil with frustration. I can't believe he had the nerve to call *me* an "at risk" student. The only thing I'm at risk of is succeeding brilliantly and becoming a world-famous journalist. And do you think I'm going to thank him in my speech when I win my first Pulitzer? I don't think so.

I open my laptop and do a search for my personal essay document. I'm surprised, however, when two results appear on the screen:

Kennedy Rhodes—Personal Essay—Version 1
Kennedy Rhodes—Personal Essay—Version 2

Version 1? Other Me wrote two versions? The first must be a rough draft because it's in the trash folder, while the second is in the AP English folder, meaning it's the most recent one. I click on it and get to work implementing Mr. Fitz's notes from the paper he handed back yesterday.

As I suspected, it only takes me forty-five minutes to finish. I check it off the list and continue on to the next item.

By the time my two hours are up, I've managed to complete my problem sets for AP chemistry, my new schematics for the Robotics Club, my weekly stock trades for the Investment Club, *and* thirty pages of reading for AP history.

I'm really starting to get the hang of this Windsor Academy thing.

Cracks under pressure? Ha! Take that, Mr. Fitz!

More like *excels* under pressure. Kicks pressure's butt. Eats pressure for breakfast!

Eagerly, I close my schoolwork and pull out my new notebook. Unfortunately all the pages are still blank after my unsuccessful first interview today, but I try not to let that deter me.

I flip to the first page and start writing.

Facts That I Know for Certain:
- Someone has been stealing tests and selling them to students
- Lucinda Wallace and three others were caught with stolen exams
- The administration has forced teachers to change their log-in passwords

Speculations:
- Additional students who haven't yet been caught might still be in possession of stolen exams
- The culprit most likely hacked into the teachers' server to access the test files

Suspects:
- Dylan Parker

I carefully read back over what I've written. If Dylan won't talk, then I'm going to have to find another way to get enough information to nail him.

I tap my fingernail against my teeth before adding:

Next Steps:
- Find out how students contact test thief to purchase stolen exams
- Determine how stolen exams are delivered

I pause and take a deep breath before adding the final bullet point. The thing I know has to be done before anything else. Although I'm definitely *not* looking forward to doing it.

- Interview Lucinda Wallace

Then Frankie Is Enlightened

"I've got it!" Frankie barges into my room in the middle of the night. His hair is sticking up in a hundred different directions, like a model of an atom.

I roll over and check the clock on my phone. "Frankie," I moan. "What are you doing? It's two in the morning."

He sits on my bed with a bounce, ignoring my complaints. Then he switches on my lamp. I blink against the bright light, squinting at him. It's only now I notice his notebook is open on his lap and the page is covered with diagrams and symbols.

Oh, no. It's *way* too early for Frankie's diagrams.

I pull a pillow over my head. "Go away," I mumble.

Frankie promptly removes it. "I've been up all night. You have to hear this."

"Is this about your board game? Because if it is, I don't understand how to play anyway, so you're wasting your breath."

"Don't understand how to play?" Frankie says, aghast, as if I've just admitted I've never seen *Star Wars*. "What's the Matter?

is only the easiest game in the world. You pick a Cosmic card, it tells you what to do. It's basically Candy Land." He stops, thinking for a moment. "Well, except if you land in the Forest of Relativity and you don't have a Time Dilation card or a Space Contraction card, then you have to wait until someone crosses the Bridge of Dark Matter and offers you an Electromagnetic Radiation Boost. Or if you get stuck in the Absolute Zero Tundra. Then you're pretty much screwed unless you can manage to find the Thermodynamic Key. But let's face it, no one ever found it so—"

"Frankie!" I sit up. "Could the Forest of Thermodynamics wait until morning?"

"Forest of *Relativity*," he corrects. "Not Forest of Thermodynamics." He snort-laughs. "How ridiculous would that be?"

"Get out," I say sternly.

"Wait!" he cries. "I didn't even come in here to talk about the board game!"

"I don't care. Get out."

He stands up but doesn't leave. I switch off the light and roll over, trying to fall back asleep. But a few seconds later, I hear Frankie whisper, "Psst. Kennedy. Are you awake?"

I groan. "I said leave."

"But I figured it out!"

I sigh in bitter surrender. "What?"

He turns the light back on. "Why I'm exactly the same in both universes."

I seethe quietly. For some reason, he takes that as a sign for him to continue. "You see, time is like a domino effect. Every tiny choice affects everything around us in small, subtle ways. And I thought it was really strange that everyone else in this family seems to have been affected by your decision in some way. Mom has a different role at her firm. Dad has a totally different job. You go to a different school. Why am I exactly the same?"

"Yeah," I mutter. "So?"

"So," he repeats, thrusting the notebook into my hands and pointing at some dotted line between two complex-looking diagrams, like I'm supposed to make sense of it. "I've been thinking about it all wrong!"

I stare blankly at him.

"I've been trying to figure out what *variable* I am when in actuality I'm not a variable at all!"

His face lights up as he waits for my reaction to what he obviously sees as a *huge* breakthrough. Except I have no idea what he's talking about.

His face falls. "Don't you get it?"

I shake my head. "No."

"I'm a constant!"

"A what?"

"A universal constant! I don't change from dimension to dimension!"

"Is that a thing?"

His face falls. "I don't know. But it really only leads me to one logical conclusion."

"That you're weird?" I intone.

"No." He smiles a handsomely devilish smile. "That I've achieved enlightenment!"

I roll my eyes, thrust the notebook back at him, and shut off the light. "Go to sleep, weirdo."

"But I'm Yoda!" he whines in the darkness.

I roll over and close my eyes. "Go to sleep, Yoda."

Then I Become a Scapegoat

Lucinda Wallace lives in the same subdivision as Sequoia, on the other side of town. Fortunately, Mom seems to be over the whole grand theft auto incident and lets me borrow ~~my~~ *her* car.

When I knock on the door of the two-story mini-mansion, a middle-aged woman appears on the other side. She's dressed in skinny jeans, an angora sweater, and so much bling I fight the urge to shield my eyes from the glare. I mean, the woman is practically *dripping* with diamonds.

I don't recognize her but she certainly recognizes me, which means she must be Lucinda's mother.

"Hello, Mrs. Wallace," I say in a light and friendly tone. "How are you today?"

"What are you doing here, Kennedy?" she asks tersely. Her hostility takes me by surprise and I instinctively step back from the door.

I clear my throat. "I came to speak to Lucinda."

Anger flashes over her face. "She doesn't want to speak to you."

Her answer confuses me. "Why?"

"Because none of this would have happened to her if it weren't for *you*."

I stand there, completely aghast. What is this woman talking about? "I . . ." I stammer. "I don't think that's a fair statement."

The woman takes a step toward me, her body blocking the entrance to the house. I take another step back. She's a slight woman with a body that's clearly seen the inside of a Pilates studio more than once, but there's something about her presence—her whole demeanor—that's surprisingly intimidating. Maybe it's the weight of all that bling.

"Fair?" she asks. "You want to talk to me about fair? My daughter has been expelled from the Windsor Academy. There's no way she'll get into a good college. She'll have to attend *community* college." The way her nose wrinkles, you would think she was talking about picking up after her poodle. "While *you* are sitting pretty on your little top-of-the-class throne. Are you happy now that she's out of the way? Are you relieved to have one less person to compete with?"

"Of course I'm not happy," I reply. "Lucinda is my friend."

Mrs. Wallace snorts. "Friend. Some friend you turned out to be."

I shake my head, completely stunned by this woman's attack. Does she honestly blame *me* for Lucinda's expulsion? But I had nothing to do with it. It's not like *I* convinced her to buy the stolen test.

Wait. Did I?

"I . . . I still don't understand what this has to do with me."

"Everything has to do with you!" she barks, causing me to flinch. "Don't you get it? Ever since you came to this school, she's been competing with *you*. Talking about how smart Kennedy is. How accomplished Kennedy is. How easy Kennedy makes it look. How Sequoia likes Kennedy better. The teachers like Kennedy better. Everyone likes Kennedy better. Kennedy. Kennedy. Kennedy. She pushed herself too hard because of *you*. Because she was trying to keep up."

"The Windsor Academy is a very competitive school," I say shakily. "I don't think it's reasonable to place all the blame on—"

But she doesn't even let me finish. "You know what I heard? I heard you weren't even accepted right away. That's why you didn't start until the ninth grade. I heard you were *wait-listed*."

Her words are like a series of bullets shot right into my chest. *Pow. Pow. Pow.*

I struggle to stay upright and keep my expression neutral, but I must not succeed because Mrs. Wallace's lip curls into a snarl. "That's right," she continues maliciously. "*Wait-listed*. And if I could go back in time and make sure you never got off that list, I would. Because I'm convinced that my daughter would have been better off if you had never stepped foot in that school."

Then she slams the door in my face.

I stand motionless on the front steps, feeling like the air around me has gotten too thin. The earth's atmosphere has disappeared.

Deep breaths. In. Out. In. Out.

Is all of that true? Did Lucinda really cheat because of me? Is she gone because I'm here?

I think about my other life. All of those times I lay in bed scrolling through Sequoia's SnipPic feed, analyzing her life. *Idolizing* her life. And who was in almost all of those pictures before I hit my head and bounced into this universe?

Lucinda.

As soon as I woke up in this life, she had disappeared from the photos altogether. Which means maybe Mrs. Wallace is right. Maybe this *is* my fault.

Or maybe it was only a matter of time. Maybe Lucinda would have gotten expelled in either version. After all, this happened because someone sold her a stolen test and she got caught. What if the time line is just off? What if she just hadn't been caught *yet* in the other universe? Maybe she would have eventually disappeared from Sequoia's SnipPic feed in that life, too.

If anything, this is Dylan's fault. If he is the one selling the tests—and every bone in my body is telling me he is—then he's the one to blame for Lucinda's expulsion. Not me. He's the one who should be standing on that front porch getting reamed by the frightening five-foot-one Mrs. Wallace and her army of jewels.

I need to get to the bottom of this. I need to get what I came here for.

The answers.

The story.

And right now, Lucinda is my only lead.

I'm going to have to come up with a new plan.

I take a few steps back and glance up at the house. There's a tree that leads to a second-floor window. I could climb it, but there's no guarantee that the window is open. Or that it's anywhere near Lucinda's room. For all I know, they could be keeping her locked in the basement. Plus, if I knock on the window and Mrs. Wallace is the one who opens it, she'll probably push me right out of the tree to my death.

Just then, I hear a low rumbling sound and I quickly duck behind a hedge. I watch as the garage door of the mini-mansion groans open and a Range Rover backs out. I peer through the leaves of the hedge, trying to determine if Lucinda is inside.

She's not.

After the car is safely down the street, I take a deep breath and approach the front door again. I ring the bell and wait.

A few seconds later, I hear the sound of quiet footsteps padding on hardwood floors. Then the door swings tentatively open and Lucinda's head pokes out. She's dressed in flannel pajamas and her dark pixie-cut hair is mussed, like she hasn't bothered brushing it for days. But she's still the same girl I saw in those photos. And the sight of her makes my chest squeeze.

I study her face closely for a reaction, expecting to see the same hate and blame and rage that I saw in her mother.

But it never comes.

Lucinda crosses her arms, flashes me a wicked grin, and says, "It's about time one of you losers came to visit me."

Then I Walk into a Crime Scene

Lucinda grabs us sodas and leads me up to her bedroom. When I walk in, I worry that maybe she's been robbed or the CIA has been looking for some top-secret document in here, because the place is a disaster.

She must notice my stunned reaction because she lets out a low belly laugh. "Pretty awesome, isn't it?"

Oh God. Has she lost it? Has the expulsion caused her to truly crack?

"It's . . . nice," I say stiffly.

She grabs a throw pillow and tosses it at me. I'm so unprepared, it hits me squarely in the face, nearly causing me to spill my drink. "C'mon, Crusher. You don't have to walk on eggshells around me. I'm fine. In fact, I've never been better."

Glancing around her room, I highly doubt that.

She falls onto her unmade bed and starts swinging her arms and legs like she's making a sheet angel.

"I feel free!" she announces to the ceiling.

I take a tentative sip from my soda. Not because I'm thirsty but because I don't know what else to do with my hands.

"Your mom seemed to imply that you were—"

"My mom is nuts," Lucinda says, sitting up abruptly. "*She's the crazy one who needs to be locked up. She blames the school. She blames the teachers. She blames . . .*"

"Me," I finish.

Lucinda giggles. "Yeah. She *really* blames you."

I swallow. "Do you?"

She grabs another pillow and sends it flying in my direction. This one I'm ready for. I duck and it hits a picture frame on the wall, bringing it clattering to the floor. Lucinda barely even blinks an eye. "Of course not, Crusher! Don't be ridiculous. I mean, you and I have always been competitive, right?"

I take another sip and clear my throat. "I guess."

"It's just how we are. You and I battle it out and Sequoia sits on the sidelines and cries a lot."

I can't help laughing at that one. "She does cry a lot, doesn't she?"

"If the girl were a space on the Monopoly board she'd be Water Works." She takes a long pull from her soda, finishing what looks like half of it in one gulp. Then she burps and guffaws proudly at the sound.

"Anyway, I don't blame you. It was my own fault. But actually, I'm kind of glad things went down the way they did."

This surprises me. "You are?"

"Yeah, I've never been happier. Or more relaxed. That school"—she pauses, deliberating on her next words—"it was toxic. At least for me. It turned me into a person I didn't even recognize anymore. There's so much freaking pressure to not only *do* everything but *excel* at everything. That whole 89 percent Ivy League acceptance rate they push in your face, it's like poison being pumped right into your veins. If you don't get into an Ivy League, you're basically chalked up as a failure and they forget your name. It's ridiculous."

She takes another gulp of her soda and releases another loud belch. "Of course my parents didn't help either," she goes on. "I felt like I was already carrying around a thousand-pound boulder, and then I'd get home from school and my mom would be like, 'Hey, here's a rhinoceros to put on top of the boulder.' It's no wonder I cracked. It's no wonder I bought that test. I just couldn't hack it. But now . . ." She glances around her room with a sudden air of calm. "Do you hear that?"

I listen and then shake my head. "Hear what?"

"Nothing," she whispers dreamily. "No Achiever app beeping every five seconds with a new task. No calendar reminders going off for club meetings that I have absolutely no interest in. It's so quiet. So peaceful."

"But what will you do?"

She shrugs and throws her hands in the air. "I don't know! And you have no idea how amazing that feels!"

She's right. I have no idea. Although I can't imagine that *not* knowing what you're going to do with your life would feel anything but terrifying.

"That place was killing me a little bit every day," Lucinda goes on. "I just couldn't feel it. It was the frog in the pot of boiling water. You know, the temperature rises so gradually, the frog doesn't even know he's burning to death . . . until he's dead. So, yeah, in a way, I'm glad I got caught with that test. It was a wake-up call. It was someone screaming, 'The water! It's too hot! Get out of there!' "

I squirm in my seat. Everything Lucinda is saying is starting to make me uncomfortable. I'm reminded too much of that first conversation I had with Dylan outside the dean's office, when I was waiting to try to get my spot back, and he was waiting to . . .

Actually, come to think of it, why *was* Dylan sitting outside the dean's office that day? I still have no idea. He seemed to freak out when I accidentally brought it up at his literary magazine meeting.

I make a mental note to return to that later and focus back on Lucinda. "Can I ask you about the stolen test?"

She finishes her soda and crushes the can between her fingers. "Shoot."

"Do you know who sold it to you?"

She rolls her eyes. "Dean Lewis asked me the same thing. She drilled me for hours, offering me all sorts of bargains. They'll let me back in if I give up the name. They'll make sure my future isn't completely destroyed if I cooperate. Jeez. I thought I was in a bad cop movie. And no, I have no idea who sold me the test. Not that I would have taken her deal if I had. By then, I was so done. So ready to leave her office and never step foot on that campus again."

I reach into my bag and pull out my notebook and pen, jotting down a few things.

"What are you doing?" Lucinda eyes my scribbles.

"Oh," I say awkwardly. "I forgot to tell you. I'm starting a

school newspaper and I thought this would make a good story."
I see panic flash in her eyes and quickly add, "Not about you!
About the guy stealing the tests and selling them to students."

"What makes you think it's a guy?"

I avert my gaze to my notebook. "I don't. I'm just speaking generally. So would it be okay if I asked you a few more questions?"

She shrugs and leans back against her headboard. "Go right ahead. I've got nothing else to lose. But you should probably keep my name out of it. You know, so my mother doesn't hire the mafia to off you."

I force a smile even though I think we both know she's not fully joking. "No problem." I tap my pen against the page. "So, if you don't know who's selling the tests, how did you arrange to buy one?"

"Oh, that's easy. There's an email address."

This gets my attention. "An email address?"

"Yeah, you send an email to TSM4@youmail.com with the name of the class and the date of the test you want and then you get a response telling you where to leave the money."

I scribble furiously, my heart starting to pound as the adrenaline rushes through my veins. This is what I loved most about writing for the *Southwest Star*. That thrill you get when you know you're close to breaking a story. It's a feeling like no other. "And where did they tell you to leave it?"

"In a book in the library," Lucinda says, grabbing one of her pillows and hugging it to her chest.

"Which book?"

"Which test?" Lucinda fires back.

My eyes widen. "You bought more than one?"

I notice a flash of something in her eyes—guilt maybe?—before she covers it with a shrug. "Yeah, so?"

"I . . ." I hesitate. "I didn't know that. What were the two . . . or more books?

"Just two," she confirms. "*The Count of Monte Cristo* and *Madame Bovary*."

I write the names down in my notebook and then tap the pen against my teeth. For some reason those two names together ring a bell in my mind. Like they're connected somehow. "Do you think those titles have any significance?"

Lucinda's forehead crinkles. "Like what?"

"Like because Madame Bovary cheats on her husband and—"

"And I'm a big fat cheater, too?" Lucinda snaps, her gaze hardening. She must hear the terseness in her tone because a second later she breaks into hysterical laughter, throwing her head back. "See! There it is again. The monster returns! Sometimes it's like second nature. I can't even hear myself."

I laugh, too, although mine comes out more like a nervous stutter.

"Anyway," Lucinda goes on, back in her normal voice, "no, I don't think the titles have any significance. I think you give the culprit too much credit."

I stare down at my notes again. I'm not sure I agree with her. This criminal seems smart. Organized. Why would he choose a random book? Plus, the email address obviously means something, too.

I underline the book titles and the email address, reminding myself to look more deeply into them later.

"So, you put the money—how much was it?"

"Two hundred dollars. Cash."

I swallow hard. "Okay, so you put the two hundred dollars in the book and then what?"

"Then forty-eight hours later, you check the same book and the test is there. In a sealed envelope."

"That's it?"

She squints at me, a knowing look flashing on her face. "You're going to try it, aren't you?"

My head pops up. "What?"

"That's why you're here. There's no newspaper. You're not writing a story. It's all a ruse, right? Columbia early decision is coming up. They're going to be looking at your second quarter grades and you want a little boost. Let me guess. AP history. No. *Chem.* Chem is the worst."

I gape at her, feeling flustered. "N-n-no!" I stammer. "I really am writing an article. I'm not the kind of person who would cheat just to get ahead."

As soon as the words are out of my mouth, I wish I could take them back. That was mean. And insensitive. I search her face for signs of insult, but I honestly don't find any. All that stares back at me is smugness. A trickster who knows a secret and can't wait to tell you what it is.

Then she lets out a low, unnerving chuckle that rattles my bones. "Crusher, no offense, but you're *exactly* the kind of person who would cheat to get ahead."

Then I Get Domestic

I've only cheated once in my life. I was playing Uno with Frankie two years ago and I was just so tired of losing to a nine-year-old that when he got up to go to the bathroom, I rearranged the cards so that I would be dealt the most awesome Uno hand in the history of mankind.

Needless to say, it was a slaughter of mass proportions. Frankie lost in less than a minute. I waited for the glee to kick in. That satisfying sense of accomplishment. The pure, unadulterated glory. But all that came was the guilt. It was relentless, chasing me around like a cat chasing a mouse, batting at me, teasing me, playing with my emotions.

I admitted my crime to Frankie the very next day, in an attempt to ease my conscience. I expected him to reprimand me. His moral compass is even straighter than mine. But he didn't. He just smiled and said, "No more Uno for you, Kennedy. Obviously the pressure is too much."

I think about that day the entire way home from Lucinda's house. I think about how I stacked the deck because I was tired of losing. Because I just wanted to win.

But that was a game. It didn't mean anything. It wasn't some huge, significant moment. It wasn't my *life*.

I would never cheat at school. I'm not that kind of person. Lucinda doesn't know anything. She doesn't know *me*.

But then that small voice in the back of my head gently reminds me that she does. She knows *Other* Me. She's one of her best friends. She might even know her better than I do.

Would she really cheat?

Would she really purchase a stolen test?

Has she already?

When I get home, I'm anxious to go straight to my room and start researching some of these new details I collected for the story, but I'm stopped when I hear my mom in the dining room, yelling at someone on the phone again. At first I think she must be on with another poor legal assistant about her latest case, but then I hear her say, "You think I want this? You think this makes me happy? You being in New York for Thanksgiving?"

New York?

Thanksgiving?

Is she talking to Dad?

Curious, I take a step closer.

"I don't give a crap about the money!" Mom bellows into the phone. "I want a husband who lives here. I want the man I married back."

My head swims with questions.

What is going on? Why is Mom yelling at Dad? Are they fighting? But they never fight.

There's silence as my mom listens. Then she lets out an indignant snort. She seems to be doing a *lot* of snorting lately. "Yeah, sure. Fine. I'll tell the kids. I'll tell them that you'd rather be in New York for Thanksgiving than be here with them."

There's another long pause before Mom snaps, "To be honest, Daniel, I don't know what the truth is anymore."

Then I hear a crash. I assume it's her cell phone hitting something, because a moment later she comes storming out of the dining room empty-handed. When she sees me she freezes, her jaw tightening.

"Your father won't be coming home for Thanksgiving tomorrow," she says flatly. Then she grabs her laptop from the kitchen table and vanishes down the hallway. A moment later I hear footsteps plodding up the stairs.

I stand speechless in the middle of the kitchen.

What just happened?

And how could Dad not be home for Thanksgiving? It's his favorite holiday. He would never miss it. Every year he cooks an epic over-the-top feast in an attempt to outdo his last year's dinner. He takes it very seriously. He makes us all fill out score sheets rating the turkey, the side dishes, the decorations, the entertainment, even his choice of music. He started with a ten-point scale, but over the years, it's evolved to a sixty-point scale because none of us can bear to give him a lower score than the previous year.

I drop my bag on the table and collapse into one of the chairs.

I can't believe he's going to miss it. It won't be Thanksgiving without him. It'll be just . . . Thursday.

I dig my phone out of my pocket and send him a quick text, asking him if it's true. He replies almost immediately.

Dad: Unfortunately, yes. I'm so sorry. The client hates the campaign we've been working on and wants a complete redesign. We're going to be working all weekend and next week.

Then, a moment later, he adds:

Dad: Take care of your brother. And tell your mom I really am sorry.

I drop my phone back into my bag and glance around the kitchen. There are dishes stacked in the overflowing sink, crusty food stuck to the counter, and used pans still sitting on the stove. Dad would hate this mess. He'd freak. Not that he's going to be around to see it.

But still, I do the only thing I can think to do. The only thing that momentarily distracts me from the fact that tomorrow we'll be celebrating Thanksgiving as a threesome.

I start cleaning.

Then I Get Quantumly Entangled

We end up ordering pizza for Thanksgiving dinner because nobody wants to cook. Dad always cooked. I suppose I could Google a few recipes and give them a try, but what would be the point? It's not the same without him here.

I don't see much of Mom. After she disappeared into her room with her laptop yesterday afternoon, she barely came out at all, except to say "We're ordering pizza" and then to actually eat the pizza.

I haven't had a chance to work on my cheating story because I've been too busy keeping the house clean and trying to distract Frankie so he doesn't fall into a depression, too.

On Thursday night, after I've cleared the pizza plates, broken down the box, emptied the dishwasher, and folded the three loads of laundry I started this morning, I head upstairs to find Frankie sitting on the floor of his bedroom with his board game spread out in front of him. After moving one of the game pieces, he crawls to the other side of the board and draws a card from the deck.

"Are you playing against yourself?" I ask.

He doesn't look up. He stares at the new card he's just plucked and taps his teeth in concentration. "I've been thinking about what you said the other night. About how you don't understand how to play. I'm trying to figure out how to make the game more user-friendly."

He sets the card in the discard pile and moves the game piece three squares.

Then he crawls back to his original seat.

With a sigh, I plop down across from him and assume the second player's hand.

Frankie picks a card, puts it in his hand, and then plays a different card, moving his pawn six spaces. "I want to make sure that everyone can play. Not only scientists. What's the Matter? is a family game."

I pick up the cards in front of me and fan them out in my hand. Then I pick a new card. It's a Quark card. I have no idea what that means. "Frankie. I think you should know your audience. I don't think this game will ever be played by anyone but scientists."

"That's not true!" he argues. "I just have to make a few tweaks."

I sigh and toss my Quark card into the discard pile.

Frankie's eyes grow wide. "You can't play that card now! It's a building-block card. You can use it to create matter if you get stuck in a black hole. This is one of the most valuable cards in the deck!"

I shoot him a look and pick the card back up. I study my hand again. But I must take too long because Frankie grows impatient and says, "Just play your Inertia card and stay where you are."

I do as I'm told.

"Frankie," I begin cautiously as he scribbles something down in a nearby notebook. "Have we ever played any other games? Like, I don't know, Uno?"

He twists his mouth to the side as he studies the game board. He plays a Speed of Sound card and moves forward five spaces. "Not in forever."

I immediately play a Speed of Light card and move ahead ten spaces. "So, I never cheated at Uno two years ago."

He peers at me from over the top of his cards. "No. But if you did, I would tell you you're not allowed to play anymore."

I stifle a smile. "So, what about other types of cheating?"

He sets down a Quantum Entanglement card and swaps places with me on the board. "What about it?"

I study my hand, trying to figure out what to play next. But I honestly have no idea what I'm looking at. I turn my cards around and Frankie chooses for me. "Have you ever known me, I mean *Other Me—this* me—to cheat?"

"Like Lucinda?"

I suck in a breath. "So you know about that?"

"Yeah, you told me. You were really upset about it."

"Do you think *I'm* capable of cheating?"

"Like at school?" Frankie asks.

I've completely given up on the game. Frankie has gone back to playing each of the hands alternately.

"Yeah."

He shrugs. "I guess it depends on what you consider cheating."

My forehead crinkles. "What do you mean?"

"I mean," he goes on, pulling a card from my hand and playing it, "what are the definitions? What are the parameters? Do sleeping pills count as cheating?"

I scoff. "No."

"Does coffee count as cheating?"

I shake my head. "No. Don't be silly."

"It cheats your body's natural chemistry."

"I mean, like cheating on a test."

He thinks about that for a second. "I don't think you've ever cheated on a test."

I feel the knot in my stomach unravel slightly.

"But," he adds thoughtfully a moment later, "I honestly wouldn't be very surprised if you did."

Then I Question Myself

Later that night, I open my Windsor Academy email account and click on the sent folder. With my heart in my throat, I scan the list of sent emails. Most of them are to teachers or Sequoia. There are no emails sent to TSM4@youmail.com.

Not that you would keep them in your mailbox for anyone to find, my inner voice remarks.

To be honest, I'm starting to grow a little tired of that voice.

Nor would you use your school email address to send them, the voice adds indignantly.

As much as I hate to admit it, she's right.

I open up the web and navigate to my personal email address. I type TSM4@youmail.com into the search box and hold my breath.

No results.

With a huff, I close the lid of my laptop and lean back in my chair.

What if Lucinda and Frankie are right? What if this version of me *is* the kind of person who would purchase a stolen test? What if she already has?

I launch out of my chair and start scouring my room. I empty drawers and bags and boxes. I check pockets and under the mattress and inside books. And then I end up in the exact same place I did a week ago: staring down that ugly black lock-box in my bottom drawer. The one I still haven't been able to open.

I shake it next to my ear, trying to gauge what's inside. The mystery contents make a swishing sound. Like paper.

Oh God.

My heart starts to thud and I feel a jolt of desperation stream through me. I need to get inside this box. I have to know what's in there. It's a stolen test, I just know it! Maybe even *multiple* stolen tests.

Maybe I'm a repeat customer. Maybe I have a freaking loyalty card.

I dial combination after combination to no avail. I try wedging everything I can find in the metal gap, but nothing seems to make a dent. I even watch a YouTube video on picking locks, but I'm decidedly *un*skilled in that department.

There's a small amount of comfort to be found in that. If I *have* resorted to cheating at school, at least it's not likely I've become a car thief as well.

Finally, I toss the box aside in a fit of rage. I watch it roll twice before finally coming to rest against the frame of my bed with a *clank*.

What is in there? What did *Other Me* want so desperately to hide that she had to lock it up in a box with an impossible-to-guess combination? It has to be a stolen test, right? What else would she go through so much trouble to hide?

But then an absolving thought comes to me.

Why would I keep it?

If I purchased a stolen test and used it to get an A, why not destroy it instantly? Burn it. Shred it. Erase all evidence that it ever existed? Why lock it up for someone to find and incriminate me with later?

If Lucinda was caught with a stolen test and expelled from school, you would think Other Me would be smart enough to destroy all evidence of her own guilt.

If she was guilty.

Which I'm still not convinced of.

I sigh, pushing myself to my feet, and sit back down at my laptop. The box is a dead end. I need to get back to the story. I need to find out who is selling these tests. I can worry about my own culpability later.

I grab my notebook, flip it open, and start typing up my notes from Lucinda's interview. Then I make a decision.

I'm going after the test stealer. I'm going to catch him red-handed. If you want to catch a criminal, you have to act like one. Cops don't catch drug dealers by being cops. They catch drug dealers by being drug *buyers*.

I navigate to YouMail.com and click the button to start a new account. I pick a random string of numbers and letters and choose a password.

Then, once my new address is set up, I compose my first email.

To: TSM4@youmail.com
From: PPYU991@youmail.com
Subject: Help

Hello. I'm a Windsor Academy senior and I'm struggling with AP biology. We have a test coming up next week (12/1) and I've heard you can help. Please reply at your earliest convenience. I'm desperate.

Thank you.

Then I Get My Exercise in the Fiction Section

By Monday morning, I'm eager to go back to school. The trap has been set. The email has been sent. So far, there's been no response but I'm not discouraged. I know it's only a matter of time before the culprit responds with directions on where to leave the money. Then I'll set up the sting. I've already ordered one of those nanny cam things online. It arrives tomorrow.

This will work.

I will catch Dylan Parker red-handed.

In the meantime, I've typed up all my notes in a document on my laptop, so I can keep them organized and searchable when I need to quickly reference anything.

And now it's time to see if *Madame Bovary* can offer me any leads.

During our first Student Mastery Hour, I tell Sequoia I'm going to work alone in the library again. She gives me an almost-hurt look, like she's offended that I don't want to study with her, but eventually she brushes it off.

I head straight for the fiction section and make a beeline for the Fs. Gustave Flaubert is the famous French author of *Madame*

Bovary and the Sanderson-Ruiz Library has five copies. I check each one, surreptitiously flipping through the pages, but I find nothing. I do the same with all three copies of *The Count of Monte Cristo* by Alexandre Dumas, but those pages are empty, too.

Maybe the test thief only chooses books by French authors. Maybe *that's* the connection.

I move through the fiction section, checking every French author I can think of from Balzac to Proust, but there's nothing out of the ordinary in any of the books.

There has to be a pattern. There's always a pattern. If you think about all the great journalists in the world and all the epic stories they've broken, it was because they found the pattern. They linked things together. They connected dots.

But I only have two dots. Yet I know there's some connection between the titles. I can feel it.

I check my new anonymous email account on my phone. Still no response from TSM4@youmail.com

Frustrated, I find a table near the back and sit down. I open my laptop and review the notes I typed up over the weekend.

<u>Facts That I Know for Certain:</u>
• Lucinda Wallace was asked to leave money in copies of *Madame Bovary* and *The Count of Monte Cristo*

<u>Questions:</u>
• Were other test purchasers asked to leave money in other books? Or other places around school?

- What's the connection between *Madame Bovary* and *The Count of Monte Cristo*?

"Whatcha doing?" a voice says, startling me out of my thoughts. I look up to see Dylan leaning on the table, trying to peek at my screen.

I angle it away from him. "None of your business."

"Still playing detective?"

"If by detective you mean still trying to prove you're guilty? Then, yes."

He grins. "Maybe I can help."

"Doubtful." I roll my eyes and focus back on my notes, hoping eventually he'll take the hint, go back to his sacred little corner, and mind his own business. Why is he *always* in here when I'm trying to work anyway? Does he live in the library or something?

My head pops up, an idea suddenly forming.

He's *always* in the library.

Is he working in here? Or is he doing *more* than working? Is he possibly conducting some *other* kind of business in here?

"Did you know," I begin, trying to sound conversational, "that Lucinda Wallace was asked to put the money for her stolen tests in copies of *Madame Bovary* and *The Count of Monte Cristo*?"

I study his face, hoping again to catch one of those micro-expressions. A flicker of guilt. A momentary glimpse of surprise. But Dylan's face is blank. He's either somehow learned how to hide his micro-expressions, or I'm still not quick enough to identify them.

All he says is "Huh."

I'm about to return to my notes when, a second later, I see something. It's just a flash of a reaction. But it's there.

Except it doesn't look like guilt or shame. At least not to my novice eyes. It looks more like confusion. As though he's trying to piece his own mystery together.

"So," he continues after a moment, "the school is totally okay with you doing this? Snooping around trying to catch this person?"

I hesitate, averting my gaze. "Um, not exactly."

He lets out an overdramatic gasp. "What? Unsanctioned investigative work? Going against the almighty Windsor authority? What kind of zombie are you?"

"I'm trying to convince Mr. Fitz to let me start a school newspaper," I retort in exasperation. "He said no, but I know he'll come around if I can break this story."

"No, he won't."

I glance up at him. "How do you know?"

"Because it's too out of the box. It requires too much free thinking. They don't like free thinking. Free thinking leads to questioning which leads to anarchy. Trust me, I know. I have to fight with them over *every* single issue of *Writer's Block*. They don't want the content to be too 'edgy.' They just want us all to keep our heads down, study on our little computers, join their sanctioned clubs, and maintain the 89 percent Ivy League acceptance rate. Anything beyond that is a waste of time."

"That's not true."

"It's absolutely true."

"That's not why Mr. Fitz said no to my request to start a news-paper. He told me it was because he thought I was overextended and—" I stop. Why am I explaining all of this to *him*? He's my primary suspect. I shouldn't even be conversing with him. Unless it pertains to the story. "Never mind," I mumble, focusing back on my laptop. "Can you please leave me alone now?"

He sighs. "Sorry. No can do. If the Zombie Queen is doing something unsanctioned by the school, I can't walk away. I'm an interested party now." He pulls out the chair across from me and sits.

"Excuse me," I protest, horrified. "I was sitting here."

"Yeah, yeah, you were here first. I know." He grabs my lap-top and spins it around so he can read the document on my screen.

I stare at him in stunned silence for a few seconds before brusquely snatching back my computer. "Um, hello? What do you think you're doing?"

"*San Francisco Chronicle* '25 Books to Read Before College.'" He leans back in his chair and crosses his arms, looking mighty pleased with himself.

I scrunch my nose. "What?"

"*Madame Bovary* and *The Count of Monte Cristo*. The con-nection. The test thief is using books taken from that list."

My mouth falls open. "How do you know that?"

"The *Chronicle* is my favorite newspaper."

I do my best to conceal my shock, but I'm certain *my* micro-expressions give me away instantly. In fact, mine are probably more like *macro*-expressions.

"What?" he asks, smirking. "You don't think I read newspapers? Newspapers are the last great journalistic art form. Too bad they're dying. Nothing quite compares to the tactile feel of newsprint in your hand."

"I-I—" I try to say something but only stunted syllables come out.

Dylan Parker reads the *San Francisco Chronicle*?

Dylan Parker and I have something in common?

Actually, come to think of it, I do remember that he was reading a newspaper during the school assembly last week. I was just too infuriated with him to think anything of it.

"B-b-but," I try again for words, this time managing to get out a whole sentence. "How do you know about that list?"

"Because I read it. And all the books on it."

This might come as more of a surprise than his previous statement, momentarily distracting me from my investigation. "What?"

He gives me that patronizing smirk again. "I may not be a Windsor Zombie but I still care about going to college."

"Where did you apply?"

He glances away, like the question makes him uncomfortable. "Columbia. Among others."

"Columbia?" I spit, my throat constricting.

He snickers. "Don't sound so shocked."

"I . . . I'm sorry. That's not why I . . . that's where I applied, too."

He raises his eyebrows. "Oh yeah? What do you want to study?"

I think back to the application on Watts's coffee table. The one that said "economics" on it. I cast my gaze to the floor. "It's . . . I'm still deciding."

"Well, I applied for their writing program. They have one of the best in the country for undergrads."

I swallow hard. "You want to be a writer?"

"A novelist. Yeah." He gets a far-off look in his eyes for a moment and then mumbles, "But I probably won't get in, so it doesn't really matter."

"Why not?" I ask, genuinely curious.

He gives his head a shake, like he's coming out of a disturbing dream. "Never mind. Anyway. The *San Francisco Chronicle*'s '25 Books to Read Before College.' I would check other books on that list."

He switches subjects so quickly, it takes me a moment to keep up. "Right," I say, refocusing on my notes. "So what makes you so sure the books are coming from that list?"

"Because the other day I found two hundred dollars stuffed into a copy of *Robinson Crusoe*, which is also on the list."

I lean forward excitedly. "You found two hundred dollars in a copy of *Robinson Crusoe*?"

"Yeah. And until this conversation, I thought it was just some kid who had left his lunch money in his book. I mean, it *is* the Windsor Academy, after all."

I stifle a laugh. "What did you do with the money?"

He shrugs. "I took it. Obviously."

"You took it?" I screech, a little too loudly. I glance around to see if anyone heard me and then lower my voice. "You can't just take that. It's evidence. You messed with a crime scene."

He laughs. "Slow down there, Columbo. It was money in a book. Not a dead body."

"But why do you think it's *that* list? Those three books are classics. I'm sure they're on a lot of reading lists together."

He scratches the back of his neck. "Just a hunch."

I shoot him a suspicious look. "A hunch, huh?"

He shrugs. "Check it out. Maybe I'm wrong."

I close my laptop, rocket out of my seat, and dash back to the fiction section. I can feel Dylan on my heels as I round the corner to the Ds.

If he's right, this could be it. The connection I've been looking for.

When I locate Daniel Defoe, I find three copies of *Robinson Crusoe* on the shelf. This was the book I'd been trying to get from the Southwest High library for the past few months but it was always missing.

I quickly flip through all three copies, finding nothing. My shoulders slump in disappointment. "When did you say you found the money?"

"Right before Thanksgiving break."

"And there's still no test here," I think aloud. "Lucinda said the test appeared in the book forty-eight hours later, in a sealed envelope."

"Yeah," Dylan says condescendingly, like I'm a little slow on the uptake. "Because I took the money. Why would the culprit leave the test if there was no money?"

Dang it. He's right. I should have thought of that myself.

I point at him. "Unless *you're* the culprit. And *that's* why you took the money."

"Yeah," he says again with the same annoying inflection. "And that's why I'm helping you. Because I'm the world's stupidest criminal."

I bite my lip in frustration. He makes a good point. Why *would* he help me if he was guilty? To throw me off? To lead me in the wrong direction?

There's only one way to find out.

I hurry back to my laptop and Google "25 Books to Read Before College—San Francisco Chronicle."

The result pops up right away, and all at once the article comes rushing back to me. I remember reading this list for the first time when I was twelve. I found it right after I decided I wanted to go to Columbia University and figured I better start preparing now. I did all the research, read article after article about college prep.

I scour the list of titles that I've been slowly working my way through since middle school.

Frankenstein by Mary Shelley.

Emma by Jane Austen.

Great Expectations by Charles Dickens.

Then I'm out of my seat again, running back to the fiction section. Somewhere behind me, I hear Dylan whine, "This is a lot more physical activity than I was anticipating."

I ignore him and reach for a copy of *Emma* on the shelf, right as the bell signaling the end of Student Mastery Hour chimes.

I hastily flip through the book, stopping when a chill runs up my arms.

There, nestled between pages 84 and 85, right at the part where Emma says, "You must be the best judge of your own happiness," are two crisp hundred-dollar bills.

Then I Quiz Sequoia

I would love to stay in the library all day and keep working, but I can't miss the rest of my classes. I still have to prove to Fitz that I can handle this. That I'm not stretched too thin. And in order to do that, I need to be sure to stay on top of my schoolwork.

"Is everything okay?" Sequoia asks as we make our way to Bellum Hall for chemistry. "You've been acting so strange and distant since before Thanksgiving."

"What happened on my date with Dylan Parker?" I blurt out.

"You went on a date with Dylan Parker?" she asks, looking scandalized. "When? Over Thanksgiving break?"

"No. Freshman year."

"Oh," she says with a chuckle. "I don't know."

"Did we have a good time? Did I like him?"

"Kennedy," she says, sounding confused. "What is this about?"

"I just want to know how the date was. Was it miserable and we fought the whole time or did we . . . you know . . . *like* each other."

She gives me a strange look. "Why are you asking *me*?"

I bow my head, averting my gaze. "Because I don't remember."

She laughs. "Well, I think that answers your question."

"Do you remember anything?"

We turn left to circle around Waldorf Pond. "Not really," she admits. "I mean, I guess you had a good time. You were going to go out with him again."

I stop walking. "I was?"

"Yeah, remember? But I talked you out of it. Because of the boycott."

"Right," I say, my voice thick. "The boycott."

The reason my name is listed in the number-one spot of that class ranking. Because I chose this. I chose *me*. And my future.

As it should be.

"Is that what's been bothering you?" Sequoia asks. "Or is it something else?"

"I went to visit Lucinda," I tell her.

Sequoia skids to a halt in the middle of the paved walkway, causing other students to have to veer around her. "What? *Why* would you do that?"

I don't miss the disdain in her voice. Is she that quick to cast her off? Just because she made a mistake? Just because she cheated . . .

The thought catches me off guard.

Isn't that exactly what I did to Laney? Wrote her off the moment I found out about her and Austin?

But that was totally different. She cheated with my boyfriend. The guy I'd been dating for three years.

Except now *she's* dating him.

I flash back to her SnipPic feed and all of those photos of them. Photos that make them look happy together. Photos that would make anyone say they were meant to be together.

Sure, maybe in *this* life. But in my other life, she betrayed me. She went behind my back. That's what counts.

"Because she's our friend," I tell Sequoia. "And she misses us." Then, a little less earnestly, I add, "And because I wanted to ask her some questions about the stolen test thing."

"WHY?" Sequoia screeches, and I can hear the break in her voice. The crack. I'm starting to sense the patterns. There'll be tears running down her face in less than five seconds. "Are you thinking about . . ." she tries to ask, but a sob gets in the way.

"Cheating? No! Don't be ridiculous. I'm just trying to figure out who's behind it so we can turn him in and save our grades. I would never buy a stolen test."

I expect Sequoia to wholeheartedly agree with me but she doesn't. She stays quiet. I look to her, studying her face. "Do *you* think I would do that?"

"No. Of course not," she responds. But there's the slightest squeak in her voice, and the slightest pause before she says it.

I don't need to be a human lie detector to decipher that.

Then I Defile
the Sacred Uniform

Every day this week, I go to the library to work on my story during Student Mastery Hour. And every day, Dylan is there. At first, he pretends like he's not at all interested in what I'm doing. He just casually stops by my table a few times, asking how things are coming along. But by the end of the week, he's spending almost the entire period hunched over my laptop with me, pitching out ideas, helping me research, suggesting possible leads.

At first, I was reluctant to let him help, given that he's still at the top of my suspect list, but he did kind of give me my first big break in the story. Plus, if he *is* the culprit, I'll want to keep him close, right?

I don't only work on the cheating story. I start brainstorming and fleshing out other stories as well. After all, if I'm going to put out an entire newspaper, I need more than just a front page. And Dylan actually has some really good ideas for articles.

On the following Monday, when the chime rings signaling the end of the second Student Mastery Hour, Dylan says, "I had a thought."

I snicker. "Did it hurt?"

He rolls his eyes. "I think I might have another way to figure out who's behind the test stealing. Do you want to meet for coffee after last period?"

The idea of spending time outside of school with Dylan is not exactly appealing to me, but I admit I'm intrigued by what he has in mind.

"Okay," I agree. "Where?"

"There's a little coffee shop on the other end of town. Near the public school. It's called Peabody's. Do you know it?"

I nod, feeling a lump form in my throat. "I know it."

"Great," he says. "I'll meet you there at five."

Sequoia drives me home that afternoon and I walk to Peabody's. The place is packed, but I find Dylan sitting at a quieter table in the back.

He heads to the counter to order us some coffees and pastries while I boot up my laptop. I glance around the small coffee shop, a knot instantly forming in my stomach when I remember that *this* is the place. This is where Laney and Austin went together the morning before I caught them in the basement. Laney told me she was catching an early ride with her dad so that she could work on her newspaper story when actually she was here with him. How many more times did they come here together? Was it every morning for three whole months? Where did they sit? At this very table? Did they kiss while waiting in line for their coffees? Did they feed each other bites of muffin? Did they . . .

Stop, I command myself. *Let it go. You have other things to worry about. Things that are happening* now. *In* this *life.*

I blink and focus back on my laptop screen. Checking to make sure Dylan is still waiting on our coffees, I log in to my secret email account. The one I used to send the sting email to the test thief. The inbox is still empty.

That's over a week.

What is taking so long?

Why hasn't he responded?

Maybe because he's been hanging out with you, my inner voice says. I look up to see Dylan returning to the table with a tray and quickly close the window.

Dylan takes the seat next to me so he can see my screen. He's a little too close for my comfort. I can smell his amazing citrusy shampoo again.

He sets my Pumpkin Spice Latte in front of me and takes a big swig of his black coffee. The scent of it immediately masks all evidence of his shampoo and I'm reminded of the morning before I caught Austin and Laney kissing.

His breath smelled like coffee.

And so did hers.

A familiar pang of frustration wells up inside me. I should have put together the clues. I'm a journalist, for heaven's sake. All the pieces were there. I was just too blind or stupid, or both, to see them.

I suddenly wish I had suggested another location to Dylan. This place is suffocating me with the memories of their betrayal.

"So, this is what I think we should do," Dylan begins, taking a bite of muffin.

I come out of my reverie and instinctively scoot my chair away.

"Sorry," Dylan says, wiping his mouth. "Am I chewing too loudly? My mom says I have a problem with that."

I laugh. "I don't remember you being so concerned about it when you were crunching carrots in my face."

He nods and sips his coffee. "Ah, well, that was back when I still thought you were captain of the zombies. I had to take preventive measures."

"Captain of the zombies? I thought it was *queen* of the zombies."

He cracks a smile. "Don't worry. The positions are interchangeable."

"But you don't think that about me anymore?"

He swallows his mouthful of muffin, looking pensive. "Hmm. Jury's still out on that one. Check back with me tomorrow."

I slap him with the backside of my hand.

He throws his arms up in surrender. "Hey, I'm just following the evidence."

"What evidence?" I challenge in a mocking tone.

"Let's see." He drops the muffin and dusts crumbs off his fingers so he can count on them. "Top of the class. Student fundraising captain. Member of all the clubs."

"I'm not a member of *all* the clubs," I interject.

He ignores me and keeps counting. "Immaculate uniform."

I glance down at my gray skirt, white blouse, and blazer. "What's wrong with my uniform?"

"What's wrong with your uniform?" he echoes. "Where do I start? Your shirt is perfectly pressed and tucked in. Your blazer looks like you lint-roll it daily. Your socks are never slouched. And your skirt is . . ." He reaches out and touches the gray fabric, his fingertips grazing my bare skin.

For some reason, this little action sends a shiver through me. Even though his hands are warm. Surprisingly warm.

He tilts his head and studies me for a moment, almost as though he can sense my reaction. I play it off quickly by continuing my act of annoyance. "What's wrong with my skirt?"

But he doesn't answer right away. I lift my eyes to meet his and suddenly our gazes lock. Involuntarily. Unexpectedly. Irreversibly.

He clears his throat and looks away. "It's . . . um, very clean."

"Would you rather it be filthy and wrinkled like *your* uniform?"

"Yes," he replies. "Yes, I would."

"Fine." I reach for the pastry on the tray in front of us, run my fingertip through the chocolate cream filling, and smear it across my lap.

Dylan stares at me with his eyes wide and his mouth slightly agape.

"Happy now?" I grin.

It takes him a while to reply. But when he does, he says, "Yes. And admittedly a little turned on."

Then My Past Catches
Up with Me

"*So, what was this big idea of yours?*" I ask, sipping my latte.

Dylan stuffs the last of his muffin into his mouth. "I think we should try to hack the password of the email account."

"Or," I say thoughtfully, "you can just *tell* me the password. Since, you know, *you* created it."

He gives me a devilish smirk. "Where would be the fun in that?" He bypasses the stack of napkins on the table and wipes his hands on his pants, leaving behind an unsightly grease streak. I guess that solves the mystery of why he always looks so disheveled. He turns the laptop toward him. "What email address is the perp using?"

"I'm sorry," I say teasingly. "The perp?"

"Yes, the perpetrator. Keep up."

"I know what *perp* means," I argue. "I just . . . You know what? Never mind. It's TSM4@youmail.com."

He nods and navigates to the YouMail site. He types the email address into the log-in box and clicks the Forgot Password link.

"Look, the perp set up a password hint." He squints at the screen, his eyebrows knitting in confusion as he reads aloud. "I know what you're thinking . . ."

"What?" I grab the laptop and spin it toward me so I can read it for myself.

I know what you're thinking . . .

He turns and looks at me. "What on earth does that mean?"

I shrug and shake my head. "I don't know. Maybe it's a warning message to us. Or whoever is trying to hack the password. Like, I know what you're thinking about doing, so don't even try it."

Dylan takes the computer back and stares at the password hint.

"I know what you're thinking," he repeats with a curious inflection. "I know what you're thinking."

Every time he says those words aloud, something stirs in me. Something I can't quite identify. I can almost hear someone else saying them. Someone in my past. A faint, clouded memory that's struggling to break through.

He raps his fingers against the keys, contemplating. "Maybe it's a line from a book. Like on the *Chronicle* list."

I nod. "It's as good an idea as any."

He opens a new tab in the browser and Googles the exact password hint along with the word "book." There are no obvious results.

I don't know what the password hint is referring to, but for some strange reason I'm positive it's not a book. And my conviction is starting to unnerve me.

"What about . . . ?" Dylan starts to ask but I don't hear the rest of his suggestion. I don't hear anything, actually. Because just then, the door of Peabody's jingles as two customers come tumbling into the restaurant and all of the blood instantly drains from my face.

Oh my God. This isn't happening.

Why, oh why, did I agree to come here? Why didn't I suggest we go somewhere else?

I should have known they'd walk through that door. I should have been more cautious. I should have protected myself from this very situation.

I watch in a mixture of shock and horror and jealousy as my ex-boyfriend and my former best friend order coffees from the barista and carry them to a nearby booth. They slide into the same side, leaving the opposite bench empty, and immediately snuggle up to each other.

And in that moment, all I can think is *Austin never did that with me.*

We never snuggled on the same side of the booth. Not even in the beginning when things were new and exciting. He always insisted on sitting *opposite* me. He said it was so he could see me better. I never argued because that sounded so sweet.

But maybe it was a lie.

Maybe he just didn't want to be that close to me. Maybe the thought of being separated from me by a foot of table didn't bother him in the slightest.

"Friends of yours?" Dylan asks, crashing into my thoughts.

I blink and face him. "No," I mumble, trying to focus on my laptop screen. But my attention keeps getting diverted. I keep looking up to see what they're doing. What they're saying. How many times they turn to just look at each other. Not talk. Not smile. Just gaze into each other's eyes.

"They look happy," Dylan remarks, and once again I realize that I'm staring.

"Whatever," I mutter. "Let's get back to work."

But I can sense Dylan watching me. I have a feeling he won't let this go. "Is that your ex-boyfriend or something?"

I bark out a laugh. "No. I mean, not really. We went on one date in middle school."

I notice his body tense for a moment before he leans back in his chair. "Is that like a pattern with you? One date and then you're done?" It sounds like a joke, but I can hear the hostility behind the words. I know he's referring to us. To *our* one date. The one I don't remember, but he obviously does.

"N-n-no," I stammer. "It wasn't like that."

"So, did you stop responding to his texts, too?"

I startle at this. Not just because he's no longer even trying to hide the resentment in his voice, but because I can't believe I would do that. Or *she* would do that. Did she just ignore him until he got the point and went away? That seems kind of harsh. And incredibly cowardly.

I bite my lip, struggling for words. "No. It just didn't work out." I see a flicker of something on his face and quickly add, "With him."

Because the truth is, I don't know what happened with us. With Dylan and me. All I know is what Sequoia told me. That we had one date. That I was planning on going out with him again but then I met her and she convinced me to focus on school instead of boys.

"Why didn't it work out?" he asks, and then after a moment, he also adds, "With him."

But I have a feeling he's asking me for more than that. He's asking me for something I can't give. An overdue explanation that I simply don't have.

I swallow. "Because I went to Windsor and he went to Southwest High. It just kind of fizzled out."

"So," Dylan presses, folding his hands in his lap like a TV talk show interviewer. "If you *hadn't* gone to Windsor, you two might still be a couple?"

Yeah, and he would have eventually cheated on me.

My body tenses. My heart thumps in my chest. I don't want to think about that. I spent the last three and a half years wondering about what-ifs. I'm done. This is my life now. This is where I belong. I've already made that decision.

"It doesn't matter what *would* have happened," I say. "This is what *did* happen."

"So you're bitter," Dylan guesses. "About the one that got away?"

"What?" I ask, flustered. I can feel my face turning red. "No.

I'm not bitter about anything. That was more than three years ago. In *middle* school. I don't care about him. I barely even think about him."

Dylan's expression is inscrutable. But apparently mine is not. "That's not what your face says," he points out.

So, now *he's* the micro-expression expert?

"Admit it," Dylan prods. "You're totally still in love with that guy."

"*No!*" I screech. "I will not admit that."

"Why not?"

"Because it's not true! He and I . . . we were . . . we didn't . . ."

Dylan's hostility gives way to amusement as he sits back and watches me struggle.

"We were terrible together," I finish. "We didn't work. We had different interests and he made weird sounds with his teeth and laughed at fart jokes. *And* he misuses the phrase 'for all intents and purposes,' which is just annoying."

"That's a lot of specifics for one date."

I don't like where this conversation is heading. Actually, I don't like where it already is. "Let's drop it. We weren't meant to be and that's that."

"Unlike them," Dylan prompts, and I get the sense from his goading tone that he's trying to get me riled up again.

"What do you mean?"

"I mean, those two are clearly meant for each other. Just look at them."

Reluctantly, I turn back to the booth where Laney and

Austin are sitting. Of course, it happens to be the exact moment when he chooses to kiss her on the forehead. I avert my eyes. For some reason this gesture seems more intimate than watching them swap spit in the parking lot for five minutes. This hits me in a more vulnerable spot. So instead, I let my gaze wander to the empty bench across from them.

In the old days, when the three of us used to go out together, Laney and I would always take one side of the booth and Austin would sit by himself on the other. I did it because I didn't want Laney to feel like the third wheel. I never wanted her to be uncomfortable hanging out with us. But it turns out, she *was*. Just maybe not for the reasons I thought.

Is Dylan right?

Is there a reason they ended up together in both versions of this life?

Were they the ones meant to be together all along?

"I should probably get home," I say, closing my laptop and returning it to my bag. "We're not making much progress here."

"Okay," Dylan agrees, still looking at me like he's trying to X-ray my brain. "I'll drive you."

"That's okay," I say quickly. "I can walk."

Dylan laughs. "Are you crazy? Have you seen what it looks like out there?"

I peer through the darkening window of Peabody's at the rivers of rain streaming down the glass.

Crap.

When did that start?

Probably the moment Laney and Austin walked through the door. Like some kind of dark omen.

"You're not walking home in that," Dylan insists. "I'll give you a ride."

I sigh. "Fine." Then I remember my manners. "I mean, thanks."

Then the Truth Comes Out

By the time Dylan drops me off in front of my house, we've suffered through five minutes of awkward silence, punctuated only by the sounds of the rain pounding on the windshield, the wipers swishing, and the hard-hitting guitars of whatever heavy rock music he has playing on the stereo.

Dylan keeps asking if I'm okay, to which I repeatedly respond, "I'm fine."

I feel like I've been saying that for the past month. When Mr. Fitz told me he was worried about me. When Sequoia told me she was worried about me. Even when I woke up in Nurse Wilson's office and she insisted I wasn't, I still repeated it.

"I'm fine."

"I'm fine."

"I'm fine."

Like a parrot who's only learned to speak one phrase.

But I'm starting to wonder if that's really true. *Am* I fine? My face looks like it's been left out in the rain for too long. My body is always tired. I've been renting out space in my brain to a permanent headache that doesn't want to leave no matter how much coffee I drink. My teachers think I'm going to crack. Dylan thinks I've been brainwashed and turned into a zombie. Three people who are important to me have told me that they think I'm capable of cheating my way through life.

Am I really fine?

Is that what Lucinda told everyone before she did what she did? Is that what the Windsor Academy trains you to say no matter what?

The song on the speakers kicks into a final chorus as the main singer croons something about trying to figure out the mind of a girl.

Yeah, good luck, buddy, I think. *We can't even figure ourselves out.*

"Who is this?" I ask, nodding toward the radio.

Dylan immediately lowers the volume, as if interpreting my question as a dislike for the song. "Some new band I just discovered online. They're called Whack-a-Mole." He shrugs. "They're pretty good."

I give Dylan directions to my house from the main road and he pulls up to the curb and puts the car in Park.

I reach for the door handle, fairly desperate to get away from the awkward energy of this car. "Thanks for the ride."

"Wait," he calls out. And suddenly his hand is on my arm. Even through the thick fabric of my blazer, I feel a tingle shoot through me. The kind of tingle I haven't felt since Austin McKinley kissed me in that movie theater lobby. The kind of tingle I never thought I'd ever feel again the second I saw him kissing someone else.

And yet there it is. Scorching through wool and cotton and skin. Traveling up my arm, spreading across my skin, rushing right through my heart.

Originating from the least likely of places.

I glance down at his hand and suddenly find myself wondering if this happened before. Three and a half years ago. Did he touch me then? Did I feel what I just felt? Did it scare me away?

Dylan notices me staring at his hand and quickly pulls it away, taking that glorious rushing, heart-skittering sensation with him.

"I—" he starts to say, but he stumbles over the words. Starting and restarting like an Olympic sprinter who can't manage to synchronize his feet with the sound of the gun. "I'm not good at this." The sentence finally tumbles out.

Despite everything, I manage a thin smile. "Not good at what?"

He rubs his hands on his pants. "Um. You know . . ." He gestures ambiguously between the two of us. Back and forth, faster and faster. "I'm not good at . . ."

"Finishing sentences?"

He laughs. It's a genuine one. Not the sarcastic chuckle that I've grown accustomed to over the past few weeks.

"I think I owe you an apology," he finally says.

My forehead scrunches in confusion. "Excuse me?"

He blows out a breath. "I've been kind of a jerk to you lately."

"*Kind* of?"

He laughs. "Okay. I've been a big jerk. But you haven't exactly been a picnic either. I mean, sometimes you're just so infuriating and rude and—"

"Whoever taught you to apologize did a horrible job."

He looks at his lap. "Sorry. You're right. I'm just trying to say that I *might* have misjudged you. I . . ." He stops and restarts. "For a while, I suspected . . . I mean, I'm in the library a lot. I see things. And you're at the top of the class. You seemed like the most obvious choice. So I thought . . . well, the point is, I was mistaken. And I'm sorry."

I squint at him through the darkness of the car. "What are you talking about?"

He shakes his head. "Nothing. I'm rambling. It happens when I'm nervous. I was trying to say that I was wrong about you."

I'm not exactly sure what he means but I still feel a squeeze in my chest. I look down at my lap. "I think I've been wrong about a few things, too."

He flashes me a toothy grin. It's kind of adorable. "Does that mean you don't think I'm the perp anymore?"

"I didn't say that," I correct.

He chuckles, then falls quiet. "It wouldn't be so bad, you know."

I squint. "What?"

"If I was guilty. Maybe then I could get out of here."

I'm suddenly no longer interested in leaving the car. I train my eyes on him. He runs his hands anxiously over the steering wheel. "What do you mean?" I ask.

"Never mind," he mutters. "Just forget it."

"No. What?"

He sighs. "I don't exactly love it at Windsor."

"Tell me something I don't know," I joke.

He gives me a thin smile. "My dad is the only reason I'm there. He thinks if he can put me on the right track, I'll stay on the right track."

"You're ranked in the top 20 of our class. I'd say that's a pretty good track."

He shakes his head. "Not for him. Until I agree to go to business school and follow in his footsteps, he doesn't take anything I do seriously." He glances out the window with a sigh. "He thinks writing as a profession is a joke."

I chuckle. "Then I guess we're both screwed."

He pulls his questioning gaze back to me.

"I'm a writer, too," I tell him.

He looks extremely dubious.

"I know. I know," I say. "I'm in the Robotics Club and the Investment Club and the National Economics of Boredom Club. But actually, I want to study journalism."

He barks out a laugh. "So this newspaper thing, you're serious about that?"

"Yeah," I say earnestly, then I turn and face out the window, as though I'm no longer talking to him. As though I'm announcing it to the whole world. The whole universe. "I'm a writer. It's what I do."

He's quiet for a moment, like he's digesting this new piece of information. "I think I remember you saying something about that. About loving to write."

"On our date?" I ask, finally voicing the word that has seemed off-limits for so long.

"Yeah," he says quietly, looking away. "On our date."

I want to ask him for more details—Where did we go? What did we do? What else did we talk about?—but I know that admitting to him I don't remember any of it will only make things worse. So instead I just say, "We had fun, didn't we?"

He laughs to himself, like he's reliving a memory I will never be able to share with him. A moment in time that I will never experience. "Yeah. We did. I mean, I *thought* we did. I asked if you wanted to go out again and you said yes, but then . . ."

"I never responded to your texts," I finish, an ugly knot forming in my stomach. An ugly truth forming in my mind.

"Yeah," he replies distantly. Then, as though pulling himself out of a trance, he shakes his head and adds, "Anyway, I remember we talked about writing. How much we both loved it. I always wondered what happened to that. Why you never pursued it."

I glance down at my pristine Windsor uniform with the single dark streak on the skirt. Suddenly it feels like more than just a smudge of chocolate. It feels like a stain on my whole life.

I know the answer to his question. It's obvious to me now. This world—this choice, this place—it changed my priorities. It changed who I thought I was.

"Do you believe in the multiverse theory?" I ask him.

"Is that the one that states that every decision we make creates an entirely new universe?"

I nod. "Yeah."

"It's a cool theory, I guess."

"Do you ever wonder about all those other versions of you out there? What they're doing. Where they are. If they're happy. Is this really the best possible version of your life?"

He scoffs. "I will now. Thanks a lot. As if I didn't have enough to worry about."

"Sorry," I offer.

He smiles to let me know he was joking. "Do you? Think about that stuff?"

What if I had just broken up with Austin years earlier?

What if Dylan and I had gone on that second date?

What if I'd never applied to the Windsor Academy to begin with?

"Pretty much every day."

"And?" he prompts. "What have you come up with? Is this the best possible version of your life? Are all those other Kennedys Crushers, too?" I don't miss the sarcasm he places on my nickname.

I let out a sad little laugh. "The truth is, I'm not even sure this Kennedy is." Then I reach for the door handle and step onto the curb. "Thanks for the ride."

Then I Know What You're Thinking

By the time I reach the house, I'm completely soaked. Wool definitely wasn't meant to stave off moisture. I peel off my blazer and hang it in the laundry room before heading upstairs to my room.

I lie on my bed and scroll through Laney's SnipPic feed, staring at happy picture after happy picture, until I grow too disgusted and toss the phone aside. Then I pull out my laptop, carry it to my desk, and plop down in my chair, vowing to get some work done.

The computer opens to the same window that I closed it on: the log-in page for the test thief's anonymous email address.

I lean in and stare at the password hint.

I know what you're thinking . . .

Why does that sound so dang familiar? Why does it seem like the answer is on the tip of my tongue?

I know what you're thinking . . .

"I wish I knew what *you* were thinking!" I yell at the screen, maneuvering the mouse to close the window. But just before I click the little red X in the corner, words flood into my memory. Like water filling holes.

It's a deep, masculine voice that speaks them.

"I know what you're thinking . . . and you're right."

It's from Dad's favorite TV series. *Magnum, P.I.* It aired in the early eighties. Dad used to make us watch countless old reruns when we were growing up. Frankie and I always thought the show was lame. The effects were outdated, the pacing was slow, the dialogue was cheesy. And Tom Selleck, the actor who plays Magnum, always did this corny voice-over throughout each episode, narrating his reaction to what was happening on the screen.

Whenever he would get into some kind of trouble, he would always say to the audience . . .

"I know what you're thinking . . ." I repeat aloud, a chill running down my back.

Then, he'd usually follow it up with "And you're right." Or "But you're wrong."

That's the question of the day, isn't it?

The question of a lifetime.

Am I right? Or am I wrong?

I pull the laptop closer, click on the empty password field, and position my shaking hands on the keys. Then, slowly, I type: M-A-G-N-U-M.

The name of Dad's best camera. The name of Dad's favorite character on his favorite show.

His full name was Thomas Sullivan Magnum IV.

I gaze at the email address in the log-in box and feel my stomach clench.

TSM4@youmail.com

As my finger hovers over the Enter key, I close my eyes, not wanting to see it. Not wanting to admit what I'm fairly sure I'm going to have to admit in a matter of seconds.

I press down, holding my breath. When I open my eyes again, my heart starts to hammer and I feel sweat pooling on the back of my neck.

I'm staring at an inbox.

And not just any inbox.

The inbox of a thief.

There are a zillion questions banging on the doors of my mind, begging to be let in. I try to keep them all at bay as I skim the messages on the screen. Most of them are from gibberish email addresses, anonymous accounts like the one I set up. I spot my own sting email near the top of the list. It's still unread.

As are the next twenty messages.

I follow the trail of unread emails all the way down until I find the last message that was responded to. I click on it and read the familiar exchange.

The name of a class, the date of a test, the title of a book, forty-eight hours.

Emma is the book.

This was the money Dylan and I found in the library last week. But how long was it just sitting there? When did this exchange take place?

I glance up to the email heading and read the date stamped into the reply.

November 15.

The date instantly sets off a series of alarms in my head. Why does that date sound so important? Why does it seem to be engraved into my mind like an inscription?

I quickly grab my phone and search my calendar, but there's nothing out of the ordinary about that date. Just the usual. School, clubs, homework.

In this life, the voice quietly reminds me.

I'm starting to wonder if it's really a voice of reason.

Or a sign that I'm going crazy.

But once again, it's right.

My vision starts to shimmy. The walls of my bedroom start to shake, like they're getting ready to collapse around me. They're just waiting for someone to plunge down on the detonator.

November 15 was the date of my Columbia alumni interview. In my *other* life.

When I bombed it. When I didn't speak German. When I mistook the Kalahari Desert for New Mexico. When I flipped out and drove straight to the Windsor Academy to beg for my space back.

When I hit my head and woke up here.

November 15, the last time this inbox was checked, was the day I swapped lives with a girl named Kennedy "Crusher" Rhodes.

Then I Make a List and Check It Twice

It's a coincidence. It has to be. A lot of things happened on November 15. It doesn't mean anything. So what if I happened to know what the password hint meant? That was a lucky guess. A shot in the dark. I'm sure a lot of people watch *Magnum, P.I.* and would get that reference. I mean, it's like basically common knowledge.

It doesn't mean anything.

It doesn't mean anything.

It doesn't mean anything.

I skim through more returned emails, reading the same conversation over and over again. Another class. Another test date. Another book title.

I get out my notebook, flip to a blank page, and start writing them all down as a list.

History—November 22—Jane Eyre

Spanish—November 23—The Scarlet Letter

Algebra—November 21—Great Expectations

English—November 18—Don Quixote

I stop and stare at the list, tapping my pen against the page. There's something about those dates that feels so familiar.

November 22

November 23

November 21

Those are all dates that I was here. In this life. But what significance do they have?

I write them out in numeric format, trying to bring to flame the tiny spark that keeps flickering in the back of my mind.

11-22

11-23

11-21

I stare at the sequence for what feels like hours, until my vision blurs and my eyes water.

And then, as I'm blinking away the moisture, I notice it.

I remember where I've seen those numbers before.

With a lump in my throat, I go back to my first list and write each entry in shorthand next to the original.

History—November 22—Jane Eyre / HI-1122-JE

Spanish—November 23—The Scarlet Letter / SP-1123-TSL

Algebra—November 21—Great Expectations / AL-1121-GE

English—November 18—Don Quixote / EN-1118-DQ

I don't need to look at my phone to confirm what's in front of me. I don't need to reexamine those strange, coded tasks in my Windsor Achiever app to verify that they're an exact match.

I don't need to see anything else to know, without a shadow of a doubt, that it was me.

It was me the whole time.

Then I Become Her

I leap out of my chair and start pacing the length of my room as Dylan's cryptic, seemingly nonsensical words from the car come flooding back to me.

"For a while, I suspected . . . I mean, I'm in the library a lot. I see things. So I thought . . . Well, the point is, I was mistaken."

He knew. Or at the very least, he *thought* he knew. The whole time I was suspecting him, he was suspecting *me*. Was that why he was so interested in helping me? Because he was trying to prove his own theory? Because he was trying to prove I really was the brainwashed zombie he always thought I was?

". . . I was wrong about you."

No! I want to scream aloud as tears spring to my eyes. *You were right.*

He must have thought I was crazy. Investigating a story that he was so sure I was behind. He must have thought I really *had* cracked.

I continue pacing, struggling to take deep breaths. To calm the deafening racket in my head. Then, as I reach the end of my room and turn around, my gaze lands on my desk. On the bottom drawer.

I run over to it and, with shaking hands, yank open the drawer.

There it is. The big, black monstrosity. Sitting there like the heavy stone that's settled in to the pit of my stomach.

I kneel down next to the drawer and run my fingertips over the smooth metal surface of the box, stopping when I reach the four-digit combination lock.

It's time to crack this code. It's time to solve this mystery once and for all.

Again, I try every combination I can think of. My birthday, Dad's birthday, Mom's birthday, Frankie's birthday. I even look through my phone to find Sequoia's birthday and try that, too. Nothing works.

How long would it take to try *every* possible combination?

I do a quick calculation in my head. There are 10,000 combinations. If I can input one every ten seconds, I'd be done in . . .

Just over twenty-seven hours.

I collapse onto my back with a sigh and stare at the ceiling. There's got to be a better way.

Think, Kennedy. THINK.

She's the same person as you. We share the same brain. The same first fourteen years of our lives. You cracked her email password, you can crack this, too.

What was important to her?

What was important to *me*?

Dad. Mom. Frankie. But I tried all of those.

What else?

The newspaper. That was important to me. But not to her. Other Me never had a chance to cultivate that passion. She never had the opportunity to feel the thrill of commanding a room full of writers. Of putting an issue to bed after fifty straight hours of reading and rereading and proofing and last-minute cuts and last-*last*-minute additions. Of handing over a flash drive to the printer like she was handing over her whole life.

She never got to feel the satisfaction of holding that Spartan Press Award in her hand. Of framing that prized issue and hanging it on her wall.

My gaze drifts up to the place where those frames used to hang. I would look at them every day. For strength. For courage. For motivation. On good days and bad days. They were my reminders that no matter what happened, no matter what regrets lived in my heart, something was good.

Life was good.

That life was good.

And now, as I stare at the single frame hanging in their place—my acceptance letter to Windsor—I wonder if life can ever be good again.

Tears blur my vision as I gaze up at the letter. At those familiar words that I memorized oh so long ago.

Dear Ms. Rhodes,
Congratulations! It is on this date, May 12, that we are
pleased to inform you . . .

On this date, May 12.

That was the day that my life split into two directions. Where the choice was offered to me. Where I was so convinced that I took the wrong turn.

That I chose poorly.

But as I lie here on the floor with a lockbox full of dark secrets, I wonder which way was really the wrong turn. I wonder if the mistake that haunted me for more than three years wasn't a mistake at all. If maybe, it was the best decision I ever made.

But what did Other Me think? What has been going through *her* head for the past three and a half years? Did she have regrets about that exact same moment in time? Did she think back to that day she got the letter and wish she had taken another path? Did she look at her deathly reflection in the mirror every morning and wonder how her life could have been different?

On this date, May 12 . . .

Two roads diverge.

On this date, May 12 . . .

I choose Austin.

On this date, May 12 . . .

I choose Windsor.

May 12.

I bolt upright and glance at the black box next to me. The keeper of my secrets. The truth I didn't want anyone to see.

On this date, May 12 . . .

I become who I am.

With shaking, uneven fingers, I dial in the combination.

0512

Then, somewhere in the farthest dark corner of every single universe, I hear a faint *click*.

Then I Open Pandora's Box

The money pours out like a gushing fountain. Piles and piles of hundred-dollar bills. They've been stuffed to the brim inside this box. They've been hidden from sight like a skeleton in a closet.

I don't bother counting. I don't even want to know how much is here. How deep the secret goes.

It's enough to see it.

It's enough to feel the cash slithering around my ankles like a swarm of snakes. I jump to my feet and back away. Afraid of being bitten. Afraid of being infected. Afraid of my very existence.

I don't understand.

My life was perfect. I was at the top of my class. I was a member of too many clubs to even keep track of. I raised thousands and thousands of dollars for the school. I was a shoo-in for Columbia. Why on earth would I risk it all?

I can't, I decide in one sweeping emotion. *I can't risk it all.*

I need to shut this down. I need to erase all the evidence, pretend it never happened, go on with my life. I need to get into Columbia, become a rock star journalist, live a fulfilling life. That's how I'll fix this.

Not by getting caught and suspended, ruining my future, and maybe even ending up in juvie.

No. Not gonna happen.

It wasn't me who did this. It was *her*. She's the culprit. The thief. The perp. Whatever Other Me did was her problem. Not mine. And I won't take the fall for her mistakes.

I run to my bedroom door and turn the lock. Then I get to work. I start by deleting both of the anonymous email accounts (TSM4@youmail.com and the one I set up last week). Then I clear my cache and erase my browsing history. I rip out all my notes from my notebook, light a match, and burn them in the shower, washing away the ash with a blast of cold water. I stuff the cash back into the box and lock it. When I get to school tomorrow, I'm going to have to search through every book on that reading list and get rid of any money that's still hidden in them.

There won't be any front-page story or any school newspaper. That's gone. Not many people knew I was working on it anyway. Mr. Fitz turned down my request. For all he knows, I took his advice to heart and didn't pursue it further.

The only loose end is Dylan.

The person who suspected me from the very beginning.

I grab my phone, find his contact information in the Windsor Achiever app, and tap out two text messages to him, choosing my words carefully.

Me: Looks like I've hit another dead end.
Me: Couldn't figure out the password. Got locked out. Oh, well.

I rap my fingers anxiously against the phone as I wait for him to respond. A few seconds later, a message appears.

Dylan: Don't give up! We can figure this out. The perp shall pay!

I feel the knot in my stomach twist.

Me: No. It's over. I'm dropping the story. Fitz was right. I don't have time. I need to focus on my other commitments.

I sigh and press Send. His response is exactly as I expected.

Dylan: I thought you were braver than to listen to Fitz.

He thinks I'm a coward. He thinks I really am a brainless zombie. But I don't care. If it keeps him off my back, I can live with that.

Getting kicked out of school for a crime I didn't commit? That I *can't* live with.

Me: I guess you were wrong.

I power down my phone before he can respond and toss it onto my bed.

I'll just have to lie low. Keep my head down. Do my work. Follow the rules. Be a good Windsor student. Eventually the administration will realize that the test stealing has stopped and maybe—hopefully—they'll just let it go. Maybe— *hopefully*—everything will return to normal. And I can go on with my life and forget this ever happened.

I navigate through the folders on my computer until I find the document where I typed up my story notes. Without a second thought, I delete it. Then I click on the little trash icon in the corner of my screen. Other Me tried her hardest to screw up our lives. She tried to take me down with her. But I won't let her.

It's time to take out the garbage. It's time to erase Other Me forever.

I hover the pointer over the Empty Trash button, sucking in a huge, courageous breath. But before I click, I notice something out of the corner of my eye.

Another file.

Kennedy Rhodes—Personal Essay—Version 1

I remember seeing that before. When I was revising my PE for Fitz's class. Other Me must have deleted it but then forgot to empty the trash.

I tell myself to let it go. Erase it all and move on. But some invisible force is tugging on my finger. Call it curiosity. Call it intuition. Call it whatever you want.

But I open the document.

I read what's inside.

Then I collapse into tears.

The Choices That Define Us—First Draft

Kennedy Rhodes

AP Language Arts, Period 7

Mr. Fitz

The topic of this personal essay is "The choices that define us." But the topic itself is a flawed one. Or, at the very least, incomplete. Choices don't just define *us*. They define everything around us. When we make a decision, we don't only decide for ourselves, we unknowingly decide for every soul connected to us. It's impossible to do anything without affecting the world around you.

That's what makes choices so significant. And also what makes them so destructive.

Three and a half years ago, I was faced with such a decision when I received my acceptance letter to the Windsor Academy. And now, three and a half years later, from the outside, it would appear that I made the right choice. I'm currently ranked number one in my class. I am liked and respected by my peers. I am single-handedly responsible for raising a total of more than a quarter of a million dollars for the school that I chose.

But that's the thing about the outside. It doesn't tell the whole story. It conceals. It hides. It *lies*.

Underneath, I feel like a shell of a person. I'm tired. I'm empty. I'm plagued by guilt.

Because, as it turns out, my choice wasn't just about me. Perhaps it started out that way. In that single decisive moment—when I signed my name on the acceptance letter, when I licked the envelope, affixed the stamp, dropped it in the mailbox—perhaps then, for just a brief flash of an instant, it was all mine. It was a choice that belonged solely to me.

But then the moment was over. The choice grew. It expanded. It multiplied and poisoned like a plague. It affected people outside of just me.

People like my dad, who gave up on his dream of becoming a photographer and sold out for a high-paying corporate job, just so he could afford the Windsor Academy's exorbitant tuition.

People like my mom, who watched her husband lose his identity, sell his soul, and then get farther and farther away from us because of it. Until he felt like a ghost in our house.

And that's what led me to my next life-defining decision. The one I made six months ago when I installed a piece of software on the school server that logged every keystroke, every username, and every password of every faculty member. When I began stealing exams and selling them to students for a price.

It was the only way I could think to pay my parents back. For everything they gave up. For everything I stole from them. Because I'm selfish. Because choices are selfish.

But then, that choice, too, started to grow and infect and spread its poison. To people like Lucinda Wallace, my best friend, who is now expelled. Because of me.

In the end, there is no escape. No matter what you do, no matter what you choose, someone suffers.

Our choices don't define only us. They define everyone around us. They are powerful, evil things full of a dark, dark magic. They ruin lives. They wreak havoc on worlds. They turn good people into villains. Innocent people into victims. And promising students into criminals.

Some people weren't meant to make life-altering decisions. Some people simply can't handle that much power.

Some people just wish they could go back and do it all over again.

Then I Try to Go Back

A cold chill blows through my room, making me shiver. Freezing the tears on my cheeks. Turning my whole world into an endless ice age.

During all of those years I dreamed of going to Windsor, and pored over the online catalogs and obsessed over the pictures of green grass, I never even considered the price. How much it costs to keep that grass so dang green.

I never considered what it would do to my family. But now the cold, hard truth is written right in front of me. In an essay far too personal to be read by anyone else. In a confession my other self never had the courage to turn in.

It's impossible to ignore now.

Impossible to deny.

My dad traded his dream for mine.

He took that job to pay my tuition. He took that job to make sure I could have everything I always wanted. Now, instead of doing what he loves, he's doing something he hates. He gave up on his passion. His big project. The one that would have eventually landed him a sold-out gallery show. But he'll never know that because he'll never get there.

I erased it all. I cut and pasted it right out of his life.

He was on his way to something huge. He was going places. He was finally on the precipice of success and I took it away. All because I wanted to go to some fancy school where they wear fancy uniforms and sit in fancy classrooms and track their tasks on fancy apps.

Is that what's been keeping her up at night? Other Me? Is that why she has five different kinds of sleeping pills? Is that why her reflection looks like she's just survived the apocalypse?

The guilt was eating her alive.

And I can already feel it doing the same to me.

I stuff the cash box back into my bottom drawer, unlock my bedroom door, and dash into the hallway.

"I need to go back!" I cry as I barge into Frankie's room.

He's sitting on his bed, drawing. "What?"

"I don't want to be in this life anymore. I want to go back. I don't want to be her. I want to be me again. I choose my other life. I choose Austin and Southwest High and locker doors that fall off and libraries with mysteriously missing books. I choose all of it. Please. Tell me how to get back."

Frankie studies me for a long, agonizing moment before setting his drawing pad aside. "Kennedy," he says in a serious tone. "It doesn't work that way. You can't just *go* back."

"Sure you can!" I argue, tears rolling down my cheeks. "You said something about an overlap. The exact same thing happening at the exact same time in two different universes. You said that's how I got here. By hitting my head on the stairs in both lives. So let's create another one of those."

Frankie looks at me like I'm crazy. "You can't *create* an overlap."

"Why not?"

"Because," Frankie says, fumbling for words, "you just can't! It's not like a special order at McDonald's. I'll take one overlap, hold the pickles. For starters, I'm not even one-hundred-percent certain that's *how* you got here. It's a theory. *One* theory. And even if it *were* true, it was a fluke. A miracle. I mean, the odds of you and one of your other selves being in the exact same place, doing the exact same thing, at the exact same instant are like billions to one. Even if I'm right, even if that *is* how you got here, there's no way of *making* it happen. It's like predicting where lightning will strike . . . twice!"

I wilt in defeat. "So you're saying I'm stuck here? Forever?"

Frankie offers me a waxen smile. "I'm saying it's a high statistical probability."

Then I Visit Two Best Friends

"Mom!" I call out, swatting tears from my face as I stagger down the stairs. "I'm taking your car!"

I don't wait for permission or acknowledgment. I grab the keys and go. I have to get out of here. Away from that money. Those emails. That reflection in the mirror.

It's still raining when I back out of the garage. I drive straight to Sequoia's house and sprint for the front door. I need to talk to someone. Someone who gets it. Gets the pressure. Gets the stress.

Gets Windsor.

I ring the doorbell and she answers a few seconds later wearing her pajamas. I can tell from the crease between her eyebrows that she's been staring at her computer screen for hours. Studying. Always studying. Always trying to maintain that 89 percent Ivy League acceptance rate they've been drilling into us since day one.

"Crap!" Sequoia swears, gaping at my face. "What happened to you?"

It's then I realize how horrible I must look. With my

tearstained cheeks, messy hair, and chocolate cream still on my uniform.

"I think I'm having a meltdown."

She nods rapidly. "Hold on. I'll get the Xanax."

"No," I say, grabbing her arm. "I don't need a Xanax or a sleeping pill. I just need to talk to someone. I did something horrible. And I don't know what to do or how to fix it."

Sequoia stares at me like she doesn't understand a word I'm saying. And I can't blame her. I'm rambling so fast and more tears are streaming down my face and sobs are cutting off my words.

"I was with Dylan. In the library. And then Peabody's and we were trying to figure out the whole test-stealing thing and then—"

"Stop," Sequoia says, in the most forceful tone I've ever heard come out of her mouth. "Stop talking right now. I can't do this. I can't hear this. I can't be implicated. Not when early decision letters are being sent out next week!"

"Sequoia," I beg. "Please. Can you stop being a Windsor Academy student for one second and just be my friend?"

She holds her hands over her ears, blocking out the sound of my voice. "No. I'm sorry. I can't."

Then she slams the door. And I'm left crying alone in the rain, feeling even emptier than I did before.

I can't believe she would close the door on me like that. I can't believe she would just shut me out when I needed her the most.

She's supposed to be my friend!

Or maybe we never really were friends. Maybe we were just

horses in the same race, keeping each other company while we sprinted for the finish line. Always secretly knowing that, in the end, only one of us could win.

I wander back to my car and start the engine. I'm freezing and shivering so I blast the heat, but it doesn't seem to make any difference. The cold is coming from somewhere inside me. Somewhere I fear will never be warm again.

I shift into Drive and pull away from the curb. I don't even know where I'm going until I find myself parked in front of Laney's house.

I stare out the window at the darkened, two-story brick home. The porch light is on, illuminating the familiar red door that I've knocked on so many times. I know which window is hers. It's the second floor, last one on the right. I spent so many nights in that bedroom. Sleeping on her blow-up air mattress, talking until the wee hours of the morning, giggling about everything under the sun.

Laney would know what to say to me right now. Laney would know how to make everything feel survivable. She could make Everest look climbable. The entire Atlantic Ocean look swimmable. The farthest star in the farthest galaxy look like nothing but a plane ride away.

That's what she did. She turned mountains into molehills. She talked me down from so many ledges. She was my life jacket.

And without her, I drowned.

The front door opens a moment later and Laney exits holding an umbrella. She starts skipping toward my car, like she's been waiting for me. Like she always used to do when I would pick her up to go to school or to the movies or out for a late-night snack. She would always skip out her front door like a little kid.

And for a brief second, I dare to think that maybe Frankie was wrong. Maybe it's not impossible to create an overlap. Maybe I just did it. Simply by driving here. Maybe somewhere in a far-away universe, in another version of this life, I'm doing the exact same thing. I'm here to pick up my best friend on a Monday night and we're going to spend the rest of the night laughing and goofing around and being Laney and Kennedy again.

But that brief moment comes to a crashing halt when Laney suddenly stops in the middle of her front lawn and tilts her head to the side, studying my car in the limited light. Her expression quickly turns from one of excitement to one of trepidation and she takes a few steps back to the safety of her front porch.

I'm not who she was expecting, I realize with a twist of my stomach.

I'm not Austin.

I watch as she deliberates whether or not to go back inside or wait on the porch. She continues to eye my car warily, wondering what this stranger is doing parked at her curb with the motor running.

Finally, she makes a decision. She turns toward the front door and inserts her key in the lock.

I kill the engine and hop out.

"Laney!" I call.

She stiffens and turns, squinting through the darkness. I step into the light of the streetlamp so she can see that I'm harmless. I'm just a girl.

A girl she once knew. But doesn't anymore.

"Hi," she says tentatively. I know that inflection in her voice. She's trying to fight her incessant instinct to be polite. Laney never had a mean bone in her body. She was the least confrontational person I knew. She had a hard time saying no to people. It's how she always got roped into feeding dogs and watering plants and bringing in the mail for all her neighbors when they went on vacation.

She can't even be unkind to a stranger who pulls up to her curb at eight o'clock at night and calls her by name.

Because that's Laney.

She would never hurt anyone. Least of all me.

As I stare at her face lit by the porch lights of her house, I get a sudden flashback to that night in Austin's basement. To the look in her eyes when she saw how much pain she had caused me. When I asked her how long it had been going on and she bravely told me the truth, even though it was like releasing an arrow aimed straight for my heart.

"I never wanted to hurt you."

And now, on this strange moonless night, as I stand in the shambles of my perfect life, suddenly I believe her. I know she was telling the truth.

I know she didn't fall in love with Austin out of spite or jealousy or malice. She just fell in love with him. Like she fell in love with him in this life, too.

They were always the ones meant to be together.

It was never Austin and me. It was always them. I was just the conduit. And then, I was just the obstacle.

"Do I know you?" Laney asks from her front porch, and it's not until then that I realize I've been standing here staring at her like a creepy stalker.

Yes! I want to scream. You know me! I'm your best friend! We do everything together. We brought a newspaper back from the brink of death. We won three Spartan Press Awards. You were my rock and my balloon. You lifted me up and kept me grounded. And I never realized how little I gave back to you. How long you stood in my shadow without ever complaining about the cold. You betrayed me but I betrayed you, too. Because I was never the friend to you that you were to me. You were one of the best things about my life and I gave it all up. I traded it in because I thought this would be better. I thought I would be better. But I'm not better without you. I'm worse.

Obviously, however, I don't say any of those things. They're words that have no meaning. At least not to her. They will stay where they are forever. Trapped in my mind as echoes of the past.

Instead, I say, "No. Sorry. I must have the wrong house."

I turn back to my car and open the door. Laney watches me. No longer with concern, now with genuine curiosity. I glance back at her one last time. Then in a whisper, I add, "But I forgive you. And I hope you can forgive me, too."

Then I Run Away from It All

"*The captain has turned on the fasten-seat-belt sign,* indicating our initial descent into New York's LaGuardia Airport. Please return to your seats and fasten your seat belts for the remainder of the flight."

I watch the city far below appear through a blanket of clouds. I already feel better. I can already breathe easier. See more clearly. Think without all that noise in my head.

As soon as I got back from Laney's house last night, I made a decision. I figured out what to do with the money in the lockbox.

I used it to get as far away from the Windsor Academy as possible.

When I woke up this morning, I called a cab to the airport, I bought a plane ticket, and I left. I didn't tell anyone I was going. I figured it wouldn't take long for the school to call my mom and my mom to call me. I'll explain everything to her then. If I can even explain it.

When we land, I grab the small bag that I packed and my winter coat and follow the stream of people eager to get back on solid ground. I found the name of my dad's hotel in an email on my phone from a few weeks back. When he first started the job for Cuddles Diapers.

He won't be done with work until much later in the day, so I direct the cabdriver to Columbia University.

He drops me off at the entrance on Broadway, between the Miller Theatre and the journalism building. I immediately feel the chill as a gust of wind blows across my face. I zip my coat up to the top, burying my face behind the nylon fabric.

I stick my hands in my pockets and walk down 116th Street toward the iconic Low Memorial Library where the famous *Alma Mater* bronze statue of Athena sits, welcoming you to the school with her open arms.

As with Windsor, I visited Columbia University once and immediately knew I wanted to go here. The campus, the buildings, the leaves, they called to me. They sang enchanting melodies to my soul. Later, in high school, when I found out they had one of the best journalism programs in the country, my resolve solidified.

It was Columbia or bust.

I didn't even want to apply to any safety schools, but my dad made me. He said you should always have a backup plan. I said I didn't need one. I was going to Columbia. I was so certain.

I was so certain about so many things.

As I stand in front of the grand columned building and stare up at the statue of Athena, I try to imagine what it would feel like to stand here as a student. A freshman on her first day of class. With my entire future laid out ahead of me. Nothing but promise and possibilities.

I wonder if Other Me felt that way on her first day at the Windsor Academy. The first time she drove through those black iron gates and ascended the grand staircase of Royce Hall. She must have. There must have been a time when she was happy. When she thought she had everything she always wanted.

I wonder how long that lasted. How many days, weeks, months did it take for her to realize her happiness had soured? How long was it before she realized that she was the frog in the pot and the water had boiled around her?

As I walk alongside the snow-covered lawns of the beautiful city campus, I think about that personal essay I found on my laptop. The *first* version. The one Other Me wrote and deleted. Those pages were so saturated with sorrow. And bitterness. And regret. The Windsor Academy had turned her into someone she didn't recognize anymore. A shadow of the girl she thought she was.

And I know exactly why she never turned it in.

It's the same reason I never broke up with Austin.

Three and a half years passed, and somewhere deep down, I knew we weren't right for each other. I knew we would never last. But I wanted to believe I had made the right decision in choosing him. I wanted to believe that I had followed my heart and that my heart would never mislead me.

And so did she.

If she had turned in that essay—if she had admitted she was unhappy and her world was flawed and her family was falling apart—she would have invalidated her entire life. Her entire existence. It would have confirmed what she didn't want to admit: that she had made the wrong choice.

But in the end, both choices came with their own varieties of heartbreak and regret. Neither life was perfect. Neither path was free of obstacles.

Which means maybe the problem was never the choice.

Maybe it was me.

I stop and sit on a park bench, bristling against the cold. I remove my phone from my bag and scroll through my SnipPic feed, staring at the countless pictures of my so-called perfect life. Me and Sequoia studying in the student union, me and Sequoia dressed to the nines at the fund-raising gala. Me and Sequoia with the wind blowing through our hair, smiling in front of the steps of Royce Hall.

Up until a few weeks ago, I was so certain about so many things. My future. My past. And all the mistakes I had made in between. I was so certain I knew what I wanted and exactly how to get it. But now I'm not certain of anything anymore. And I wonder if I ever will be again.

I always thought certainty was one of my biggest strengths. A character trait I could lay claim to and proudly write on a college application in between "meticulous" and "strong leader."

But maybe certainty is more of a weakness. A flaw. A limitation. After all, when you're so absolutely certain about what you want—about the life you are meant to lead—you miss out on everything else that's out there. Every other possible happiness.

Every other potential road that could have led you exactly where you're supposed to go.

Instead, you end up here.

Cold and confused. Sitting alone in the middle of a city you don't know. Haunted by a version of yourself you don't recognize. Surrounded by a place you thought you could call home.

Then My Father Grows Up

When I show up at the hotel later that night and knock on room 717, I almost don't recognize my own father when he opens the door. His clothes are all wrong. He used to wear ratty jeans with holes and T-shirts with funny photographer puns on them like "Warning: At Any Time I May Snap!" Now he's wearing a collared shirt and slacks. I didn't even know my father *owned* a pair of slacks.

But it isn't even his attire that most shocks me. His skin looks ashen and almost thirsty. His hair is graying at the temples. And there's something about his eyes that sends a chill through me, followed by another wave of guilt.

This life, this *choice.* It's changed him. In more ways than I even realized.

It takes a long time to convince my dad not to put me right back on a flight home. It takes even longer for my mom to stop screaming at me on the other end of the phone. But eventually, things settle down and the world seems somewhat at peace again.

I told my dad that I needed a break from school. That it was just getting to be too much. I didn't elaborate beyond that.

Maybe he could see it in the shadows under my eyes, or hear it in the break in my voice, but he eventually agreed to let me stay for a few days, on the condition that I come to work with him tomorrow so he can keep an eye on me.

I want to argue that I'm eighteen years old now. I don't need anyone to keep an eye on me. But I decide not to press my luck.

He calls for a rollaway bed to be brought to his hotel room. I order room service. And we both sit in our pajamas eating pasta and watching episodes of *Magnum, P.I.* on Dad's iPad.

The next day I go to the set of his photo shoot and Dad puts me to work as his photographer's assistant. I run around swapping cameras, bringing him lenses, fixing stray hairs on the heads of babies, ordering lunch. It's nice to feel busy without all the pressure. It doesn't erase any of my problems, but it does make them fade into the background for a few hours.

After a long day, Dad and I return to the hotel for another room service dinner.

"Is this what your life is like now?" I ask after we've eaten. I'm sitting on my rollaway bed, playing a game on Dad's iPad.

Dad is propped up on his bed with his laptop, reviewing pictures from today's shoot and marking the ones he likes. His face is so serious as he clicks through page after page of the same stupid baby. Like the fate of the world rests on this one diaper ad.

"Is what my life now?" he asks without looking up.

"Room service and twelve-hour shifts with toddlers?"

He cracks a smile. "Pretty glamorous, huh?"

For just a flicker of a moment, I see a glimpse of old Dad.

The one who lives in a universe far, far away. The one who makes waffles with chocolate chips in them on special days. The one who wakes me up every morning by singing horribly off-key.

The one whose eyes, close up, look like the whole world.

But then, just as fast as it came, the moment is gone. His smile fades. His jaw tightens. He goes back to sorting through photographs.

"Dad?" I ask, setting down the iPad.

"Hmm?"

"Do you ever take pictures of people's eyes anymore?"

"Eyes?" he asks, his brow furrowing. Then, a moment later, recognition flashes over his face and he looks up at me, leaning back against the headboard. "Oh, right. The eyes. God, I haven't thought about those in a long time."

"You called the project Portals," I remind him.

He chuckles. "That's right. Your mom's eyes were always my favorite."

"The sunflowers."

He smiles, looking nostalgic as he stares off into the distance. "Yeah. The sunflowers." Then, like he's silently scolding himself for getting distracted, his wistful expression vanishes and he goes back to work.

"So you don't take those pictures anymore?" I confirm. "I mean, not even as a hobby?"

He laughs like this is the funniest thing he's heard in a while. "Yeah, in all my spare time between photographing diapers and bottles of shampoo."

"But the eyes were your passion. You lived for those photographs. They were good. And maybe, if you had kept at it, they would have taken you somewhere amazing."

Dad studies me for a while, like he's trying to read between my words. Finally, he sighs and says, "Sometimes we have to do things we don't want to do. Give up on things we love to allow other things to flourish. Sometimes our responsibilities and obligations outweigh our silly whims and childish dreams."

Tears well in my eyes at the reminder of what Dad gave up for me. At the sight of this man—this *stranger* in a hotel room—who bears so little resemblance to my father. My dad is the kind of person who lives for silly whims and childish dreams. He embodies them. He makes adulthood look like an amusement park. Or at least he *did*.

In another life.

But this person sitting on that bed has none of that. The child in him has been stamped out long ago. I can see that now. He's lost his whimsy. He's lost the thing that makes him . . .

Dad.

I watch him for a long time, taking in his studious expression, wondering where the manchild inside is hiding. Is he even still in there? Or is he gone for good?

I listen to the quiet *click, click, click* of his selection process for a few moments, then I ask, "Will you take a picture of *my* eyes?"

The clicking halts. "What? Now?"

I shrug. "Why not?"

"Because I'm busy, Kennedy," he says, a slight edge to his voice. "And because I don't do that anymore."

"Please," I say quietly. Urgently. It's enough to make my dad look up.

"Why?" he asks.

"I . . ." I start to say, my voice cracking. "I can't explain. I just really need you to do this for me."

Dad studies me for a few seconds, his brow pinched together to form a lopsided question mark between his eyes. Then he places his laptop on the bed next to him and grabs Magnum from the nightstand.

"C'mon," he says, standing up and heading toward the bathroom. "This is where we'll get the best light."

Then I Grow Up

Thirty minutes later, I'm staring into an endless icy blue tundra. At least that's what it looks like to me. My dad has taken several pictures of both my eyes and blown them up until all that's visible on the screen are interwoven threads of blue and white. Like the snow-covered branches of the trees on the Columbia campus.

I click through the shots, leaning forward and back and tilting my head from side to side, trying to see the images from every angle. But the longer I gaze at the pixels, the more certain I am that there's been some mistake.

"This isn't it," I determine.

My dad leans over my shoulder to get a clearer view. "What do you mean, this isn't it?"

"There's been a mix-up. These aren't my eyes."

He laughs. "Of course they're your eyes. I don't have any other eyes on this computer."

I turn back to the screen and examine the pictures again. Is it the sleep deprivation? Is it all the stress? This can't be my eye.

It's too different. Where are the spiderwebs? Where's the good luck my Dad always put his faith in?

"But . . ." I start to argue, my voice lacking conviction. "They've changed."

"Of course, they've changed. The last time I photographed your eyes you were only thirteen. Eyes change. Just like faces."

No, I want to argue. *You photographed my eye a month ago. For your gallery show. There were spiderwebs there. There was magic there. You said so yourself.*

This eye has no magic. There is no life in these strands. No shimmering energy. This eye looks . . .

Dead.

Frozen over.

Broken.

I close the laptop screen, unable to look at it anymore. It reminds me too much of what I've lost. What I fear I'll never be able to get back. I rise from the desk chair and walk back over to my little rollaway bed. I sit down and pull my legs up to my chin, wrapping my arms tightly around them.

"I'm sorry," Dad offers. "I didn't mean to upset you. You said—"

"I know," I interrupt him. "It's fine. I just . . ."

Didn't expect to see what I saw.

Didn't expect to feel what I feel.

Didn't expect any of this . . .

"Do you ever think about quitting your job and going back to the Portals project?" I ask.

Dad chuckles, but it's an empty, soulless sound that makes me shiver. He grabs the laptop from the desk and brings it back to his bed. "No."

"Why not? Don't you ever wonder where another path could have led you? What choices could have resulted in different outcomes?"

"The Portals project was a silly dream. It would never have led to anything."

"Maybe it would!" I shoot back, feeling tears of frustration spring to my eyes. I have to make him see. I have to make him realize that he made the wrong choice. He never should have given up on his dream because of me. If I can't fix my own mistakes, then at least I can try to fix his. "You don't know. Maybe it would have been huge!"

"Kennedy," he says, softly but urgently. "We make our choices and we have to live with them."

He sits down, props his feet back up, and reopens the laptop. My own lifeless zombie eye instantly pins me with an accusing stare.

I avert my gaze so he can't see my tears, but the crack in my voice gives me away. "I know you gave it up for me," I whisper. "I know you only took the job so I could go to Windsor."

He sucks in a breath as he looks over at me, his face pale. He struggles to say something—the *right* thing—but in the end he goes with "I always had a feeling that you knew."

I'm crying now. But I don't care. I turn to him. I confront him with my tears. "Why didn't you just tell me?"

"Your mom and I decided not to. We didn't want to burden

you with the financial stuff. I always thought you deserved to know, though."

"What if I gave it up?" I fire back before I can think of what I'm saying. But as soon as the question is out of my mouth, I know it's what I want to do. What I *have* to do. Dad gave up everything for me. It's time I return the favor. "I'll quit the Windsor Academy. I'll do it tomorrow. You won't have to pay the tuition anymore. You won't have to work this job. You can do whatever you want. You can—"

"You're not quitting Windsor," he says sternly. "Stop talking nonsense. You have a little more than a semester left. I don't know what's been going on at school. Obviously something or you wouldn't be here. I realize you're probably under a lot of stress, but you can't quit now. Not when you're this close to the finish line."

The finish line.

It's always about the finish line.

"I have to," I whisper. "I've made too many mistakes. I can't go back."

Dad laughs softly. "Kennedy, mistakes are a dime a dozen. Everyone makes them. Not all of your choices can be winners. But you make the most of the outcome. You learn what you need to learn and you move on. Some mistakes *need* to be made. So we can teach ourselves how to get back up. You're not a quitter. That's one of your best qualities. You see things through. To the very end."

A chill runs through me. He's right. I do follow through. That's always been one of my strengths. But maybe I don't do it for the right reasons. Maybe I can't let go because letting go would be the same as admitting I'm wrong. So I keep digging myself in deeper and deeper to avoid facing the fact that I made the wrong choice.

But Dad *did* make the wrong choice. I'm certain of it.

"Neither are you!" I reply, my voice rising much higher than I anticipated. "You were never a quitter. But you gave up on your dream, Dad. You could have been something amazing but you quit. For me. I can't live with myself knowing you did that. I can't. You have to take it back. You have to!"

My final words are strangled in sobs. The tears are falling so fast, I fear I might drown in them. Dad rushes over, sits down on my bed, and pulls me into his arms. I collapse against his chest and cry like I used to do when I was a little girl. When all I needed to stave off the nightmares was my dad's strong, unrelenting arms.

But it's going to take a lot more than a hug to stave off this nightmare. It's going to take a miracle.

"I don't regret anything," Dad whispers into my ear. "I promise."

I shake my head, most likely leaving unsightly smudges on his white undershirt. "But your job," I mumble. "You hate your job. You must regret taking it."

"Never," he says, with such certainty it almost startles me. I lift my head and look at him through my blurry, tear-filled eyes.

He laughs and reaches out to wipe my face. "Look what it did for you! You are at one of the best schools in the country.

You've practically been accepted to Columbia. How could I ever regret that? I'm so proud of you."

I open my mouth to speak, but no words come out. How can I tell him? How can I possibly admit that I wasted it all? I can't. I won't. I refuse.

Dad offers me an encouraging smile. "Look. Jeffrey and Associates might be how I make money but it's not my *job*. My job, first and foremost, is being your dad. I made that choice eighteen years ago when I left my 'edgy phase' behind and decided to be a husband and a father. It was the best choice I ever made. Every parent makes the decision to put someone else's life first when they have children. My job is providing for you and Frankie and giving you guys everything you want. However I can. And you know what?" He reaches out and catches a stray tear that rolls down my cheek. "I did that. I've succeeded. So, no, I regret nothing."

I sit there for a moment, letting his words sink in, letting my tears dry a little. And then I ask, "Remember when I used to write captions for you?"

He smiles. "Of course. You were always a great writer." He nudges his chin toward his open laptop on the bed. "What would you caption this?"

I wipe my nose and glance at the screen. At the lifeless eye that stares back at me. I think about all the things those eyes have witnessed. All the late nights of homework and staring at computers and lying awake feeling the strain of too little sleep. I think about how those eyes have watched my father leave and my mother struggle to cope. They've watched one friend fall apart while the other fought so hard to keep it together. I think about Dylan and how he saw something in those eyes that I couldn't see until right now.

But mostly, I think about the girl behind those eyes.

The girl who gambled with her future and lost.

The girl who thought she had everything she always wanted until she realized it was an illusion.

She's not me. She's some other me.

And yet somehow we are connected. Somehow we are the same. It was our same mind that got us here. It was our mutual decisions that led us down this path. It was both of our hands that dug this hole. And now we need our combined strengths to get us out.

I sniffle and look back at my dad. "I would call it 'Resurrection.'"

Then I Make Another Choice

I click Print on my laptop and watch the crisp sheets of paper appear on the printer tray. I grab the stack, tap the pages against the table, and staple them together. I spent the entire flight home from New York and the rest of the night working on the final draft of my personal essay and now it's ready.

It finally feels personal. It finally feels like the truth.

It's Friday and school let out a few minutes ago. I've been waiting all day to turn this in. I stand up from the small computer bay in the Sanderson-Ruiz Library and glance around the beautiful building. I don't know how many times I scoured the Internet for pictures of this place. I don't know how many times I lay in bed thinking about what it would feel like to be here. But now I see the truth behind the glossy exterior. I see the true cost of this building. These books. This privilege.

It's a price I'm not willing to pay anymore.

I'm just about to start for the door when I see Dylan. He looks like he's searching for something. When he spots me, he smiles and heads my way.

I hurriedly stuff my laptop into my bag and start for the door.

I don't want to talk to him right now. I can't be distracted from what I'm about to do.

I bolt outside, into the cool December air. It's barely four o'clock and the sun is already setting, coloring the campus in the most amazing yellow-pink glow.

"Hey! Kennedy!" I hear Dylan call from behind me. "Wait up!"

I don't slow. I curve around Waldorf Pond and head for Royce Hall. This paper is burning a hole in my hand. I need to get rid of it. I need to be done with this.

Dylan finally catches up with me at Bellum Hall. He falls into step beside me. "I've been looking for you all day. Where have you been?"

Hiding is the answer that comes to mind. "Working" is the answer I give.

The truth is I've been avoiding everyone today. I went to class. I kept my head down and my mouth shut. One last day, I kept telling myself. I just have to get through this one last day and then it will all be over. I'll turn in my paper. Fitz will read it. He'll tell the dean. She'll call my parents. Expulsion papers will be drawn up and that will be it.

"Look," he says, somewhat breathless from trying to keep up, "I've been thinking all week. About your story. And I think I found another way in."

"I told you," I say curtly. "There's no more story. I'm dropping it. And you should, too."

The pathway splits and I veer left toward Royce Hall. Dylan

walks briskly beside me. "Kennedy," he says, an edge to his voice. "Don't do this. Don't let them get to you. Don't let them keep you from doing what you want. That's their M.O. They try to keep us all in chains. They turn us into monsters. But not you."

"It's too late," I tell him. "They've already gotten to me. I'm already a monster."

"No!" he says. "That's the thing. You're not. I mean, yeah, I thought you were. For a long time, I was convinced you were basically their leader. But now I've seen the other side of you. I've seen who you really are."

Yeah, I think bitterly. *So have I. That's the problem.*

I reach the front steps of Royce Hall and Dylan finally grabs my arm and pulls me to a stop. He gazes into my eyes with an intensity that makes my limbs go weak.

"Finish the story. Don't give up. We'll figure out who did it. We'll find a way."

"I did it!" I yell, finally losing my patience. "There is no story, because it's me. It's been me all along."

He blinks. "What?"

I hold up the paper. "It was me. I'm the perp. I opened the email account. I stole the tests from the server. I sold them to the students. I'm the monster you always thought I was. And now I'm turning myself in."

He looks from me to the essay, confusion etched into his face. "But . . ." he says, rubbing his temples.

"Oh, come on. I know you already suspected me. That's what you were trying to tell me in the car."

"No, I was trying to tell you that I was *wrong* to suspect you."

"Well," I say indignantly, "it turns out you weren't. You were right. I'm exactly the person you always thought I was."

A flicker of something passes over his face. Pain? Recognition? More confusion? I can't tell. "But if it was you all along, why were you investigating?"

I push past him toward the stairs. "It's a long story. You wouldn't understand."

Dylan catches up with me again at the top of the steps. "Kennedy. Wait. Think this through. They're going to expel you."

"I have thought it through." My voice softens. "And this is what I need to do."

He steps in front of me, forcing me to a stop again. "No, you don't."

"Yes, I do." I move around him, through the front doors, up to the second floor. I can hear Dylan's feet pounding behind me. I march determinedly toward Fitz's classroom—211—and rap on the door. There's no answer. I try the handle but it's locked. He must have already left for the day.

"Kennedy," Dylan pleads, panting from the chase. "Don't do this. You'll ruin your whole future. Think about Columbia. Think about becoming a journalist."

I close my eyes, trying to put up a fortress to protect me from his words. They're not unfamiliar. I've heard them all before. In my own head. They echoed inside my brain the entire flight home from New York. But I can't keep living this lie. I can't keep hiding from my mistakes. I have to face the consequences.

My dad was right. I'm not a quitter. I follow through with my decisions.

And this is how the decision ends.

I'm tired of lying.

I'm tired of ignoring the truth that's been closing in around me for more than three years.

I'm tired of saying "I'm fine."

"I know," I say quietly. To Dylan. To the universe. To myself. "But I can't stay here. I ruin people's lives here. I destroy other people's futures here. I can't keep doing that just to save my own."

"No," I hear Dylan say, and suddenly the paper is ripped right out of my hands. Dylan stalks toward the nearest trash can, preparing to tear the essay in half.

I groan and follow him. "Dylan. Stop. What are you doing?"

"I'm keeping you from making the biggest mistake of your life."

"This isn't your decision to make!" I cry. "It's mine!"

He stops at the trash can, his chest rising and falling rapidly, his hands poised on the sides of the paper, ready to destroy. He looks at me, then at the essay. "You're right. It's your decision." He proffers the pages to me. "Now make the right one."

I glance down at the essay. It's creased and a little bent from his grip. I take it, smooth it out against my leg, and turn back to room 211.

"But before you do," Dylan says, "you should know something."

I exhale and turn back to face him. "What?"

"Until last week, this place sucked. I hated it here. I just wanted out. But I felt trapped. Because of all the expectations that were shoved onto my shoulders from the minute I was born. But do you know what changed that?"

I feel tears welling up in my eyes. I shake my head.

He takes a purposeful step toward me. "You. I met *you*. Not the brainwashed, stuck-up girl who went on one amazing date with me and then never returned my texts. Not the zombie queen I thought I knew. But some other version of you. One that I didn't even realize existed. And then, suddenly, this place became bearable again. You think you ruin everyone's life by being here. Well, you don't. Not everyone's. Some lives you make better by being here."

He grabs my hand and squeezes it. I feel that same shiver I felt in Peabody's when he first touched me. I open my mouth to speak but my words are cut off. Suddenly the shiver is every-where. In my feet. In my hands. In my hair follicles. And mostly on my lips.

Because Dylan is kissing me.

With urgency. With desperation. With longing.

His lips plead against mine. His hands wind into my hair like he's trying to keep me here. His body pushes me against the wall. And I feel it like I've never felt anything before.

It's the kind of kiss that can make someone reconsider their choices. It's the kind of kiss that can sway someone's judgment, change someone's mind, alter the course of someone's entire life. I know because I've felt it before.

The kiss was different, the boy was younger, but the sensation was the same.

I chose to stay after Austin kissed me in that movie theater. I chose to give up everything I thought I wanted, everything I thought defined me, because of the promise of that one kiss. And I can feel myself wanting to do it again. Wanting to defy my instincts, take the easy road, turn my back on what I know to be right.

"Stay," Dylan pleads, his breath on my face, his hands cupping my cheeks.

I lean my forehead against his. I breathe in that delicious scent. I take a moment to think about what it would be like. If I said yes. If I ripped up this paper and threw it away. If I quietly finished out my last semester here. Not bothering anyone. Not breaking any more rules. Just keeping my head down and my nose clean. If I had Dylan beside me.

It could work. It could be amazing. It could be exactly the life I envisioned.

But it won't. Because the life I envisioned turned out to be an illusion. A lie. And I would always carry the truth around with me in the back of my mind.

I would always know that I hadn't played fair.

"I can't," I whisper. Then I duck away from him, walk the three paces back to room 211, and slide the paper under the locked door.

Then Everything Becomes Clear

I finally have a full appreciation of the term "dead man walking."

Every second that ticks by feels like I'm waiting for my own funeral. It's agonizing. But these are the choices I've made. And I'm going to live with them. This is my universe now. And I'm going to make the best of it. Who knows what will happen when Fitz reads that essay? But whatever the outcome is, I'll be ready for it. Monday is sure to be a very interesting day.

I spend the weekend getting my affairs in order. I fold up all but one of my Windsor Academy uniforms and place them in brown paper bags. I take the black frame down from my wall and remove the acceptance letter inside, returning it to my bottom desk drawer. I collect the remainder of the cash in the lockbox and stash it inside an envelope. I've addressed it to the Southwest High School library with an anonymous letter suggesting they buy a new copy of *Robinson Crusoe* to replace the ghost copy.

And then finally, when everything else is done, I go to the website for the county's public school department, print out an enrollment form, and sign my name.

Fortunately, because I'm eighteen, I don't require a parent's signature to register. I just need to hand deliver it to the office. Starting January of next year, I'll be an official student of Southwest High again.

I'm actually looking forward to going back. To sitting in the smelly cafeteria and walking on the sticky tile floors. It's only for five months. Maybe I'll use that time to relaunch the newspaper.

On Monday morning, I wake once again to the sound of elephants trumpeting and dogs barking and roosters crowing. I lie in bed and stare at the ceiling. Maybe after I go back to Southwest High I'll finally be able to get some sleep again.

I roll out of bed and check my phone for messages. So far, nothing from the Windsor Academy. I take a shower, get dressed, and wait outside for Sequoia.

We ride to school in silence. We haven't said much to each other since that night in front of her house. When we drive through the beautiful black iron gates of the school, I stare at the Windsor Academy logo that parts to let us in. I remember the days when the ornate WA letters signified so much to me. Hope. Dreams. A guaranteed future.

Now, they just feel like an empty symbol that has lost its meaning.

I fully expect the SWAT team to be waiting for me outside of Royce Hall, but all seems normal. Sequoia chatters about our AP history quiz today and how she wishes she had more time to study and I nod and agree in all the right places.

Throughout the entire day, I wait for the backlash to come. Every time a door opens in one of my classrooms, I'm convinced it's Dean Lewis coming to "retrieve" me or the police coming to drag me off to jail, but it never is.

I check my phone after each class, expecting to see a barrage of missed calls from my parents or alerts in the Windsor Achiever app or an email in my inbox, but none of those come.

And when last period finally rolls around and I walk into Mr. Fitz's classroom, I'm convinced that he'll give me a stern look and say, "Stay after class, Ms. Rhodes. We need to chat," but he barely even glances my way. And when he does, I see nothing in his face that gives me any indication he's mad or disappointed or even smugly arrogant for correctly predicting my ultimate demise.

It isn't until the final bell chimes that I come to the conclusion that he simply hasn't read the essay yet. He probably found it on the floor when he came in this morning and tucked it away in his desk to read later, with the rest of the final PEs.

I don't know how I'm possibly going to wait. How long will he take to read them? What if it's days? Weeks? Months?

By Thursday, I just can't take it anymore. The anticipation is killing me. I need this to be over with. I need to move on with my life and put this awful part of my past behind me.

After class, I wait for the room to empty before taking a deep breath and approaching his desk. I'm going to make him read it.

I'm going to stand there while he does and I'm going to accept whatever punishment he dishes out.

He barely glances up from his laptop. "Yes, Ms. Rhodes?"

I can feel my legs shaking beneath me. "I turned in my final PE last week."

He nods absentmindedly. "Yes, I received it."

"I'd like you to read it." I swallow. "Right now."

He pulls his glasses from his nose and stares up at me. "And why is that?"

I feel sweat form on my upper lip. "I just need you to read it."

He studies me with a curious expression. Then, in one decisive motion, he slides his glasses back on and returns his attention to his computer. "I've already read it."

I nearly collapse in shock, my eyes growing wide. "You have?"

"Yes," he says nonchalantly. "And I'm rejecting it."

For a moment, I'm certain I misunderstood. "Rejecting it?"

"Yes."

"What does that even mean?"

He types something into his laptop. "It means I'm not accepting it as your final draft. I'd like you to try again."

"But . . ." I argue, suddenly at a loss for words.

Did he read the wrong one?

Did I forget to put my name on it?

"I don't understand. You must not have read the whole thing."

Fitz looks up at me again, this time with an air of impatience. "I read every last word. Twice, actually. And I've decided it's not your best work."

I stand there, openmouthed and completely stunned. "Not my best work? But aren't you going to show it to Dean Lewis? Aren't you going to expel me?"

Mr. Fitz sighs and removes his glasses again, this time cleaning them with a small cloth on his desk. "Kennedy," he begins in a somber tone, "you are one of the best and brightest students I've ever had. If not *the* best student I've ever had. I'm not going to let you throw your whole life away because of one misjudgment."

"*Misjudgment*," I spit back in astonishment. "I think stealing tests from teachers and selling them to students is more than just a misjudgment."

"I don't," he says decisively. "I've worked here for ten years and I've seen so many good students go down bad roads. It happens all the time. If I could have saved all of them, I would have. But I couldn't. I *can* save you."

I stand up taller. "I already told you, I don't want to be saved."

"I know," he says, and I don't miss the subtle eye roll. "You want to take the noble route. The high road. You want to pay for your mistakes. You want to throw away everything you've worked for because you believe it's the *right* thing to do."

"Y-y-yes!" I stammer, unable to believe what I'm hearing. This is definitely *not* the reaction I was expecting.

"Well, I won't let you. I'm not going to watch another one of my students drown. Not while I'm five feet away in a working lifeboat. I've already ripped up your essay and I'm going to pretend I never saw it. Then, tomorrow, you're going to come in here with your other draft. The one you turned in a few weeks ago. I'm going to give you an A and we're never going to speak of this again. Are we clear?"

I stare at him in utter disbelief. Then, as he repeats the question—"Are we clear?"—I see something in his eyes. It's just a flicker of an emotion—maybe even a micro-expression—but it's there. I recognize it because I've seen it in my own face. And in the face of Sequoia.

It's fear. Fear of not living up to your potential. Fear of failure.

And, in that moment, I realize something for the very first time.

The students aren't the only ones who are pressured to succeed in this place. The students aren't the only ones pushed to exhaustion to fulfill an Ivy League quota. The teachers feel the exact same thing. They suffer the exact same debilitating stress. Fitz probably gets even less sleep than I do.

They're just another link in the chain. The administration passes it down to the teachers, the teachers pass it down to the students, the students kill themselves until they get those acceptance letters in the mail, and the statistic is upheld.

Then the whole cycle starts all over again the next year.

As I look into Mr. Fitz's pleading eyes, I know that I'll never escape. It's just like Other Me wrote in that original version of her essay. My decisions affect everyone around me. No matter what I do. No matter what I choose.

I chose to come to Windsor and my dad's life suffered.

I chose to stay at Southwest High and Laney's life suffered.

If I choose to turn myself in now, I won't be the only one

who suffers the consequences. My teachers will, too. And my parents. And Sequoia. And probably the whole student body.

It's a never-ending cosmic cycle and I'm trapped in the center. We all are.

"Yes, Mr. Fitz," I say quietly. "We're clear."

Then Someone Else Makes a Choice

I stand in the middle of the grand staircase of Royce Hall and stare out across the campus. At the immaculate green grass and beautiful buildings that once populated my dreams.

This is the very step that started it all.

This is where I slipped and fell and woke up in another world. Another life.

This is where my journey began and this is where it must end.

I think about all the things I did to get here and all the things I did to stay here. And then I think about what I have to do to leave here.

I could ignore everything Fitz told me and turn myself in to the dean. Or I could simply drop out without hurting anyone else.

Either way, I'm not coming back here tomorrow.

I turn and start back up the steps, but I'm halted when the front doors of Royce Hall burst open and Sequoia rushes out in a flurry of tears.

"Sequoia," I call out her name, and she stops at the top of the stairs, staring down at me like a frozen rabbit stares down at the fox that's about to consume it. "What's wrong? What happened?"

I assume she's going to say something like "I got an A minus on a test" or "They ran out of coffee in the student union," because let's face it, pretty much anything can set that girl off.

But she doesn't. She just continues to stare at me, tears streaking her face. And then she starts crying even harder. "I'm sorry!" she blubbers. "I'm so sorry, Kennedy. I didn't have a choice."

I climb up the stairs to reach her, my eyebrows knit in confusion. "Slow down. What are you talking about? What did you do?"

"I did what I had to do!" she yells, startling me. "They already started docking our grades. Just like they said. I was about to lose my A. I couldn't . . . I . . ." Her words get swallowed by her shudders. "I . . ." she tries again, wiping her face. "I'm so sorry."

With that, she hurries down the stairs and disappears into the parking lot. A moment later, my phone vibrates in my bag and I pull it out to see Dean Lewis's name on the caller ID.

I don't even bother answering it. I already know what it's regarding. Sequoia made the choice for me. She turned me in. She must have assumed it was me behind the cheating scandal after I came to her house blubbering that night.

She must have seen it as a chance to win the race.

Or at least a chance to keep herself from losing.

I turn and walk slowly into the building, trudging down the administration hallway until I find myself back where I started: in the little waiting area in front of Dean Lewis's office. Where I first met Dylan. Where he first told me about the zombies. Where I refused to believe him.

Turns out he was more right than I could ever imagine.

The door to the office is closed, so I take a seat in the same chair and drop my head in my hands. This is it. This is what I wanted. It's just not the way I thought it would go down.

Twenty minutes later, the door finally opens and I stand, ready to face the music. But my whole body freezes when Dylan walks out of the office. He catches my eye and winks at me.

"What's going on?" I demand.

But he doesn't respond, and a second later Dean Lewis pops her head out. "Hello, Kennedy. Please come in."

I gape at her and then back at Dylan, trying to put pieces together, trying to make sense of this.

"What's going on?" I repeat to Dylan.

"You made your choice," he says, that devilish smirk returning. "Now I've made mine."

"Please come inside, Kennedy," Dean Lewis repeats, her voice leaving no room for argument.

I take one last look at Dylan before stepping into the office. Dean Lewis closes the door behind me and takes a seat. She gestures for me to do the same. I sit in the chair across from her.

The last time I was in here was when I begged for my spot. Now it appears I'll be begging again.

"Dylan had nothing to do with this!" I rush to say. "I don't know what he told you, or what Sequoia told you, but he's innocent."

Dean Lewis cocks her head to the side and studies me. "Interesting."

"What?" I ask, panicked. "What's interesting?"

"He said the same thing about you."

I frown in confusion. "About me?"

She sighs. "He said *you* had nothing to do with it. That he acted alone. That he hacked the teachers' server, stole the tests, and sold them to students. He even gave us the email address he used—which no longer exists—and he told us which books he hid the money in."

I think I'm going to faint. I struggle to take deep breaths.

"He can't do that! He can't take the blame for this! It was me! I did it all!"

She squints at me, like she's trying to figure out what to believe. "Sequoia named you both."

"What?!" I roar. How could she possibly name us both? Why would she even associate Dylan with this?

But then I suddenly hear my own words in my head. The words I said to her that night I stood there crying on her doorstep.

"I was with Dylan. In the library. And then Peabody's and we were trying to figure out the whole test-stealing thing and then—"

I was sobbing. I was rambling. I wasn't making any sense.

But apparently that didn't matter. Sequoia made her own sense of it.

"No," I say, flustered. "She's wrong. I did this. You have to believe me. I hacked the teachers' server. I set up that email address. I sold the tests. *Alone.*"

"Can you prove it?"

Yes! I think automatically, my hopes lifting. But a second later they come crashing back down to earth when I realize that I can't. I can't prove it. Because I destroyed the evidence. I deleted the email account. I burned my notes. I mailed the cash to Southwest High. All I have now is my personal essay, but it doesn't prove anything. It'll be my word against his.

"No," I say, sinking down in my chair.

Dean Lewis rubs her eyes, looking distressed. "I'm sorry, Kennedy. I just don't believe you. If you and Mr. Parker are having some kind of fling and you're trying to protect him, I would strongly advise against it."

"I'm not trying to protect him," I mutter. "I'm trying to tell you the truth."

Dean Lewis sighs deeply, looking torn. "You're a promising student, bound for great things, Kennedy. You're one of the best we have. I won't let you throw your future away for a boy."

"Fine," I say, launching out of my chair. I reach into my bag and pull out my beautiful navy blue Windsor Academy laptop and place it on Dean Lewis's desk. "Then I'm dropping out."

Then Dylan Finds a Way

I find Dylan's address in the Windsor Achiever app. I'm surprised they haven't already deleted him from the record. I bang on the door until someone answers. I assume it's his mother. She looks just like him. Same wide-set brown eyes. Same dark hair. Same slender face.

"Can I help you?"

"I need to talk to Dylan," I say, not even bothering with pleasantries. I'm pissed. He had no right. No right to do this. This was my consequence. My punishment. My choice.

"He's upstairs in his room," his mother says, "but—"

I don't bother letting her finish. I mutter a thank-you and charge up the stairs. It's not hard to tell which room is Dylan's. I just follow the sound of the grungy rock music blasting. When I enter, he's standing by his dresser, holding a pile of jeans. I notice a suitcase open on his bed.

"What do you think you're doing?" I shout over the music.

He grabs a remote and lowers the volume. "I'm packing," he replies nonchalantly, placing the pile in the suitcase.

This catches me off guard. "For where?"

"Minnesota!" He grins, and gives me two sarcastic thumbs up. "Why?"

"My father is sending me there to live with his brother and his wife. As punishment for my crime."

I feel my face flare with angry heat. "But it's not your crime!" I yell. "It's mine. You can't do this. I can't watch any more lives being destroyed because of *my* choices."

"Hey," he argues, opening another drawer. "Don't take all the credit. I had a say in this. It was my choice, too. I'm the one who confessed, remember?"

"To something you didn't even do! And you never would have even confessed if it weren't for me!"

He purses his lips. "That might be true. But I would have found another way out eventually. I told you, I've been trying to leave that school for months. Sequoia just stumbled upon the answer before I did. I'll have to send her a thank-you card when I get to Minnesota." He reaches into the drawer and pulls out a stack of T-shirts.

"I'll find a way," I vow. "I'll make them believe me somehow."

Dylan drops the shirts into the bag. "They'll never believe you."

I cross my arms over my chest. "And why not?"

"They have their culprit." He flashes me a winning smile. "I make sense to them. I'm the slacker who's been trying to get himself expelled for years. You don't make sense to them. You're the straight-A student with too much to lose. You're the very best puppet in their puppet show!"

"I'm not a puppet," I seethe through clenched teeth.

"No," he says quietly, rearranging the clothes in his suitcase, "you're not."

"I dropped out, you know."

He cocks an eyebrow. "Really?"

"Dean Lewis wouldn't believe I had anything to do with it. So I expelled myself."

He cracks up. "Well, I guess there are *two* more spaces open now. It's a double miracle."

I have to laugh at that, despite my still-simmering anger. I remember when *one* spot opening up felt like a miracle.

"So, where will you go?" he asks.

I sit down on his bed. "Southwest High."

He closes his suitcase and zips it up. "You're better off there."

"And you?" I throw the question back at him. "Are you better off in Minnesota?"

He sighs. "Only time will tell, I guess."

"It's far," I say flatly.

He looks at me for a moment, then sits down and places his hand atop mine, sending those delicious shivers up my arm again.

"I'm still mad at you," I tell him.

"I know."

We stay like that for a long time. Hands touching. Hearts beating. Eyes asking questions we'll never be able to answer.

"Before I leave," he says, his voice breaking ever so slightly. "There's something I have to know."

I nod.

"Why *did* you stop answering my texts after that first date?" he asks.

"Honestly?"

"Honestly."

I exhale. "It was Sequoia. We became friends and she convinced me to give up boys altogether. Something about how if I want to succeed in this place, I need to be one-hundred-percent laser-focused on school."

He chuckles. "Well, it worked."

I smile, thinking about everything Other Me gave up to reach that coveted number-one spot. "Yeah. I guess it did."

He sighs. "I have to say, I'm relieved. I always secretly thought it was me. That something was wrong with me. That you just weren't interested."

I shake my head. "No. That definitely wasn't it. She was interested."

He cocks his head in confusion.

"I mean, me," I correct. "*I* was definitely interested."

Then he kisses me.

And it's like we both know. We both understand. We weren't meant to be. Not in this universe anyway. Maybe in another one. A distant one where I made different decisions.

Frankie says there's a universe for every decision. For every possible road. Every possible outcome.

Maybe there's one where Dylan and I end up together.

But this isn't it.

Then I Get a Special Delivery

When I get home, I change out of my Windsor uniform for the final time and slip into some jeans and a T-shirt.

"Kennedy!" Frankie calls from his bedroom as I pass by on my way downstairs.

I poke my head through his open door to find him on the floor working on his board game. "What?"

"I figured out how to fix it! How to make it *way* simpler."

"That's great! What is it?"

He beams proudly at me. "I'm going to add an Antimatter Tower! To counteract all the matter."

Even though I don't have the slightest clue what he's talking about, I still give him my best smile and say, "Good idea!"

I head downstairs to the basement and pull on the cord to turn on the light. I take a glance around at all the dusty boxes lining the shelves, Mom's old treadmill in the corner, holiday decorations, boxes of clothes that Frankie and I never wear.

Dad is finally coming home this weekend and I want everything to be ready. It shouldn't be a problem. After today, I'll have a lot of free time on my hands.

I switch off my ringer, blast my music through my head-phones, and get to work. Clearing boxes, making piles, dusting shelves, sweeping floors.

I'm so engrossed in the process, I don't even hear the basement door open a few hours later. I don't hear the heavy footsteps on the stairs. But I do hear my father's gruff voice when he appears in the doorway.

"Kennedy?"

"Dad!" I yank my earbuds out and stare, flabbergasted, at him. He's still dressed in his work clothes and he has a pile of mail in his hand. "What are you doing here? I thought you weren't coming home until this weekend."

"I wasn't," he growls. "Until I got a very interesting call from your school a few hours ago and I was forced to take an earlier flight."

My face falls. "Oh."

"What is this about you dropping out of Windsor?"

I tuck my hands behind my back and nod. "I did. I dropped out."

"What were you thinking? Are you crazy? We're going straight back there in the morning and getting you your spot back."

"No," I say as sternly as possible.

My dad balks. "What do you mean, no?"

"I mean, no. I'm not going back. I'm eighteen years old. I'm a legal adult. This is my choice."

"B-b-but," Dad stammers, "what are you going to do?"

"I already enrolled at Southwest High down the street. I start

January 5. I'll finish out my senior year there. It will be fine. Everything will be fine."

He sighs and rubs his forehead. "Kennedy."

"It's good," I tell him. "This is a good thing. You can quit your job. You can go back to photographing things you love." I gesture to the half-finished space around me. "I'm turning this into a studio for you."

"What?"

"You'll need a place to work. You can stay home and take photos and Mom can go back to the office if she wants and everything will be better."

"Kennedy," he repeats. "Not this again. I told you. The photo thing is never going to work out. There's no money in photographing people's eyeballs. If you did all of this just so that I would quit my job—"

"Oh!" I say, ignoring him. I reach into my pocket and pull out a piece of paper. "Here's the phone number of the woman who owns an art gallery downtown. I've been emailing with her. She wants to talk to you about putting on a show."

My dad looks at me, completely stunned, then down at the piece of paper in my hand. "A show?"

I nod, beaming. "Yeah. I emailed her some of your old pieces from the Portals project. She flipped. She loves them. And she wants to meet with you."

He continues to stare at the small scrap of paper with the handwritten phone number on it. I nudge it toward him and he eventually takes it, accidentally dropping the stack of mail under his arm in the process.

The letters fan out across the floor. One larger envelope peeks out from the pile and I freeze when I see the logo on the top left corner.

Columbia University.

The blood in my veins congeals as I slowly bend down to pick it up.

"Dad," I say uneasily. "What day is it?"

"Thursday," he replies absentmindedly, still hung up on the fact that I basically just handed him the artistic break of his career.

"No, I mean, the date."

"December 15," he says. "Why?"

December 15. Oh my God. This is it. This is what I've been waiting for. Early decision letters. I've been so preoccupied with everything else going on around here, I completely lost track of the date.

Dad leans in to see what I'm holding and I can feel him stiffen beside me. "It's big," he remarks.

I run my fingers around the edge of the envelope. He's right. It is big. Which usually means good news.

"Well," he says, nudging me excitedly. "Aren't you going to open it?"

"I'm scared," I say, turning to face him. My heart is pounding in my chest. This was it. This was everything I'd been waiting for. Everything I'd worked for. For the past three and a half years, this had been the goal. The finish line. The destination.

"You got in," Dad assures me. "With all of your accomplishments and your GPA at the Windsor Academy, there's no way they'd reject you."

Unless they knew the truth, I think bitterly.

"Open it!" Dad urges.

With trembling fingers, I slowly peel away at the top of the envelope, feeling my breath grow heavy with each passing second. I reach into the open slit and pull out a single sheet of paper.

I turn it around so I can read the words.

All I need to see is the first one.

Congratulations!

My knees go weak. All the blood rushes out of my head. And then, just before my legs give out from under me, I swear I feel something pass *through* me. Like an energy. A spirit. The ghost of everything that I could be and won't ever become.

And then, I'm falling.

Falling through time.

Falling through space.

Falling onto the hard cement floor of the basement.

Then Lightning Strikes Twice

When I come to, my head is throbbing and sore. I open my eyes to see my dad kneeling over me. "Kennedy!" he says. "Can you hear me? Oh my God, you scared the bejeezus out of me!"

I touch the back of my head. It's tender but not bleeding. I struggle to sit up. The room spins. I put my hands on the floor to steady myself, feeling the soft fuzzy rug beneath me. I rub it with my fingertips.

This rug wasn't here a second ago . . . was it?

No, I've been sweeping the floor all afternoon. I would have remembered a rug. There hasn't been a rug down here since . . .

I scan the room, taking in the towering lights, the stacks of photography backdrops, a desk with a computer on it. A shelf with a single camera positioned in the middle.

Almost like a shrine . . .

"What happened?" I ask dazedly. "Where am I?"

"You're in my studio," Dad says.

His studio.

But I was still working on his studio. It wasn't done yet.

"I have no idea what happened," Dad goes on. "You ran down here to show me the envelope. Then you opened it and the next thing I knew, you were dropping like a dead horse."

I ran down here?

No. I was already down here. He's the one who ran down here. He's getting the details mixed up.

I try to stand. Dad jumps to his feet to help me. I glance around the basement again, searching for the dusty boxes and Mom's treadmill. But they're all gone.

"You were *working* down here?" I confirm.

"Yes. Been at it for weeks. I think I finally got enough pictures to fill the gallery order. I'll tell you, being successful is hard work." He chortles to himself.

"Where's my phone?" I demand, spinning in a circle. "I need to see my phone!"

Dad startles at my outburst. "It's in your pocket."

I feel around my jeans and pull out the device from my back pocket, letting out a tiny gasp. My newspaper-print case. It's back. I touch it curiously before turning on the phone and navigating to my SnipPic app.

The first picture on my feed is from CoyCoy55. She's wearing her Windsor uniform, posing in her kitchen. She's holding up an acceptance letter from Harvard. And standing right next to her, also in a uniform, holding an Ivy League acceptance letter of her own, is Lucinda Wallace.

I'd recognize her anywhere.

But I check the caption just in case.

"Well," Dad says, nudging me. "Don't keep me in suspense. What did the letter say? Did you get in or not?"

"What?" I peer around the room before finally spotting a piece of paper lying on the rug. It must have slipped from my hand when I fainted. I bend down and scoop it up, turning it around again so I can see the front page. Just under the Columbia seal, it says:

Dear Ms. Rhodes,
Congratulations!

"I got in," I say numbly. "I can't believe it."

Dad lets out a whoop, picks me up, and twirls me around. Just like he did to Mom at his gallery opening. In that other life.

Or *was* it another life?

This is Dad's old studio. This is my old phone case. Lucinda is still a Windsor Academy student. I glance down at my clothes and notice that I'm wearing Dad's brown leather jacket again. I touch my hair, feeling my same old braid.

A jolt of electricity travels through me.

"Dad!" I say urgently. "What is your job?"

He squints. "Huh?"

"Just tell me what your job is!"

He guffaws and gestures to his wrinkled T-shirt, which reads, "I flash people for a living."

I feel my pulse start to race. "Who do you work for?"

"Kennedy, what's gotten into you?"

"Just answer the question!"

He puts his hands up like he's surrendering to the police. "Easy there, cowboy. I work for myself."

A shiver runs down my arms. "And what school do I go to?"

"Is this a game?" Dad asks. "Or did you really bonk your head that hard?"

I give him a pleading look. He sighs. "Fine. You go to Southwest High."

"You mean, as of today?" I confirm.

He scrunches up his face. "No. As of . . . always. What's going on?"

Frankie said it was impossible, but I did it. I made it back. I created another overlap. The exact same event occurring at the exact same moment in time.

I stare down at the piece of paper still gripped tightly in my hands.

Dear Ms. Rhodes,
Congratulations! We are pleased to offer you admission to the class of . . .

It was the acceptance letter. That was it.

I really did accomplish the impossible.

I got into Columbia in *both* lives.

Then I Freak Out Frankie

I stare speechlessly at the letter in my hand. How did this happen? How could I have possibly gotten in? I bombed my alumni interview. I totally freaked out in that woman's living room. They never should have let me in.

But a moment later, my thoughts are interrupted as my phone vibrates in my hand and I jump, staring down at the new text message on the screen.

Mia: Where are you? The whole staff is waiting! Chief, we're dying here!

Mia? Who's . . .

Oh my God! Mia Graham. My features editor at the *Southwest Star.*

I really am back!

I glance at the clock on the phone. It's 4:50 p.m. What am I doing here? I should be there right now. I should be in my newspaper office with my staff.

I let out a giddy yelp and run for the basement stairs. "Dad! I gotta go. Can I borrow your car?"

He frowns. "What's wrong with your car?"

"Oh yeah!" I exclaim. "I have a car again!"

I bound up the steps and find my schoolbag hanging from a chair at the table. I rifle around inside until I locate my car keys. I smile when I see the familiar Columbia University key chain and run my fingers affectionately over the metal.

"Hey," Frankie says, running into the kitchen. "You're here. I have great news!"

"Frankie!" I yell, pulling him into a hug.

He backs away. "What's with you?"

"Nothing."

He gives me the strangest look. "I think I figured out how to fix my game. To make it *way* simpler."

"Let me guess. You're going to build an Antimatter Tower to counteract all the matter?"

His mouth falls open. "How did you know?"

I grin. "I'll explain it to you later." I clutch my car keys, swing my old schoolbag over my shoulder, and head for the garage.

"Um, are you sure you're feeling okay to drive?" Dad asks, appearing at the top of the basement stairs.

"I've never felt better," I announce.

"She's acting weird," Frankie says.

"And you're acting exactly the same!" I say with a laugh, reaching out to ruffle his hair, but he dodges me just in time.

"Someday I'll understand my own offspring," Dad mutters, shaking his head.

I walk up to him and kiss him on the cheek. "It's good to have you back, Dad."

"Did I go somewhere?"

I smile and wrap my arms around him, squeezing as tightly as I can. "No. But I did," I whisper into his chest.

Dad pulls me back to give me another quizzical look. "Hey. *I'm* the photographer. I'm supposed to be the weird one."

I laugh. "What can I say? It must be genetic."

Then I Remember Myself

"Woody!" I exclaim, plopping down in the front seat of my car and running my fingers over the newsprint-wrapped steering wheel. I lean forward and kiss the dashboard. "I missed you."

I turn the key in the ignition and Woody hums to life. With a huge grin, I shift into Reverse and back out of the garage.

A few minutes later, I zoom into the parking lot of Southwest High, park in a spot near the front, and dash through the front doors, the familiar smells hitting me all at once.

Ahhh. There's that mix of sweat and beef Bolognese that I missed so much.

I dart up the stairs and head toward room 212. But as soon as I round the corner and see the display case in the distance, I have to stop. With my heart hammering in my chest, I inch toward the glass.

When I see the flash of gold, I start running again. Running until I reach them. Until I can see them in all their glory. Our three Spartan Press Awards, lined up like goddess soldiers going into battle.

As I press my nose to the glass and stare at those beautiful statues, my heart swells to the size of a blimp inside my chest.

It's real. I truly am back.

I glance to the left of the case where we always keep a metal stand with copies of our latest issue for students to take. I recognize the new layout immediately. I spent weeks perfecting that layout.

It's the issue we put to bed right before I hit my head on the steps of the Windsor Academy. Our latest achievement. I reach for the paper and run my fingertips across the soft, silky newsprint. I missed this feeling so much. The butterflies. The blood pumping on high speed. The tingling in my muscles.

It came every single month.

With every single newspaper we printed.

It never got old. It never faded. I could always count on that high. Like an addict.

Like an artist.

I flip through the pages, skimming all the familiar sections and articles that I edited and approved, remembering every hour I logged in that office to put this issue together. Every single skipped heartbeat when I thought that a story wouldn't be finished in time. Every single roll of my stomach when I found a last-minute typo. Every single molecule of air that I breathed out when I handed the drive over to Eric at the printer's office.

It's all buried inside this issue. Every emotion. Every high and low. They're written into these very pages.

When I flip to the end, I stop and peer down at the little box in the bottom left corner. Tears fill my eyes as I read the names of the newspaper staff.

Delaney Patel—News Editor
Mia Graham—Features Editor
Ethan Rice—Photo Editor
Ana Perez—Sports Editor

But it isn't until I see my own name that the tears start to fall.

Kennedy Rhodes—Editor in Chief

I've never been prouder to see my name on anything.

Not on an acceptance letter to Columbia.

Not on a fancy navy blue computer.

Not on a Windsor Academy student record.

This is where my name belongs. This is where I belong. At the newspaper I built. At the newspaper I saved. At the newspaper that saved *me*.

Just then, I'm distracted by the sound of distant chatter and I glance over to see that the door to the newspaper office is propped open. I recognize the familiar sounds flooding into the hallway. A little bit of laughter. A little bit of harmless bickering. A few stressful sighs. But always an underlying spirit of camaraderie and dedication. A group of people who have devoted their days and nights and boundless talent to something that they love.

And Horace.

I take two steps toward the door, suck in a huge breath, and come home.

Then the Second Miracle Arrives

The moment I walk through the door, everyone stops and looks at me. Mia pushes her way to the front. "So?"

"So what?" I ask, not quite understanding what she's referring to.

She groans. "Don't do that to us, Chief. That is so *not* funny."

I glance around the room at my staff. My amazing, wonderful, talented staff. I want to hug all of them. But they're staring at me like relatives in a hospital lobby, waiting for me to announce whether someone has lived or died.

Well, everyone except Horace, who's hunched over his computer, playing his game.

I scan the room, taking in each and every one of their faces. Until my gaze lands on Laney and my breath catches in my throat. She's sitting way in the back of the room and she'll barely meet my eye.

I don't know why everyone is staring at me like that, but first things first.

"Laney," I say in the gentlest voice I have. "Can I talk to you outside for a minute?"

"Oh God," Mia says, collapsing into a chair. "It's bad. It's bad news."

Laney tentatively rises to her feet, looking nervous. She follows me into the hallway and I close the door behind her.

"I have to talk to you about something," I say.

Laney's eyes dart left and right, like she's looking for witnesses. There's actually fear in her eyes as she asks, "Is it about the newspaper?"

"No, it's about us."

"Us?" she repeats, like she's never heard the word before.

"Yes."

She looks completely distrustful. "You've barely said two words to me in a month and now you want to talk about *us*?"

I let out a relenting sigh. So I've been ignoring her this whole time. I assumed as much. I was so angry at her, I was so blinded by that anger I could barely see straight. Whatever version of myself I left behind—whoever has been living this life, walking these halls, manning this paper for the past month—had no reason to forgive her. But I'm not that person anymore.

I'm not the Kennedy Rhodes who chose Austin. And I'm not the Kennedy Rhodes who chose Windsor.

I'm somewhere in between.

I'm some combination of the two.

And this new version of me wants her best friend back.

"I just wanted to tell you that I'm happy for you." I swallow. "And Austin."

She squints at me like I'm out of focus. "Is this a joke?"

I shake my head. "I've had some time to think about

everything. And I realize that you two belong together. He and I were never meant to be. I know that now."

"But . . ." she begins to argue. "I was a terrible friend to you. I never should have done what I did."

I shake my head. "No. *I* was the bad friend. I was never there for you. And I want to be better. I want to fix this. Do you think we can do that? Do you think we can be friends again?"

Laney looks like she's about to say something, but just then we're distracted by the sound of yelling. "Ow! Get off my foot!"

Laney and I both look over to see practically the entire newspaper staff pressed against the window in the door, trying to hear what we're saying.

She laughs. "Everyone's been waiting for you to get back."

"Back?"

"Yeah, you went home to check the mail, remember." Her eyes suddenly light up. "Oh, wait! Did you get in?"

I beam. "Yeah!"

"That's incredible!" She leaps forward to hug me. It's not hesitant or cautious. She doesn't hold anything back. She hugs me like she used to hug me. When she was congratulating me. When she was comforting me. When she was supporting me. The way I need to start supporting her.

It feels so good. And in that moment, I know that her answer is yes.

We *can* fix this.

We *can* be friends again.

I laugh. "Yeah, it's incredible, all right. Especially since I totally bombed my alumni interview."

Laney swats this away with her hand. "I'm sure you didn't *bomb* it. I'm sure you did better than you thought. Columbia was probably so impressed by you, the interview didn't even matter! You probably could have kicked the interviewer in the balls and still gotten in!"

I crack a smile. "The interviewer was a woman."

"My point is," Laney goes on, undeterred, "you're always so hard on yourself."

I release a sigh. Maybe she's right. Maybe I would have gotten in no matter what I did inside that woman's living room. Maybe I didn't need the fancy school or the fancy résumé, or even the perfect interview. Maybe I did it all on my own.

Maybe I can start cutting myself a little slack.

"Eew!" Mia shouts through the newspaper office door. "Ethan! Stop breathing in my face."

"Well, then stop putting your face near my mouth!" Ethan shouts back.

Laney chuckles. "You should probably get back in there and check your email before Mia bursts a lung."

"Check my email?" I ask in confusion.

Laney snorts. "Two minutes after getting into Columbia and you've already forgotten about us? Hello? The Spartan Press Award? The committee sent out the results via email at four o'clock. Ring any bells? We've all been dying in there."

Oh my God! I completely forgot. Today is the day. December 15. Early decision letters *and* the Spartan Press Award results!

I dash back into the room, shoving through the crowd by the

door. Laney pushes her way after me and hovers behind my chair as I log in to one of the computers and navigate to my school email address.

Everyone sees the email at the top of my inbox and a simultaneous yelp pierces the room, followed by a hushed, anticipatory silence.

I reach for Laney's hand. She squeezes reassuringly. I pause with my finger on the mouse button, ready to click. Ready to see my future. All of our futures.

As I sit in that chair with my best friend by my side and my entire newspaper staff huddled around me chanting "Four years in a row! Four years in a row!" I realize that it doesn't matter what that email says. It doesn't matter if we fill that display case with a thousand more gold trophies.

Because, right now, I feel like I've already won.

Epilogue

Three weeks later . . .

I drop my paper teacup into the trash and head for the door. "Are you two lovebirds coming?" I call back to Laney and Austin, who are still cuddled together in the booth. "We're going to be late."

"Hold your balls," Laney says, downing the last sip of her coffee.

Austin slides out and offers Laney his hand, pulling her to her feet.

The three of us leave Peabody's and climb into my car, Laney in the passenger seat and Austin in the back like always. As we drive the few blocks to school, Laney tries to give me a recap of the latest episode of some new comedy show they've been watching, but it sounds just as horrible as that other one they both like.

"Is this one full of fart jokes, too?" I ask, grinning at Austin in the rearview mirror.

"No!" he says earnestly. "Well, not really. Okay, maybe there's a few. But for all intensive purposes, it's fart-joke free."

Laney and I share a conspiratorial look, then both burst out laughing.

"What?" Austin asks, leaning forward to stick his head between the seats.

"Nothing!" we sing in unison.

When we get to school, Laney and I say goodbye to Austin and make our way to the newspaper office, pausing in front of the display case to admire our latest gold statue that arrived last week.

On this one, the plaque says:

SOUTHWEST STAR

EDITORS IN CHIEF:

KENNEDY RHODES AND DELANEY PATEL

Laney fought me again. But this time I was insistent. Enough is enough. She deserves the title just as much as I do.

"It really does look good," she says, pressing her fingertips against the glass.

"I agree. Awards should come in fours."

She laughs and we walk into the office together. Tomorrow night is another Drop Dead. The issue is due in two days. But I'm much more relaxed this time. Or at least, I'm trying to be.

I sit down at my station and turn on the computer, cringing when that nauseating melody from Excavation Empire blasts through the speakers. "Ugh," I whine. "Horace has been using my terminal to play that stupid game of his again."

"I'll talk to him," Laney promises.

I close the game and open the file for our latest issue. "I doubt it'll do any good," I say, pressing Print on the front page and then leaning over to grab the proof from the printer so I can check it for typos.

"It will if I threaten to cut off his balls," Laney says nonchalantly.

I stifle a laugh. "That's a good point."

"Uh," a tentative voice says. "Is this the newspaper office?"

I glance up and my heart sputters to a halt when I see who's standing in the doorway.

It's none other than Dylan Parker.

His hair is still messy and falling into his face, but he's no longer wearing his disheveled uniform that looks like it hasn't been washed in weeks. Instead he's dressed in a pair of jeans and a plain black T-shirt.

He looks amazing.

I launch out of my seat, tripping all over my feet as I stumble toward him. "Y-y-yes," I stammer. "This is the newspaper office."

He chuckles. "Oh, good. I heard some talk about ball chopping and I wanted to double-check."

I flash a look at Laney, but she stares back at me with a clueless expression.

Of course she would.

She has no idea who this is. Dylan is a ghost from another life. Another universe. Another choice.

"What are you doing here?" I demand, trying to keep the shock from my voice.

"Uh," he mumbles, sounding a little scared, "I just transferred here and I was hoping to join the paper."

My mouth falls open. He just transferred *here*? To Southwest High?

Dylan chuckles at my reaction. "Hey, easy there, Crusher."

I gape at him. "W-w-what did you call me?"

He points down at my hand and I realize I'm still holding the front-page proof. Although, *holding* is a generous description.

"Crusher," he repeats. "You're being pretty merciless on that piece of paper."

I release my clenched fingers and the proof drops to the ground. Dylan bends down to pick it up and I catch a whiff of that delicious citrus scent of his.

It's exactly the same.

He smooths out the page and looks at it. "I've heard great things about your paper. Do you have any room on the staff?"

I close my eyes and shake my head in an attempt to clear it. I fully expect him to be gone when I open my eyes, having vanished back into the depths of my imagination where I'm positive this whole conversation is taking place. But no. He's still there. Still looking at me. Still waiting for a response.

"I'm sorry," I say. "You transferred *here*?"

He laughs again. It's such a beautiful sound in my ears. "Yes. From the Windsor Academy." He rolls his eyes. "Thank God. I couldn't stand to be there a second longer. I tried everything to get out of that place."

I suddenly have a flicker of a memory. Something Dylan said to me in his room after I discovered he'd confessed to my crime.

"I would have found another way out eventually."

"How did you finally manage to get expelled?"

He flashes me that scrumptiously wicked smirk. "Expelled? I like the way you think. But I didn't have to get expelled. I turned eighteen yesterday and before the wax could even melt on my birthday candles, I dropped out, and voilà! Here I am."

"Voilà," I repeat softly. Wistfully. "Here you are."

He stares at me and, for just a moment, our eyes lock. I can feel that same tingle I felt when he first touched me at the coffee shop. "Do I know you?" he asks somewhat dazedly.

I chuckle. "Yeah, maybe in some other life."

He shakes his head. "No! I know you! You came by the Windsor Academy about two months ago. I met you outside the dean's office."

I smile. "That's right. Good memory."

"You were kind of hard to forget."

I laugh. "I must have come off a little crazy."

He holds his thumb and forefinger an inch apart. "Just a *little*."

I cross my arms over my chest in mock offense. "And you really want to join our newspaper?"

He grins. "If there's room."

I turn back to Laney, who waggles her eyebrows at me. "There's room," I reply. "In fact, we need a story by tomorrow night about the school board election debate this afternoon. It's supposed to get pretty nasty. Do you want to take it?"

He looks pleasantly surprised. "Really? Just like that? Are you sure? It sounds like a big story. You don't even know if I have any talent."

I shrug. "Something tells me you'll be great at this. I have very good hunches."

"Cool." He grins and turns back toward the door, pausing just long enough to ask, "Hey, did we meet anywhere else? I mean besides outside of the dean's office. Because you look really familiar." He scratches his head, seemingly at a loss for words. "I mean, you *feel* familiar. Kind of. It's weird. Like déjà vu or something."

I bite back a smile as I shake my head. "Nope. It was just that one time."

He stares at me for a long moment and I hold his gaze, daring him to challenge me. "Huh," he finally says. "Okay then. I guess I'll see you later."

I nod. "See you later."

Then he turns and heads out the door.

I float back to my computer, no longer able to keep the stupid grin off my face.

"Um," Laney says, gawking at me, "what was that?"

I shrug and slide into my seat. "I haven't the slightest idea what you mean."

"You are totally into that guy."

I scoff. "Don't be ridiculous. We only met once. Like I said."

But I can feel Laney's glare on my face. I print another copy of the front page, pluck a red pencil from the basket on my desk, and go to work proofing.

"What were you even doing at the Windsor Academy?" she asks.

I circle a misspelled word. "Oh, nothing. I stopped by to see if they had any open spaces. There was a time when I really wanted to go there."

"Well, it sounds like there's an open space now," she points out.

I look up and stare curiously at the doorway where Dylan was just standing. Five minutes ago, it was just a doorway. Now it feels like some kind of magic portal to another world. Another life. One that happened all on its own. Just by letting it.

I guess you never really know who's going to walk right into your life. Unexpected. Unplanned. Uncertain of what it all means and where it all goes.

I guess that's the whole point.

"Nah," I tell Laney, returning my attention to the newspaper. "I think I'm good where I am."

Date: April 29
From: My Friend the Printer
To: Kennedy Rhodes
Subject: RE: Retirement

Dear Ms. Rhodes,

Thank you for your recent email informing us of your imminent retirement from the award-winning *Southwest Star* school newspaper.

Although we are sad to see you go, I can promise you that we are not, as you surmised, throwing a raging party to celebrate your departure. Nor have we opened any bottles of champagne, expensive or otherwise. And I do not even own a copy of "Ding Dong! The Witch Is Dead!" nor would I play it over the loudspeakers if I did.

We will unquestionably miss working with you, as you were, by far, the most dedicated and devoted client we've ever had the pleasure to do business with. And, without a doubt, the only client who has ever offered to hire bomb-sniffing dogs to ensure our shop has not been rigged with explosives set by pirates who only target print shops.

I can assure you that we will work closely with the new editor in chief, Mia Graham, to help make the transition as easy and seamless as possible and, as you requested, we will make every effort to search out any unauthorized articles about Excavation Empire that have been unlawfully inserted into the paper. Although, I do feel the urge to remark, as a side note, that I am an avid fan of the game.

We wish you the best of luck at Columbia University next semester. It has been an honor to be your printing partner for the past four years. We look forward to receiving your final farewell issue, and as always, we will handle it with the utmost care and meticulousness that you have come to expect from us.

Regards,

Eric Nettles
General Manager
My Friend the Printer

Acknowledgments

Maybe in some other life, I could have written this book completely on my own, but certainly not in *this* life! Thank you to everyone who made this book possible. And special thanks to my superb agent, Jim McCarthy; my fabulous editor, Janine O'Malley; and my superstar publicist, Mary Van Akin. Also, thanks to the stellar team at Macmillan Children's Publishing Group: Caitlin Sweeny, Joy Peskin, Allison Verost, Molly Brouillette, Angus Killick, Simon Boughton, Jon Yaged, Lucy Del Priore, Liz Fithian, Katie Halata, Holly Hunnicutt, Kathryn Little, and Mark Von Bargen. And an extra-sparkly thanks, once again, to Elizabeth Clark who blows me away every single time with her amazing cover designs!

Many *many* thanks are due to Morgan Matson, Jessica Khoury, and Jennifer Bosworth for the plotting help, the late-night brainstorm sessions, and the longest list of possible titles I've ever had . . . for any book. You guys are the best.

Thanks to Stephanie Uehlein for the German help and to the incredible students at the *Chaparral Crier* newspaper at Chaparral High School for letting me crash your Drop Dead night.

Thanks to my sister, Terra Brody, for dressing yet another cast of book characters; my parents, Michael and Laura Brody, for their endless support; and to Charlie. There might be a universe out there where you're not in my life, but it's certainly not a universe I'd want to live in!

And finally, thanks to *you* for reading this book. For reading any of my books. And for proving that words and stories matter . . . in every life.